WILDHEART

THE STARCHASER SAGA
BOOK VII

R. DUGAN

DEDICATION

To JD
who, like this book, brought the end of one saga
and the start of something beyond what I could ever imagine.
Your Mama loves you, Little Man—with her whole heart, for her whole life.
Thank you for being my new dream. <3

And to SZ
who shares a birthday with this book, whose heart is truly wild, and without
whose Mama I would not be the writer I am today.
Your Ciocia Renee loves you and is always rooting for you, buddy. Never stop
chasing your stars.

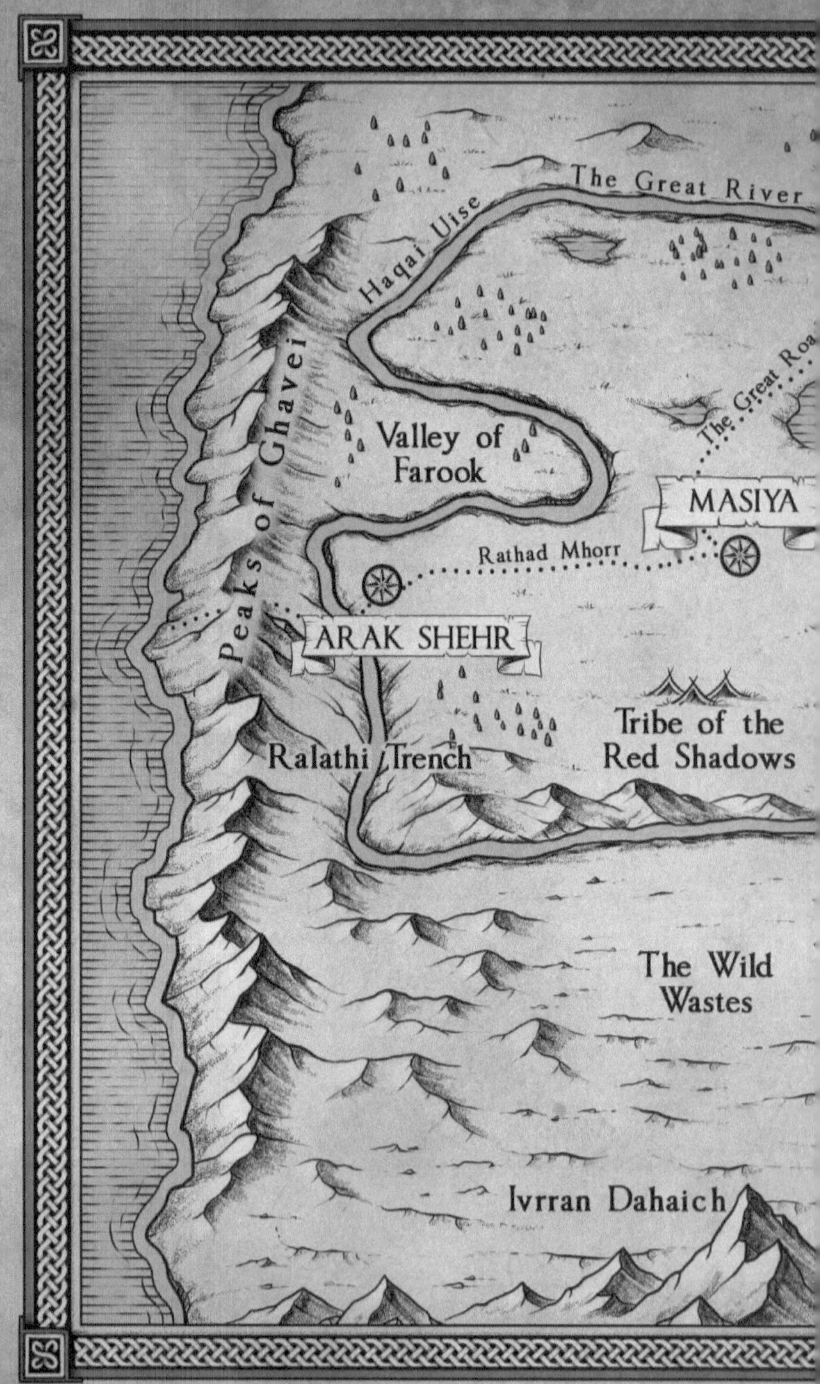
The Great River
Haqai Uise
Peaks of Ghavei
Valley of
Farook
The Great Road
Rathad Mhorr
MASIYA
ARAK SHEHR
Ralathi Trench
Tribe of the
Red Shadows
The Wild
Wastes
Ivrran Dahaich

KHORARRIS
MAHASAR

THE PRINCESS

OF

CUNNING AND MIGHT

CHAPTER ONE

IN THE VIVID lavender glow of late autumn lightning, Princess Cistine Novacek of Talheim fled for her life, fifteen Mahasari Enforcers in pursuit.

The thick undergrowth snapped against her armor while she bent nearly double, scaling the slope of the lower Calalun Peaks. Everywhere her fingertips brushed the last valiant threads of autumn foliage, they crumbled away from her touch. She did not look back to watch them die or to spot her enemies in the gloom. Eyes trained forward, vision cut with snaking tendrils of augment-shocked silver hair spilling from the knot behind her ears, she ran with all her might.

Only a half-mile to go.

She burst over the crest of the hill and skidded down the far slope, arms windmilling to break her fall. Arrows peppered the vegetation around her, smooth-tipped and reeking of Mahasari paralytics, and panic closed her throat. If she'd misjudged the distance or the direction...

There was no time to question the plan. Popping to her feet at the base of the hill, she dodged another volley of arrows and tore forward, legs pumping, lungs heaving.

The half-mile blurred by in a wash of rain and crackling thunder, and with every bolt of lightning she fought not to think of augmented energy, diamond-hard skin, or midnight eyes. Heedless of the death fuming from her body, she punched through the last wall of living undergrowth, killing it in her wake, and skidded to a halt on rain-slick rock.

She'd reached a ledge looming into the deep valley between the Calaluns. Shadow-dipped hills rolled before her, limned in lightning flashes and soaked in rain. There was nowhere else to run.

She spun back, hand to her dagger Nail, as the sounds of pursuit slowed and the Mahasari patrol prowled into the open. Their leader's familiar, pale face reared up a memory of a late-night ambush, striking pain into an old scar on her side. Setting her teeth, she regarded his approach.

"*Faes alykar,* Princess." The musical Mahasari syllables rolled from his tongue, but he bit out her title in the common language of the Three Kingdoms. "We've been looking for you."

"You'd think I'd be used to that by now," Cistine muttered, half to herself.

"You are quite the prize. And now you have nowhere to go." He extended a hand.

"I don't think you want to do that, Vezzik." Cistine crept back from him, nearer to the ledge. "You've probably heard the stories."

"Of the princess who can kill with a single touch?" he scoffed. "Talheim has always been keen on tall tales. I'm willing to take my chances." On either side, his men fanned out—a fourteen-bowed falcate with their weapons primed. Training clamored in Cistine's mind, half a dozen voices warning her against sudden movements. "Come with us, and you can live in luxury until the game is over."

Her heels snagged the edge of rock and sky. "*Game?*"

Bowstrings twanged. Vezzik lunged for her. And she jerked back.

The ledge vanished. She plummeted.

A great roar cleaved the whistling wind; a blur of gold streaked past her, shooting up toward the ledge where the Enforcers' cries of shock turned to screams of terror. Fire lit the sky, burning the rain to steam.

For a heartbeat, Cistine closed her eyes and envisioned a river below her, a gorge above, and strong arms shielding her body.

Glass pinged and shattered, and wind wrapped around her. Power surged through her fingers like breath blown from the True God's nostrils, and then she was rising—a star falling in reverse, alighting with bent knees and hair ripped loose from its tie to find the stone aflame and a battle raging across it. Fifteen Enforcers dueled five warriors in a halo of dragonfire, bows traded for blades in close quarters. A summoning whistle cut through the clash of Valgardan steel and Mahasari metal, and with brilliance that seared Cistine's vision in bright mint dapples, a fire flagon exploded.

Tatiana, limbs striped in trembling heat, ducked and swiveled, hurling a globe of flame to Quill. He flipped over two opponents to catch it from the air, handspringing backward to clap hands with Ashe, who portioned the fire to Ariadne. All of this while Maleck, braided death-god and swordmaster, dueled ferociously against six Enforcers at once, drawing their ire; and in the sky above, Bresnyar slithered through the clouds, cutting off their escape with his own fire.

Cistine's chest swelled with fierce love for her cabal.

Before she could gather her wind and leap into the fray, it was already over; Maleck drove the Enforcers back toward the others, and in a cage of fire, one by one, they brought them to their knees. Quill discharged the fire augment and pounced on Vezzik, driving him face-first into the rock and perching on his back. Eyes battle-bright, he tossed a grin at Cistine. "You know, I'm not usually one for using our own as bait, but that went better than expected. Good strategy, Stranger."

She sketched a curtsy. "We aim to please."

"We succeed." Sending out her fire in a gust, Ashe sheathed her blade Starfall, kicked an Enforcer onto his back, and planted her knee on his chest. "Why are you hunting the princess?"

"Don't answer that," Vezzik mumbled against the rock.

"Do answer that." Maleck spun Stormfury into its harness. "If you value your lives."

When no Enforcer spoke, Ashe craned her head back. Flickers of gold speared through her eyes, and the man in her grip squirmed under the heavy press of her knee to his chest. "What—what is she doing?"

"Cleaving." Tatiana's smile was a feral glint. "If I had to guess, she's summoning her dragon for an evening feast of Mahasari flesh."

"It's for the game!" A younger Enforcer, barely Cistine's twenty-one years if that, broke first. Vezzik spat a curse Cistine ignored, passing him and Quill to crouch before the Enforcer—though not near enough to touch.

"What *game*?" she demanded.

Dark eyes, round with terror, fixed on her. "You really don't know?"

Ashe's ragged scream burst across the rock; in the clouds above, Bresnyar roared, and the cleaving severed so suddenly Ashe pitched from the Enforcer's chest, saved from crashing into the stone only by Maleck's arm swooping around her shoulders and spinning her back to her feet.

"They have *gods-damned dragons!*" Ashe bellowed.

In a flash of lightning, a small, dark streak shot through the clouds, colliding with Bresnyar's golden bulk; from the treeline, through the dragonfire still gulping the dead grass, a line of scaled bodies emerged, driving against the cabal like a scythe.

Sulfuric breath blasted Bresnyar's wall of flames to deadly whips. The cabal dove left and right with shouts of shock and rage, and the dragons bowled into their midst; not sharp-edged, horned creatures like Ashe's dragon, but snake-sleek with tapered muzzles agape, foul breath pluming the wet air. The rotten-egg stench sent Cistine gagging as she scrambled up and dodged the barbed whip of a tail aimed for her legs.

While the cabal evaded the dragons' vicious breath, the Enforcers rallied and struck again. Steel sang, and not for the first time in this war, Cistine heard the cruel slice of deadly Mahasari metal cleave through threads she'd once believed all but indestructible. With a bark of pain, Maleck fell to one knee, blood streaming from his upper arm; Ashe's answering cry was world-ending in fury, Starfall a glistening flame in her hand when she sprang over her *valenar's* bent form and kicked his attacker down, running him through.

Despair gripped Cistine's throat. The plan was crumbling. Above, blood mingled with rain as Bresnyar and the Mahasari dragon shredded one another, ripping the clouds with bass roars and owl-like shrieks; all around her, fighting raged, Ariadne dueling three Mahasaris, Ashe towing Maleck back to his feet, Tatiana and Quill guarding one another's backs but still overwhelmed when the dragons charged them.

Cistine knew what must be done. Even as her conscience rebelled, stomach cringing at the choice; even as she stripped off her gloves, flexing her cold fingers into the blood and rain—into the power lying dormant beneath her skin, girdling her bones. The augment that would never be fully spent, never dispatched like the fire dazzling in the lines of Ariadne and Tatiana's armor still.

This was her curse. But she would use it to defend her family.

She hurtled toward Vezzik, arm extended, death unspooling between her fingertips—

The rain stopped.

For a moment, the battle halted as well. Cistine stumbled to a standstill, hair prickling on her nape and gooseflesh pebbling her body.

Augmented power rode the wind's currents, and a sensation three months buried reared within her so violently her heart staggered its pace. She sucked in her breath, choking on a Name.

Starchaser.

The rain descended all at once, flooding the rock, driving Mahasaris and Valgardans alike to their knees; two warriors drove from the scorched treeline, crashing into the enemy flanks, sending the dragons into a spinning, spitting whirlwind. Arms slashing in tandem, the men smashed their water augments into the Enforcers once, twice, three times...buying Ashe a moment to break a healing augment against Maleck's arm, Ariadne to fall back with Quill and Tatiana, and all five of them and Cistine to rally and attack.

Overwhelmed, the Enforcers broke, lunging onto their mounts. Vezzik led the charge, swinging onto the back of a piebald dragon and drawing a whip from the saddle; hatred burned in his gaze when it found Cistine's across the ledge, promising theirs was not the last patrol who would hunt her personally. Just as it hadn't been the first.

In that moment he paused to convey his silent rage, Quill reached him. When the whip reared back to snap against his mount's hide, Quill leaped, catching the lash against his armor and yanking with all his might. Vezzik hauled back, cursing and driving his heels into the dragon's flanks. With a pained screech, the creature lofted, dragging Quill up with him. Steel flashed as Quill drew his dagger Fjadar, driving toward the dragon's brow—then hesitated.

Heart in throat, Cistine watched him dangle. Then he let go.

The crack of boots on rock boomed in tandem with thunder and more than a dozen pairs of dragon wings slashing down all at once, and in a torrent of rainfall the beaten patrol vanished into the same peaks they'd haunted for nearly a year.

Tatiana was at Quill's side in a heartbeat, dragging him up from his landing crouch. "What was that? Why did you let him go?"

He brushed his hands off on his thighs, furious gaze scouting the clouds that shuttered to hide the Enforcers from their view. "Those scales felt like a red adder's. Didn't want to blunt my dagger if I couldn't break through."

Cistine blew out a long breath, spraying rain from the tip of her nose. Her body didn't know whether to slump with defeat or straighten with relief when she sheathed her weapons and swiveled to face the newcomers who'd turned the tide. Their leader shoved back his hair, dark marriage band snagging in strands far too silver for his age—barely thirty years old. "Honestly, that wasn't the worst scrape I expected to find you all in when we returned."

Cistine flashed a sheepish smile. "Hello, Thorne."

Soft blue eyes swung to her. "Hello, *Logandir*."

A rough sigh. "I'm here, also."

Laughing, Tatiana burst forward to fling her arms around the other man's neck. "*We* missed you, Aden."

"The new *valenar* glow just hasn't worn off for those two quite yet," Quill added wryly. "How's Pip?"

"Good. Missing you," Aden chuckled, squeezing Tatiana.

Thorne shaded his eyes as Bresnyar descended in a blur of gold, smashing into the ledge and staggering toward them. Ashe swore and hurtled to meet him, the last silver threads of the healing augment gliding from her fingers and running over his golden scales. "So, I wasn't seeing things. Those were *Iteilach Tayir* the Enforcers rode out on."

"Yes, my delightful southern cousins," Bresnyar spat. "Fireless, but full of venom."

Quill flung up his hands. "Here we go again. Shei, Thorne, and Bresnyar, our walking bestiaries."

Tatiana chucked a crumbled bit of stone at his head. "At least they bother with books every once in a while, Featherbrain."

Ashe's gaze swung from her dragon to Thorne. "So now Jad has dragons in his army?"

"Judging by the look of those spurs and whips, they were not drafted of their own volition." In Ariadne's tone hung a *visnpresta's* indignation for all abused creatures formed by the True God.

Aden scratched his thick golden beard. "For what purpose? Fireless dragons do little at long range, and less for stealth."

"And their poison wasn't even that potent," Quill pointed out. "Mostly putrid. Seems like all they're good for is a quick escape."

"Speaking of that." Thorne's gaze leaped back to Cistine. "Your father seems to think the cabal is on a reconnaissance mission to the east, not the south."

Cistine sopped her rain-soaked hair from her brow. "That's because I didn't want him to know what we were doing. He'd never agree with it."

He cocked a brow. "With his only heir making herself bait to his decades-long enemy?"

"Well, when you put it that way," Quill muttered under his breath. Tatiana jabbed him in the ribs.

"We know they've been targeting her," Ashe said grimly, laying a hand on Bresnyar's shoulder until he stood steady again. "Patrols have twice as much engagement when Cistine is with them. She can barely set foot outside Astoria without encountering a slew of Enforcers. We want to know why."

Concern drew a divot between Thorne's brows. "What did they give you?"

"Nothing," Maleck sighed. "And with the aid of their dragons, we have no one left to question."

"You'd think we'd be used to that by now," Ariadne said wryly, squeezing Thorne's shoulder on her way to embrace Aden.

"How did *you* know where we were?" Cistine demanded.

A half-smile crooked her husband's mouth. "By following the scent of danger and desperation." She jutted her tongue, and he snorted. "You know how, *Logandir*."

Of course; he'd sensed her power. Few but the cabal were so attuned to the way she could wield many augments when they only managed one at a time. He'd likely set off into the wilds the moment he'd returned to the Citadel and realized she was gone, then waited for the bond between their blended hearts to strum with the Key's power, showing him the way.

"I'm sorry I wasn't there to greet you." She sidled closer to him, still maintaining distance.

"I didn't fall in love with a princess who pined for the people she loved to come home. I married the warrior who took up her sword to save her Warden."

"Can we *please* let that go?" Ashe groaned, and Thorne laughed, leaning into a sideways embrace from Quill. One by one, the others surged forward to greet each other—first Ashe, then Maleck knocking foreheads with Aden, Tatiana joining Quill in embracing their Chancellor.

Left on the fringes, Cistine could do nothing but tug on her gloves, shielding her fingers once more from the rain. Thorne's gaze followed her, watching tan skin disappear beneath armored threads that could win a few precious seconds if she touched the wrong person. She hadn't slipped once since that first time on the Deathmarch...but once was enough.

Sadness and concern stamped his eyes when they flicked back to her face. She offered him a smile that felt braver than she truly was, and he knocked his fist against his armored shoulder three times.

Tears sprang to Cistine's eyes. She'd missed that silent cipher of beats—had missed *him* more than she'd thought possible during his furlough home to Valgard. She knocked her shoulder in return, three times, then burst into shaky laughter when Quill slung an arm around Thorne's neck. "So, how was it? I can't believe we had to miss your first cycle as Chancellor!"

"Later," Thorne chuckled, shaking him off. "Let's get all of you back to the Citadel."

"Someone journeyed back with us," Aden added with a nod to Cistine. "Someone who very much wants to see you."

She blinked at him. "Who?"

Kanslar's High Tribune flashed her a wild smile reminiscent of the Lord of the Blood Hive he'd once been. "I'll give you just one hint: your mother had to pull your old cradle out of hiding."

CHAPTER TWO

CISTINE SPENT FAR too long in the bath, thawing limbs frozen by the cold autumn rain and the swift but brutal journey back to the Citadel by wind augment. That power was the only way to and from Astoria over the trench Aden and Ariadne had dug the day of King Jad's siege on the capital; it made their augur allies utterly indispensable, something the King's Cadre Commander, Rion Bartos, absolutely despised.

But she cared far less about his opinions today and more about what they'd learned from that patrol—or hadn't.

There was a knock at the door of her spacious bathing chamber, and she leaned her head back against the tub's sculpted edge, peering upside-down at Thorne standing propped in the doorway. He'd changed out of his armor, donning a loose linen shirt and sleep pants from their bedchamber closet, and he tugged the embroidered hem that ended just shy of his waist. "I'm not entirely certain blue suits me."

Cistine grinned. "Maybe, but I was getting bored with all that black in your wardrobe. It's nice to see you in color for a change."

"I just spent three months being forced to dress like a peacock. I'd prefer nothing to this."

"I'm not going to argue, if that's an offer."

He snorted. "What are you doing in there?"

"Pruning." She wiggled her fingertips above the water. "Look at me, I'm hideous."

"I still see beauty." He toed the door shut and dragged the footstool to the end of the tub. Perching on it, he folded his arms against the edge. "Are you hiding, or thinking?"

"Thinking," she sighed, fanning the water with her breath. "That patrol...they mentioned a game."

Thorne pillowed his chin on his elbow. "They see this war between our kingdoms as a game?"

"Maybe. Vezzik didn't want to elaborate. That makes me think there may be something more to it, at least from Mahasar's perspective. That worries me."

"Me as well, particularly when the opposition's ruler is a sadistic madman." Thorne's eyes flashed with rage on behalf of the family he'd married into when he became hers, and the kingdom that was his by oaths and titles. "I'm sorry we didn't arrive quickly enough to help you capture them."

"I don't blame you. The plan was always a risk."

Thorne's gaze sharpened. "Do you intend to tell your father about this so-called *game*?"

Cistine shook her head. "Not until there's really something *to* tell him. For all we know, the patrols are trying to confuse us. Once we have tangible proof of whatever game they think they're playing, we'll bring it to the war council."

"Wise words." Smiling, Thorne dipped his fingers into the tepid water. Cistine jerked her knees up to her chest, out of his reach, and he stiffened. "We know water doesn't conduct the augment, Cistine."

She banded her arms tightly around her ankles, tucking herself as far from his reach as possible. "I know." But she could muster no explanation for how his closeness terrified her; and a small, resentful part of her pulsed with fury that it should even need explaining after what she'd done to him on the Deathmarch. Had three months apart already made him forget what she was capable of?

"I did some research while Kanslar was in session," Thorne offered after a beat. "They said nothing of the *Stor Sedam*, but it's possible, in time—"

"Don't." Cistine surged from the tub and snatched her freshly-laundered towel from the floor. "I can't listen to this."

"Why not?" Even with her back to him, she knew he'd risen to his feet. "Wildheart—"

Stricken by her Name, she snapped around to face him. "Because I'm tired of false hope, Thorne! Do you know how many times my father has asked me whether it's different today? How often my mother's invited me to touch something, just to *see*? I'm cursed, and I'm trying to manage that as best I can. I don't have the strength to carry everyone else's grief, too!"

Wounded eyes traced her face. "I thought we agreed our grief makes us one. You can't shut me out of yours if you want to be part of mine."

"But I *don't*." The words emerged wearier than she'd meant them. "I can't hold onto your pain *and* mine. Not tonight. I have too much to think about."

His bright blue eyes dimmed. He dragged a hand through his hair, nodded absently, and turned for the door. "Not tonight, then."

"Thorne," Cistine groaned when he stepped into the bedchamber. "I didn't mean...you don't have to *leave*."

He paused, one hand to the doorframe. "What do you want from me, Cistine?"

Your arms. Your hands on me. To remember what it feels like to kiss you. "My robe is on the footboard," she whispered. "If you don't mind bringing it."

With a nod, he vanished. Cistine sank her haunches back onto the tub's edge, banding the towel tightly around herself. She hadn't expected to be so relieved he'd returned and yet so miserable that as near as he was, he'd never be closer than an arm's length away. Because of *Haval*, the Death Augment; because she'd already taken his life with it once, and every moment since was a gift from the gods themselves. For six months, they'd warred against Mahasar together; for three months after, he'd been gone, fulfilling his duty as Chancellor of Kanslar Court in Valgard.

She hadn't considered how being reunited might hurt differently than being apart.

A clatter from their bedchamber roused her, and she raised her head. It sounded like he was rooting through her empty breakfast tray. "Thorne?"

"Guess again."

Cistine caught her breath at that calm feminine voice. Dread and excitement twisted together in her gut, and she lunged to her feet, then hesitated. She knew precisely what awaited her in that room. Did she dare face it?

The door swung wide, her silk robe dangling from the knob. "Come out, will you? There's tea."

Stomach pinched with hunger, Cistine relented, tossing the robe on and slipping into the vast bedchamber she and Thorne shared. Already, his mattress on the floor looked lived-in again, his rucksack tossed onto the foot as if he'd dashed to and from on his way through the Citadel to find the cabal. But Thorne himself was nowhere in sight; their dining table was taken up instead by a dark-haired, tawny-skinned Valgardan woman, cradling a bundle of cloth to her chest.

Cistine bit her lips, but still a smile slipped through. "Mira!"

"Hello, Cistine." Mirassah's gaze raked over her, full of delight. "Look at you! So...pruny."

"Look at *you*...a mother!" The words bubbled out giddy, then fizzled when she remembered whose child Mira carried in her arms and the lonely figure their family of two cut at the table. "How...how are you?"

"There are good and bad days." Mira adjusted the bundle in her arms. "Do you want to see him?"

Fear planted her feet firmly on the plush rug, imagination dancing with impressions of her hands slipping, touching that child by accident. "Oh. I don't know if that's wise—"

"I don't fear you, Cistine. I trust you."

Heat branded her throat. Carefully, she sidled up beside Mira's chair, peering over her arm at her slumbering child: a cap of dark wisps that would someday be curls, a broad nose and thick, long lashes tickling his plump cheeks, twitching in dreams.

"He's stunning." Cistine's heart tugged with melancholy. "I can see his father in that face."

"He does have Sander's roguish good looks, doesn't he?" Wistfulness crept through Mira's tone. "His attitude and desperation for attention, too."

Some of Cistine's bitterness from the bathing chamber melted away. Here she was, forcing Thorne away and focusing on her own anguish, but she was not the only one who'd lost something precious on the Deathmarch. At least she had her *valenar*, though she couldn't touch him; Mira had been forced to grow and birth this child alone. "What's his name?"

"Nadeem." Joy rounded the word. "For my father. It's an ancient Valgardan name."

"It sounds...princely."

Mira winked. "It means *arguer*."

Laughter dissolved the last of the tension from Cistine's shoulders. She pulled out the chair beside Mira and poured them both cups of peppermint tea. "Before he left for Valgard, Thorne told me he was going to make you Tribune over Nordbran in Sander's stead. How was that?"

Shaking her head, Mira shifted Nadeem to one arm and picked up the tea. "Exactly how you'd imagine, being the first woman Tribune outside Yager's secret Court. I've never faced so much scrutiny...and you know how my profession is looked on."

Cistine grimaced. Mira's occupation had no name, but if she had to call her anything, it would be counselor or healer; not just a medico treating the body, but a clever woman unraveling wounded hearts and troubled minds. Though both the poor and the elites had paid her visits now and again— even some Chancellors—few spoke of it for fear of being mocked; Valgard still had some ways to come in accepting its infirm and mentally challenged.

"Well, I can't think of anyone better to take that battlefield." Cistine settled back and drew her feet onto the chair. "I don't know how you did it, raising a newborn and helping rule a kingdom at the same time."

A quandary she herself would never face. She parried a stab of sadness and sipped her tea.

"Well, I had plenty of help. Hana, Kendar, and Elsin have been wonderful, though I worry Elsin's decided motherhood suits her too well. She was off searching for a man to make her one when we left." They both burst into giggles. "Kristoff was brilliant, of course, an absolute trove of knowledge about everything. And Aden..."

Here she tapered off, and Cistine's gossip ears, long dormant in weariness of more and more bad news, perked. Feet smacking the floor, she bent forward in her seat. "What *about* Aden?"

A faraway look entered Mira's eyes. "His time helping raise Thorne, Quill, and Tatiana did him credit."

"He's good with Nadeem?"

"Incredible. He's been up with him at night more than I have, I think." She sipped her tea, then slowly settled the cup on the tabletop. "He was there when Nadeem was born. Pippet, too. It was on the journey from Holmlond to Stornhaz for the start of Kanslar's session, and we were cornered by bandits during a storm..."

For several minutes, Cistine drank tea and listened to her friend weave a tale of caves and cliffs and angry men determined to ensure Kanslar had no female Tribune, even at the tip of a sword; a story in which Quill's younger sister, Pippet, had proved her mettle and months of training by holding the cave mouth with Vihar, Mira's trained wolf, while Aden coaxed her through labor pains, bringing Nadeem into the world.

"It certainly wasn't the birthing I expected," Mira finished wryly, taking up her own cold cup again. "But here we are."

Only now did it strike Cistine how odd that was. "Why *are* you here?"

"I thought that was rather obvious. I'm here for you."

Precisely what she'd feared. "I don't...you didn't have to—"

"Cistine, I'm your friend," Mira interrupted gently, "and as your friend, I can tell you aren't all right. None of us really are after the war against the Bloodwights, granted...but your war's continued, not just here with Jad. You're facing a grief no one in the kingdoms ever has before."

Shrugging, Cistine traced her fingertip along the rim of her cup. "I suppose. But you didn't have to uproot your entire life for that."

"Are you seeking help from anyone else?" Ruefully, Cistine shook her head. "Would you accept it from me?"

Eyes budding with heat, she held Mira's earnest gaze. As usual, there was no will forcing itself over her; Mira never gave of her talents without consent, and Cistine loved her for it. For everything she was, really. "Can I take a day to consider it?"

"Take all the time you need. I know this came without warning." Mira settled back in her seat. "And don't feel like you have to agree just to make my journey here worthwhile. Honestly, I needed a reprieve...I'm not certain I'll ever look at Valgard the same way after serving as a Tribune."

"Do you wish you hadn't taken the position?"

Mira's brows rose. "I think we both understand what a woman can do in a place of power. The need for our voices often surpasses our own need for comfort."

Cistine smiled, raising her cup. "To women of strength."

"May we be them. May we inspire them," Mira laughed, and they knocked their cups together. After pausing to sip, she added mildly, "Why does that matter to you?"

Cistine froze, the cup still pressed to her lower lip. "Why does what matter?"

"Being a woman of strength. Particularly now?"

"Shouldn't it always? Being weak was what got me into this entire mess to begin with."

Mira pointed to her around the mug. "Ah, but not all strength is strength of arms."

An unbidden smile cocked Cistine's lips. "I feel like I've heard that somewhere before."

"It may have been from me. The number of braggart men I've had to teach that lesson to..." Again, laughter, but it hitched in Cistine's throat this time. After a pause, Mira added, "What strength are you striving for?"

"I'm just trying to remain true to myself in light of...everything." Setting aside her cup, Cistine ticked off her fingers. "Keeping up my training, continuing my studies, fighting, finding a way to end this war with

Mahasar..."

"If only there were several thousand others who could help carry those burdens." Mira raised a brow. "If only there was a King, a Queen, a Commander, and a Chancellor on your side."

Cistine considered throwing a beaded pillow at her, then thought better of it for Nadeem's sake. "Point taken."

"I can't tell you how to be a princess. I wouldn't quite know where to begin. But it's good to remember you aren't alone, Cistine. You don't have to be the one who saves them all."

"Not yet. But I'll be Queen someday, and then their lives *will* be in my hands." She refilled her cup. "Besides, I've seen battle more recently than anyone in Talheim, even my father. They need my help. They need me to lead them."

Mira shifted Nadeem, nodding. "I suppose my counsel is this: don't let yourself believe you have to save every life to atone for the ones you could take. And don't put on your crown before it's yours to wear. If this past season has taught me anything, it's that leading is a burden no one should crave before their time."

CHAPTER THREE

A KICK TO the boot roused Thorne Starchaser from dreams of soft lips and green eyes, sitting him up sharp and wild on the lush sofa. A book slid off his chest, clapping hard on the floor; dawn light gleamed on the shelf-ribbed walls of Astoria's library and broke around Ariadne's body at the foot of his impromptu bed.

"Good morning," she greeted with a wry smile. "The King is looking for you. Patrol."

Groaning, he pinched the bridge of his nose. Cyril had mentioned something about that in passing before he and Aden had left to retrieve the cabal. "If you love me, you'll cripple me before I have to do this."

Ariadne's eyes flashed with humor, but it quickly faded when he swung off the reading couch. "Have you been here all night?"

Guilt jabbed Thorne's chest. He'd meant to return to the bedchamber and make amends with Cistine, but in the interest of giving her and Mira space, he'd come down to the library instead—and promptly fallen asleep, a book of Talheimic culture still open on his chest.

He shelved the book and beckoned his strategist. They hurried through halls already buzzing with activity despite the early hour, and Thorne slipped into his and Cistine's room, snatching up his armor from the chair beside the door. The Citadel's launderers had already washed the smells of Stornhaz from the threads, leaving them fit to be bloodspattered again—a future that still made more sense than the months of laws and governance he'd just accomplished.

Cistine was deeply asleep in the bed, flat on her back with arms outflung, drooling open-mouthed. Thorne wished he could shift that one stubborn lock of hair from across her brow, kiss her forehead, and tell her he was leaving. All he could give instead was a crumbled piece of paper he'd written to her at the beginning of this war. She'd given it back to him when he'd left for Valgard, and now he dropped it into her open hand and let himself out.

He and Ariadne walked together to the throne room, crossing half the Citadel before she said, "You never gave us a report from Valgard last night."

"I was preoccupied." He swiped his thumb absently against the marriage band on his finger. "How has Cistine been?"

"Managing. Sleeping, eating when she can. Unfortunately, busyness is its own form of distraction. She's hardly ever still, always dashing off to the next crisis."

"She needs to take better care of herself. Talheim will be in no less dire straits if its only heir drops dead of exhaustion once the war is over."

"Try telling her that. She'll remind you that her father managed during the war with the North, and why should she be any different?"

"Cyril didn't have the added burden of knowing his touch could kill the very people he fought to save."

Though Ariadne's face remained perfectly schooled, her silence was heavy. "How are you managing with...that?"

"It's not about me. Cistine is—"

"Your *valenar*, and you're walking this road beside her. When was the last time anyone asked how this augment has affected *you*?"

A flash of dark fields, a stripe of bright sky, chapped lips pressed to his and the feeling of his heart stopping in his chest—

Thorne checked over his shoulder, then ahead. No Talheimic maids or Wardens lurked in sight. No one to carry his words to the gossip circles...or to Cistine. "I thought I'd reached a balance while I was away, but the moment I saw her, all the old urges came back. I wanted her in my arms, I wanted to hold her, to kiss her...and I *can't* have her that way. I'm a parched man in a desert facing strange water. I could drink if I was desperate, but the cost..."

"Too high," Ariadne murmured.

He shoved his hands into his pockets. "In some ways, it was easier to be a kingdom apart. I couldn't touch her then either, but distance was a more bearable excuse than my own mortality."

"Your desire to be apart is a natural step of this grief-journey. Don't hold yourself in contempt. You're allowed to feel what you feel."

"I *should* feel happy. We're reunited. We have months to sort out this war before I go away again."

"But winning this war won't change the war within you both, and that's why you *aren't* happy. You know that solving the broader issue won't resolve the one that matters most: you're separated by a chasm neither of you can cross."

Though true, for once her counsel offered little comfort. Thorne halted at the throne room doors, scowling, flicking a hand through his hair again and trying desperately to reclaim the poise of a Chancellor.

"Thorne." Ariadne touched his shoulder. "We do still need that report."

He offered her a smile. "Over lunch. You have my word."

With a brisk nod, she hurried down the hall. Thorne squared his shoulders, tossed a prayer to the gods, and entered the throne room.

Only two people were present this early: Lord Rion and King Cyril. The latter had abandoned his crown long ago, leaving it on the ebony throne; Cistine had explained that he could not pick up the thin circlet again until Mahasar was driven out. On the ivory chair beside it, Queen Solene's diadem glittered in the early light. And on the porcelain throne, Cistine's tiara was already dusty, a diamond-flowered circlet left behind by a princess who'd descended that dais to go to war—first for Valgard, now for Talheim.

"Thorne." Cyril's voice jerked his attention to the long table littered with maps and effigies of warriors. "I'm glad you could join us."

Rion's face conveyed none of that sentiment; the father of Cistine's previous suitor, Julian Bartos, had a scowl that mirrored his son's. Thorne had never held any personal contempt for Julian apart from anger at the arrogant, brattish, and ignorant way he'd often treated Cistine—but Rion was the viper to his son's harmless garden snake. Where Julian's inexperience had been his greatest flaw, Rion's streak of scorn toward Valgard was a blade Thorne did not like having to dodge. Nor did he appreciate the many ways Rion condescended to Ashe and Maleck.

When no one spoke, Cyril straightened, laying a hand on the sword belted at his hip. "Rion, see to it these patrols each have an augur with them. Coordinate with Cistine, she should be at breakfast within the hour."

"Augurs for a simple patrol *inside* the trench?" Rion argued. "We risk seeming too dependent on them for protection. Is that the impression we want to give to Mahasar—or Valgard?"

Cyril's eyes settled on Thorne. "In your assessment, Chancellor Thorne, is Valgard positioned to see our use of its augurs' flagons as greed or weakness?"

The question struck Thorne as strange, though perhaps it shouldn't; Cyril never questioned him in any way that suggested entrapment or mockery. He seemed to truly esteem Thorne's opinions the same way his daughter did; though that unsettled him, he kept his answer honest: "We consider it a show of trust. We're not searching for vulnerabilities to exploit, we're here to shore up the ones that already exist."

Rion scoffed, but Cyril's lips twitched, fighting a smile. "You have your orders. Assemble those patrols."

The Commander's parting glare might've rattled a lesser man, but Thorne was not beneath Rion Bartos.

The door closed with a snap, and Cyril chuckled. "If I perish before Rion, gods help you, Thorne. You'll have a fight on your hands when I'm not here to cool his temper."

"I'm more concerned with the enemies beyond your walls than the quarrels within them."

The King straightened, knocking his fist on the table. "I trust Valgard is well?"

Thorne kept his posture straight and tried to ignore the stream of sweat flirting down the back of his neck. Holding the King's singular attention was always difficult; it flickered like a memory of dark halls and scarlet doors. "As well as can be expected after the chaos of the past year. You wanted me for patrol?"

Cyril rounded the table. "Since you just returned, I thought I'd answer any questions you might have about the state of the war while we take a shift along the eastern edge of the city."

Despite the discomfort curdling his stomach, Thorne said, "It would be my honor."

Thorne had never seen catapults before his first day in Talheim. In the aftermath of that battle, homes had been devastated, bodies smeared to the cobblestone streets, and everywhere the house-sized boulders had landed, aid was slow to come. The eastern quarter of the city had at last recovered, the shops opening their doors, the sounds of daily life interspersing with the familiar clatter of chisels and mallets where architects struggled on, discontent to wait for the end of the war before they rebuilt.

Thorne admired their tenacity as much as he admired their pastry-making talents. It wasn't really a surprise why Cistine was so sweetly spoiled and food-obsessed when he'd first met her. He and Cyril ate their breakfast of cream-filled rolls while they walked, leaving the populated districts for the edge of the city.

"The people seem happier than when I left," Thorne remarked.

"I think their trust in us has returned," Cyril said. "It's been generations since anyone came as close to invading Astoria as Jad did that first day. But over time, they've begun to believe we'll keep the wolves from their door. And the trench helps." He winked. "Tell me about yourself, Thorne. How was your first season as Chancellor?"

Unease strummed Thorne's muscles, sending a tingle of warning down through his fingertips. "As can be expected, I suppose."

"Was it?" Cyril's tone remained amiable, but his eyes sharpened. "Cistine mentioned how trying it can be to navigate the waters of leadership when you share your throne—forgive me, your Judgement Seat—with four other rulers."

Thorne's skin felt hot and slick. "May I ask what your interest is?"

"Is it shocking that a father wants to learn more about the man who's captured his only daughter's heart?" Cyril's tone was bright, but sadness stamped his eyes when he looked down the avenue. "To see a life of leadership through the eyes of a son is something I was twice deprived of."

"Cistine's brothers, you mean."

They paused on the city's edge, facing toward the devastated harbors in the west. Though Thorne and Cistine had ripped that finger of Jad's fleet apart, the men who'd made it ashore from the Mahasari navy had made quick work of setting the town alight. Not even augmented waters had quenched the blaze in time to save all the docks and fisheries.

"Jakob and Mikolas," Cyril said quietly. "We never told Cistine their names back then...we hoped it would soften the blow. Now I don't think Solene or I could bring ourselves to say them to her at all."

Thorne shifted his feet, resting a hand on the augment pouch belted to his hips. "It wasn't the leading that was difficult this past season, it was the people themselves. I wanted to help them all, but I couldn't."

Cyril was nodding before Thorne finished speaking. "Leading is like that. You want to mend every issue, populate every storehouse, provide for every person."

"But you can't." Thorne's tone echoed the gaping hollowness he'd struggled with every night he sat on the Judgement Seat, staring in the face of his own inadequacies.

"You can't, and sometimes you have no more than the turn of a moment to decide who you can help, and how you'll help them...and what it will cost your kingdom if you do. What it will cost you as a man."

Thorne dropped his hand from his belt and his gaze from the horizon, staring at the stunted grass between his feet. Though the rest was beginning to grow brittle as winter enclosed them, there was a special sort of death here between his boots...a mark of where his *valenar* had stood, casting augments to drive Enforcers out of the harbor district. "I sentenced my mother to death during Kanslar's season."

In that moment, he decided the Novaceks all carried some darker power than the Key's might under their skin: the ability to loosen his tongue when he ought to keep it in rein.

Cyril's head snapped toward him. "On what charges?"

"Sedition. Aiding the enemy. Murder." Thorne tugged a hand backward through his hair and started walking again, soothing the ache that built in his calves. "She didn't act alone...my father's greatest supporter, Devitrius, faced the same charges. They both confessed without shame, and my Tribunal convicted. I carried out the sentence myself." Wretched laughter burst from his lips. "What kind of man puts his own mother to death?"

After a long, quiet moment, Cyril broke his remaining pastry in half and offered a portion to Thorne. "It's never simple to carry out justice on those we consider family, but sometimes they fall so far beyond saving it's merciful to serve the law. You didn't sentence her out of spite or malice, it was an act of legal justice. Your hands are clean."

"You sound as if you speak from experience."

"I do. When I was away at war, one of my cousins tried to usurp the throne. Not that he came very far...he was more ambitious than clever, and Solene easily held him at bay. Unfortunately, he did just enough damage that my hand was forced. Since he attempted to poison my mother and my wife, the law decided his fate. It removed the choice from my hands, and that was easier."

"Do you still think of him?"

"Often. But the key to leading is to think of the people ahead of you, not the ones behind you. Just in the few battles we've fought together, I've seen you walk through fire for those you love. You are a good man who fights for his family...his *true* family. One day, you'll understand the meaning of that...and why it matters more than the ones you couldn't save."

Thorne's reply cut short when someone shouted the King's name. A Warden sprinted from the warren of Astoria's streets, sweat-sopped and puffing, and slid to a halt abreast of them. "King Cyril, your presence is requested by Lord Rion in the Citadel."

Cyril sighed. "Well, I expected him to find a way to interrupt this patrol much, much sooner. He's losing his touch."

Thorne took a moment to make peace with the fact that he would not be giving the cabal a report at lunchtime after all. "What is it?"

The Warden swallowed, still heaving for breath. "A Mahasari warrior just revealed themselves at the trench...and turned themselves in."

CHAPTER FOUR

THE SMELL OF brine and wild places seeped through the open balcony doors, chasing out dreams of blood and battle from Asheila Kovar's nostrils. The softness of a well-loved shirt hung aslant on her frame as she stood in the doorway, rubbing away the phantom pain of Bresnyar's injured wing on the Deathmarch from her shoulder.

She could barely see her dragon, a distant slice of gold against the Agerios Sea. When she shut her eyes, the bond between them snapped taut, and she cleaved straight through his eyes, watching the waves pass below.

ASHEILA! His roar rattled in her head. *WHAT HAVE I TOLD YOU ABOUT CLEAVING WHILE I FLY?*

Ashe bit back laughter. *Calm down, Scales. Bank left.*

He tilted his wing, talons skimming the water as he turned. *MOST BEAUTIFUL AND DEADLIEST OF ALL WINGMAIDENS, WOULD YOU PLEASE GIVE ME BACK MY SIGHT?*

Now she did laugh, and released the cleaving, letting her own vision fill with the sprawl of the city before her and the dragon swooping over the water. *Just trying for a change of scenery. Anything I need to know about?*

A BIT OF UNREST ON THE LINES NEAR THE TRENCH. NOTHING TOO UNUSUAL. I'LL HAVE A CLOSER LOOK ONCE I'M CERTAIN NO MORE SHIPS ARE TRYING TO CRAWL UP THE COAST, THE ABSOLUTE INSECTS.

Good. No sign of Mahasari dragons, either?

NONE. DO YOU FEAR THEM?

Ashe shifted, leaning heavier into the gilded frame. *I don't like surprises. Especially the kind that can cut past* your *armor.*

I'M FLATTERED. BUT DON'T FEAR FOR ME. YOU KNOW AS WELL AS I, ITEILACH TAYIR *ARE NO MATCH FOR A DRAKON.*

Even so. Alert me if you find anything.

I WILL. DO HAVE FUN WITH MALECK IN THE MEANTIME.

Ashe cleaved again, stealing his sight just long enough to send him plunging into the water.

Hoarse laughter drew her back to her own vision this time—her rooms in the Citadel, the mother-of-pearl walls shivering into focus as she turned away from the balcony and back into the room she shared with her *valenar*. She found him smiling, and it was easy to match it with the weight lessening some around her heart. It had been a better night for them both: their entire cabal back under the Citadel's glass roofs and Bresnyar on watch. A slow awakening of kisses on cheeks and necks and shoulders had led to something more before dawn; Ashe could get used to a life like this, if the world would stop going to war for two gods-forsaken minutes.

But at least Maleck was still relaxed, sprawled on his back on the bed, shirtless and in his undershorts with one arm tucked behind his head and his face angled toward her. The sunlight through the open window traced the Atrasat inkings spread across his torso from right shoulder to left hip, partially obscuring the knots of augment scars across his chest.

Ashe sat on the bed's edge and let her fingertips explore those clots of tissue, making her way to her favorite of all his scars—nestled in the center of his palm, light and long, twin to the one she bore above the Wingmaiden Rune on her hand. The *valenar* mark they'd forged after the Battle of Braggos, the first time Ashe knew what it was like to belong and be seen, to be loved so deeply and fearlessly it had utterly wrecked her and rebuilt her anew.

She was waste and wild for this Valgardan who was more than a friend, more than her husband, more than her *selvenar*. Every day they fought and plotted and lived together was a blessing, even in the midst of war.

She flopped down beside him, gazing up at the vaulted ceiling. "What did you make of those Enforcers last night?"

He rolled to his side and slid a hand down her thigh, gaze distant with thought. "What we've always believed…that there is something more to this than mere warfare. And that we might've known months ago, if—"

"I know," Ashe muttered. "If Rion would give the gods-damned order to take prisoners instead of killing every Enforcer his patrols encounter."

A hard knock at the door startled them upright in the sheets. "Is it safe to come in? I'm not going to give myself any new nightmares, am I?"

Ashe slid free from Maleck's hands. "Don't be an infant, Quill."

He broke into the room, then slapped a hand over his eyes and waved the other before him. "Oh, gods, it's worse than I thought! Is that Mal's shirt you're wearing? Is *he* wearing anything under those covers?"

Maleck picked up his pillow and slung it at Quill's head so hard, it knocked him back into the wall.

"What do you *want?*" Ashe snatched her clothes from the bedside floor.

Quill hurled the pillow back at Maleck. "Cistine just sent for us. Thorne's on his way back from patrol. Something's wrong, we're meeting in the dungeon."

"The dungeon?" Ashe whistled lowly. "What did he *say* to Cyril?"

"Hilarious, Shei."

Maleck sighed. "We'll be right there."

"Take your time. At least put on some pants," Quill laughed on his way out the door, dodging Ashe's pillow this time, which she flung at him with all the force of a battering ram.

"As far as Warden patrols are concerned," Maleck offered as they slid into their armor, "you could speak to Rozalie and the others who fought in the north with us. Request that they make capture a priority over killing."

"I've considered that." Ashe crouched to lace her boots. "But I don't want to undermine Rion's authority. He's a bastard and a bully, but he's their Commander as long as they choose to serve in the Cadre. I'm a Wingmaiden now, not a Warden. It won't help anything if I start sowing division. We'll just have the augurs redouble their efforts to capture someone, since Thorne at least can be reasoned with."

Maleck snagged her chin and guided her upright in one smooth pull, his hungry, reverent gaze igniting fire in her core. "Have I mentioned of late how much I admire your nobility? Rion would not show the same regard if your roles were reversed."

"I know. But at least *I* can sleep at night."

"That can be changed, if you so desire."

Ashe groaned as he dropped his head, planting a kiss on her collarbone. It required all her considerable self-restraint to catch him by the throat and shove him back. "Later. First, let's go see what crisis Thorne's stumbled into this time."

"As you wish, Commander."

Ashe flicked his nose. "Don't call me that."

"Very well, Warden."

"Augur."

He kicked her haunch, and Ashe, laughing, snatched up Starfall and led the way out into halls teeming with whispers and rumors about a *prisoner*.

She and Maleck swapped wide-eyed glances and broke into a sprint for the steps down to the rarely-used dungeons.

CHAPTER
FIVE

Rozalie Dohnal despised the Citadel dungeons. They reminded her too much of the carts and hovels she'd been stuffed into after the brothel masters stole her from her family's farm. But there was no excusing herself this time—not with the whole cabal, the royal family, and Rion Bartos crammed into one tiny cell.

At least she wasn't the only one tense. Everyone was shifting their feet and looking around at one another by smoky silver ghostlight. It seemed to take forever for the sound of footsteps grinding on rock to reach them, and another lifetime for the Wardens to actually appear, leading a woman between them, arms bound behind her back. Dark hair, dark eyes, skin a sun-loved brown, billowing pants and a loose shirt meant for warmer climes. Mahasari, without a doubt. The part that caught Rozalie's attention was the mess of scars marking her cheeks and scouring her lips.

She had seen war, this one; or at least been its victim.

The Wardens dragged her to a halt in the middle of the cell, and Rion jerked his chin, dispatching them into the hall. The moment the iron door swung shut, he addressed the woman: "Who are you, and how did you cross the trench?"

"Are you the King?" Her voice was deep, the accent markedly Mahasari as well.

"I'm the Commander of his forces."

"I will only speak to Talheimic royalty."

Cyril stepped forward, hand to his sword. "I'm the one you're looking for."

The woman studied him, nodding slowly. "This doesn't surprise me. You certainly have the look of a king."

His eyes narrowed. "Tell us how you crossed the trench."

"Rope. Climbing. Perseverance. I have gone in and out of much, much more difficult places."

Rion cut a look toward Aden and Ariadne, like it might be their personal fault someone had crossed their trench without using an augment. Ariadne cocked a brow in reply. Aden cinched his arms and paid Rion all the respect of a scuffmark on his boot.

"What do you want?" Cyril asked the prisoner.

"To put an end to the slaughter of our people," she said. "For more than half a year, Talheim has killed us, and we've killed you. And to what end?"

"Ask *your* King," Rion snapped. "He's the one who lopped off the hand of friendship we offered in Middleton."

"An act of dishonor, yes. He's known for those."

Cistine tilted her head. "Who *are* you?"

"My name is Sacha ra-Fyra. I come bearing information that can turn the tide of this war in your favor if you're wise enough to heed it."

Rion scoffed. "As if we would allow a Mahasari to direct us in the war against her own kingdom. This is ridiculous, even by Jad's standards."

"You're right, it is ridiculous," Sacha said. "I've spent years ducking into doorways and dark holes, hiding from the eyes of Mahasari royalty and the Enforcers...yet here I am, showing my face to you who hate us. You ought to at least hear what I say before you dismiss me."

"She's right," Thorne interjected. "Listening costs us nothing."

Cistine nodded. "I spent too much of my life ignorant and prejudiced. I'm willing to hear her out."

"We have enough to sort through without adding lies to the heap!"

Rion argued. "Mahasaris can't be trusted, none of them have clean hands. They give Jad their land, they fund his conquest...they're all just as guilty as him!"

"I would agree," Sacha said, "if they'd made those choices of their own volition."

That statement silenced the cell. Rozalie swapped a look with Ashe and found her eyes churning with thought.

"What do you mean?" Solene asked.

"The whole kingdom is under the influence of a poison Jad calls *Sorcel*. It strips the inhibitions, leaving its victim vulnerable to persuasion," Sacha explained. "The more a suggestion is repeated, the more it takes root, until no other thought can sway it. Whole villages have given up their inheritances and priceless heirlooms to pay for this war against Talheim."

Cyril cursed quietly. "Is that why he feigned talk of peace? Buying time for that drug to settle into his Magnates?"

Sacha nodded.

"Impossible," Rion muttered, but even he didn't look so sure anymore. "No one could possibly enslave an entire kingdom with a drug."

"Yes, they could." Ashe's stare was fixed on Sacha. "When the Mahasaris held me captive in the Calaluns, they used that drug to wrestle the truth about the treaty out of me. It's more powerful than you can imagine."

"One woman broken, that doesn't surprise me. But an entire *kingdom*?"

"You know very little about Mahasar," Sacha said. "Do you even know how our water is gathered?"

"Manmade aqueducts," Cistine offered. "I've read about them. They draw water from the mountain rivers that girdle the heart of the kingdom."

"Poison the aqueducts," Ariadne murmured, "and your drug will spread to every household in every populated city."

"The deed was done before the people even realized they were being poisoned," Sacha said. "Did you really believe we *all* supported Jad's schemes?"

Rion shifted in the uncomfortable pause.

"Mahasar's own people suffer worse than yours," Sacha added. "Jad murdered his own siblings long ago and stole their son and daughter for his heirs when no woman fell pregnant by him. Prince Kashar and Princess Tirzah terrorized the people until the princess became such a skilled assassin, Jad ordered her brother to kill her for fear she'd take the throne." Cistine sucked in a harsh breath at that, head cocking back. "Now the prince sits poised to rule when Jad dies, and he will inherit an ensorcelled kingdom with his own mind corrupted."

"Kashar," Ashe growled, and Maleck's brow darkened. Hate twisted in Rozalie's gut. "We've met that bastard."

"Would he carry on his uncle's war?" Cyril asked.

"Yes," Ashe and Sacha chorused.

Rozalie studied this woman, poised and proud and handing over her kingdom's secrets for practically nothing. "How do we know *you're* not under the influence of Sorcel?"

"For many years, I was. But an accident put me at the brink of death, and the drug lost its hold on my mind. It will do that if people go long enough without drinking it, so Jad has made them depend on him for everything. He takes their wealth for his war and promises them rations in return, and into those rations he puts his drug. So they give more and more, fed on the lie that he will restore them to glory with riches taken from other kingdoms."

Like ours. Rozalie's fists trembled from furious clenching.

"I came here because I believe there is a chance you can help save all our kingdoms. I've heard tales of a Valgardan cabal and the warrior princess with the power of death in her hands who leads them." Sacha's gaze lit on Solene. "And I know of the huntress who burned Khorraris and the prince who risked everything to save her. I've come to appeal to that noble bloodline."

Fierce pride swelled in Rozalie's chest, but none of the Novaceks dropped their guard.

"What exactly do you want from us?" Cyril demanded.

"To make an exchange. Your aid for mine."

"And what aid is that?" Rion asked.

Sacha didn't even grace him with a look. "Mine are not the only people ensorcelled. Jad's Enforcers brought a ration into your city, Middleton...and dispersed it from there."

Horror dripped into Rozalie's stomach. Her eyes found Ashe's again, wide with the same disbelief and outrage.

"Do you mean to tell me," Cyril growled, "that some of my own *people* are in Jad's council?"

"They would serve him before you."

"That's absurd!" Rion barked. "If our people had become gods-damned Mahasari sympathizers, we would know it!"

"The fact that you *don't* should make you very, very afraid," Sacha retorted. "It's difficult to tell someone is ensorcelled. Sometimes it's no more obvious than a glint of strange light in their eyes, the sheen of the drug doing its work. When was the last time anyone could bear to hold *your* gaze, I wonder?" Rion cursed her under his breath, and Sacha's scarred lips twitched with triumph. She addressed Cyril again. "In my kingdom, they call me an alchemist. I've managed to craft an antidote that will stop the effects of Sorcel altogether. I'm prepared to offer some to you, to free your enslaved people...for a price."

Cyril regarded her a long moment. Then he said, "No. I will not strike a bargain with you."

Rozalie deflated. *Damn.*

"Why not?" Cistine burst out. "Papa, if we could end this war...if our own *people* are already his—"

"It's a trap," the King said, and the hair on Rozalie's neck prickled at the certainty in his tone. "If not by her hand, then by Jad's. Something to make us doubt our own, to resort to infighting."

"You don't know that!"

"I know this madman's mind better than I'm comfortable with." Cyril's fingers tapped a beat on the pommel of his sword. "It's a trick, and I won't allow it."

"Will you even *consider* it? What if she *is* right, what if our people are working against us? How can we expect to win a war like this?" Cistine waved a hand at Sacha. "We can at least hear her full terms! How many months have we *prayed* for something to end this war? An antidote could help turn Mahasar against its King, we could all dethrone Jad *together*—"

"Cistine!" Cyril's voice sharpened. "You heard me."

Rounding his lips in a silent whistle, Quill shot a glance at Tatiana. Her palms flicked at her sides, a helpless shrug. Rozalie's guts writhed with embarrassment for her princess, visibly seething while her father swung away from Sacha.

"Everyone, out."

They left the cell, Sacha standing in the middle of it, still bound. Rion clapped the door shut, locked it, and pocketed the key. Then he leaned against it for good measure. "I agree it's a trick."

"But a clever one." Cyril skimmed this thumb along his lower lip. "If this Sorcel is real, and we know Jad *is* clever enough to manufacture it..."

"All the same concerns remain," Solene said. "Real or not, it could be used to draw us out of safety."

Cistine cinched her arms at her waist. "Is protecting the royal line really paramount to ending a war that's left thousands of our people displaced or *dead*?"

Rion shot her a look that made Rozalie want to punch him, duty be damned. "You know the answer to that."

"*However*," Cyril stressed the word carefully when Cistine's mouth leaped open, "I'm not willing to discredit her claims outright. Rion, I want the names of every Warden who has served in Middleton since just before Jad sacked it until the last handful escaped. Find out who they've had dealings with since. Make sure you speak to Dorminger's daughters as well."

Rion nodded, straightening from the door and hiking a thumb over his shoulder. "What about that one?"

"We keep her detained until we can verify her claims. If they prove true, we'll speak with her again."

"Brother." Rion glowered at everyone else in the dungeon hall like their entire presence offended him. "Should we postpone—?"

"No," Solene cut in swiftly, and Rozalie's ears perked at the thinly-veiled hint of a secret. "If Jad does have informants among our own, any shift in strategy could incite violence."

"She's right," Cyril agreed. "We behave as if we know nothing. In the meantime, Rion, get me those names."

He started up the hall, Rion and the Queen on his heels, leaving the cabal standing in darkness. Sighing, Tatiana shattered a fire flagon, the light tracing every contour of her frame. Rozalie was delighted to find the old shiver of dread no longer coiled in her chest when she saw it; thanks to these people, she'd come to see the use, the magnificence, even the brilliance of augmentation. But today, wearing her Talheimic armor, she could only watch Tatiana toss a clot of fire to Aden. "*That* went well."

"Thorne, if you were any quieter, I'd check for a pulse." Aden hurled a portion of the flames to his cousin. "What are you doing over there?"

"Thinking." At the rear of the bunch, Thorne passed the globe of fire from hand to hand. "It's not without reason that this Sacha would want our aid. If repute has spread enough for random Mahasari patrols to sniff us out..."

"The patrols," Cistine burst out suddenly. "*That's* how they keep finding us!"

Ashe let out a low breath. "You think they're getting information from ensorcelled Wardens?"

"If that's the case, everything we know is compromised." Ariadne caught a handful of flame Thorne tossed her way. "Strategies, maps, formations, future tactics..."

"And the royal family is no safer here than out in the wilds." Quill flicked up a hand just in time to take the fire she threw him. "Maybe less, even."

"Because they believe they're secure inside the Citadel walls," Maleck murmured. "But no one truly is."

A beat of silence broken just by the crackle of augmented fire.

"Do you think this is the game?" Cistine directed the question toward Thorne.

His gaze hardened. "It may very well be."

"One way to find out." Quill shipped the last spare scrap of fire to Cistine's open palm, then flicked a cinnamon stick from his pocket and jammed it into his teeth.

Cistine tossed him a hopeful look. "Do you feel like breaking a few rules?"

"Already ahead of you, Stranger."

"We need the key to Sacha's cell," Ashe said, "and we need to meet with her somewhere Cyril and Rion won't find out."

"The usual place?" Aden asked dryly.

"Midnight." Quill struck Maleck's chest with the back of his hand. "With me, *Storfir*?"

"Where are you two going?" Rozalie called after them as they started up the corridor.

Quill tossed her a grin. "We're going to pick a fight."

When they vanished, Rozalie sighed. "In that case, I'll reassign some Warden patrols. I can buy them time to get back down here without being noticed, at least. Beyond that, it's up to them."

Gratitude glowed in Cistine's eyes. "Thank you, Roz."

"Are you sure the Wardens will listen?" Ashe asked.

"Some won't, but the ones who came to Valgard with me certainly will." Rozalie winked. "And believe me...they're good at looking the other way."

CHAPTER SIX

ADEN BLOODSINGER HAD not slept well in three months, and tonight held little hope of being different.

Not that he minded, given the circumstances; like the rest of the cabal, he'd developed a certain affinity for this place Quill and Tatiana had stumbled upon during their first few weeks scouting the Citadel. Fortressed between a bathing room on one side and a weapons reserve on the other, the siege chamber was accessible by only two doors: one behind a tapestry on the Citadel's lower level, the other a long shaft leading out into the moat. Even Cistine hadn't known about it before Quill and Tatiana discovered the false wall, so it was a fair guess her less-curious parents were unaware of it as well. In the last nine months, the cabal had stockpiled the rotunda with spare bits of furniture stolen from burn heaps around the city, a brassy drink cart, and heaps of training equipment. Amber ghostlights swung from the flat, high ceiling, and by their golden sweeps Aden paced the ring of mismatched sofas and chairs, rocking Nadeem.

He loved this room, and the people in it, with a ferocity that occasionally unnerved him. Much as he'd enjoyed three months spent with his father in Stornhaz, helping Thorne oversee Kanslar Court as its High Tribune, he'd missed the late-night strategizing and drinks and card games; Cistine taking up one seat, Tatiana and Ariadne on a couch together, Ashe sprawled across the plush sides of an armchair, and Thorne stretched out at his *valenar's* feet, almost close enough to touch. Maleck and Quill's absence would soon rectify itself, and in addition to them...

Strange, but fitting, having Mira squeezed onto the sofa next to Ariadne, laughing while she sipped tea.

Sleepless or not, it was the most relaxed he'd been since setting foot back in Valgard for Kanslar's season. Life was a battle wherever he went, but it made more sense with his cabal around him—just as strangely as it made sense with this child in his arms, though Nadeem was not his.

He peered down at the boy in the crook of his arm, raising a brow at the large eyes gazing back at him. "Tell me how a child of three months has more stamina for late nights than a seasoned warrior."

Nadeem gurgled, depositing a healthy amount of drool on himself, and Aden smirked.

"Fine, keep your secrets, *Arofir*." He thumbed Nadeem's chin clean. "Just know when you're large enough for training, I'll repay the favor."

"Who says he'll be training?" Mira's teasing voice heralded her arrival at his side to reclaim her child.

Aden surrendered the boy to his mother. "You're the one who brought him into a midnight consortium of warriors."

"I did, didn't I?" Mira hefted her son fondly above her head, then swooped him down, rubbing her nose against his until he giggled. "And I still trust him to keep secrets better than Quill."

As if waiting to be summoned, the warrior arrived at last, swaggering down the hidden hall with thumbs hooked in his belt and blood crusting his upper lip. One look at him, and Tatiana sighed. "So, this time you actually *meant* a fight?"

"What *happened*?" Cistine yelped, leaping to her feet.

"Picked a fight, Stranger, keep up." Quill went to the drink cart and poured himself a tumbler of Talheimic spirits, then dropped onto one of the open sofas and rested the cool glass against a bruise on his brow.

"Did you get what we needed?" Ariadne demanded.

Grinning, Quill cocked a finger.

The splash of wet boots on rock echoed from the opposite corridor, and Maleck padded into view, soaked and sporting a freshly-blackened eye. Behind him, hands unbound, strolled in Sacha.

Thorne pinched the bridge of his nose and sighed. "A better man would ream you both for this."

"Let us know if you ever meet one," Quill chuckled, opening his palm. Maleck pitched the dungeon key underhand to him, bumped fists with Aden in passing, and made his way to the chair with Ashe, sliding his body effortlessly under hers.

Mira studied Sacha as she paused abreast of them, and those dark eyes pierced her right back. Subtly, Aden's muscles tightened.

"I don't know your face from the war stories," Sacha remarked.

"I'm the secret weapon." Mira's smile was gentle, but her eyes gleamed like new steel when she offered her hand. "Mirassah."

"Sacha." The so-called alchemist gave her hand a firm squeeze, then directed her attention to Cistine. "Why such cloak and dagger, Princess?"

Cistine held that stare without blinking. "Because I think my father's wrong. *I'm* going to help you end this war."

Thorne shifted fully upright, turning to peer at her. "I thought we brought her here to listen, not that our next steps were already decided."

"The longer we deliberate, the more lives are lost. Why wait if we already know where this ends?" Rising, Cistine jerked her head toward a table shoved off to the side of the rotunda, splayed with maps of Talheim and Mahasar. Uneasy energy nipped Aden's fingertips, the same he'd felt on those rare occasions when Noaam circumvented his authority and forced matches in Siralek that were too steep, too bloody, too soon.

That feeling rarely ended well.

Sacha joined Cistine at the map table, and one by one the others trailed over to join them; Thorne gave Cistine a wider berth than usual, and Mira, propped against the wall with Nadeem mouthing on fistfuls of her dark hair, watched the Princess through narrowed eyes.

"So, what are we up against?" Cistine asked.

Sacha splayed her hand on the map of Mahasar, gazing at it in silence for so long that the others began to fidget. "Jad began his campaign by taking your city, Middleton," she said at last, gesturing to the pike-walled lakeside city Aden had heard so much about from Rozalie, Ashe, and Maleck. "He murdered its Lord and established an Enforcer presence there, then retreated."

"How did he manage to retreat without being caught in the open?" Quill demanded. "We've had eyes on Middleton for *months*."

"Through tunnels bored under the crust of your kingdom."

"Burrow wyrms," Thorne and Ashe chorused, and looked at one another wryly.

"And what is a *burrow wyrm*?" Tatiana demanded.

"Eyeless, legless, flightless dragons," Thorne said.

"Inbred," Ashe added.

Sacha nodded. "When you unleash them underground, they will plow through any obstruction. Their holes have swallowed entire Mahasari cities."

"And as your sands closed over the holes again," Maleck said, "it would be as if such places never existed at all."

"This is how Jad is refreshing his ranks," Aden growled. "Marching his people into Middleton below our feet."

"It seems he's more interested in dragon breeding all around than we thought," Ashe muttered.

"Ah," Sacha said. "You know of the *Tayir*."

"Had a run-in with them." Quill lounged, hands hooked in his collar, thumbs tapping his clavicles. "What's their story?"

"They're Mahasar's best tool to harvest Sorcel. The plants used to brew it grow in a chasm full of fatal fumes. Men's lungs can only survive it for minutes at most, but the *Tayir* are immune. Enforcers send them into Ralathi Trench to harvest the flowers."

Tatiana's finger followed a dark furrow in the map's surface. "Someone needs to cut off those supply lines."

"And Middleton must be dealt with," Ariadne added. "Not all its inhabitants escaped when Jad invaded. Anyone still inside is liable to be poisoned with Sorcel and turned loose into Talheim."

"Do you really think they're already here?" Cistine posed the question softly toward Sacha. Aden's heart ached on her behalf.

The alchemist's stern countenance eased as well. "I know it's difficult to accept, but Dyalmun as my witness, I do."

Quill cocked his head. "Who?"

"The Maker." Cistine blew out a long breath. "If we help you, you'll give us enough antidote to save our people?"

Sacha laid a hand to her heart. "I swear it."

"And what is it you want in return?" Thorne asked.

Sacha's mouth curled up at the corner. "I want your princess to accompany me back to Mahasar and speak to *Alhuru en-Asgaid*—the Free People, the unensorcelled in Mahasar."

Warning rived through Aden's chest. He glanced at Mira and caught her frowning as well.

"Speak to them?" Cistine echoed. "Why?"

"Because they have been fighting this war far longer than you. They are weak and tired...they have need of inspiration. And they hear stories, just as I have, of you and your family. If your father won't come to help spread hope, perhaps you will."

"All this for a speech," Ashe muttered to Maleck. "Where have I heard something like that before?"

"This speech, I hope, will lead the *Alhuri* to rally and push back against Jad one last time," Sacha said. "And with the thrust of all our kingdoms at once, we may end his reign."

Cistine tapped the maps, then looked up at Ariadne across them. "What are you thinking?"

"That it is a four-pronged mission." She slipped around the table to Cistine's side, gesturing at the maps. "Middleton must be liberated. Who holds control there now?"

"Kashar replaced Jad there many months ago." Sacha's torn mouth twisted viciously. "And I agree, stopping him is of supreme importance. Jad may have begun the war, but he left Kashar here knowing his ensorcelled nephew would whip that beast until it runs its full race. We must find a way to grab the bridle." She dipped into her pocket and laid a small tincture bottle on the table. "If you slip this to Kashar, it will undo the ensorcellment and prove my word is true."

"Will he help end the war?" Aden asked. "Or underneath that drug, is he just as ruthless as his uncle?"

"I can't be certain, but the stories say he and Tirzah loved their kingdom before their uncle took them into his custody. They were Sorcel's first victims, the ones he perfected it on. If time hasn't ravaged Kashar beyond redemption, and if those stories are indeed true, you may find an ally in him once the ensorcellment lifts."

"And if not, I'd be glad to kill him." Ashe shrugged. "Problem solved."

"Either way, we drive the Enforcers out of Middleton," Tatiana said, "and collapse those burrow wyrm tunnels. Then they'll have to cross the border to replenish their ranks, and we're already watching."

"And that, stars willing, reduces the spread of Sorcel in Talheim," Ariadne agreed. "But someone will need to find Jad's influencers already here in the capital."

Aden met Mira's eyes. She'd grown somber again, cradling Nadeem tightly to her chest, but the set of her jaw and the glint in her eyes were pure steel.

"Leave that to us," he said, and she nodded.

"Are you certain?" Thorne asked.

Aden flashed his cousin a smirk. "We learned during Kanslar's season that Mira and I have a penchant for politicking, *Mavbrat*."

"You'll protect my family, too?" Cistine asked. "Watch over my mother and Eboni especially?"

"Of course we will," Mira said, and the Princess visibly relaxed.

"We'll take Middleton." Ashe gestured between herself and Maleck. "We know that place better than anyone here."

"Take Rozalie with you," Aden suggested. "Freeing Middleton from Mahasari control is paramount for the success of everyone involved."

Tatiana nudged Quill. "We've got the Sorcel supply lines."

"Just the two of you?" Sacha asked.

Thorne snorted. "Believe me, they move better as two than ten would. They'll have the lines destroyed in no time."

"Besides, it won't be only them." Ariadne smiled at Tatiana. "I'm with you, *Malatanda.*"

"Then we'll join you afterward, I take it," Quill said to Cistine.

She nodded, turning back to Sacha. "Where do we find this *Alhuru en-Asgaid*?"

Sacha tapped the map. "Masiya, the Trade Haven. This is where the largest gathering has laid roots. If they can be mustered, every other arm of their enclave will rise as well."

Cistine tossed a hopeful smile across the table, where Thorne watched her, gaze inscrutable.

If Aden could have, he would have given them the room.

Thorne turned his attention to the map after a moment, thumb snaking across the border down into Mahasar. "You're all committed to this...to treason. To outright defying the King of our allied kingdom and risking that this may very well be a trap, even considering what rebellion has cost us before?"

"My father isn't like Salvotor," Cistine snapped.

Thorne grimaced, withdrawing his hand. "He is still a ruler. He is *your* father. And no father takes kindly to direct defiance of his orders."

In the silence, Quill's swallow was audible. Ashe grimaced. Maleck folded his arms and traded his weight heavily.

"He doesn't have to know. He leaves tomorrow on a tour at the southern barracks with Rion," Cistine said after a beat. "No one knows but my mother, Rion, and me. That's what Rion wanted to postpone...and that's our chance to move."

Thorne's head jerked back slightly. "Were you already planning to sneak away from the Citadel again?"

She scowled. "I didn't hear you complaining the last time I did."

"Which time are you referring to? The one when your ambush in the Calaluns went awry, or when you came back to Valgard for the war?"

"The war I helped *win*, thank you!"

"At what *cost*, Cistine?"

"Enough," Ashe cut in. "Obviously, this isn't quite settled. But whether anyone goes to Mahasar or not, we still need to solve the problem with Middleton."

"And the ensorcelled Talheimics," Aden agreed. "The supply lines as well."

"We'll decide the rest by tomorrow morning." Cistine's gaze burned into Thorne with nothing short of venom.

Quill whistled quietly and shrugged up from the wall. "All right, well, you two enjoy that. Let's get the prisoner back to her cell before the Wardens change shifts."

"Thank you, Princess," Sacha said. "I know you have little reason to trust a Mahasari. But we want the same thing: an end to Jad's schemes."

When Cistine peeled her glare away from Thorne, her smile was genuine. "I believe that."

Quill guided Sacha down the hall to the moat. Aden, practically sweating at the tension in the room, jerked his head at Mira. "Shall we?"

"That may be best, if we ever want this one to sleep." She gave Nadeem a bounce, then fixed her eyes on Cistine. "But I'll be awake a bit longer if anyone needs me."

Together she and Aden slipped into the outer hall, walking its comfortable width in silence. They needed no light, and in the shadows Nadeem cooed to himself, soothing toward slumber.

"What did you make of that?" Aden asked quietly.

"I saw no indication that Sacha lied, if that's what you're wondering. But as for the rest of it..." Mira blew out a breath. "Cistine is desperate to prove herself a capable leader despite her curse. And desperation makes a poor dance partner. It will trip you more often than not."

"Clever words."

"Thank you, I like to keep a repertoire."

Light filtered ahead around the seams of the false wall behind the tapestry, and Aden slowed. "I'm sorry for this. I know you didn't agree to come along with us to investigate drugged Talheimics."

"I doubt I agreed for any of the reasons *you're* thinking." Mira brushed ahead of him and fitted her shoulder to the wall, but her strength wasn't quite enough to shift it alone.

Chuckling, Aden leaned his forearm into the seam, grinding it open effortlessly. "Enlighten me."

Mira's unburdened shoulder bobbed, jostling Nadeem slightly. "That chamber in Kanslar's wing is lonelier than you can imagine, even with Hana, Kendar, and Elsin always there. Sometimes it's lonelier *because* they are, and Sander...isn't."

Pain lanced through the blood-oath scar on Aden's palm. "You could have asked for any other room. Thorne would give it to you."

Secrets danced on the edge of Mira's half-smile. "I'm aware."

They shut the false wall and slipped into the moonlit corridor, lined with Talheimic artifacts and tapestries of horses galloping on open plains.

"Do you know, the biggest struggle with pain isn't the sensation," Mira added as they walked. "It's the identity of it. Do you remember how you struggled to release the Blood Hive after you left?"

Aden slid his hands deep into his pockets. "It was part of me. The largest part, I thought, of the man I was."

Mira nodded. "Pain can be a raft we cling to that keeps us from casting out into safer waters. Because, however safe they are, they're still unknown."

"Better the suffering you know than the risk of worse."

A burst of rowdy laughter from ahead silenced Mira's reply—Warden voices, raised in banter. Normally Aden would pass them by with a glare and his head high, but tonight, with Sacha's warnings in his ears and he and Mira out long past sensible hours, coming from a secret meeting in a hidden place...

He grabbed her arm, spinning her and Nadeem behind another tapestry. The boy fussed, rousing slightly, and Aden slid a hand under Mira's, supporting his head the way he liked. Silent and unbreathing, they listened.

"...would still rather have a Mahasari here than a Valgardan. But who asked me?" one man scoffed.

"True that," a woman replied. "If you'd asked *me* a year ago if the King would let those rat-eaters inside the Citadel, much less that his daughter would be *married* to one..."

"Inez! That's our Princess you're speaking about!" A second woman's harsh voice preceded the slap of an open palm on hair. "Show some respect!"

"You can't honestly be all right with having a Valgardan married onto the throne, Adela!"

"Well, no, I'm not, but as for Cistine..."

"She's one of them. We'd be better off if she went north when all this is over."

The whispers swelled, then vanished down the hall. Aden let loose his breath, trembling with anger on behalf of Cistine and Thorne. He all but flinched when Mira tapped his arm. "Aden. You can let go now."

He was still gripping her tightly by the bicep, locked against his body. Grimacing, he released her, towing the banner aside, and they stepped out to watch the Wardens vanish up the hall.

Though he wouldn't be the one going into battle on this mad mission, things would by no means by simpler for him and Mira—finding ensorcelled traitors in a Citadel already divided was a war all its own.

CHAPTER SEVEN

I T WAS ONLY by sheer willpower that Cistine held her temper in check until she and Thorne were alone in their room. Slamming the door, she rounded on him, anger sparking in her nerves. "You don't support this."

He lowered himself onto the foot of the bed. "I believe there are reasons for and against going."

"Then tell me about it privately! But back there, in front of Sacha, we needed to present a unified front!"

"Then why didn't you tell me you were already committed to going?"

Pressing her back to the door, she slid down to a crouch, looking up into his earnest face. Concern, not anger, darkened his eyes. "Our kingdoms need this, Thorne." She swallowed heavily. "*I* need this."

Thorne came to sit against the wall beside her, an arm's span apart. "We may be separated by touch, *Logandir*, but that doesn't mean you have to make decisions alone. I thought you knew that."

Cistine laughed bitterly, plucking at her armored sleeve. "I want to, more than anything. But there's so *much* to prove to my people, and it's my duty to save them. I have to show I can be as good a queen as my father is a king, even if I can never touch them."

Thorne studied her sidelong. "And this is how you do it. By going into danger for them, traveling to Mahasar like you did to Valgard."

She raised her shoulders helplessly. "Who else can I send? I won't risk our cabal on that mission."

"Nor would I. But if there's any merit to Cyril's fears, we can't afford to risk you, either."

"I think that's a risk worth taking if it stops Jad from hurting our people. You told me once that a princess brings hope...it sounds like that's precisely what Mahasar needs. And if it wins us the antidote for our people, how can I say no?"

"You can't. Which is why I'm not letting you go alone." Thorne rocked his head back against the door. "I'm with you."

Relief spilled down her throat. "Thank—"

"Consider deeply what that means, Cistine," he interrupted quietly. "I'm with you to ensure you come home regardless of any plans Jad has set in motion. That means if it becomes a choice whether you return or I do, I *will* choose you."

Her breath caught, relief blackening to dread as she held his stare.

Not just her own life being risked. She was betting his against the odds that Sacha told the truth; that this was not the elaborate trap her father believed it to be.

Her resolve wavered, and she clapped it with steel. A queen did not put her own heart first; she did not think of her own needs before her people. "I have to do this, Thorne."

The words tasted of betrayal, but his expression didn't change. "Then we go."

They were silent for some time, backs to the door, watching shadows shift on the walls as moonlight dipped lower and lower through the curtained windows.

"I missed you." The semidarkness swallowed Cistine's voice. "I can't remember if I told you that. I spent every night you were in Valgard trying to make a pillow nest the same size as you."

A low chuckle rumbled through him, vibrating the door. "I drenched my bed in so much lavender and lemon, I went to every Tribunal session with a headache."

She burst into giggles. "I stole all the sandalwood soap from the baths. Papa thought the Valgardans were hoarding."

"I drank my weight in tea every day."

"I drank *mead* more than tea!"

"I wrote you letters I never sent."

Her breath hitched, and she turned her head to the wall, meeting his anguished gaze. "So did I."

Thorne's arm dropped, hand inching across the floor. So near, and yet so far—a fathomless chasm between them. "*My dearest Wildheart,*" he murmured, and her heart skipped. "*I thought I'd learned all the ways I could miss you. I was wrong.*"

"*My Starchaser,*" she whispered, and his chest stopped rising and falling. "*I don't feel as strong without you supporting me.*"

"*I dream every night of holding you...*"

"*I dream of being held.*"

Her fingertips were a whisper from his. A thrill of terror and excitement spiraled through her.

"I'm always with you," Thorne finished, and somehow it felt like consent...grace for their mission. A blessing that eased the knot of guilt in her chest.

"With my whole heart," Cistine murmured.

"For my whole life."

The old wound in her gut ripped wide, bleeding freely, and she pulled her hand back to safety in her lap.

Shadows reigned across a blood-spattered battlefield, the dying as lost as the already-dead, and across the expanse Cistine watched her power cut them all down, one by one. The cabal, the Bloodwights, the unified Courts...all victims of *Haval,* the cruel augment fuming from Cistine's fingertips. Killing, killing—

She woke with a start, back drenched in sweat, captive in her silken sheets. Gasping, she kicked loose and rolled to her feet, backing away from the bed; on the other side, Thorne's snores went on from the floor. But she'd seen him fall, seen him dying again.

Shivering, she snatched up her robe and bolted from the room.

The Citadel halls were quieter than usual, the servants and Wardens given the night off so few would know which way the King departed in the black hours before dawn. The ruse would be that he traveled to the east to ensure the coastal defenses there; only Cistine's family, Rion, and now the cabal knew how near he would be to Jad's borders. A precaution she'd thought almost paranoid before, but now she was grateful for it. A day she'd been dreading for weeks was now her first and perhaps only chance to end this war with minimal risk to her kingdom.

But with great risk to her cabal.

Stomach churning, she slipped into the dining hall to find it quiet, only one lonely figure seated at one of the long tables. A book was open before him, a bowl of whipped cream and shaved chocolate tucked in the crook of his arm.

Cistine almost turned and walked back out, but it was too late; he caught sight of her.

"Couldn't sleep?" Cyril asked with a half-smile.

Cistine rubbed the lingering gooseflesh from her arms. "Bad dreams."

"That makes two of us." He gestured to the chair two seats down. "I can't promise I'll be good company, but the cream is delicious."

Her gurgling stomach decided for her.

With her own bowl retrieved from the kitchens, Cistine sank down in the chair near him. He shut the book and leaned back, bowl gathered onto his stomach, studying her. "Do you understand why I made the choice I did with the Mahasari woman today?"

Irritation racked through Cistine's body, but she nodded anyway, spooning down a bite of sugary cream.

"I know you don't like it," Cyril said when she didn't speak. "You may even think I'm being cowardly. But I'd rather be thought a coward than play loosely with the lives under my command. Or with my family's."

"But you're leaving tomorrow anyway," Cistine argued. "Won't we be in danger regardless?"

"It's different. I'm going to assess the southern forts, not stepping onto Jad's own land where he holds every advantage. There's necessary risk, and then there's foolishness. You're straying dangerously close to the latter."

Stung, she looked down, stirring the fluffy mounds of cream. After everything she'd done in the war against the Bloodwights, the narrow victories and daring strategies, it sat heavy as iron in her gut that her father trusted her so little; that he'd given her so few chances to prove herself.

"I know this is difficult for you," Cyril added gently. "You sacrificed much to keep this war from happening, and now there's no end to it in sight. But I need you to trust me...I know what I'm doing. These choices you find so unpalatable will keep our family safe."

"Meanwhile, our people keep being hurt."

"People will be hurt in either case, Cistine. By not stepping into Jad's schemes, I hope to give them a fighting chance."

"I know, Papa." Just as she knew he was wrong. War in the north had taught her an enemy left to fester too long became more and more difficult to kill. She couldn't allow her father's caution to become Jad's weapon.

The rumble of another late-season storm growled through the walls, and Cyril raised his eyes to the dark, vaulted ceiling. A mischievous smile teased his lips. "Shall we go watch?"

Cistine bit back her dismissal. Just for tonight, they could be father and daughter—not King and Princess, not warriors of different minds taking the same battlefield. He was leaving tomorrow, and so was she. Gods knew what things would be like when they reunited; but tonight, her father loved and trusted her. She couldn't waste that, either.

"I'd like that." She snatched up her bowl. "I'll race you!"

With him laughing behind her, she sprinted out into the lightning-striped halls.

CHAPTER EIGHT

SHOCKING AS IT was, Tatiana Dawnstar would miss the Citadel. She'd miss its glass courtyards and alabaster stone, its hidden passages and glittering bridges. She'd miss having the cabal all together again.

She would miss moments like this, too, with her favorite people sprawled on her bed in the early-morning light, assessing maps of Mahasar.

"Ralathi Trench." Quill slung his long, white topcoat of hair across his head, the dark bristles below rasping on his callused palm. "That's where they're harvesting this plant for the Sorcel."

"It's near the capital, Arak Shehr." Ariadne traced a finger along the rendering of the city's domes and minarets. "Separated by only a finger of mountains. That's almost too near for my liking."

Tatiana's nape prickled, and she stopped stuffing rations of dried fruit and beef and waterskins into her bag. "Trap?" She didn't trust Sacha's word for much, and Cistine was known to walk headfirst into danger; it was Ariadne's assessment Tatiana trusted most.

"Possibly. But it's sensible Jad's kept the mining of his greatest resource close to his dwelling place. Perhaps he visits there to evaluate their work."

"Good. Hope he shows his face while we're there." Quill cracked his knuckles. "I wouldn't mind taking a swing at the *Mad King* myself."

Tatiana rolled her eyes, securing her satchel and dropping onto the bed between them. "Save it for the Trench, Featherbrain."

He tossed her a brash grin, sprawling back on his elbows. "I've got enough of it for both."

Ariadne coughed, gesturing to the map. "Wind augments will carry us to the Trench, but we'll need to establish a presence nearby, to assess its workings before we strike."

"Just like the Black Coast mines." *And just like Selv Torfjel.* Stretching on her stomach with arms folded, Tatiana studied the map. Its dusty paper notes filled her lungs and quieted her jangling nerves at the horrific memories of that place—and its aftermath. "This looks like an oasis here, just to the east."

Ariadne nodded. "Shinar, yes. We're likely to encounter Mahasaris there...even Enforcers."

Quill shrugged. "So we play traveling merches, get the lay of the land."

"And bring down those lines," Tatiana added. "No matter what. Then we get to Masiya..." Trailing her fingertip down to the trade city, she tapped the marker. "And rally with Thorne and Cistine."

Ariadne heaved a sigh. "I suppose we can refine the plan once we have a better understanding of what we're facing."

"That seems to be the strategy of the hour." The voice came from the bedchamber doorway; Thorne gripped the stone arch above his head with one hand and sloped casually inside, but one look at his eyes and the old tension snapped through Tatiana's body.

Quill stretched and groaned, gripping the bed's corner post and swinging to his feet. "Time to go?"

"The King and Rion have left Astoria," Thorne confirmed. "Cistine's bringing word to her mother of a disturbance in the Calaluns. That should give her and I a fortnight in Mahasar at least. If we don't report by then, Aden will tell the Queen he received a cipher from us, that we need more time. Tati, the key?"

Grinning, she pitched him the dungeon cell key. "You know, Viktor Pollack is a lightweight. A few drinks bought by the pretty girl down the counter, and he didn't even question whose hand was in his back pocket."

"Just remember to return it before you leave the city," Thorne reminded her.

"Have a little faith, will you?"

"I do." He smiled, stepping into the room. "In all of you."

"But just a little." Quill clapped him in an embrace. "See you on the dunes, *Allet*."

"It was good to see you for two entire days," Tatiana added wryly, taking her turn to wrap their Chancellor in her arms. Weariness stooped his back, and he held her a little longer and tighter than he had Quill—like he knew she could feel the weight in him, and he needed someone to share it with.

Once he moved past her to Ariadne, Tatiana excused herself and went hunting for their princess.

She found Cistine in the library, gathered into a windowsill, arms wrapped around her ankles, staring across the vast sprawl of Astoria. The princess didn't turn her head when Tatiana arrived, but said in greeting, "I wish you could've seen this place when everyone wasn't so afraid. We would've gone shopping."

"We will, once this is all over. Trust me, *Yani*, we'll drain those royal coffers dry on the best clothes." Tatiana hopped into the sill with her, and Cistine curled against the sleek oak frame, giving her as much space as possible. "How did it go with the Queen?"

"Too well. All she said was to be safe and come back when the task was finished." Cistine sank her chin onto her knees. "I don't know what's worse anymore...how easy it is to lie to them, or how quickly they believe me."

"Well, we've always known they spoiled you to the core."

Cistine shot her a dry look, but didn't manage so much as a smile. "Will that make me a better queen, do you think, or a worse one?"

"I think that's something you don't need to worry about just now." Reclining against the opposite frame, Tatiana drew the knife from her boot and scratched Old Valgardan runes into the supple wood. "Is that why you're sitting here when you should be packing or saying goodbye to the others?"

"I'm tired of goodbyes. I've been tired of them since my wedding."

Tatiana grimaced. "Well, stars willing, this will be the last for a while."

"It won't be. Even if we end the war, you're all going to leave again. Even Ashe." Now the smile made an appearance, limp on her lips. "I have to betray my family to win this war, and even if I win, I still lose."

If it had been anyone else, Tatiana would've reached for their hand and squeezed until they felt every bone in her grip holding their broken edges together. Instead, she bored the knife into the sill, arresting Cistine's attention. "We're not losing today. Do you hear me? You wanted this, and we're supporting you. Don't lose your courage now."

Cistine wiped her knuckles beneath her eyes. "I'm not." Taking a deep breath, she vaulted from the windowsill, peeling her shoulders back. "Rally the others."

That task didn't take long, though Thorne's absence was notable once they gathered in Cistine's private chamber; Tatiana tossed up a silent prayer to the gods that he'd be quick, breaking in and out of the dungeon.

"You all know what to do?" Cistine asked the moment Tatiana slipped into the room, Aden and Mira in tow, and shut the door.

"Let you get out of the city, then stage a prison break," Quill said around a cinnamon stick. "Frame Pollack for shirking watch, just for fun."

"Not just for fun, he's the one who followed a girl to the tavern where his key went missing," Tatiana pointed out. Though he hadn't known the girl was Valgardan, and a friend of Tatiana's, working under her orders. "It will be well-deserved."

"Roz and I will pretend to track Sacha to Middleton," Ashe said, "with Mal and Bres along for support. We'll find a way in through the tunnels and deal with Kashar."

"With Sacha in the wind and most likely a Mahasari informant, we're heading south to reinforce the King." Quill tossed a smirk at Cistine. "On your orders."

"By the time either Solene or Cyril realizes we're not where we said we were, stars willing, this will be finished," Ariadne concluded.

"Meanwhile, Mira and I will be here," Aden added, "searching for the ensorcelled among your father's council."

Cistine nodded. "Remember, the ensorcelled *can't* know we're on to them. If word reaches Jad of what we're doing, everything will be twice as difficult."

Mira winked. "Don't worry. We'll lie like all our lives depend on it."

Silence pinched off every voice, and for a moment they simply looked at one another. Melancholy roiled in Tatiana's stomach, and she laid her hand over the old scar there...the permanent reminder of the thief that was war, and how it spared no one. Not the young, not the old, not even the unborn. Not even the ones they couldn't afford to lose.

"None of us wanted this," Cistine said at length. "I came to Valgard to stop a war, not make you all fight one. But I want you to know how grateful I am that you're willing to do this. And how much I wish I could hug you all goodbye."

A smattering of chuckles burst from the cabal, Tatiana's among them. Quill said, raspier than usual, "Us, too, Stranger."

"One last push," Ariadne said. "For Talheim."

"For Talheim," they all echoed.

Bright-eyed, Cistine snatched up her satchel and swung it across her body. "Be safe. We'll see you all when this is over."

"And perhaps you and I will have our talk." Mira's accent hung heavy with things unspoken, and color bloomed in Cistine's cheeks.

"We'll have to."

"You and Thorne watch each other's backs," Ashe ordered.

"The rest of you as well," Cistine answered quietly.

Tatiana stepped out with her into the hall while the others went back to murmuring about their plans. "Be careful out there, *Yani*. Sacha may want the same things we do, but there's something about her..."

Cistine's eyes narrowed. "What do you mean?"

She shrugged. "I can't place it, exactly. Just keep your eye on her."

"We will." Cistine backed away down the hall. "After all, what else will I have to look at?"

"Thorne's backside?"

Rolling her eyes, Cistine blew her a parting kiss, then twirled on heel and jogged down the hall. Tatiana watched her go, a pang echoing in her chest.

She didn't flinch when a warm smell of cinnamon and steel enveloped her and an arm looped around her chest from behind. "I hate it, too, Saddlebags."

"The worst part is knowing ending this war won't make *everything* right," Tatiana sighed, resting her chin over Quill's wrist where it settled over her collarbone.

"Maybe not, but it's easier to deal with problems when you're not worried about someone sticking a knife in your back while you solve them." Quill turned her in his grip, holding the length of her body flush to his. "You know what will cheer you up? Staging a prison break."

Though touched with emptiness, it felt good to grin. "You always did know how to show a lady a good time."

CHAPTER NINE

CISTINE, THORNE, AND Sacha entered the trade haven of Masiya under the cover of night after a brief journey by wind augment; while the alchemist traded her loaned Valgardan battle threads for a shirt, pants, and half-veil to mask her scarred face, Thorne and Cistine bedded down in a tight, dark gap between two sandstone buildings.

It was a colder night than Cistine had expected, and she didn't know what dawn would bring. She lay awake for hours, listening to the faraway hum of city life, stomach churning with guilt at the deceptions that had brought them this far.

Perhaps she wouldn't even have to be gone a full week; perhaps she'd return before anyone in Astoria realized she'd lied.

Those hopes chased her off to sleep, and she woke in what seemed like a different world altogether: the warmth of Thorne's armored leather jacket flung over her shoulders, and outside the awning-draped alley, a street glowing like the inside of a prism.

Breathing Thorne's name, Cistine hopped to her feet and slipped quickly to the alley mouth, finding that under last night's shadows, Sacha had led them to a blown-glass market. Heated with the fire of a hundred kilns, the air pulsed and shimmered despite the early hour—but not just from the warmth. Heavy cords strung across the market-top hoisted blown glass of every shape and color, from spearlike twists to thick pomegranate globes, spirals and feathers and even rune-like renderings bright as fire. Cistine's heart squeezed so fiercely with wonder, tears leaped to her eyes.

Thorne's low whistle ghosted her ear; he was right behind her, arm propped to the wall above her head, peering past her. "Now, *that's* a sight."

"You should see them after it rains." Sacha's tone was oddly wistful, and Cistine twisted to find her already on her feet, boots tugged on, veil fixed over her scarred mouth. "Come, we've no time to waste." Cistine's stomach growled in protest, and Thorne chuckled. Sacha's cheeks plumped with a smile beneath the veil. "We'll eat while we walk."

Just beyond the glass market, a wide avenue sported food stalls and booths just beginning to roll up their goathide sides. Sacha haggled at one, and though no money traded hands, they walked away with three cloth-wrapped flatbreads, a bowl of some thick, white sauce, and an envelope Sacha tucked into her waistband.

"Just a detour," she explained when Cistine's gaze caught on the envelope. "In Mahasar, we often trade with favors."

"Are three flatbreads really worth one letter?" Thorne asked as Cistine accepted the flatbread, nostrils stuffed with the aromatic smell of yeast and garlic.

Sacha winked. "It is when he can sell five times that in the hour and a half it would take him to cross the city and deliver it himself."

"In that case, should we have asked for more?" Cistine half-joked.

Sacha tapped the envelope's corner. "Oh, I believe this will be worth its weight in gold."

Foot travel was sparse at this hour, sunlight just beginning to slide between shops and stalls, paving the well-worn dust red-gold. Buildings of every shape, state, and color lined their way, from towering blackwood edifices to short brick homes and clay huts. Residences and shops wove together, all likened by the smells of sage, saffron, and sweat riding the air. Excitement had Cistine twisting on heel when they passed through a cloth district under silk and cotton banners braiding the shop balconies together in a lurid dome. "There's just so *much* to see!"

"I'm surprised we don't stand out more." Thorne slid a hand under his hood, fingering the augment-shocked hair beneath.

Sadness tugged the corners of Sacha's eyes. "Mahasar was once a haven of commerce. Ours were the most diverse markets, the most resplendent coasts. People of every tongue and tribe, every color and kind, came to our spice markets and made their homes in our cities. Even your Valgardans came here, half a century ago. But when Jad rose to power, people soon found these shores were unfriendly places. The only ones who haven't fled are the ones who can't."

"Well, that's going to change."

Thorne's calm certainty drew Cistine's focus back to the task at hand. *Stop behaving like a princess on market day,* she chided herself. *You're here as a future queen to stop a war, not to shop.*

They reached a place where the road broadened suddenly into another marketplace teeming with shoppers and vendors, the murmurs of conversation sliced intermittently with hawking shouts. Cistine's skin pebbled at the sight and sound; she would never be able to walk among them without brushing into someone.

Thorne stepped nearer to her, jerking his chin at the flat roofs above. "Keep watch?"

Relieved, she nodded and slipped down a side alley full of mismatched awnings. Flexing her fingers, she took a running leap, kicked off the wall, grabbed onto the nearest awning and started to climb.

Quill would've been proud—she'd never scaled a rooftop so quickly. Scrambling onto its railed platform, she darted past clusters of seats and potted ferns, keeping Thorne and Sacha within sight while they delivered the letter; her *valenar* had knocked back his hood, baring the beacon of his silver hair for her to follow. They stopped at a stall hanging with burlap satchels, ducking inside, and on the roof's corner Cistine sat to wait.

Despite the early hour, heat crawled up the nape of her neck, and in the market below women shed their cloaks and linked arms; men toasted cold cups of water and laughed at the weather. The sight birthed an ache in Cistine so deep, her breakfast threatened to make an untimely return.

Was this her curse for the rest of her life? To be so separate from everyone else, everyone who didn't carry death beneath their skin, that they might as well have been flickers in the dust shrinking away from her grasp?

She sat alone with her miserable thoughts while the sun crawled higher, and worry for Thorne and Sacha had braided with the ache in her middle when they emerged at last—Sacha bereft of the letter, and Thorne carrying one of the shop's satchels in his fist. They made straight for the alley where she'd first vanished, and she clambered down to meet them. "What took you so long?"

"You can blame this one." Sacha hiked a thumb at Thorne. "It seems a dangerous mission is, to him, the perfect time for shopping."

Cistine shot him a quizzical look, then yelped when he pitched the satchel to her. The moment it struck her palms, bursting the smell of herbs into her nostrils, she knew what it was.

"Orange spice tea," Thorne said anyway. "For the road."

Gratitude tightened Cistine's throat. She might not be as much a part of the world anymore, but he always found ways to remind her she was the center of his.

Pocketing the satchel, she followed Sacha from the alley's opposite side out into a warren of streets, Thorne close on her heels. While Masiya's main thoroughfare was patterned and pleasant, the streets around it proved to be a hopeless, tangled mess. She would've been lost in minutes if not for their confident guide; though they doubled back and took cross-streets more times than Cistine could number, Sacha's stride never faltered. Finally, she led them along an aqueduct's railed edge—the water below furrowing at the base of stone arches and columns plunged deep into the current—and came to a halt at last. Looking both ways, she pried up one of the stones in the middle of the walkway, revealing a hole below. The sunlight directly overhead barely illumined a metallic glint in the shadows.

Thorne crouched and stretched out a fist, knocking on the metal. "Rungs?"

"You can only see them at certain times of day. Otherwise it appears like any other hole." Sacha nudged his fingers away with her foot. "You two go down first. I'll set the stone behind us."

Cistine slid over the edge of the hole, reaching blindly where Thorne had touched, and began her slow descent into pitch-darkness through a shaft so narrow her breaths closed in tightly around her ears. It was an effort not to think of dark mountain wind vents or gauntlets deep beneath the earth when Sacha pulled the stone back into place, plunging their way into shadow. The sound of Thorne's breathing kept her going—and the knowledge that if she paused to panic, he might crash into her. Still, a bark of shock escaped her when her foot left the rungs and slammed into rock instead.

"It's the bottom!" she hissed up at Thorne, then stepped back until her shoulders struck a wall. He dropped before her, the wind of his movement the only tell of where he stood; then Sacha landed, boots scuffing stone.

"This way." Her voice guided them to the left, and for a time they walked in blackness. Cistine curled her fists and measured her breaths, chanting silent reminders that she had survived far worse places than this. But still, the shadows felt like fetters around her ankles and enemy skin beneath her hands.

"Wildheart." The sound of her Name jolted her out of the spiral of dark memory. "I'm right here."

Heat pricked her eyes. "I know."

No sooner had the words left her lips than light ignited before them, and Cistine slammed to a halt, shielding her face. Sizzling ropes of ultramarine crisscrossed her vision in the echo of the fire pulsing ahead— torches, held by a cavalcade of men and women in varying attire. Some wore marketers' dayclothes; others wore armor. Cistine tensed, and behind her, Thorne's sabers whispered in their sheaths.

"There's no need for violence," Sacha said. "Sabir, Mairin, it's me."

The dark-skinned, dark-haired man at the head of the gathering shot a glance at the woman beside him, light and narrow-featured, his opposite in every way. Their stares held for a moment; then he broke into a grin, slid two fingers into his mouth, and whistled.

At once, all the others dispersed. The man named Sabir stepped forward, extending his torchless hand. "It appears your mission was successful."

"I've brought aid, yes." Sacha clasped his hand briefly, embraced Mairin, then gestured over her shoulder. "Cistine and Thorne Novacek, the heirs of Talheim."

Cistine winced, but Thorne didn't correct the assumption, slipping past her to offer a hand to Sabir. "We heard your kingdom was in need. We've come to help."

"Dyalmun bless you." Sabir gripped Thorne's hand in both of his. "We'll take all the help we can get."

"Have things worsened in my absence?" An edge crept into Sacha's voice.

"Thankfully, no. But the other captains grow restless, and Ez...well, you know." Sabir's face fell for a moment; then he flashed a charming smile at Cistine and changed the subject. "I see the rumors are true. Talheim's princess is fairer by far than ours ever was."

Sacha snorted, and Cistine flushed. "I don't know about *that*."

"I do." Thorne grinned, and Cistine stuck out her tongue at him.

"Come." Sabir draped an arm around Mairin's shoulders. "*Alhuru en-Asgaid* welcomes you, friends."

He led them out of the dark tunnel into a tall, broad chamber edged in torch sconces and lanterns, stretching some distance back before the shadows swallowed it whole. The middle was flagged with old cobblestones, the edges riddled in canvas and goathide tents and booths like the market stalls. Small fires burned in stone pits, and men and women raised their hands in greeting. Smiling shyly, Cistine fluttered her fingers in return.

"Welcome to *Via Hosial*," Mairin called back to them, "the way beneath the world."

"Ancient caravan tunnels," Sabir explained. "Built by our ancestors to ferry goods during the sandstorm season, when the crossing between Masiya and the coast was too dangerous."

"That's not *this* season, is it?" Cistine asked.

"No, only in the summer," Mairin laughed. "Besides, these old tunnels were bricked over when Jad took the throne. He doesn't like things happening where he can't see them."

"Which makes it the perfect place for us." Sabir planted a kiss on her temple.

Freckles of water plopped onto the stones beside Cistine's feet. She jerked away, craning her head back to peer at the ceiling, but it too was swallowed in shadow.

"We're directly beneath the aqueduct," Sacha explained. "A danger with Sorcel in the water, but these tunnels are still safer than anywhere aboveground for the *Alhuri*."

They halted before a dark slit in the tunnel wall, and Sabir waved an arm. "He'll be eager to see you, Sacha."

"Isn't he always," she sighed. "Thank you. I'll see you and the other captains at dinner." With a final nod and a smile at Thorne and Cistine, Sabir steered Mairin to one of the fires.

"And who, precisely, is eager to see us?" Thorne's casual tone held a faint undercurrent of tension.

"Esmail, the *Alhuri* leader." Sacha led them down the short tunnel into a darker, drier room, the roof tarred and sealed tightly—and no wonder. It was a library of sorts, mismatched shelves crowding the walls, overflowing with volumes both ancient and new. The sight of them, even with spines sketched in Mahasari words she couldn't fathom, lifted Cistine's spirits so high a smile leaped to her lips.

Motioning them back at the tunnel mouth, Sacha approached a man bent over a table strewn with charts at the back of the room. He spun when she cleared her throat, hand to his sword, and the look on his face set Cistine's hair on end.

Until she'd gone to Valgard, she hadn't truly fathomed how war could paint the contours of someone's features, shifting their countenance like a mountain ravaged by landslides. But even having never seen this man before, she knew the flint-hardness of his gaze and the cool set of his mouth were strikes of battle chiseled into his flesh. Even when he smiled, recognizing Sacha, there was little warmth to his face. "Hello, sparrow."

"Hello, Ez." Sacha's greeting wasn't quite cold, but it still made Cistine's arms prickle. "Keeping busy while I've been away?"

"As busy as can be." His gaze leaped past her to Thorne and Cistine. "And who are these?"

"New friends. I would be less concerned with them and more with your enemies," Sacha added briskly. "I just delivered a message this morning from one Enforcer to another, posturing as vendors."

Cistine glanced at Thorne; judging by the sharp flicker of his jaw, he hadn't realized the men they'd couriered for today were Enforcers, either.

Esmail didn't seem surprised by the report; in fact, he smiled. "It's being taken care of."

Sacha folded her arms. "You had no idea, did you?"

He swept a hand through his dark hair, paying Cistine and Thorne an irate glance. "Must we do this now?"

"We must. I'm concerned."

"Of course you are." Esmail's face softened in a way that reminded Cistine too much of Julian. How many times had he preempted a valid argument with the same gentling of his gaze? "Look at you...back in the city a day at most, and already you've found Enforcers hiding in plain sight. That's more than any of our patrols have managed."

"Then I think you and Sabir need to have words about who you're recruiting."

"Or perhaps we're not the ones for the task." Esmail's eyes sparkled with such vehemence even Cistine leaned back from him. "There's never been a woman more fit to captain the *Alhuri*."

"A woman who doesn't kill, leading those who seek Jad's head." Sacha shook hers with an indulgent smile. "You're the one for the task, Esmail az-Lochan. Not I."

"I know, I know...you're an alchemist, and that's all you care to be." Esmail sighed, as if they'd had this conversation before. "Still a pity. With you at our head, we'd be certain to succeed."

Curiosity arched against Cistine's ribs, but she bit it back. Queens couldn't always satisfy their interest on the first morsels they found.

At last, Esmail's hand fell from his blade. "And these friends of yours, have they come to fight and die for the cause?"

A low protest rumbled in Thorne's chest, but Cistine stepped forward, flashing a smile. "Not exactly. Princess Cistine Novacek of Talheim. This is my husband, Thorne—"

"What are you doing here?" Esmail interrupted, his gaze lacking even a lick of the warmth he'd shown Sacha.

Cistine faltered on the verge of a curtsy. "We came to offer our assistance. We heard *Alhuru en-Asgaid*—"

"Whatever you heard was a lie. We are not weak, we are not wanting, and we have absolutely no wish for your help."

"Ez, enough," Sacha sighed. "They've come as friends."

"They're Talheimics, I know precisely why they've come." Esmail's frigid gaze held Cistine fast like a snare, stopping her protest. "I was born in Khorraris. I know what the Novacek family is capable of. Mark my words, no princess, prince, queen or *king* of yours will ever be welcome here."

"Esmail!" Sacha snapped. "*Alhuru en-Asgaid* opens its arms to *all*."

"To all who fight for the cause," Esmail snorted. "Don't think I don't know why you've come, *Princess*. Hoping to force a change of power like your father did with Jad?"

"No!" Cistine protested. "The only reason I came was to help inspire your people to fight for their home!"

Esmail stepped so near, Cistine was forced to recoil or risk killing him outright. "Let me be clear. The *Alhuri* obey *me*. I inspire, I lead, I tell this one and that one where to go. Unlike Talheim, we do not require another kingdom to rescue us." His disdainful gaze leaped to Thorne, then dropped back to Cistine. "Clever of you, using Sacha to get close to me. But I know the ways of your family. There is nothing but death in your hands."

Cistine flinched, and Thorne stepped forward, slamming a hand into Esmail's chest, forcing him back a step. "Enough. A true leader shows respect for others of title."

"Your titles mean nothing here. *You* are nothing here." Esmail jerked his chin. "Go home. No one wants you in this place."

It demanded all Cistine's strength not to flee before him. Humiliation stained her cheeks, but she held his glittering stare for a moment before she stalked from the room, Thorne and Sacha a silent, grim presence behind her.

In the heart of *Via Hosial*, Cistine halted, the fire-striped walls blurring before her eyes. Sacha slipped past her and beckoned, leading her and Thorne to a pattern of steps up the tunnel wall to a shelf high above. They sat, and Cistine cradled her head in her hands. "That was a *disaster*."

"Not by your doing." Thorne's voice deepened with rage. "There are few things worse than a leader without civility."

"I'm sorry," Sacha murmured. "I'd hoped, with things as desperate as they are, that Esmail might be ready to accept help."

Cistine flashed her a glance. "You had to know how he saw my family. Did you bring me here just to see the pain we've caused?"

Sacha's gaze hardened. "No. This is not about you, it's about Esmail and what a poor leader he is. How much these people need help, hope...and true guidance."

Thorne's eyes narrowed. "How do you mean?"

"Esmail az-Lochan is interested in two things: glory and vengeance." Sacha's tone dipped with her gaze. "The King's Shadow, Tirzah ra-Kyrian, murdered his family. Disemboweled his sister and mother, nailed his father and brothers to a tree. He has more reason to hate Jad than anyone I know. His fury makes him good for some tasks, but his fear makes him unfit to lead."

Cistine pressed a hand to her roiling stomach. "If that's the sort of woman Jad's niece was—"

"What of his nephew?" Thorne finished grimly.

"Oh, Kashar's hands are far less dirty. They've had to be. Women aren't permitted rulership in Mahasar, we do not even have a formal Queen...so it was always going to be him on the throne. Tirzah did the King's cruel work, Kashar grew muscle and flexed it in public view. The truly gruesome things were left to the King's Shadow...that's why Jad grew to fear her so much he had her killed by the one person she'd never expect to willfully harm her."

Sacha shook her head. "But enough about the past. As for Esmail, I'm afraid there's no helping him. It's the people who need your aid."

Cistine followed her gaze down to the braziers and makeshift tents; most people she spotted were of fighting age, some with youthful faces, others craggy and hardened. But here and there were families with children even younger than Pippet. Refugees, she guessed; the unensorcelled who truly had nowhere safe to go.

"Maybe it's not *our* help they need," she ventured slowly. "Esmail wanted you to lead."

Sacha scoffed under her breath. "He'd like me to lead because he relishes the thought of our unified front. But you saw how he lives...spending all his time reading maps, mustering strategies, but never acting on them. Dismissive of anyone or anything that doesn't fit to his plans. He would never fully remand control of the *Alhuri* to me, no matter what he believes of himself...and even if he did, I wouldn't want it."

Cistine swiveled to face her. "But why not? If you could have that power without even fighting him for it, why wouldn't you take it?"

"Rulership is not for everyone, Princess. There are more ways to help people than by leading them. And there is plenty of life to be lived without the weight of other people's wellbeing hanging on your shoulders."

Cistine could no longer fathom why anyone would not want the power to lead, especially if it meant saving their people; she hardly remembered what it felt like not to want the throne, not to dream of the day she'd be Queen. But Sacha's expression was cool and unmovable, and that was that.

"Could anyone else lead them?" Cistine ventured. "What about his captains, like Sabir and Mairin?"

"You heard him...they do as he says, go where he commands." Sacha's lips tugged in a mirthless grin. "Short of invoking the Rite of *Bar Resam*, I don't see anyone wresting power from him, and in the blade no one here is better than Esmail. So they endure it, but you can see in their faces how little hope they have."

She could—and it was no surprise. While Esmail plotted, the people here festered in darkness; above, their fellow Mahasaris fell deeper into poverty and Jad's clutches. Once, she might not have cared...she might've been like Rion, seeing no innocents, or like her parents, razing cities without a care for who was displaced.

But then she'd gone to Valgard.

Sacha rose, dusting off her hands. "I'm sorry to have dragged you all this way for nothing. I wanted to believe he'd be inspired, not threatened, by an offer of aid from your kingdoms. Forgive me."

"There's nothing to forgive," Cistine said slowly, searching Thorne's gaze. The silent question danced between them, and by the crease between his brows she knew what he weighed out—all the odds and the lost time against the plea in her face.

At last, he dipped his head.

And that settled it. They would not be returning home by tomorrow, after all.

"We'll stay a bit longer," Cistine spoke for them both. "Maybe Esmail doesn't want our help, but that's only because he doesn't know us yet. We can still do good for these people. Just give us a few days...we'll think of something."

CHAPTER
TEN

DESPITE THE TORRENTIAL rain that caught them after Bresnyar departed, and stayed steady on their way to the burrow wyrm tunnels revealed by the patrol they'd caught and thrashed in the foothills, nothing washed the stink of the Enforcer's sweat from Ashe's stolen armor. The stench of his fear was still in her nostrils when she, Rozalie, and Maleck entered Middleton's central square. The cobblestone plaza was broken up, the fountain gone, the bricks turned to gravel. The steep slope through which they emerged was bitten with wagon tracks from supply carts and convoys of Enforcers riding up into the city.

Indignation choked Ashe at the sight of this place where she and Maleck had made their stand for their kingdoms united, where she'd realized she loved him. Her throat tightened when they passed between homes and shops where dead-eyed Talheimics swept their stoops and farmed out their goods at a fraction of their worth to Enforcers who patronized them in every sense.

She was glad to get off those familiar streets after only a few blocks; she wasn't certain she could keep from punching the next Enforcer she saw.

It was Rozalie who found an apartment above an abandoned shop, untouched for months judging by the cobwebs and neglect. The only thing Ashe worried of was alerting Enforcers to their presence with a coughing fit at the dust they kicked up.

"So," Rozalie said while they broke up their rations of jerky and hardtack, sitting in a circle in the one-room loft, "Lord Dorminger's estate is one of the most heavily-fortified in Talheim, and now it belongs to Kashar. Pose as household guards and assess the state of things here?"

Ashe nodded. "To start with."

Maleck leaped on the opportunity and was gone for most of the day, leaving Ashe and Rozalie to secure the boards more tightly over the windows and lay out their weapons. In the last vestiges of light before sunset, Rozalie drowsed against the wall and Ashe sharpened Starfall, content to brood about the Mahasari presence in this city in silence for a time; then, growing tired of her own familiar anger, she tipped her head back against the wooden column in the center of the room and shut her eyes.

Traces of gold filmed the darkness. HELLO, *ILYANAK*.

A smile stretched across Ashe's mouth. *Hello, Scales.*

I TAKE IT YOU'RE INSIDE MIDDLETON NOW?

I am. Where are you?

The world opened up before her through her dragon's eyes: Astoria from a distance, its familiar avenues popping with color. From this angle, she knew he was down by the beaches, keeping watch over both land and sea. Her heart ached at the city's emptiness.

The tethered bond between them twinged. THIS DISTRESSES YOU.

I hate seeing it so desolate. Usually the streets are packed this time of day. The trench may keep Astoria safe, but if the people don't feel it, we've missed something.

AND WHAT WOULD YOU DO DIFFERENTLY?

I'm not sure. But their King is gone, and their Princess, and the Cadre Commander. I wonder if they feel like we aren't fighting for them.

A beat. YOU CARE VERY MUCH FOR THEIR PLIGHT.

Well, they are *my people, Bres.*

AND THEY ARE FORTUNATE TO HAVE YOU. I WONDER IF THEY EVEN REALIZE HOW FIERCELY YOU FIGHT FOR THEM.

Ashe snorted, stirring dust. *Do you think it matters without my old titles?*

I THINK IT DOES, YES. PERHAPS FAR MORE THAN YOU REALIZE. DO YOU SUPPOSE THE PEOPLE BELIEVE RION BARTOS FIGHTS FOR THEM, OR FOR HIS OWN IDEALS?

Ashe was still mulling over that question when the loft door sprang open, severing the cleaving, and Maleck slipped inside. Rozalie sat up at once like she'd never been asleep at all. "*There* you are! What did you learn?"

He disrobed rapidly of his stolen Enforcer armor for the simple Valgardan clothes beneath. "That it is inherently difficult to mine information your first day on watch." He caught an apple Rozalie hurled to him, sitting on the other side of the post from Ashe. "I didn't press for fear of raising suspicion."

"But you found out *something*, I take it," Ashe coaxed.

Maleck nodded. "The rotation schedule of the garden patrols."

"That's not very exciting." Rozalie took another side of the post, palming her own fruit from hand to hand. "What else?"

"The estate is sealed tightly, the front door welded with a new lock."

"Mahasari make?" Ashe asked.

"Undoubtedly. It's like nothing I've ever seen before...I doubt even Tatiana could pick it."

"Two guesses as to who holds the key," Rozalie said wryly, and Ashe rolled her eyes.

"I saw nothing of the Prince. Apparently, few people in the estate ever do. He slips away often, never at the same time or for the same duration. Rumor has it he likes to spend his days in the lower town. Doing what, though, few would say. Only speculation."

"What else?" Rozalie drummed one hand on her knee. "Any more gossip?"

"Plenty. It seems they *all* gossip when he's out of earshot. There is no end to the tales of Kashar az-Kyrian and his infamous fallen sister, Tirzah ra-Kyrian. She was the King's Shadow, so when he felled her, he gained great status with his people. Now they call him the Shadow-Slayer."

Rozalie went still, staring at the boarded window across the loft.

Abruptly, she swung to her feet and grabbed Maleck's discarded

Enforcer armor. "I have an idea."

"Are you going to tell us what it is?" Ashe sighed.

"Later." She was already halfway to the door. "But if I'm not back by sunrise, come look for me in the taverns. And bring some of that antidote."

And on that unsettling note, she was gone.

Ashe and Maleck passed most of Rozalie's absence sorting rations. They'd brought plenty of water skins and nonperishable food, enough to last them several weeks if they were careful. Still, Ashe didn't like the thought of creeping out and back into Middleton with fresh supplies if their water stores ran low.

"This would be easier if we could tell which rations in Middleton were tainted with Sorcel," Maleck sighed, stuffing the skins back into the darkest, draftiest corner of the loft.

"We have to assume they all are." Kneeling at his side, Ashe slid a hand up his back. "We'll manage, Mal."

He pressed a kiss to her temple. "We must. Spar with me, *Mereszar?*"

Grinning, Ashe popped to her feet. "I thought you'd never ask."

It was past midnight, but they were still awake, resting from their sparring session with Maleck's head in Ashe's lap and her sprawled against the wall, when Rozalie returned. She shed Maleck's too-large armor and went straight to the waterskins, drawing from the first one she touched. Tension banded the line of her shoulders, sparking Ashe's nerves when she sat up, Maleck with her.

"What did you find out?" Ashe demanded.

"Something I've learned watching Rion and Viktor strut around for years...an insecure man never feels like he's proven himself enough." Rozalie dropped cross-legged onto the floor, capping the waterskin. "He'll keep trying to measure up...usually by making others seem small."

Ashe blinked, comprehension dawning swift and sharp with a tang like desert sun and gritty sand. "He's fighting."

Rozalie nodded. "There are fighting circles in the lower town where the Enforcers *encourage* ensorcelled Talheimics to brawl. Kashar likes to hone his metal there."

"If someone should beat him," Maleck mused, "and slip the antidote to him when he's at his weakest, and his reputation scarred..."

"The perfect cover," Rozalie agreed. "If *someone* could get close enough."

Ashe held her friend's wild, glittering stare. "If anyone, it should be me. I fought in the Blood Hive, I've seen more combat—"

Maleck arched a brow. "And who was battling for his life in the wilds while you guarded your princess for twenty years?"

"Unless you want to battle for it again, *stay out of this*."

"Ashe, it can't be you," Rozalie argued. "He knows you too well from the peace treaties. And no offense, Maleck, but you have something of a distinct face, you know?" When Ashe scoffed, Rozalie rocked forward, fists pressed into the floor, eyes flashing. "It has to be me."

Everything in Ashe rebelled, remembering the horror of seeing girls like Rozalie broken in Siralek; but this was not the Blood Hive, and Rozalie was an experienced, competent Warden, not an untrained criminal.

Bearing a breath deep down into her lungs, Ashe looked away. "Then I suppose we need to get you into a fight, Dohnal."

CHAPTER ELEVEN

BRIGHT GOLDEN DUNES scaled the horizon, shifting unpredictably in gusts of wind funneling down from the mountains around Mahasar's central desert that cut them off from the Agerios Sea. Tatiana longed for a taste of wetness on that wind, a glint of water beyond this oasis, but it was a hopeless dream; the sea, a three-week trek on foot through those vicious peaks, had become nothing but a storybook setting after Jad collapsed Rathad Mhorr, the great road to the coast.

No wonder word of his navy had never reached Talheim before the war. And no wonder the people were so easy to poison, cut off from the sea on every side. At least they had the Oasis of Shinar, though it was a bit crowded for Tatiana's tastes. She sat beneath a palm tree on the spring's edge, grateful for the arid breeze drying the sweat on her navel and back. She'd forgone her armor for a handkerchief top and billowing pants, baring the sharp-angled, winged Atrasat inkings down her bare arms. None of the merches scattered across the oasis paid her attire any mind; in fact, a handful were dressed similarly, ducking in and out of striped traveling booths and goathide tents.

It was a pity none of them stayed and drank Shinar's water long enough to break their ensorcellment; or maybe a few did, but they were too terrified to speak out. They didn't *look* like their minds were swayed to Jad's wicked schemes, but if Sacha's warning about the state of Talheim was true, that meant absolutely nothing.

A shadow fell across her outstretched legs, and Quill swung up onto the dune with a hand around the tree, collapsing on his haunches beside her. "No sign of Enforcers north or east. Ari should be back soon." And that would tell them if the south and west were clear, so they could make a move on those mountains—and on Ralathi Trench.

"You know what I see out there, Quill?" Tatiana braced her weight back on her palms and tucked her chin to her chest. "Poverty. The kind my father couldn't claw out of before he and Kadlin forged the *valenar* bond."

A note about that had come with a new batch of augurs six months ago; it bothered her less now that the shock had worn away.

Quill squinted across Shinar, its sun-kissed waters fringed with green palms, hardy bushes, and wild wheat-colored grass. "Show me."

Tatiana gestured across the oasis. "Booths with waterlogged shiplap. Tents with three, maybe four patches to the same place. And even the nicest clothes here must've been darned six or seven times. You remember what Sacha said about the people?"

The crease between Quill's brows smoothed. "He used Sorcel to take their wealth."

She nodded. "Now they're passing through on their way to eke out a living, just like Papa with his inventions."

Quill was quiet for a moment; then he twisted suddenly and stretched out, pillowing his head in her lap. "Well, now we're definitely going to win this thing."

Smirking, Tatiana threaded her fingers through his hair. "How do you figure, Featherbrain?"

He caught her hand and pressed his lips to her knuckles. "Because the fight just turned personal for Tatiana Dawnstar."

Her smile softened the same way every other part of her did when he spoke her Name. Cocking her knees, she brought his head up just enough to press her lips to his; then they settled in again, his head heavy in her lap, her fingers following the line of his scalp and flaking loose sand gathered there from their wind-swift journey to Mahasar. Gradually, Quill's breathing evened into slumber; of the entire cabal, he was always the most susceptible to the strain of augments, the quickest to fall asleep after a hard battle with them. He was nearly snoring when Ariadne returned, flitting over the dune like a specter and settling at Tatiana's side. She cast Quill a look of exasperated fondness—like most people did—and reported in a whisper, "No sign of Enforcers west or south."

Tatiana let out incremental breaths. "So. The Trench it is."

Ariadne nodded. "And this will be the perfect place to cast off from."

"I have everything we need. Already traded for a tent and some blankets."

"And your trinkets?"

She patted the satchel at her side. "Self-made. Nothing else like them. They're bound to catch a few eyes if we feel like trading for something else."

Now it was just a matter of finding this noxious Trench full of Enforcers and dragons...and putting their lives to the test again.

"What's wrong?" Ariadne asked. "You have that look in your eye."

"Just wondering if we'll *finally* have peace when all of this is over." She tugged absently at a snarl in Quill's hair. "Or whether we'll go home to find some plague has gripped the north, or man-eating serpents are procreating in the Sotefold, or maybe Valdemar has a wild notion to put us all on trial for, I don't know, being prettier than him..."

Ariadne laughed. "What's *really* bothering you?"

Tatiana's breath caught when her fingers did on the next tangle. "Thorne told me he found out the house Quill gave me on Darlaska is gone. Burned down during the war. Not that it matters, it's just a house, but it makes me wonder...will we really have a life to go back to after this?"

"Yes," Ariadne said firmly. "And we will love it twice as much, because unlike so many of our ancestors, we *fought* for it. Every day, every moment of that peace will be earned."

"You're awfully optimistic."

She shrugged. "I have faith in our future, *Malatanda*. Faith that the gods will lead us into it."

"But there are things we don't get to bring with us into that future," Tatiana argued. "How do you reconcile with that? When things happen, like Cistine and *Haval*, or..." She grazed a hand over her abdomen and shot Ariadne a glance. Her friend's focus hung on her, gentle and full of compassion. "Does it make it harder to believe the gods are for us?"

Ariadne took a long time answering, funneling sand through her fist. "Never, for me. You know how I perceive the world in balance. When I see unconscionable evil, it is proof there must also be good beyond comprehension fighting against it. Good that turns wickedness to victory."

"How do you see that in Cistine and me? Or in *your* story?"

"Because I have this family...something good that came from the ashes of what I once wanted. And you are still alive, despite what you lost. And Cistine's journey is not over yet. So, no, Tati, I don't doubt the True God exists, or that he and his vassals are for us. We may not have everything we wish we did, but that isn't proof against good. The proof is that we are still fighting." Ariadne slipped an arm around her shoulders. "And that keeps me believing."

The burst of unease faded, rocked to slumber by her friend's quiet trust. Tatiana turned her eyes west—toward the Trench, at least a day's walk according to the map, still far from view. But she could feel it out there, a source of malevolence buried deep in the cracks between the mountains. "So, do you think we'll find something good in those trenches?"

"Stars willing." Grimness returned to the set of Ariadne's mouth. "Because I have no doubt we will find evil there, too."

CHAPTER TWELVE

THE FIRST SPARKS of intermittent crying woke Aden from dreams of blood and battle on the Deathmarch. Untwisting his fingers from the knife hidden beneath his pillow, he stumbled up from his cot and out of the servant's quarters in the room adjacent to Mira's, reaching the bassinet before Nadeem could dredge a real cry from the bottom of his lungs.

"It's all right, it's all right." He swept the boy up, blankets and all, swaying back and forth to preempt his cries. "Who needs a warning bell when we have you?"

Cradling Nadeem's head in one hand, he checked the bed over his shoulder. Mira slumbered on, the depth of her sleep a testament to the day she'd had, and Aden bit back a sigh.

Sander had told him of Mira's fits during their investigation of Siralek during Salvotor's trial, but he hadn't truly comprehended how those shaking assaults could unravel her mind, leaving her ill and dazed for long stretches. In the months since Nadeem's birth, he'd noticed lack of sleep and an abundance of stress made them more frequent and difficult to revive from, so he made it a point to be the one who tended the boy's cries when it wasn't a feeding he needed; and tonight's fussing, mercifully, was not the hungry sort.

Today had already seen one of Mira's fits, and for a few hazy minutes she'd struggled to find Nadeem's name on the tip of her tongue. She needed rest; so Aden gave it to her, slipping from the room with the boy tucked in his arms.

He always struggled to find comfort and rest in the Citadel; though he'd certainly lived in worse, and with greater threats looming on every side, it was impossible to miss how some of the Wardens looked at him with equal parts fear and loathing, and he couldn't forget how men like Viktor Pollack had behaved while Aden helped search for their captured princess.

He would never feel fully comfortable on Talheimic soil the way Thorne did, slipping effortlessly into a role of leadership, learning to bump elbows with the royal family. Most of the time, and particularly on nights like this one, he fiercely missed the chilly north, its solid soil under his feet, his father's near and comforting presence, and the walls of the city he'd grown up in. The sooner they routed Jad, the better for everyone bound to this war.

And to accomplish that, Aden had work to do.

He sequestered himself with Nadeem in Cistine's study, adjacent to the throne room; she'd made it known the moment her father gave it to her that the cabal was welcome to it whenever they pleased. The floor-to-ceiling windows at the aft allowed splashes of moonlight to coat the walls of bookshelves and shorter, stockier cases of maps and scrolls. The worktable down the middle rippled with shadows from unbroken ghostlamp-chandeliers strung along the ceiling, those deep blue recesses above patterned with golden stars—the constellations of Traisende, Yager, Tyve, Skyygan, and Kanslar.

Aden recalled with a fond shake of his head the day Thorne and Cistine had decorated this ceiling; how they'd both come to dinner sweaty and smiling, cheekbones, hands, hair, and clothes streaked in residue like they'd been slinging paint at one another. It was the widest he'd seen the Princess grin since the Deathmarch, the most relaxed his cousin had seemed since his wedding day. This room held the echoes of laughter and love sealed into its very pores; Aden felt it the moment he settled on one of the couches clustered at the windows, Nadeem tucked to his chest. Feet kicked up on the low table between the sofas and chairs, Aden turned his face to the moon—and began to plan.

It had been a tumultuous few days since the others departed; a mysterious breakout from the dungeons, their tentative Mahasari informant vanished. The Queen had dispatched Wardens in every direction to hunt for her, but they'd lost the trail at the trench around the city; on its other side, no trace of Sacha could be found. He was still waiting for murmurs to die down before he began his hunt for the ensorcelled traitors; but in the meanwhile, he'd watched the council in particular for their reactions to Sacha's sudden appearance and equally-sudden departure.

A few piqued his interest, lords who'd either been too concerned or not concerned enough about an escaped Mahasari prisoner.

It was nearly time. The Queen had made it firmly clear she wouldn't allow Sacha to distract them any more than she already had; and with that temporary chaos nearly over, Aden was ready to move.

For tonight, though, he was content with peace and plotting.

The study door whispered on its hinges—an old cabal trick, keeping doors creaky enough to signify an approach—and Aden twisted on his seat, hope rising and then perishing when he saw it was not Mira, but Queen Solene who joined him. She was still dressed for the day, her diamond-studded dress catching fistfuls of moonlight as she approached. The smell of wind and wild places floated ahead of her.

"I hope you don't mind...I saw the door was cracked." She greeted him with a warm smile that scrunched her nose and crinkled her eyes, similar to her daughter's. "Is it all right if I sit?"

Aden spanned the arm not holding Nadeem. "It's your Citadel."

"Sometimes it doesn't feel like it anymore." Solene lowered herself on the divan across from him, toeing off her mud-caked flats. "After what that woman Sacha told us, of our own *people* being ensorcelled..." Her hand leaped to her throat and she shook her head as if to ward off the mere thought.

Whatever comfort Aden might've offered arrested itself with Nadeem's renewed squirming and fussing. He bounced the boy, meeting Solene's eyes.

"May I?" she asked almost shyly, holding out her arms.

"I insist." Aden gently passed the boy off to her, and Solene settled against the divan's winged back, Nadeem nestled perfectly in her plump arms. A strange expression crossed the Queen's face, battling between bliss and grief in the tremble of her mouth and the wideness of her eyes.

"So, what do you truly make of Sacha's accusations of ensorcelled men in our midst, now that she's gone?" Aden ventured.

"I wish her disappearance was proof she was a liar," Solene sighed. "After all, no one wants to think their own advisors and friends might be working against them. But Jad is clever...of course he would make weapons of those we trust. And it's not as if we treated that girl with great kindness. In her situation, I would've snatched any opportunity to escape as well." A beat of thoughtful silence reigned between them. "However, that she was able to escape at all suggests if there *are* ensorcelled people here, they're allies of hers. Cyril must be right that it was a trap."

Aden prayed silently and fervently it wasn't—that Cistine and Thorne weren't bolting straight into a snare laid on Sacha's heels. "The question is, how do we sort out the loyalists from the traitors?"

She met his eyes over Nadeem's head. "You have opinions?"

Aden shrugged. "Cistine requested I lend my service seeking out these ensorcelled allies while she and Thorne are in the Calaluns."

Solene studied him with such royal scrutiny it stiffened his spine and set his shoulders back. He'd endured the same calculative look from Chancellors and Tribunes throughout the courthouse during his recent tenure as Thorne's High Tribune; he would not falter before the Queen.

After a long, silent minute, Solene nodded. "Whatever aid you need, you have it. This is my kingdom, but if Cistine asked for your help, I know it's with good reason. We'll do this thing together, Aden."

He dipped his head. "Quietly and diplomatically."

Solene's eyes crinkled at the corners. "I'm glad someone else understands the delicate line we walk." She bent forward, passing Nadeem back to him. "He's a good child. You must be very proud."

"He isn't mine," Aden corrected hastily.

Solene stood, dusting off her dress. "Isn't he?" She squeezed his shoulder and strode from the room, the diamond gown throwing a moonbeam's array across the floor until the door shuttered behind her.

Freeing his breath, Aden peered down at Nadeem's drowsy face. "Are you?"

The words bounced, strange and foreign, off his ears and around this room sealed in love and joy. They found no answer, and he was strangely glad for that.

He had enough to contend with already.

CHAPTER THIRTEEN

A S MUCH AS Cistine grappled with the problem in her head, the task of outwitting Esmail's suspicions and bringing hope to *Alhuru en-Asgaid* became more daunting the longer she dwelled on it.

"It feels like my mind is crawling through *mud*," she complained, kneading her temples. "Why is this so much harder than it was back in Stornhaz?"

She and Thorne lay in their private grotto portioned to them by Sacha, recently woken but not yet ready to rise; he stretched out on his bedroll, shirtless and relaxed, arm supporting his head. She curled up on hers, legs tucked, muscles humming with flighty energy.

"It's harder because now you've seen war," Thorne explained, "and the fighting can be easier than the politicking."

"A queen should be able to flow between the two. It's the only way to keep her kingdom safe. It should be *easy* for her."

"Perhaps. But for a princess?"

She ignored the question. "Sacha's right, Esmail's problem is that he's afraid. Afraid of us, afraid of Jad, afraid to act rashly. He just needs to see that action is better than waiting to be slaughtered. Someone has to teach him that."

Chuckling quietly, Thorne turned his head to look at her. "What did you have in mind?"

"We could talk to the others," she offered. "Sabir and Mairin to begin with. I know Sacha said they won't move without Esmail's word, but think of the way Sabir talked about him...when he said Sacha knew how he was. I think they want to make a difference, so let's help them do it."

"All right. But carefully, *Logandir*. Esmail tolerates our presence to win Sacha's favor, I suspect. He won't take kindly to subversion."

A grin crept across Cistine's face. "Don't worry. You know how crafty I can be."

They found the two captains sitting alone at a fire together, sharing a blanket and a bowl of spiced molasses beans. Even from a distance, the smell made Cistine's mouth water, but she reminded herself queens did not put appetite before duty. So with Thorne at her side, she breathed out the intoxicating aroma of sugar and starch and flashed her brightest smile at Sabir and Mairin. "May we join you?"

"By all means!" Sabir grinned, spanning an arm across the fire.

"I'm surprised you're still here," Mairin said once they sat. "Esmail made it seem like you'd return to Talheim in a heartbeat."

Of course he had. "Well, even if there's no welcome for us in *Alhuru en-Asgaid*, we hoped we could learn a bit about outsmarting Jad from the people who have done it the longest."

Thorne's cheek ticked at her flattery, and perhaps she was laying it on too thickly. But Sabir's mollified smile suggested otherwise. "Stay around a bit, and we'll teach you all the methods to outwit him."

"Except how to actually kill him," Mairin reminded him dryly. "You know, what would actually *win* this war."

Sabir deflated with a sigh. "True."

"The time will come," Thorne assured them. "Someone will land the killing blow."

"Maybe even Esmail," Cistine suggested innocently.

Sabir and Mairin tackled their bowl of beans together, avoiding their eyes, and Thorne struck in like a warrior finding an opponent's broken guard. "So, what do you make of the Enforcers hiding in Masiya's markets?"

Sabir's spoon halted halfway to his mouth. "Come again?"

"The Enforcers?" Cistine echoed. "The ones disguised as vendors?"

"Here in Masiya?" Mairin demanded. "How do you know this?"

"Sacha told Esmail. Didn't he tell you?"

The brief glance they exchanged was answer enough.

"It's troubling," Thorne mused like he hadn't noticed, "how easily they can hide in plain sight."

"And how Esmail's not doing anything about it," Cistine added.

"That *is* troubling," Sabir scrubbed his jaw, shooting another glance at Mairin. "But still…"

"Without Esmail's orders, we do not engage or pursue." She shrugged. "*Alhuru en-Asgaid* survives on a foundation of trust. When we vowed into it, we swore to respect and honor one another, never to violate faith between us the way Sorcel forces people to do."

"But what if Esmail is *wrong*?" Cistine pressed.

"Then that is a conversation for us to have." Sabir's smile was sympathetic but firm. "I'm sorry, Princess, but these are our ways."

"And *you* would do well to learn them."

Cistine stiffened, revolving on her haunches at the scrape of Esmail's furious voice. He loomed behind them, arms folded, dislike sparking in his dark eyes.

"Why are you still here?" he demanded roughly. "Haven't you grown bored of spying on us?"

"We're not spying!" she snapped. "We want to help."

"You can help by not distracting my captains with missions other than those I give them." Esmail jerked his head. "Sabir, Mairin, may I speak to you? We have supply runs to discuss."

With a last apologetic smile, Sabir was up, following his leader away. Mairin's gaze lingered longer on Cistine before she joined them.

Left alone with her *valenar*, Cistine deflated, rubbing her arms and staring into the flames. It was several minutes before her irritation at Esmail simmered low enough that she could think around it—think of other ways to help these obstinately loyal people.

Thorne watched her with that kind of heat-stirring intuition she'd long loved about him. "Tell me what you're thinking."

Scraping a pebble from between the stones, she bounced it into the crackling fire. "That if Esmail's too afraid to do something about those Enforcers in the market, maybe *we* should."

CHAPTER FOURTEEN

THE RALATHI TRENCH was a wound ripped through Mahasar's skin, black and infected, spewing a malevolent fume Tatiana could taste through their last half-hour scaling the jagged black peaks. She hated those more than the buckling dunes they'd mounted for most of the day; vicious slivers of obsidian rock threatened to pierce the soles of her armored boots, and though her darker hair and skin blended with the crude stone, Quill's silver locks and Ariadne's pale complexion popped like snowpiles. One wrong move, and they'd be spotted.

Hoods cast up, slinking low, they found a perch above the Trench to keep watch. Pressing her wrist to her scarred nose and mouth, Tatiana peered into the deep slit, stomach roiling. "Quill? Remember that time we stumbled into that bog in the Wildwood and I told you if we ever found somewhere more disgusting, I'd owe you a hundred mynts?"

"Right?"

"It's a good thing we're sharing coffers now."

Ariadne cupped a hand over her nose and mouth. "No wonder humans can't survive this place. *Look* at it."

Tatiana wished she weren't. Not only was the Trench itself rancid as a pus-filled wound, spewing sickly greenish-gray vapors, but the work being done over it made her skin crawl. The *Tayir*, hobbled and muzzled, poured from clefts in the mountainside and streamed toward the slit; men in metal facemasks drove the lines from a distance, cracking whips whenever the dragons slowed or hesitated.

"Jad spares no cruelty," Ariadne muttered. "Not for beast or man."

Quill lurched forward suddenly, three-fingered hand and metal prosthetic snagging the stone. Tatiana tensed as well. "What do you see?"

"That dragon at the rear, that's the one Vezzik rode out on...the one that almost took my arm."

Tatiana rocked back, cracking her knuckles. "Looks like Vezzik's failure to fulfill his latest mission landed him back on chamberpot duty."

"Good. I'd love another chance at that *bandayo's* head." Quill's grin was sword-sharp. "What do you think, Ari? Earth augment?"

She shook her head. "I can't see the end from here. There's no guarantee we could collapse the Trench entirely, and if we fail to not only seal it, but silence the Enforcers, word of our presence may spread to Jad."

"Which puts Cistine and Thorne in jeopardy," Tatiana muttered.

Quill bit the side of his fist, gazing into the valley. "Then we need to be close. Practically on top of them."

"Hence my concern," Ariadne agreed. "Even if we stole armor, three fresh Enforcers arriving unannounced is bound to raise suspicion. And if they decide to verify with Arak Shehr..."

Their gazes all swiveled north toward the dark spine of mountains that hid Mahasar's capital from view.

"All right," Quill grunted. "So we plan around their shift changes."

Tatiana nodded. "These fumes are toxic. Even with those masks, they'll have to rotate the Enforcers every few days to keep them from falling ill."

"They rotate out, we rotate in. You two take on the guards, I close the Trench."

"It's not quite a plan, but it's the start of one," Ariadne said wryly. "Let's see what we can learn about rotations from the merch camp." She slid back down the hillside, shadow-quiet, and Tatiana turned to follow—then hesitated when Quill did.

Down below, whips snapped and voices bellowed. Dragons let out those owl-like shrieks of pain.

"Quill?" Tatiana urged.

"It just doesn't seem right," he muttered, almost to himself. "No wonder Cistine was afraid of this *bandayo*...he doesn't mind turning every living thing, even his own flesh and blood, into his slaves."

"That's what we're here for. Come on, Featherbrain."

He followed her this time, slipping quickly down the slope at her side, while behind them the cries of fettered dragons shook the canyon walls.

Up close, the merch stalls reminded Tatiana of a Nordbran bazaar: airy, flocked with color, an absolute threat to her coinpurse. But this place didn't seem to trade in currency—she hadn't seen any kind of coin shift hands—and when she wandered the stalls and tents, she saw more desperation than happiness. That was no surprise; these people had lost their homes and valuables and still had to make a living. Yet ramshackle smiles hitched their lips, like they were *glad* to be in these straits.

Sorcel. It had to be.

Discord chafed on Tatiana's nerves as she wandered the booths, feasting on rations from Talheim, her friends left to keep their own makeshift booth and question anyone who wandered by to purchase Tatiana's trinkets.

She was too restless to sit and wait for impoverished people to consider trading. So she was on the hunt.

Clothiers, spice merches, blacksmiths, metallurgists. She lingered at the last, watching the semipermanent establishment working with non-precious metals, and wondered what would come of their work in a fortnight this close to the capital and the Trench.

"If you want something, you'd best buy it now." The voice, low and sweet and likely meant for singing, snagged Tatiana's attention away from the metallurgist's brick oven. "It'll be gone in a few days."

Tatiana spun to find a girl leaning at the corner-post of the makeshift forge, a basket heaped in silks braced on her hip. She was younger than

Tatiana by some years, curvaceous and faintly smiling, and the welcome in her brown eyes made answering easier. "Gone, as in bought? Or gone as in...?"

"We serve the King. The King requires metals."

Of course he did. Tatiana jerked a chin at the oven. "This is your forge?"

"My *aba's*. *Umma* owns the silk booth across the way." She rattled the basket for emphasis, and Tatiana grinned. "I'm a practicing *almalij*."

She'd learned that word from one of Cistine's books. "A family of healers and creators. I can appreciate that."

The girl considered her a moment, then offered a hand. "Yasmin ra-Taia."

"Tati...ra-Nova," she lied quickly, clasping that hand. "My husband, sister, and I are new to Shinar."

"Oh? Passing through?"

"In a sense. Heading southeast, hoping to land in Masiya."

"The Trader's Haven!" Yasmin's eyes sparkled. "I've always wanted to go there. Did you know it was the capital of Mahasar's commerce thirty years ago? It's at the dead heart of Haqat Uise...have you seen the ring of manmade trenches that circles through all the mountains, gathering up the water that flows within them? They pour through underground tunnels out to the sea. Rathad Mhorr once joined both Masiya and Khorraris to the sea, through Arak Shehr, all the way across them."

"I'd heard something about that. It might be a good place for a family of tinkers to start over."

"Anyone can be anything in Masiya, with enough luck and hard work," Yasmin said wistfully.

Tatiana studied her face, soft and full, and a pang of grief hit her heart. How many times had she looked at the elites of Stornhaz that way, wanting the same things this girl clearly did? "Maybe you and your *aba* and *umma* will make it there someday."

Yasmin laughed, shaking her head. "Not with seven children to feed and *Umma* unable to travel. We'd need enough gold to pay for a caravan, and that..." Her eyes blew wide suddenly, darting over Tatiana's shoulder, then snapping back to her face. "It's not..." she faltered. "We can't go. We serve the King."

Tatiana frowned. "Couldn't you serve him from there?"

"No, you don't understand. We serve the King, Dyalmun keep him." She hefted the basket against her hip, brown cheeks flushing pink. "I must go, *Umma* is waiting."

"Wait." Tatiana took her elbow, but the girl snapped free, eyes locking onto hers with a ferocity that almost made Tatiana brace to be hit.

"If the Enforcers hear talk of Masiya here, they will hurt my family," she hissed. "We serve the King in Dyalmun's name."

She stalked into the silk tent across the way, its brightly-colored drapes fluttering into place behind her. Tatiana's stomach roiled with equal parts dread and excitement, watching her go.

There was something more at play here, and one thing was certain: that girl knew something of the Enforcers' movements in Shinar.

CHAPTER FIFTEEN

TENSION GIRDLED THE table in Talheim's throne room, as heavy as any Valgardan Tribunal. It reminded Aden too much of the session when Thorne had sentenced his mother and Devitrius to death, a day so dreadful the memory still reared goosebumps down his arms and back.

He'd rarely seen his father weep so hard as when Aden had smuggled him into the dungeons to say farewell to his sister...and she'd turned away from him, refusing to even acknowledge he was there—the brother whose life she'd once pleaded for so fiercely it had evoked sick, vicious mercy from a merciless man.

But in the ensuing years Salvotor had driven the love out of Rakel. She hadn't even blinked an eye when Kristoff told her he would always love her, or when Thorne came to carry out her execution.

None of them had slept that night, up late unraveling their hurts with Mira. Even now, Aden struggled to keep his eyes wide and mind focused while accusations and fretting once again soared across this chamber.

"It's the west that's weak!" Lord Stannik of the south pounded his meaty fist on the table. "They never did root out those gods-forsaken Mahasari *pirates* after the Princess wrecked their ships!"

"Rich, coming from you." Lord Moravec, cold and calm everywhere Stannik was hot-tempered and snarling, faced him with hooded eyes. "Was it not the *south* from which the Mahasaris marched?"

"The problem is the middle plains," Lord Toman interjected. "The archers and horsepeople are spread too thin and aren't well-trained enough to stop any sort of march. They let the Mahasaris come straight up our spine to our Citadel and beyond!"

"I'll thank you to remember," Queen Solene interjected coolly, "that the people of the middle plains are mine and Lady Eboni's kin."

The pale, reedy northern Lord receded. "I meant no disrespect, Your Highness."

"I'm sure you didn't." Solene's soft tone took the edge off what could've been a biting retort. Aden had to admire her diplomacy. "Let's not let ourselves be distracted from the matter at hand. Moravec?"

The head of the western Lords bent one arm to the table. "It's happening more and more often, my Lady. The bands of Wardens you dispatch to shore up the western holdings and relieve those already posted...they aren't arriving."

"Not in the south, either," Stannik admitted, and he and Moravec exchanged glances; finally, some common ground.

"We must assume the north and east are suffering the same loss," Aden said, and Solene nodded.

Viktor Pollack, one of Rion Bartos's closest supporters and quite possibly the person Aden loathed most in the Citadel, speared him with a belligerent look across the table. "Why are you even here?"

Solene smoothed the air with her hand. "He's come at my request. With Chancellor Thorne away on a mission with the Princess, his High Tribune has taken responsibility over Valgard's ranks. Our Wardens aren't the only ones disappearing on these patrols."

Pollack receded, scowling, but Lord Filip—one of Cistine's uncles— leaned around the others to address Aden directly down the table. "Augurs?"

Aden nodded, fighting the urge to pinch away the headache crowding against his eyes. The report had come from Njal, his fellow Kanslar Tribune, at dawn; more than twenty augurs had vanished on dispatches in the past week.

"Then the Mahasaris might have augments." Filip sat back hard, gripping the table's edge like a mooring line in a storm.

"That doesn't necessarily benefit them," Aden reminded him. "Without armor, they're more likely to destroy their own ranks than ours. But flagons or none, I'd like to know what's happening to all our people."

"They may be striking the patrols to demoralize us," Lord Toman offered. "Without relief, the established patrols will quickly weary. And if they cut us off from our people abroad, it will weaken the whole kingdom."

And someone knew it. Someone at this very table was taking advantage of that falter in their strength. Aden's blood simmered, looking around at their faces; every one a mask of calm, but at least one, if not more, hiding ill intent.

"We should recall what patrols we can," Viktor said. "Bring our people back into the city."

Solene eyed him shrewdly. "That may signal to our Wardens holding the lines that no aid will come for them. Worse, Jad could take it as a show of weakness and close in."

"I recognize that, Your Highness. But if we continue sending patrols for the Enforcers to pick off, soon our weakness won't just be a show."

Murmurs trickled down the table. Aden cleared his throat and choked down his pride. "I agree. For now, the safest course is to gather our people and tally them. Then we can take true stock of how many we've lost...and piece together how."

Pollack's eyes flashed to him, wide with disbelief, and Aden held that pale stare. He wished it were Pollack who'd been ensorcelled—he wouldn't mind the excuse to throw him into the dungeon. But for now, they had this in common: their people were disappearing, and the responsibility fell at least in part on their shoulders.

This was what diplomacy meant. If Talheim would play, so would he.

After a long moment, Pollack dipped his head. "We can call them back within two days. Stagger their return so as not to raise alarm."

Solene reclined in the seat, rubbing her brow. "Who am I to argue an agreement between our kingdoms? Do it, Viktor. Aden, you address your

Wardens."

Rising, he bowed. "I'll see to it immediately."

He stepped from the throne room, doors peeled open by the Wardens, raking back his tawny hair as he entered the hall beyond—then halted.

Mira sat innocently on a bench outside the door, nursing Nadeem, and the sight of her made all the tension from that council abate at once. When she met his eyes, a wicked smile coursed over her mouth, setting his heart lunging in unbroken stride. "You would be surprised how hastily people avert their eyes from a nursing mother."

Chuckling, Aden beckoned to her. "I take it you heard everything."

"I heard enough." Rising, she fell into step with him. "Which lords do you suspect?"

"Stannik and Jaros from the south, to start with. They're strategically vital to Talheim's defenses. If they were convinced to stand their men down when Mahasari patrols passed through their lands, it would explain how they've made it past the Calaluns so many times."

"Yes." Mira's eyes darkened. "It almost makes *too* much sense."

Aden nodded. "Which is why I'm also considering Moravec. It may be that Jad has a broader navy than we assumed, and what Thorne and Cistine destroyed was merely an arm of it. Smaller, quieter ships may be docking and unloading Enforcers at the shore, and an ensorcelled Moravec allows it to happen."

Mira winked. "Trust no one."

"Trust *you*." Aden lengthened his stride and moved ahead of her, unlocking the door to Cistine's study when they passed by. Ever since the night he'd spoken to Solene here, he'd made this place, in effect, his war room: the table scattered with maps, a list of potential traitors written out in Old Valgardan runes. He'd plucked the study's key from under Thorne's discarded pillow—his cousin's habits laughably the same after all these years—and wore it under his clothes at all times.

Mira draped Nadeem over her shoulder and bounced him, patting his back while she surveyed Aden's work. "You've been busy."

He shrugged. "I bring Nadeem here when he fusses at night. It gives me plenty of time to think."

A smile edged Mira's cheek. "Aden."

Something strange in her tone made him stare at her harder, but the look in her eyes was somehow worse than the hitch in her tone he could not decipher; a conflict lived in her gaze, working at the knots in her visibly-gritted teeth. For an instant, he dared to wonder...

Not now. Not here.

He looked away, and she cleared her throat. "These missing patrols," she went on. "I don't like the shape of them."

Aden pushed aside books and charts pulled from Cistine's shelves, baring the map of Talheim that took up the center of the table. "Nor do I."

They'd been picked off with precision—never less than a day, nor more than two from the Citadel in any direction. Watching Mira's face as she balanced Nadeem with one hand and traced the markings with the other, Aden saw the realization dawn in her dark eyes. "These are all wild places. If you're right about where they've gone missing, then the Mahasaris know *precisely* where to strike."

She met his gaze over the map, and he grimaced. "Sacha was right. The ensorcelled are here, and they're whittling our ranks from within."

Heavy silence hung for a moment. Mira set Nadeem down and drew a glossy rattle from her dress pocket. While he banged it on the stone floor, she bent again over the maps. "Do we send word to the King?"

"Things are too unstable now, and recalling him may provoke an attack we're not prepared to face. Until Ashe, Maleck, and Rozalie subdue this ensorcelled Prince, we're still vulnerable from Middleton outward. Now we know we're vulnerable from the Citadel as well. We can't afford two bleeding wounds at once."

Mira nodded. "I agree. When you recall the patrols, I suggest you meet personally with the augurs who went along. Find out what they know, anything they might've learned."

Aden hesitated. "I would appreciate your assistance with that. Given your profession in Stornhaz, you're more likely to notice if anyone seems to be lying."

Mira's smile bloomed broad and fierce. "I'd be honored."

Stars, when she looked like that—when she looked at *him* that way...

Rubbing the back of his neck, Aden stepped away from the table. "I should send word to the augurs."

"Aden." Mira caught his arm in passing, her firm grip an ever-present reminder she had once been a warrior. But the way that touch burned his skin had nothing to do with the knowledge that if not for her fits, she might have bested him in battle. "You should sleep."

"When? Between missing patrols, ensorcelled allies, marshalling Valgard's forces and getting the boy when he cries—"

"The boy has a mother." Mira squeezed his arm. "She can manage."

"She shouldn't have to manage alone."

But she did, because of his enemies. His mistakes.

He curled his hand into a fist over his blood-oath scar. "It's the least I can do."

Mira's gaze dropped to his hand, her brow furrowing. Her grip on his arm fell away. "At least make an effort to rest tonight," she cautioned. "Something tells me in the coming days, we'll both want for it even more than we already do."

Bresnyar was impossible to overlook, a great slash of gold resting on ruined housetops in what had once been a district of the Astorian market. The span of rock reduced to rubble by great trebuchet blasts formed a perfect perch for Ashe's Wingmate, who curled up watching children play in the empty fountain below. That easy visibility was the only reason the dragon was here and not prowling around Middleton; and even as Aden approached, he recognized the near-human glaze in Bresnyar's eyes, the gold flirting with glints of blue and green.

He vaulted the rubble and clapped Bresnyar on the snout. "Tell her I said hello."

Bresnyar shook like a dog rising from water, fixing Aden with a droll stare. "She sends her regards to you, and I quote, *the greatest pain in her ass*."

Chuckling, Aden propped himself against a crumbling piece of wall, turning to look down at the children playing in the deserted market. "How are they faring in Middleton?"

"Impatient and struggling. Much as I am." Bresnyar flicked his naked tail-tip, stripped of scales by Salvotor's cruel experiments over many years. "They have no love of this separation, nor of how neatly Jad's schemes divide our numbers."

Aden rolled his shoulders loose. "He and his people excel at that."

Bresnyar's head rose higher, fiery-gold gaze sharpening. "Do tell."

Rapidly, Aden relayed what had come to light in the council sessions between the kingdoms; when he finished, Bresnyar nodded slowly, tongue swiping his lipless mouth. "A keen strategy. I take it that's why you're here?"

"It is. I need you to find what patrols you can and tell them they've been recalled. Make certain they stagger their approach to avoid raising alarm among the people *or* our enemies. But by week's end, our hope is to save all those we can."

"Save," Bresnyar sighed, steam unfurling from his nostrils. "You believe they've been slaughtered."

"Given what Mahasar did when they captured Ashe, I'm not certain survival is any better."

"Indeed." Bresnyar rose, stretching each limb and arching his back. "You'll need to make certain these returning patrols are not ensorcelled."

"I doubt entire patrols will be, but Mira and I intend to examine them, and the leaders in particular."

"I'm certain you do. Quite the pair you two make."

His scalp prickled. "What is that supposed to mean?"

"Come now, don't you realize I could smell it on you walking down the street?"

Aden's pulse kicked in his wrists and elbows. "I'll skin you."

"Ah, but then Asheila will skin *you*, and Thorne will skin her, and Maleck him, on and on, and by the end everyone will be naked and cold, and no one wants that." A pause, brief and weighted. "Don't forget that I once yearned for a Wingmaiden who wanted nothing to do with me. You are not the only creature to ever dream of what lies far beyond his grasp."

Aden gritted his teeth so hard his jaw strained. "Don't you have a report to deliver?"

With a huff, the dragon dipped into a bestial bow. "By your leave, Hive Lord."

Bresnyar took flight, the beat of his wings setting Aden back a step; he stared after him, that sleek golden body arrowing away into the dimness of the early-winter sunset, and a heavy notion pricked at his mind.

An idea stirred up by that name Bresnyar had called him...and by memories breathing in the gathering twilight shadows.

CHAPTER SIXTEEN

CISTINE AND THORNE crouched on the rooftop ledge, watching the market below. The day's baking heat had begun to fade, the eerie cold of another desert night making its way slowly through the thickening shadows down every avenue. Sweat had long since dried on Cistine's skin, her lips and eyebrows grainy with salt, but still she and Thorne watched the vendor stalls, waiting for their moment to strike.

It was one of the few things they could afford to do for the *Alhuri* with Esmail appearing everywhere they were in *Via Hosial*, deterring any planned speeches or encouraging words with his flinty glare. He hadn't driven them out—likely for Sacha's sake, as Thorne had said—but judging by their encounter with Sabir and Mairin at the fire, he clearly wasn't keen to have them conversing with his people, either.

That was fine by Cistine. After two days crammed into the tunnels, her eyes ached for the sun, and her fingertips for something useful to do.

She was tired of talking. It was time for action.

"Did you suspect the man who ran the tea stall was an Enforcer?" Cistine asked—the first thing either of them had spoken in hours.

"Sacha gave no indication." Thorne shifted his weight, frowning. "It seems she likes to keep things to herself."

"Is that really any surprise, given who she's serving under?"

"I just find it discordant. Sabir and Mairin refuse even to remove Enforcers from their city without Esmail's approval, for fear of violating his trust. Yet Sacha has no concern keeping secrets until it suits her."

Guilt rubbed Cistine's limbs. Was she really any different from Sacha, being here in Mahasar while her family believed she was in the Calaluns? "Sometimes secrets are necessary to keep people safe."

Thorne was quiet for so long, Cistine feared what argument he was preparing; but when he did speak, it was only to breathe her name, gesturing swiftly to the clearing market below. The vendor emerged from the tea stall where Thorne had bought the orange-spice satchel, tugging down the burlap covering at his back. With a swift glance right and left, he stole away into one of the most packed side streets.

Cistine groaned, but Thorne was already on his feet. "I'll deal with this one. You go to the food vendor."

Divide and attack. It wasn't ideal, but with that Enforcer melting into a crowd too thick for her to navigate, there was no other way to bring them both down before one learned of the other's death and brought word to Jad. She hoped this risk would prove to the *Alhuri* they were truly here to help— and perhaps inspire them to fight for the safety of their city and its people, even when Esmail refused to give the order.

With a parting nod to her *valenar*, Cistine went right while he went left, pursuing their separate marks.

Away from the central market, things were quieter still; the shadows thickened, broken only by desperate slivers of sunlight prodding at the hanging glass and streamers strung between buildings. Cistine moved as swiftly as she could, bending away from anyone who came close, following her memory of that first morning's jaunt back toward the food vendor's stall. She arrived to find the street already vacant, and with a sinking heart, discovered the stall she'd come for was already laced shut. When she walked to it and wiggled the halves open to peer inside, it proved deserted.

She kicked the side of the stall, then rested her back against it, rubbing her sand-stung cheeks and staring up at the deepening night. "God's *bones!*"

This was the last thing she needed; to return empty-handed to *Via Hosial* while Thorne brought down his Enforcer, proving once and for all that she was the lesser ruler, unable to stop a single enemy even with the power of death in her hands.

"Looking for someone?" The cracked, ancient voice brought her sharply upright; a woman was sweeping off her stoop across the narrow street, watching her pitiful outburst. When Cistine didn't answer, she paused and leaned heavily on the broom shaft. "If it's Solam you seek, you'll not find him here. His home is two streets that way." She gave a chin nod to the right. "The one with the violet door, you can't miss it. Though I should warn you he doesn't cook for others after dusk."

"*Thank you*," Cistine muttered fervently, and bolted down the road.

It wouldn't be quite as clean as she liked, and her stomach writhed at the notion of killing a man in his own home. But this was war, and if she was to be Queen someday, she couldn't afford the fear of dirtying her hands.

Besides, those hands would take his life quicker and kinder than any blade.

True to the woman's word, the violet-doored abode waited two streets away. The darkness thickened when Cistine approached, the first sprinkling of stars dusting the sky. She didn't dare draw steel for fear it would shine; instead she removed her gloves, the last second's barrier between her lethal touch and anyone unfortunate enough to come under it.

Her guts quivered again. This felt wrong, just like every time she'd used the Death Augment to take life—as if begging the gods to take it from her was really a sham. But this had to be done, just like she'd been ready to do it on that ledge in the Calaluns to protect her cabal.

She tested the handle and found the door unchained. With one last fortifying breath, she shoved into the narrow, one-roomed home—and found her enemy sitting at the dining table, waiting for her.

When the breath tumbled out of her, he raised his head, and Cistine looked into the face from the stories her parents, Lord Rion, and Julian had told her; a face she'd imagined above her bed, smothering her, poisoning her, chasing after her in nightmares.

He was utterly unremarkable: a thatch of cropped, curly dark hair, brown skin, and a well-groomed mustache and beard.

But those *eyes*.

Exactly the way Rion always described them, dilated and dark and glassy as marbles, not quite sane, flitting up and down the length of her as if he watched ants crawl along her armor. They reminded her of a cat's eyes just before it coiled to pounce. He even shifted his hindquarters like one in the peasant's chair, his jagged, steel-clad armor creaking. Her attention drew irresistibly to his gauntlets, where each broad knuckle jutted out in a razor point and every finger ended in a lethal, steel-tipped claw. On his thick brow, he wore an iron crown, peaked to match the rest of his attire.

King Jad. The madman who'd haunted her all her life; the villain whose threats to the southern border had first sent her north, into the arms of new danger and her own destiny.

He wasn't supposed to be here, in the vendor's home. This couldn't be happening.

"Well." His voice was a snake's hiss, scratchy with desert dust. "*Well*, the report was true. What a good little spy we have in Talheim."

Cistine's heart crashed wildly against her ribs. She gritted her teeth. *Calm. Focus.* "What are *you* doing here?"

"When I took word from my spy of little *Alhuri* insects flitting in and out of Talheim, I thought I'd pay a visit to the last place they were seen." He spread his arm. "And look what they managed to secure for me! A Talheimic Princess, playing where she shouldn't be!"

"If you want to fight me, then *fight*," Cistine snarled, reaching for her augment pouch.

"Oh, I'm not here to fight you. That's not how the game is played."

There it was again. "This isn't a *game* for me."

"Yes, it is. It *is*. We are all part of the game. Your father has been playing it with me since before you were born." Jad tapped his taloned fingertips on the dining table. "But you being here, that's not right, not at *all*. You weren't supposed to come just yet. That's breaking the rules."

"I don't care about your gods-forsaken rules!"

Jad pressed a talon to his lips. "Shh. No shouting here. This is a house of peace."

"It's about to become a house of *war*!"

"No, no, no. You can't break the rules. If you break them, then I must break them as well, to make it all match, to put the game back in balance."

Cistine's pulse throbbed in her temples and elbows. She'd expected a man like Salvotor at the end of this road, cunning and quick-witted, devious beyond measure. But Jad was staring at her like an offended child, as if she'd stolen his favorite plaything and returned it damaged.

"Let me make something very clear to you," she hissed. "I don't ever, *ever* play games where my people's lives are concerned. If you want to keep *yours*—"

"Oh, you aren't going to kill me."

"And what makes you so certain?"

Jad bent forward, ticking his claws together. "Because you want to know how the game ends. And you know if I die, my men find your father and kill him to put the game back in balance."

Cistine's fists loosened, heart stuttering out of cadence.

She would not gamble with her people's lives; even less with her father's.

"What are you going to do?" she rasped.

"Going to? It's already happening!" Jad laughed. "All the players are in place now! You are all part of it, you just weren't supposed to be here quite yet. But no matter...we'll have a game of our own, you and I. You'll take me to the *Alhuri*, and I'll stomp them out from the smallest rebel child to that alchemist whose fruits pain me so. And then, *then* we shall have ourselves a *real* game. Cyril and I, his only daughter, his son by marriage, and dear, sweet, sweetest Solene, who first started this game more than twenty years ago when she was my perfect prisoner."

Cistine took a step toward him, desperation blazing in her chest. "Tell me how it ends."

Jad's eyes danced with reverence, as if he'd waited decades for someone to ask that very question. "It ends when I've taken everything from your father. Just as he took everything from me."

Rage swelled up in Cistine so swiftly, she lost her breath—so she couldn't even cry out when hands landed on her shoulders from behind.

She felt nothing; she never did when the currents of death fumed through her body. But it seemed to take an eternity this time for the power to reach out while Jad held her trapped in his stare like a venomous serpent. Heartbeat after heartbeat after heartbeat.

Then the Enforcers crumbled dead behind her. Cistine forced herself not to wince at the dull impact of their corpses on the rug.

Jad shot up from his seat. "So, *this* is the power they tell of on the battlefield! It's true, it *is* true! What *is* it, then?" Delight raised his tone, not the rage or shock or even fear she'd hoped for.

"It's a reminder," Cistine spat, "that you aren't playing this game against my father. You're playing it against *me*. And I promise you, I'll knock it so far out of balance you will never set it right again."

Jad stared at her, the black in his eyes eclipsing any hint of color. His throat vibrated with a demented giggle. "Oh, by the Wild Wastes! Won't this be *exciting*?"

Sudden, searing pain tore through her body, throwing her backward to her haunches between the two dead Enforcers, and only then did she see the wobbling shaft of black wood protruding from her shoulder, and realize—

An archer stepped from the shadows at the back of the room, second arrow primed; the first was lodged through Cistine's armor, into her shoulder, the first tendrils of pain leaking through her shock, setting her body shaking.

"Lasso her," Jad commanded the archer, turning away. "Give her a drink, and let's find these *Alhuri* once and for all."

Give her a drink. Cistine knew precisely what that meant.

Shaking, she plunged a hand into her flagon pouch, cracked open a wind augment, and wrapped the power around herself.

But it didn't obey her will this time; it *jerked* at her, filling her core with an agony utterly different from the mess of her shoulder. Like her organs were separating from the inside of her body; like power was at war with power inside her.

The wind augment nearly slipped from her grasp, but she grabbed for it with a scream of anguish. Jad pivoted back just as the power of the gods ripped her from the house, blew off its façade, and sent her tearing across the city, into the cold desert, moving north.

She let it carry her for many miles, and when she released it, it was without grace or control. She slammed into the sand, another scream tearing from her lips when the arrow jounced in her shoulder. She rolled down a dune and fetched up in the rocks at its base, curled on her side, sobbing.

Jad was here. Jad himself, playing his game to destroy her family. The Mad King, whose death would mean her father's if she didn't strike hard and swift enough. The Poisoner King, who wanted to poison *her*, and force her to turn on the very people she'd come to help.

She had never been more afraid of anything in her life.

CHAPTER SEVENTEEN

CISTINE SHOULD HAVE returned hours ago.

It must have been nearing dawn, but Thorne paced in shadow at the mouth of *Via Hosial*, kneading his shoulder uneasily and watching the darkness down the tunnel mouth to the ladder with every rotation. Dispatching the hidden Enforcer had been simple enough; a slit throat, his body dumped in the aqueduct. He'd gone back to the rooftop to wait for Cistine—and kept waiting until nervousness drove him down to the tunnels again, thinking perhaps she'd decided not to wait for him.

But she wasn't here, either, and he'd been up all night pacing, waiting. Still no sign of her.

"Wildheart, where are you?" he muttered, taking another turn at the tunnel mouth.

Padding feet and a raspy yawn behind him. "Thorne?" He pivoted to face Sacha, who banded her silk robe tightly around her body while she approached. She was the only one who would; his pacing and hair-raking had scared off the nearest *Alhuri* hours ago. Sleep weighed her eyelids, but the grooves around her mouth were deep with concern. "Still nothing?"

He shook his head sharply. "Something's not right. This isn't like her. I should be out searching."

"She hardly seems like the sort of woman who needs a man to rescue her."

"It's not like that. We don't leave each other behind. I swore I'd always come for her. *Always.*"

Sacha propped her shoulder to the tunnel wall and studied his face. "That's fair. But I think she needs this...a simple mission achieved by her own hand."

"She's achieved plenty of things, simple and intricate. She has nothing to prove to me."

"Not everything is about you." Sacha's mouth tipped up at one corner. "There are things a woman must prove to herself."

Thorne studied her. "Cistine is not you."

Only by the faint narrowing of Sacha's eyes did Thorne know his assumption had landed true. "We are more alike than you know."

His retort died on his tongue at the muffled slam of boots on distant rock; then from down the entryway tunnel, his *valenar's* voice, breaking around a cry of his name.

Thorne whipped back toward the darkness. "*Cistine.*"

He didn't think he'd ever run so fast in his life; nor had his heart ever hurt quite the way it did when he caught sight of her at the tunnel's end, framed by the light falling past him, dragging herself along the wall with a black-fletched arrow protruding from her shoulder.

He roared her name when she broke down to her knees on the stone, and her hand wobbled up in warning. "*Stay back!*"

Skidding, Thorne slammed down before her. For one moment, he'd actually forgotten; all that mattered was reaching her. "Look at me, look at me—Cistine!" he shouted when she wove on her knees and collapsed to her side. Rolling onto her back, she braced the arrow with one hand. "What in the stars *happened?*"

"Jad," she panted. "Here, in the city...I had to flee north, then I circled back around".

Emotions punched through Thorne in rapid succession, shock and rage and pain on her behalf—and pride, so fierce it choked him. "Clever."

Cistine forced a crooked smile, but it broke rapidly into a sob. "Thorne, it hurts, it *hurts*—"

Had she ever been shot like this? His frantic mind could only cast back so far. "I know, *Logandir*." He laid his hand as near to her head as he dared, meeting Sacha's eyes when the alchemist jogged up beside him. "We need to get it out of her."

"No," Cistine panted. "Thorne, you can't, the Death Augment..."

Sacha's eyes narrowed. "She must remove it herself."

"Like Nimmus she—"

"I can do it," Cistine gasped. "I'll do anything, I just want it *out*."

Her bravery found new ways to shatter Thorne's heart. His fingers leaped to his knife belt to keep from running through her hair—killing himself just to offer a sliver of comfort. The arrow wasn't even all the way through-and-through, her armor catching it just past the head by the look of things. She would have to widen the gap to free it.

Bile surged in Thorne's throat. "Here." Unsheathing his *Svarkyst* dagger, he laid it on her heaving chest. "I'll steady. You cut."

Cistine's lips pressed together, fresh tears scraping from the corners of her eyes. She laid the blade to her shoulder, readying to widen the hole. Sacha rose without a word and disappeared down the tunnel—to keep watch, Thorne hoped, though some resentful part of him would not have minded if she'd decided that an injured princess was of no use to her, and he and Cistine went home.

"I'm sorry." Thorne locked his eyes on hers. "I love you."

With a shaky breath, Cistine started to cut.

It was worse than Thorne had braced himself for; another wail ripped from her, body jerking with sobs as she cut into her own flesh, and everything in him ached to grip her hand, to do this task for her, to take her pain into himself and leave her unscathed. But he could only kneel at her head, hold the shaft steady, and watch helplessly as she widened the wound, bit by bit, until finally her arm fell outstretched, eyes rolling to the whites, on the very cusp of passing out.

Slower and far more carefully than he thought himself capable with how badly he shook, Thorne extracted the arrowhead. Cistine roused again when it slid from her flesh, retching and vomiting at the pain, but Thorne had the healing augment ready from his own pouch. The silvery kernel of light pulsed and roped between them, godlike power damming the cascade of blood and knitting the torn sides of her wound closed.

Cistine hiccupped and sipped air, lips trembling around measured breaths. Her eyes stayed shut, tears leaking from below the lashes. Then, moment by moment, her chest steadied. The panicked leap of her abdomen eased. The lines of tension on her brow relaxed, though Thorne wished he could rub away the remnant crease at the bridge of her nose with his thumb.

At last, she whispered, "I can feel you."

He blinked. "What?"

"On the other side of the augment. I can't explain it, but the power...it feels like you." Her eyes opened, pained slits over a wobbly smile. "I *feel* you, Starchaser."

Tears scoured his stubbled cheeks. He shut his eyes and reached out for any sensation of her, a taste like her bare skin under his hands or a flicker of her constant warmth—

Darkness and bone-deep cold greeted him instead, and the sensation of his own heart failing in his chest.

He blinked back to focus when Sacha returned, dragging a canvas pallet behind her. "Let's move her to your grotto before anyone realizes what happened."

It was slow going, Cistine weaving like a drunkard onto the pallet and Thorne and Sacha carrying her through *Via Hosial*. In the grotto, she rolled gracelessly from the canvas and onto her bedroll, clutching her arm.

Thorne lingered in the doorway with Sacha. "Will you tell Esmail about Jad?"

"I must. There's too much at risk." Distress flashed in her eyes. "I shudder to think what he'll do with that information."

Thorne couldn't bring himself to speculate with Cistine's blood from the arrow shaft still staining his hands.

Sacha ducked back outside, and Thorne settled next to his trembling *valenar*, keeping careful space between them while she rested with her back to him, favoring her shoulder still despite the healing augment. "Do you want to tell me about it?"

That shoulder bobbed. "He knew I'd come for that Enforcer. He knew I was *here*. He was toying with me." She trailed off, then added, "It was all part of the game."

Thorne shifted nearer. "He told you what it is?"

"It's his idea of vengeance against my parents for what happened twenty years ago. I think..." She sucked in a damp breath through her nostrils. "I think he's trying to destroy our family."

Protectiveness roared through Thorne so swiftly and unexpectedly, it dizzied him. "That will never happen while there's still breath in my body."

"But maybe *that's* what he wants." Cistine burrowed her fingers into the bedroll. "It's just a game to him, and he wants to use us all to break my father."

"Cistine. We won't let it happen."

"We aren't there to stop it. He knew we were in Mahasar, he knew we were coming. Someone betrayed us."

Her voice cracked, and his heart with it. "It wasn't one of the cabal," he said. "Not them."

"How can you be certain? You heard what Sacha said about Sorcel."

"I know them better than anyone. If they were serving the enemy, I would have seen it. I give you my word, *Logandir*."

She sniffled, wiping her nose on her arm. "Then who?"

For that, he had no reply.

A volley of commotion broke open in the tunnel outside their grotto—Sacha's familiar shout, Sabir and Mairin's outraged questions, Esmail's strident retort. Thorne stiffened, and Cistine rolled to gaze at the grotto doorway, her brow furrowed in pain.

Esmail burst inside first, leading with the jab of an accusatory finger toward Cistine. "What have you done?"

Thorne lunged to his feet, slamming both hands into the man's chest and halting him midstride. "One more step, and you bleed."

Incensed laughter burst from Esmail's heaving throat. "This damned

Talheimic *hasac* led the *King* to this city! She might've led him straight to us!" Around Thorne's side, he snapped, "Were you followed? *Were you?*"

Thorne gripped a fistful of Esmail's shirt. "She suffered far more than necessary to ensure that *didn't* happen. *Back away.*"

"Ez," Sabir murmured, "look at her. He's right. Enough."

"No, it's not enough!" Esmail snapped free of Thorne's grip. "She's ruined everything! Brought Jad's own wrath on this city!" He ripped his fingers back through his hair. "We leave. We leave *now*."

"*Leave?*" Sacha barked. "We've just learned *tonight* Jad is here! If we flee for the hills now, there's no telling how many of us will be snatched up along the way!"

"And we're fish in a barrel if we stay!"

Thorne choked back the rage that wanted to climb his throat and pour from his mouth. Flashing his palms for peace, he angled himself more fully between Esmail and Cistine. "Sacha is right. Give it a day, perhaps two. Move now, and you hand Jad precisely what he wants."

"Don't *lecture* me on what our King desires!" Esmail's eyes were wild as a spooked horse's. "I didn't lead these people here to fight against him. We would never win! The only way to save ourselves is to leave *now*…flee to where the other arms extend." He whirled on Sabir and Mairin. "You heard me! Go, muster the others!"

They'd taken just two steps back toward the grotto mouth when Cistine rasped, "Stop."

They all looked at her, Thorne half-turning to watch as she levered herself up on her palms. Her hair straggled loose from its tie, falling in silver hanks around her sallow face. But her eyes burned in pure power. The Wild Heart of Fire blazed through the room.

"I invoke the Rite of *Bar Resam*."

Esmail's breath caught. Mairin pressed a hand to her mouth.

Sacha smiled.

"Princess." Esmail's tone poured condescension into the title. "You don't know what you're doing."

"Yes, I do. The Rite of *Bar Resam* is a battle Mahasar's tribal elders raise to take control of a rival's assets and borders. I'm invoking it for control of *Alhuru en-Asgaid*."

Thorne stared at her, his heart plummeting from his sternum to take root in his ankles. Shock warred with dread and admiration, and he couldn't summon a single word.

Esmail curled his lip. "You are not Mahasari. I don't have to accept."

"There's nothing in the law against a foreigner making such a claim," Sacha said. "Remember our roots, Ez. We are not one nation, but many that make a kingdom."

"And by the rules of the Rite," Cistine added, gripping the wall shakily and pulling herself back to her feet, "if you leave the place where the challenge is made, you forfeit those assets and borders. *Alhuru en-Asgaid* will no longer be yours."

Esmail's eyes flicked Sabir and Mairin, watching with shrewd interest; and to Sacha, whose feral grin promised that by the time he set foot out of this room, word of the Rite would spread through all of *Via Hosial*.

"Name your terms," he growled at last.

"If I lose, Thorne and I will leave," Cistine said. "But if I win, your people follow me to fight Jad."

Esmail tapped his fingers lightly on the hilt of his scimitar. "*When* I win, you won't be able to walk away."

Thorne loosed a snarl at the threat, but Cistine smiled, sharp and vicious and nothing like herself. "We'll see. For now, no one leaves."

"We will need supplies eventually. Water will run out. Food will be scarce."

"But not today. And today, Jad is stalking those streets."

Esmail tossed up his hands with a curse and stalked to the tunnel mouth, then looked back with narrowed eyes. "How is it that you know so much about our customs, Princess?"

Cistine's smile fleshed out into something far more genuine. "A well-read woman is twice as dangerous as a man with a sword."

Scoffing, Esmail departed. No one followed.

"Sabir, Mairin," Sacha said after a moment, "spread word of the Rite on the off chance Esmail decides to be cowardly." With swift nods, they left the room. Sacha fixed Cistine with a look full of respect—and perhaps even joy. But she said nothing before she, too, left the grotto.

The moment they were gone, Cistine collapsed to her seat, holding her head in her hands. Thorne sat against the wall near her; subtly, she shifted away.

"He's their best swordsman," he reminded her. "Their leader for a reason."

"And I'm Talheim's future queen for a reason. I'll be all right." Head still bent, she waved a hand toward the tunnel. "It's them I'm worried for. They need a real ruler, not a coward who flees. I faced Jad tonight, and I can't think of anything more important now than defeating him. Rousing speeches aren't enough. We have to stop him by any means we can."

Thorne watched her, his stomach twisting with dread.

Coming to a neighboring kingdom to spread hope and unity was one matter; stepping in and taking control of all its free forces was another entirely.

Cistine had crossed a line in these ever-shifting sands; and Thorne wasn't certain yet if he stood on the same side of it.

THE
QUEEN
OF
SHADOW AND
SWORD

CHAPTER EIGHTEEN

T HE INTERIOR OF the Taia family's silk shop proved much cooler than the rest of sun-stricken Shinar—a welcome relief when Tatiana ducked inside, shoulders laden down with a rucksack. Tendrils of pure silk whispered over her bare shoulders and down the scooped back of her shirt, tickling her inkings. She shivered, squinting in the dim interior; a few glass candle-shells hung from the ceiling, their flickering light and the gauzy glow of the sun over Tatiana's shoulder the only things cutting the darkness.

Well, that, and all the silk. So much material, and so many items crafted from it—shirts and pants, shawls and wraps, even neatly-folded bedclothes. Her muscles quivered at the thought of being wrapped in them every night, and with a pang she thought of how much Cistine would love this tent.

"I'll be with you in a moment." The deeply-feminine voice came from behind a dyeing station in the tent's dark corner, and Tatiana edged forward to glimpse the speaker. She knew at once the woman was Yasmin's mother—the same face, the same sheet of dark hair, the same soft curviness and wide, warm eyes. But more familiar than her countenance was the wheeled wooden chair she sat in, just like Kristoff had used ever since the Deathmarch.

Tatiana met the woman's curious gaze and smiled. "I'm here to see

Yasmin. Is she around?"

"She isn't, I'm afraid. At the *almalij's* booth for her apprenticeship now." The woman wrung out a length of silk and draped it through a hook on the tent post. "I am Imane, this is my shop. Perhaps I can help?"

Tatiana opened her mouth to say she would return later, then frowned as the woman thrust her chair forward. Hinges groaned and metal castings creaked; the left wheel rolled, but the right locked and skidded, pitching Imane forward so sharply she nearly toppled from the chair.

"Dyalmun bless it!" she muttered, cheeks reddening even in the low light. "This old thing..."

"Here." Tatiana slung the bag from over her shoulder and knelt swiftly at the woman's side. "Let me help."

"It's no trouble, I'll have my husband fix it when he returns."

"From the forge across the way?" Tatiana met Imane's eyes. "You need mobility to keep up your shop. I can give you that."

After a tense moment, the woman nodded. "If you insist."

Tatiana patted her knee. "I'll be right back."

It was a quick jaunt to their tent for her toolkit and out to Imane's tent again, and to her relief neither Quill nor Ariadne questioned her brief reappearance or sudden vanishing again. By the waxing daylight through the silk shop's doorway, Tatiana sat at Imane's feet, replacing rusted casings and rotting bolts; while she worked, Imane answered her questions about her seven children, of which Yasmin was the oldest. The youngest had just turned eleven and apprenticed with a leather crafter in Shinar.

"So, you've been here a while?" Tatiana asked casually.

"Nearly a year. When the war started with Talheim, we gave everything we had to the King, Dyalmun keep him."

"He took your home? *Everything?*"

Imane looked at her like she'd sprouted a third arm. "Took? We *gave* to him. We serve the King in Dyalmun's name." The impassioned echo of Yasmin's words sent a chill skimming down Tatiana's back. "Besides, we are cared for," Imane added while Tatiana buried her angry retort in working a particularly stubborn bolt. "His Eminence sends rations by caravan every five days, food and drink enough even for a family of seven."

Tatiana's heart sank. Rations that were no doubt tainted with Sorcel, keeping even the populations near the oases under Jad's cruel thumb. "What if you run out of water before they return? Can't you just drink from the spring?"

Imane caught her hand, squeezing it sharply. "The water is poisoned by the same fumes as the Trench. *Do not* drink from it."

She was still caught in the woman's earnest stare when whistling sounded from outside the tent, and a familiar voice sang, "*Umma*, I brought peaches—"

Yasmin ducked into the tent and froze. Tatiana smiled sheepishly up at her. "I know, I know, it's me. Again."

"Why are you here?" Yasmin snapped.

"*Yasmin!* That is no way to speak to a guest." Imane gripped her chair wheels by habit, then hesitated, eyes wide when she gave them a smooth turn. "Dyalmun's name..."

Tatiana hopped up, wiping scratched, bloody fingers on her loose pants. "That ought to do the trick. Try to oil the bolts and hinges at least every other day, that should keep them from wearing down again."

Imane's smile broke like the sun around a stormcloud. "Let me repay you, please! Take any item you like from the shop. Anything. It is the least I can do for this." She gripped the wheels and propelled herself toward the silk tendrils at the tent mouth, swatting Yasmin's rump in passing. "Mind the tent and *behave*. I'm going to surprise your *aba*." She rolled into the dusty way between booths, cackling, "Watch your ankles, Kadeen, I'm coming for you!"

The silk tendrils whispered back into place, and in the shifting dimness Yasmin regarded Tatiana with less hostility, more wariness. "What are you doing here?"

"Looking for you, actually." Tatiana let her gaze leap across the silk items. "Do you really think I should take one?"

Yasmin's suspicion melted into a smile. "You must, or *Umma* will be hurt."

Tatiana browsed the racks for a moment, chose a bright blue silk skirt embroidered with silver flowers, and stuffed it into her waistband. It wasn't her favorite color, but it wasn't for her, anyway.

When she turned, Yasmin had settled on the floor by the discarded rucksack, fingers hovering but not quite grazing it. "What is this?"

"Food. Consider it an apology gift," Tatiana said. "I'm not here to make enemies, and I know I offended you somehow, talking about..." she bit back the word *Masiya* at the last instant. "Making trade somewhere else. I wanted to put things right."

Yasmin's face relaxed a bit. "That's generous of you." Still, she didn't touch the rucksack.

Tatiana nudged the burlap closer with her foot and settled on the ground next to the girl. "Since trading has been scarce so far, we had to wander out into the desert to hunt. I'm not quite sure what it was we killed, but the meat's tender. Sweet like the oasis water."

Yasmin's tongue swiped her lips. With a glance over her shoulder, she dove into the bag and pulled out a skewer of what Tatiana could only describe as lizard meat. It was the closest she and Quill could guess about what they'd hunted the day before, anyway.

It took every inch of restraint to be diplomatic while the girl ate. "I'm sorry for putting you in that position before. It won't happen again."

Yasmin tore into the meat, shrugging. "You are new here. You'll learn the ways of Shinar soon enough."

"Your mother says you've been here since the war started. That you...gave your home in service to the King."

There was no mistaking the flicker of anger like summer-storm lightning in Yasmin's eyes, but it quickly cooled. "We serve the King in Dyalmun's name."

"In Dyalmun's name," Tatiana echoed, watching Yasmin eat like she'd been giving up her rations for weeks. And maybe she had. "Could I ask a favor?" Yasmin waved a welcoming hand, cheeks too stuffed to speak. "I understand about not mentioning...that place. But my husband is more eager and loose-tongued than me. He wants to know everything he can about it, and I can't seem to stop him asking around." She slid in a helpless laugh, shrugging her hands wide. "Is there at least *some* time he can ask his questions without getting us both in deep trouble? A time when the Enforcers are more lenient?"

Yasmin wiped her mouth on her hand, regarding Tatiana with eyes so piercing, sweat bloomed on the nape of her neck. For a heartbeat, she wondered what she would do if Yasmin accused her of ulterior motives—or worse, called down the Enforcers on her. But after a tense moment, the girl said slowly, "They come to and from the mountains every five days. On the fifth day, the new ones come into Shinar for supplies, and the old ones come for our tribute to the King."

For all their wealth, more like. Rage rattled Tatiana's hands. Even with his army marching and his navy defeated, Jad still bled his people for all their valuables. "So, every five days, I should drug my husband to sleep."

A startled giggle burst from Yasmin. "Is he really so bad?"

"Sometimes." Tatiana patted the girl's knee and stood. "Thank you. I know this must be difficult for you, having a nomad plying you for information when you have nine mouths to feed. Hopefully the meat helps."

"It does. More than you know."

Tatiana's chest hitched at the girl's forlorn tone, the way she stroked the mouth of the sack like the most priceless treasure lay inside. "You're a good woman. I'm glad our paths crossed."

Those brown eyes glimmered with gratitude, and when Tatiana went to leave, Yasmin whispered her name. "Tell your husband to watch his tongue at *all* times." Her voice was hushed—a secret-telling tone. "Even when the Enforcers are not here, their ears are. And they don't take lightly to talk of Masiya...or of strangers traveling there."

CHAPTER NINETEEN

A PIERCING HEADACHE was Aden's reward for sitting through the next council session, a litany of arguments still digging at his temples hours after he escaped the throne room. Gulping his fourth cup of a special Talheimic tea brewed for energy and focus, he stared at the documents scattered across Cistine's long table. Late nights of intermittent rest and early mornings of council sessions gave him plenty of time to study these Talheimic lords, both in posterity and in person. The trouble no longer lay in finding if any might be guilty; it was a matter of weeding out just how many were.

Shuffling reams of paper in the orange ghostlight, he glanced out the window. Rain lashed the glass, a soothing lullaby like his mother's piano playing while he sprawled on the rug, a book open before him. How simple the world had seemed then, when mind-altering substances and traitorous elites had been his parents' concern, not his.

As a child, his greatest wish had been to be just like them. He hadn't realized exactly what he was asking for.

A pattern of familiar knocks sounded at the door, and Aden rose to unlock it, letting Mira inside. The warm scents of vanilla and spice on her skin cooled his headache, even as he realized her arms were empty. "Where's Nadeem?"

"The Queen has him." She shrugged from her cloak and draped it over her arm while Aden returned to his chair. "I'm starting to fear she's going to keep him when we leave. She's absolutely smitten."

"Who wouldn't be?" Aden dropped into a heavy sprawl in the chair and stifled a yawn. "Perhaps *she* can soothe him at night from now on."

"I don't think she'd protest."

Huffing with quiet laughter, Aden raised his eyes to her. "What did she say when you told her about the latest cipher?"

"That she was unsurprised Cistine and Thorne needed more time tracking the Enforcers in the Calaluns. That she's glad Quill, Ariadne, and Tatiana are with the King, given what's happened. And she hopes Ashe sends word from Middleton when it's safe."

"She believes it all."

"She has absolute faith in her daughter." Mira's smile was calm but slightly forced. "Let's hope it's not misplaced."

Grunting, Aden tapped the desk. "And what brings you here of all places, when you could be celebrating this moment of quiet anywhere else?"

"News from the Wardens. Yours and Viktor's strategy worked well. More patrols returned than expected...it seems a handful we thought were lost were really hiding from an increase in Mahasari activity near the Calaluns and the coast."

Aden frowned. "They're being checked?"

"As best as possible. Viktor could use your help, he and his men are stretched thin as it is."

"Of course. Because I don't have enough to do with all this." Aden spanned an arm down the table, then pinched the aching bridge of his nose and squeezed his eyes shut. "Now I need to do Pollack's duties for him."

A chair scraped as Mira drew it out and sat across from him. "It's good news, Aden. Fewer people are missing than we believed."

He raised his chin and sank it, unable to muster a response, his mind far away.

"But I suppose even good news sounds like bad news to a man who's overwhelmed," she added, then let him have his peace.

At last, he looked up to her again, finding her studying him with something stronger than professional concern. Something that made everything feel dangerous, being alone in this room with her, and brought his hand curling into a fist around his oath-scar. "Let's relieve Pollack of his duty before he strangles one of our augurs."

A shadow flickered in Mira's gaze, but she didn't press him, merely stood and swept her hand in a low bow toward the door. "Lead the way, High Tribune."

⚬⚬⚬

"So, you saw nothing." Aden scowled. "You were never assailed."

"Never heard a whisper." The Warden's whole posture was belligerent, from the slack of his sprawl in the chair across the dank, windowless meeting room to his hooded gaze and carefully-enunciated speech. "Patrol was going all right until your dragon rider sent her lizard to call us back."

Aden fought down a grim smile. The ruse held—even their own ranks believed Ashe was somewhere in Astoria at the Queen's beck and call.

"Am I excused?" the man added, tone still mockingly crisp. "This uniform itches."

"We know this is difficult." Mira laid a hand on his arm. "We like it no more than you. But as grateful as we are your patrol returned unscathed, many of your brothers and sisters did not. We're just trying to learn *why*."

The Warden's gaze traveled up the length of her and softened slightly when their eyes met. Aden coughed to hide a smirk.

As the newest Tribunes in Kanslar—and Mira the first woman outside Yager Court to serve on a Tribunal—they had faced their share of petitions and meetings that felt like entrapment. This pattern had rapidly become their favorite: his brawn naturally intimidating, her beauty naturally soothing. Nevermind that with every blink, shift, and breath, they were telling Mira far more than Aden could ever frighten out of them...and they rarely thought to be cautious with her.

As usual, this one unraveled under her touch.

"I'd tell you more if I could," he said, and for the first time sounded sincere. "I don't know what to say. We went out, patrol was all right, no hint of Mahasaris anywhere. Then Kovar's dragon called us back."

Aden stifled a groan. It was the same report given by no less than six patrols over stars-knew how many hours, and he would gamble Pollack had heard the same. "If your patrol went well, why weren't you on the route you were dispatched to cover?"

"We were. Orders came from Lord Rion just before he and the King went east."

Of course Bartos had changed the patrols without telling them—likely to discourage augurs from joining the Wardens. "You're free to go," Aden said after a consulting glance with Mira.

The Warden shrugged, stood, shoved in the chair, and made his way for the thick wooden door.

"One last thing," Mira called after him. "Your name?"

A beat of silence. Then he swiveled back. "Ales. Why?"

Mira offered a disarming smile. "In case we need to call on you again. That will be all for now, thank you, Ales."

With a stiff nod, he slipped out.

Aden rolled his eyes, folding his arms over his abdomen. "You'd think we were going to use his name for some dark *Gammalkraft*."

Mira didn't share his wry amusement, wearing a frown instead. "That's six patrols, all with the same report. They go out, the patrol is all right, we call them home."

"Perhaps we overreacted with how we summoned them back," Aden allowed. "But there are still ten patrols that haven't returned in the past fortnight."

"I know." Mira stared hard at the door. "Did anything about their answers seem strange to you?"

Aden trawled backward through the thick shroud of exhausted fog in his mind. "Nothing in particular, but it clearly did to you."

"Just..." She blew out a harsh breath through her nostrils. "Something about their behavior doesn't sit well with me."

Aden studied her earnest and troubled face. He hadn't felt any stranger around them than most Wardens, but then, that was precisely why he'd asked Mira to join him. Rising, he offered his hand. "Let's speak to the Queen."

Mira led him straight to Solene's study; for having been in the Citadel only a fortnight, she found her way around with an ease that surprised him. But perhaps it shouldn't; the Queen was watching Nadeem today, after all, and it was just like Mira, now a Tribune herself, to seek out and befriend the woman who held this city in power and watched over her son.

Admiration tugged up his mouth when they reached the study door, greeted by gurgling infant giggles and the Queen's high-pitched, cooing response. Mira knocked twice, then slipped inside, Aden on her heels. Solene was on the floor, legs folded beneath her, dangling her unbound hair over one shoulder just within Nadeem's reach. He squealed and grabbed, but no matter how hard he pulled, she didn't seem to mind.

Eboni Bartos sat at the refreshment table in the corner, sipping tea and staring blankly out the window. Little to Aden's surprise, Mira went straight to her, resting a hand on the back of her seat. "Lady Eboni. How are you this morning?"

"Cold," she whispered. "It must be freezing in the house in Practica...this was always Julian's favorite time of year. Helping me prepare the estate for the winter months, sealing the cracks in all the doors and walls. He'd make up the silliest songs about it. He must be so cold..."

Mira glanced at Aden, her gaze brimming with sadness, then down at Solene. The Queen offered a halfhearted smile, her eyes lined as she stared at her friend. "Would you like to hold the boy, Ebby?"

Eboni recoiled, shaking her head. "No, I...I can't. I can't care for him."

"It's all right," Mira soothed. "That's not why we're here."

At last, Solene looked between Mira and Aden's faces. Somber at once, she stood. "What is it?"

"We need to speak with you about the patrols that have returned." Mira's tone was crisp and straightforward, one leader to another, and behind her Eboni released a visible sigh of relief.

"Of course." Solene waved to the divan under the window, and Aden and Mira sank onto it. "I take it you've spoken to them?"

"We're continuing to." Aden nodded to Mira, giving her the hunt.

Her gaze darted to Eboni, then back to Solene, a quiet question in her eyes. The Queen switched Nadeem to her opposite arm and went to her friend, laying a hand on her shoulder. "Ebby, would you mind refreshing the tea?"

She stirred as if from a bad dream, sucking in a breath. A single tear escaped down her cheek, and she wiped it away, climbing to her feet. "Of course."

She carried the tray out in trembling hands. Mira gazed after her, brow pinched with a familiar refrain, clearly decided to pursue her at a later time. But for now, with Solene settling on the sofa across from them, it was time to speak of war.

"I would suggest removing all the newly-returned Wardens and augurs from rotation for the time being," Mira said.

Solene frowned. "That's over sixty of our best."

"I know. But something about their accounts rings strange to me. I'd like more time to question them, to learn what happened...to see if perhaps they can shed light on why *they* weren't attacked, but others were."

The Queen was hesitant for a long moment, Nadeem propped against her arm, drooling happily. Aden's hands itched to hold the boy, to breathe in his scent and feel the comfort of his slight weight. Instead, he forced himself to recline, one arm stretched along the divan's swooped back behind Mira, watching Solene sort through the matter at hand. Quiet and diplomatic, just as he'd sworn.

At last, Solene blew out a sigh. "I may not like it, but I see the merit. I'll have Viktor remove the Wardens from their duties for now, if you two will handle the augurs. We'll manage the gaps somehow."

Aden dipped his head. "We understand the strain this creates."

"I know you do, which is the only reason I'm allowing it. You wouldn't suggest it if it weren't absolutely necessary." The Queen's eyes hardened like steel. "But I expect you'll both be spending plenty of time questioning them from now on. I want this issue sorted out as soon as possible."

"Of course." Mira nodded graciously and got to her feet. "We'll begin again at dawn."

She held out her arms for Nadeem, and with a last tickle of her nose to his, the Queen surrendered him and rose as well. "I don't mean to be harsh. We *will* solve this. And I'm grateful for everything you're both doing to see it so. You're great leaders...both of you."

"As are you," Aden said, and watched as she strode from the study, giving them a moment of privacy.

"That went easier than I expected," Mira confessed. "I think this matter with spies and traitors and missing patrols has worried her more deeply than she shows."

"And why wouldn't it?" Aden slid a hand under Nadeem's head, cradling it gently. "She likely feels stranded, unable to trust her lords, her husband and daughter traveling abroad. All she has for decent friends are cruel Valgardan Tribunes."

Mira laughed under her breath, her gaze warm and confident. "At least you and I have each other."

Aden's heart kicked dangerously at that notion. "True. We have that."

They shared a smile over Nadeem's head, and Mira's gaze dropped after a moment, tracing absently over Aden's mouth. Something dangerously curious burned in the back of his throat—a faint fume of desire.

What are you thinking, you clever woman? The question hovered at the tip of his tongue. *What do you want from me?*

But he didn't dare ask, and she didn't speak. They simply stood there, the boy held between them, staring at one another.

A deep, painful longing swelled in Aden's heart, so mighty it felt like he'd drown in it. An urge to hold *her*—to feel her heart beating against his, to breathe in that vanilla-spiced scent and rest against her, and let her rest in him.

It was pure mercy when Mira finally looked away.

CHAPTER TWENTY

THE SOUND OF upraised voices stirred Cistine from her attack against the sandsack dummies in a distant corner of *Via Hosial*. Her sword Kaisill dipped, her arms grateful for the reprieve, and she half-turned toward the distant sounds of joy.

Beside her, Thorne straightened, lowering his sabers from his own assault and mopping sweat from his brow with the back of his wrist. Though he'd tied his unruly silver locks at the back of his head, threads slipped loose, sticking to his temples; Cistine tried not to let the sight distract her while she sorted out the sounds.

"Well, I don't think we're under attack," Thorne said wryly. "Shall we keep training?"

"We probably should." Whatever had roused such happiness among the *Alhuri*, it wasn't hers to feel; and just that morning, she'd given Esmail the terms of the Rite—sword combat in a fortnight. Two weeks to hone her skills as much as possible.

"You could train with me, you know," Thorne offered innocently while Cistine stretched, loosening her muscles for the next assault. "Blade-to-blade poses no risk."

Unless her hand slipped. Unless she forgot for an instant and checked shoulders or hips with him, or if he pressed past her guard. She glared at him. "You already know the answer to that."

His callused palm rasped on the back of his neck. "It was worth mentioning."

Cistine wasn't sure she agreed.

They attacked their separate targets in tandem, and for a time the buzz of clanging steel drowned out both curiosity and annoyance. Cistine sank into the heaviness of the sword and the demands it made of her already-taxed muscles; she'd been doing this for hours each day since her shoulder had stopped throbbing, but every time it was the same.

Jad's face she saw on these sandbags. Jad's threats ringing in her ears. The Mad King, the Poisoner King, with his spies in her Citadel and his intimate knowledge of her movements.

What if he knew just as much about the cabal? What if he'd brought down Ashe, Maleck, and Rozalie, killed Tatiana, Quill, and Ariadne? What if his spy had dealt with Aden and Mira—what if Nadeem was an orphan now in a Citadel of enemies and ensorcelled traitors?

What of her father, at the southern forts? Her mother, carrying not only the weight of rulership but the burden of Jad's hatred from afar?

Burlap threads separated with a satisfying *rip*, and the sack toppled from its post, spewing sand across the ground. She stopped, and Thorne did as well, peering at her.

"Do you think he's still up there?" Cistine murmured, toeing some of the grains into a heap.

Thorne sheathed his sabers and leaned his hand against the empty post. "He may be. But had he followed you, we would know it by now. Never forget these people have hidden in Masiya for many years, and though Jad knows it, he hasn't found them yet."

Cistine flashed him a smile. "Let's go again."

"Not yet." Thorne shook his head. "You may never tire, but I do. Let's see what has our benevolent hosts so excited."

Though itching fingertips and impending battles warned Cistine to seize every moment for training, she hadn't forgotten some of Quill's favorite missives—how rest was as necessary for strength as physical training, and how she'd do twice as much damage tearing a muscle from overuse as going into a battle after a few days without lifting a sword.

She sheathed Kaisill. "After you, Chancellor."

Thorne knocked his knuckles three times over his left shoulder; then he led the way down the tunnel toward the heart of *Via Hosial.*

They met Sacha along the way, slipping from a side grotto with the pungent waft of strong herbs hugging her body. Thorne coughed, and Cistine wrinkled her nose. "Back to your alchemy?"

"Day and night." Sacha's smile hung with pure satisfaction. "Manufacturing this antidote is no small task, and we'll need it in plenty for both your people and mine."

If she hadn't known Thorne so well, Cistine might've missed the subtle shift in his expression—the tightening of his jaw, the spark of resentment in his eyes. She chose to ignore both. "Well, I'm grateful. And my people will be, too."

They reached the fringes of the crowd, larger than usual and peppered with more than a dozen faces Cistine hadn't seen in these tunnels before. Sabir broke free to approach them, leading an elderly man with deep brown skin folding over his kind, dark eyes. His beard and brows were white and his smile yellow, but the lines around them were from smiling. "Dyalmun bless me, there she is! Little sparrow!"

"Suljafar!" Sacha laughed, embracing him, and he kissed her on both cheeks. To Cistine and Thorne, she explained, "Sul leads the Tribe of Red Shadows, an arm of the *Alhuri.* They took me in long ago when I was sick, tended and healed me. They're like family."

"And do you always go so many years without visiting family?" Suljafar teased.

Sacha's smile hardened slightly. "What are you doing here? Shouldn't you be tending the herds near Selahba?"

His smile dipped. "Selahba has fallen. They discovered we were *Alhuri* and drove us out."

Cistine winced. Sacha laid a hand to her mouth. "Sul..."

"All is well. Not one of us died, nor did they follow us here."

"You came down through the city?" Cistine demanded. "What was the Enforcer presence like? Did you see the King anywhere?"

Suljafar frowned. "Why should he be in Masiya?"

"He was a few days ago," Sacha explained. "Hunting the *Alburi.*" Cistine was grateful she didn't mention Jad's other prize—or why she and Thorne were so important to him.

"If the King was about, we did not see him." Suljafar eyed Cistine and Thorne with keen intrigue. "And who are these new friends?"

"Cistine and Thorne of Talheim." Sacha cast them a brilliant smile. "They're helping the *Alburi* put an end to Jad's schemes. But don't tell Esmail that."

Suljafar's thick brows peeled back even further. "Still the same troublemaking Sacha."

Her laughter held an edge this time. "Come, let's get you settled. Where are the rest of your tribe?"

Suljafar pivoted, raised his staff, and whistled, and from down the tunnel came a flock of people, most carrying provision sacks and bedrolls. Children swarmed before them, shouting gleefully when they spotted Sacha and flinging themselves toward her—and Cistine and Thorne standing beside her.

Cistine recoiled, panic stabbing her throat. Thorne cast out an arm. "Fall back. I'll make excuses for you."

With a grateful nod, she slipped onto the bare culvert, keeping one eye on Thorne and Sacha moving with Suljafar and his tribe deeper into the tunnel. The children climbed all over them, hands tugging at Thorne's broad fingers, at Sacha's robes and wrists. Sacha picked up and squeezed some and measured the tallness of others, held the hands of two or three at a time on each side as they tried to drag her off to start games, boasting about how accurate they had become with their slings since they last saw her. Thorne was no less popular; one little girl mounted his back like a monkey to tug on his silver hair. Others flicked his sheathed knives and grabbed his muscled arms, forcing him to lift them off the ground.

Cistine's feet snagged, a sour burst of emotion filling her throat.

This was the sort of future she'd dreamed of; that she could be a queen who was welcomed and embraced and held like this by her people, by her family. That was lost to her now...and to Thorne.

By staying with her, he was denying himself this life. There would never be children of their own hanging from his arms or climbing his back. He'd never have the chance to break the curse of cruel fathers and angry sons passed down to him from Salvotor. She'd condemned him to an heirless future.

Anguish stabbed its cruel fingers outside the place where she usually corralled it, casting shadows through her heart.

"Sul!" The booming voice brought Cistine to a halt. Esmail appeared from his tunnel and swooped down on Suljafar like a buzzard to carrion. "It's good to see you, old friend."

"And you." Suljafar's greeting was far more reserved this time. Cistine wondered if she imagined the smugness in Sacha's face at that.

"Mairin tells me Selahba is lost." Esmail clapped a conciliatory hand on the old man's shoulder. "I'm sorry. But you've come to the right place. *Alhuru en-Asgaid* remains strong as ever here."

"I look forward to seeing that strength in practice." Suljafar's gaze danced between Esmail and Sacha, and Cistine fought not to draw her own shoulders up in pride.

Strength of a different sort *was* coming, whether Esmail wished to acknowledge it or not.

His smile fixed, Esmail raised his voice. "Tonight, we will slaughter a sheep and have a feast in your honor!"

"Unnecessary."

"I insist! These days are dark, we could all use something to celebrate. What better excuse than the Tribe's safe arrival?" With that, Esmail strutted off, gesturing to rally the *Alhuri*.

Sacha spread her hands in a broad shrug. "There will be no avoiding it, I'm afraid. And I'm sure we'll enjoy ourselves if we all loosen up a bit."

Cistine glanced at Thorne, reading the resignation in his gaze. It shifted rapidly to alarm at something he read back in hers.

"One night of feasting can't hurt, I suppose," Cistine said weakly, stepping off the side path to join them.

"Your dedication to your training does you proud." Laughing, Sacha jerked her head. "Come. Mairin will want to dress us for the occasion. It's considered poor manners to wear armor to a feast."

Cistine didn't protest; not because she was quite ready to part with her armor, but because she could feel Thorne's questions scorching the air between them. And she was even less prepared to make excuses for the pain she could feel lurking behind her eyes.

❧

"Esmail grows frightened of you."

Those were the first words Sacha spoke after Mairin left them in her and Sabir's sparsely-furnished grotto to change.

Behind the veil where she tugged on the clothing Sacha had thrown to her, Cistine hesitated. Banding both arms across her chestwrap, she peeked over her shoulder at the vague outline of the alchemist kneeling at a clothing trunk on the other side of the curtain. "What makes you say that?"

"This feast isn't just to honor Sul...it's Mahasari showmanship. The number of one's flocks, the ability to make as grand a gesture as a feast, is all rooted deeply in our culture. He's showing himself rich while you have nothing to offer." A light skirt, the waist hung with unstamped coins, plopped at Cistine's feet. "Try this."

"What does it matter how rich he is if he can't even lead his people to victory?" Cistine muttered.

"Precisely." Fabric rustled while Sacha changed on the other side of the veil. "Don't worry, the Tribe are far too clever to be taken in by his flexing. And besides that, Selahba isn't far from Arak Shehr. Sul's known more fighting than Esmail would dare to dream of. He will stand with you, not him."

Cistine yanked on the skirt. "I suppose I should make friends with his people, then, since I'll be leading them into battle soon."

"I trust you will." Sacha peeked around the curtain's edge. "You take so naturally to leadership."

"There's nothing I want more in this world than to lead and help people." Except perhaps to touch them again. But that was nothing more than a fleeting dream.

Scowling, Cistine turned to peer into the bronze looking glass propped against the wall. Tatiana would've loved this attire: beaded and belled, the top ending at the midriff and the skirt hugging low on the hips. It reminded her a bit too much of Kalt Hasa, but when Sacha tossed her a beaded shawl to link over her arms and around her middle, she conceded with a brief stroke of defiance. Every other gods-forsaken thing had been taken from her. Why not make the most of this?

"Leave the scheming to me for the night," Sacha urged when they ducked from the grotto. "Try to enjoy yourself."

"Is this your way of telling me I'm being too miserable even for you?" Cistine teased half-heartedly.

"It is my way of apologizing." Sacha squinted in the torchlight. "I know this has been difficult for you. I asked for a rousing speech, but you've faced opposition...and you haven't backed away. You've taken on far more than I ever dreamed of asking. I'm as sorry for that as I am grateful you chose to fight for a people not your own."

"It's nice to be thanked for once. I haven't managed to talk Thorne into accepting the Rite...every time I mention it, he changes the subject."

"Well, thank Dyalmun you don't need his permission to fight, then!"

Cistine mustered a weak smile; she might not need it, but anything would've been better than dancing around the subject as they'd been doing for days. She just couldn't bring herself to broach it yet, not knowing what judgement he might be holding back.

They walked on in silence until a knot of onlookers blocked their way. Gathering her limbs close and tucking her body aside, Cistine followed their searching eyes and pointing hands, and her heart somersaulted in her chest.

Thorne was corralled among the children, slinging stones at rockpile targets on the shelf at the tunnel's edge. It was of absolutely no surprise that her *selvenar* knocked every heap down with steely accuracy. How many times must he have played games like this with Aden, Quill, and Tatiana? How often had he vented angry energy in Hellidom on precise tasks like these, keeping his mind from wandering to empty plans and his father's shadow looming at his scarred back?

With a jolt, she wondered how often he did things like this now so he wouldn't think of *her*.

The small audience erupted into applause when the last pile fell, and the cackling children hurried to erect them again. Others loaded Thorne's sling, ignoring his half-laughed protests that his arm was tired. Hands braced on the heads of the children fastidiously stuffing the sling and pouch, he turned to the crowd. A blush crept across the bridge of his nose when he took them in—of course he hadn't noticed he'd attracted an audience. That was her Thorne, so fixed on the task at hand the rest of the world fell away.

Then his gaze skipped to her, and his attention utterly arrested; she felt it as keenly as a hook snagging her middle. Wide-eyed, he took in her exposed midriff, her bare shoulders, her tasseled top and beaded skirt with the same sort of slow, sensual appreciation he had on their wedding day. And night.

Heat flamed in Cistine's cheeks, and she hooked her hair behind her ear, averting her gaze. But Thorne stared so long half the people turned to see what he was looking at. The other half shouted at him to give them a show when the children shoved the sling back into his hand.

Finally, shaking himself like a man rousing from a dream, he sent the stone flying so hard he chipped a corner of the ledge when he missed the target.

The flock of children sang his praises while they dragged him toward the center of *Via Hosial* for the feast. Cistine trailed safely behind them, shawl banded around her body, alone except for Sacha—and when they reached the outer ring of mingling bodies, even she slipped away.

Cistine took a moment to gather her bearings; a swath at the heart of the tunnel was cleared, a fire stacked in the middle and a skinned sheep's body turning on a spit above it. Tambourines and pipes soaked the *Via Hosial* with their music, and the *Alhuri* danced with abandon, the relief of a moment's joy as sweet and potent as the scent of herbs and wine drifting on the air. Suljafar oversaw the feast from a hand-woven blanket, his lap strewn with four small children sporting his same dark eyes and skin—possibly his grandchildren. The man reclining to his left might have been his son; and to his right, Esmail, laughing a bit too loudly, shifting to make room when Sacha joined them.

For the first time since the long days after the Deathmarch, when she'd been banished from Stornhaz, Cistine had no one to talk to. She wished Quill was here, making jokes to distract her; or Tatiana, full of brilliant thoughts that never failed to stave off sorrow. Maleck who would sit with her in quiet refrain, Aden who would hold her attention with talk of politics, Ariadne who would remind her what was good in the world, Ashe who would force her to do something beneficial even when her hands felt useless and full of death. Or Mira, who would listen and help make sense of everything.

She tried to pray for help, for a distraction, but the words clotted in her throat; she couldn't remember when she'd last felt the gods even remembered her. Ever since she'd opened the wells with nearly the last drop of her blood, she hadn't dreamed of future battlefields or seen Baba Kallah when she slept. *Haval* hadn't just driven a wall between Cistine and her loved ones; she was divorced from the divine itself, separated by a chasm of her own choosing.

She was like the quartered meat on that spit, a sacrifice offered up of her own accord.

From her left, Cistine heard her name; with great effort, she ripped her attention from the bonfire to Suljafar's male companion, swaggering over to join her with a wine gourd in hand. He thrust it out to her, grinning. "I'm Nazir, heir of the Tribe of Red Shadows. My father tells us you've invoked the Rite of *Bar Resam* with Esmail."

Swallowing raw nerves, Cistine nodded. "That's right."

"Our wishes go with you, my friend. He's a good man, Esmail, but not a great leader, to hear Sacha tell it. He's always either too headstrong or too frightened." Nazir glanced over his shoulder. "Tonight, I think he's terrified."

The wine in the gourd was so sweet, it didn't even burn. Cistine took two deep swallows, then said, "Well, his authority was challenged and your Tribe was driven out. That's enough to frighten anyone."

"Would it frighten you?"

"Yes. But I would fight anyway."

"And that's why I'd have you lead us over him, Mahasari blood or not."

She sipped from the gourd again, stomach simmering with doubt. "I appreciate your confidence, but you don't even know me."

Nazir waved a hand. "Some people you just know are good the moment you meet them. That, and Sacha's been singing your praises to my father for the past half-hour." With a wink and a grin, he added, "Best of luck in the Rite."

Watching him stroll away to mingle with the feastgoers, a trickle of purpose budded in Cistine's chest, and she drank more greedily this time.

Maybe she couldn't touch or hold, but she was training every day to do something good for the *Alhuri*. With the power of life and death in her hands, perhaps she could do it better than most.

The crowd broke suddenly, interrupting her thoughts, and Thorne stumbled into view. He was sweat-stained, the column of his neck glistening, his stubbled cheeks pulling deeply of the warm air. He'd stripped open the front of his shirt, baring the six scars across his chest and the Atrasat inkings above them.

Cistine choked on remorse and desire, forcing herself to meet his eyes. He put out his hand, beckoning. "Dance with me, *Logandir*."

She winced. "You know I can't."

"I won't touch you, I swear by all the gods. One of the children just showed me something, and I want to show it to you, too."

She stared at that outstretched hand, his wedding band gleaming in the firelight. Boldness flooded in, carried by the wine, making her dream that she could have impossible, intangible things again.

Somehow she found herself following him, slithering like a specter through the crowd. Thorne chose an open pocket near the fire where no other dancers gathered, and turned to face her. "Do as I do."

And they started to dance.

It was more like a Valgardan line dance than a Talheimic waltz, and Cistine understood at once why Thorne wanted to teach it to her. Though they danced close, they never touched—none of the dancers did. The steps were a pattern of twists and hops and stomping feet, clapping and spinning, whirling around each other with their backs close but never brushing. Like the other pairs, they raised their hands nearly palm-to-palm and circled to the tune. Thorne held her gaze, and Cistine's heart raced at the burning intensity of it, sinking in the depths of his eyes.

Then he made a face, and an intoxicated giggle escaped her as they spun apart and back together to the building tempo of the song. The resonance of clapping and leaping filled Cistine's world, and moment by moment the weight lifted from her shoulders. The smell of wine and sweat and embers mixed on Thorne's skin, the individual strands of his hair glowing in the blaze. His palms drifted just clear of her hips as she spun, his back tangibly warm behind hers as they repeated the dance again and again.

Cistine never wanted to stop. Every time the music cycled, her feet moved back into the pattern, and Thorne followed her relentlessly as if he would never tire. As if he could do this all night, every night, for the rest of their lives.

Because this was as close as they could come: five inches between their palms. Her hips between his hands. Their backs near but never touching.

She stared at that gap from his fingers to hers as the dance started over again, and her heart plunged. Her feet stuck to the flagstones.

Thorne stopped, too, staring at her, an unspoken plea in his eyes—like he was calling to her across a chasm, begging her to stay with him in this moment, this glimpse of intimacy, this heartbeat of relief where she'd almost felt as if she belonged in the world again.

But it was already gone, the threads of fleeting happiness slipping from her fingers, and she couldn't grasp them. She wasn't certain she wanted to.

Cistine turned and walked away. She didn't look back when Thorne shouted her name, or when he followed her.

He couldn't stop her from leaving. He couldn't grab her arm and keep her here.

She walked all the way to their grotto in the shadowy depths of *Via Hosial*, her mind a wine-addled haze where everything felt too loud, too bright, too *real*. He followed her there, taking up the doorway when she went to one of the bedrolls and pulled out her fist wrappings. She'd left her armor in Mairin's chamber, but she'd train anyway. She desperately needed the release.

"Cistine. Look at me. Why did you walk away?"

Tears blurred her vision, and she blinked them angrily back. "I should be training for the Rite. You go back to the dance if you want."

"Wildheart." Thorne's bare feet padded on the stone. "Tell me why you really left. We were happy."

"No, *you* were happy. Which is why I'm telling you to go back."

"That happiness is worth nothing if you're not part of it. And I know you. You were enjoying yourself, too."

"To what *end*, Thorne?" Cistine snapped. "Even if I forget for a moment I'm *cursed* by *Haval*, you still can't touch me. You can't really dance with me. That's our whole future."

"It's still a future worth having. And moments like tonight are worth having, too."

"Why? So I can remember what I've *lost*?" Cistine spun to her feet, facing him. "I can't ever really dance again! I can't train with you, I can't lie with you, I can't play with children or walk through crowds or carry heirs of my own. *Our* heirs, Thorne!"

A tremble of indefinable emotion crossed his face. "I'm aware."

"Then you *know* why there's no point to any of that!" She gestured with a cut of her arm back toward the heart of *Via Hosial*. "I don't want to do that ever again."

Thorne tore his hands roughly back through his hair. "Stars *damn* it,

Cistine! Can't you just accept one moment of happiness? Can't you look away from that augment long enough to realize there's still a world around you, and a life worth having in it?"

His words struck like a slap, the way her mother had once popped her cheek when she'd sassed her about the uselessness of learning to shoot a bow. And now, just as then, hot rage spilled into the foaming wake of that blow. "No, I can't, Thorne! Because every time I try, something reminds me of what I'll never have again!"

"But you *don't* try! You never have. What about when I came back and you wouldn't even let me put my hand in the water?" He linked his hands behind his neck, fixing her with a passionate stare burning blue like the heart of a flame. "And now you make rash decisions without me, you obsess over your future as Queen rather than living in happiness when you have it—"

"It's my right to conduct myself how I want!"

"I know that. And you choose to focus on your own hurt," Thorne croaked. "What about mine, Cistine? Have you ever considered that moments like we shared tonight are all that keeps *me* from drowning? Nimmus' teeth, I am *barely* holding on! The urge to touch you, to hold you, to kiss you one more time...there are days it's all I can do to remind myself that it's not worth dying just to have those things. But I want us to live, not just survive, and you are making it so stars-damned hard to imagine our future when you won't let happiness into it!"

"Happiness like what I gave up to save our kingdoms?"

"What if, instead of dwelling on what we *had,* you turned your focus to what we have now and made the most of it?"

"I can't! You don't understand! This didn't happen to *you,* it happened to *me.*"

"It happened to *us,* because we're one. Blended blood, blended hearts."

Cistine shook her head. "I'm sorry for your pain, gods know I am, it's all I could think about tonight! But I can't bear those glimpses. They're just a dream, and I don't want them."

Thorne let his hands fall from their sharp fold around the back of his neck. "You haven't lost *me*, Cistine. I'm right here. But I'm losing *you*…not only my wife, but the closest friend I've ever had. It would be enough to have your laughter, your smile, your friendship, even if I can never touch you again. But you're tearing yourself away from me, and I'm beginning to think I'm the only one remembering the vows we made on our wedding day…to care for one another's needs, not just our own."

Rage reddened her vision. "I *am* thinking about other people's needs, not just ours! I'm trying to be the Queen Talheim needs—"

"That!" Thorne jabbed a finger at her. "That is *precisely* what I mean. You aren't Queen yet, but you put yourself under that burden like it's already you on the ivory throne!"

"What else can I do?" Frustration ripped through Cistine's voice. "What else do I *have*?"

"You have *me*, Wildheart! And you have *yourself*. You are still everything you ever were, but you refuse to see it. You're infatuated with leading because you think it will give you back a sense of wholeness…*that's* why we're still here."

Her head jerked back so sharply, sparks fizzed in her vision. "*Excuse* me?"

"This Rite. Taking control of the *Alhuri* at the tip of a sword? The Cistine I know would use another kingdom's ways to inspire them, to establish peace and understanding—not to take power over their forces and lead them herself."

"The Cistine you knew is *gone*, Thorne! She died on the Deathmarch!"

"No. She is still in there, I *know* she is." He shook his head. "But *you* are doing everything you can to kill her."

Cistine stared at him. A sharp whine filled her ears, like the aftermath of loud thunder. The rage built up in her chest, and the hurt and defensiveness came swift on its heels. She grabbed her bedroll and weapons and stalked toward the mouth of the grotto.

"Where are you going?" Thorne asked.

"To find somewhere else to sleep. I don't want to look at you right now."

He stepped into her path. "Cistine. Wait. I'm sorry for the way I said that, but you—"

"Get out of my way, Thorne."

"No. This is not what we do. We don't walk away from each other."

"Thorne, get out of my *way!*"

She wasn't thinking, muddled with wine and wrath, and she lashed out—shoving toward his chest, his bare skin with a cut of her hand.

Thorne fell back hard on his haunches to dodge her, his elbow smashing audibly on the rock. He swore, gripping his arm across his body, gazing up at her from under the sweat-soaked strands of his silver hair.

Jolted sober, Cistine stared down at him, her breaths tumbling out in harsh pants. The hurt in his eyes—and the concern, for *her*—

She opened her mouth, but no apology came. No argument. No breath at all.

Cistine hugged her things to her chest and ran.

CHAPTER TWENTY-ONE

O NE MORE REASON to depose Jad," Maleck announced as he slipped into the loft. "He allows no female Enforcers or leaders."

"Pain," Rozalie groaned, though Maleck didn't quite fathom why *she* was groaning; she was the one perched cross-legged on Ashe's back while she did pushups in the center of the room. Heat possessed him so powerfully at the sight of his *valenar's* strength, he considered going back out into the autumn-chilled streets.

He settled for his day's ration of water instead.

"Strictly speaking, there aren't any female Enforcers *anymore*," he added once he'd composed himself. "Princess Tirzah was the only woman ever to serve in his fighting ranks."

Rozalie frowned. "Doesn't her reputation prove his women are capable?"

Maleck shrugged. "Perhaps he fears them because of her. Her list of marks would put any of us to shame. Political assassinations, public executions, kidnappings, maimings, dismemberments...if Jad asked it of her, she accomplished it without fail."

"No wonder he felt threatened enough to have Kashar execute her." Ashe's voice was guttural with strain as she continued to heft Rozalie's weight. "And killing someone of her reputation must've been the highlight of that bastard's life."

Rozalie grinned. "Are you *certain* you're not going to try to steal this fight from me?"

Ashe dropped to her chest. "Get off."

Laughing, Rozalie rolled upright, and Maleck drew Ashe to her feet, a smile chasing the cold sting of the wind from his face when her lips grazed his jawline. "Kashar's retinue hums with talk of the fighting circles. Eleven fights in the past week, and a supposedly-ensorcelled Talheimic woman has won them all. That's enough to draw attention."

"It sounds like the gossip is as good as the fighting." Rozalie winked. "What else have you heard?"

"That Kashar only wastes his time with fighters who have won at least fifteen matches." When both women groaned, he added, "But there are hints of an exception. A powerful woman, the sort Kashar's built a reputation on defeating...he won't let it stand. When Rozalie fights next, he'll be there."

"Finally!" she crowed, punching Ashe's shoulder.

Ashe's grimace, Maleck thought, owed less to the blow and more to concern for her friend. "Beating him won't be enough. We need a way to slip that antidote to him without being noticed."

Maleck grimaced. "I've considered that."

Her eyes bored into him, shrewd pools of blue and green. "Why don't I like that look?"

He cast her a reticent smile. "Because you're also not overly fond of dressing for a part."

All evening, Maleck could feel palpably just how uncomfortable his *valenar* was with this whole affair.

It made him uncomfortable as well...if for entirely different reasons.

The barmaid-styled clothing was something he'd never dared imagine her wearing before. The soft leather strap around her neck and the thin chain above her hipbones were the only things keeping the thin top and jagged skirting in place, and he wondered if she could feel his stare branding her across the sweltering room. Not merely for the attire, but the *look* of her altogether.

She'd had to disguise herself to avoid drawing Kashar's attention: fiery hair turned dust-brown by a brick of dye, lips, lids, and cheeks so heavily adorned in cosmetics she was almost a stranger even to him. Her eyes had been the most difficult to conceal, but Rozalie had offered an old brothel trick: a glass lens that shaded her blue eye green like the other.

Besides Ashe, the only women in the room were snatched from taverns and streets, ensorcelled and cast into the middle of these sweating, black-clad bodies to deliver refreshments while the men bet on fights. A high-sided arena took up the center of the room, its sunken floor filled with sand; from the center, the familiar *thud* of fists on skin broke through veins of banter and laughter. Maleck sidled between the ranks, just one of many in the crowd, catching a glimpse of Rozalie below.

He'd known she was a good fighter; for all its flaws, the King's Cadre did not churn out deficient brawlers, and on the Deathmarch she'd warred with the best of them. Kristoff and Aden owed her their lives. But against these men who threatened her own kingdom, Rozalie Dohnal was a wild thing unleashed, all but scorching the sand she danced across, beckoning fighters and then breaking them with fists and elbows, knees and feet when they came close.

Perhaps in their cruel faces, she saw the reflections of men who'd abused her in the brothel the Cadre had rescued her from as a young woman; perhaps she fought specters, not merely men, when they approached her with lewd whistles and cruel jeers.

Those jeers—and the groans—swelled as Rozalie took down yet another fighter with a crack to the jaw, knocking him senseless on the floor.

An arm encircled Maleck's waist from behind, unleashing an arc of heat through his stomach. A mug of mead jammed into his hand, and familiar breath ghosted his ear. "Keep an eye open, Mal. Word has it Kashar is next."

Maleck leaned briefly into that arm before it unwound, and Ashe hurried to serve Rozalie, who hailed her for the marked cup of clean water.

"Another challenger?" someone called. "Who will challenge this remarkable Talheimic specimen?"

A lazy voice, dripping in a rich, mocking accent, spoke above the clamor: "I will challenge."

Silence stole the air from the stuffy room and the breath from Maleck's lungs. Hate uncoiled in him with such speed and ferocity it left him lightheaded when he caught his first glimpse of Prince Kashar—the man who'd captured Ashe and nearly thrown her to her death a year ago.

He could see the resemblance at once between this man and his uncle, whom Maleck had squared with across tables and in shadowed halls in this very city: curly black hair, dark eyes, and sun-bronzed skin. But where Jad bridled with madness, this man skulked with a wildcat's grace. He wore a heavy necklace, a sash across his narrow hips, and that was all—leaving on full display his many scars.

Maleck wondered if his sister had left those marks the night he'd murdered her—the most powerful assassin in Mahasar.

He cast his gaze to Ashe, hovering at the edge of the arena, and found his own fury reflected in her eyes. Were it not for the necessity of their mission, he was certain she'd be across the room already, her hands around Kashar's throat. But for all their sakes, she restrained her anger, her gaze hanging on Maleck's for a moment, then turning to Rozalie.

Only when Kashar dropped into the opposite side of the ring did she at last turn to face him. Maleck's scalp prickled at the vicious calm in her face, but the Mahasari Prince merely rocked his head, shifting kinks from his spine. "You've done well to rise this high, for a pitiful Talheimic *basac*."

Tension traveled across Rozalie's shoulders, yet she played her part perfectly as the subservient fighter, here only to entertain. She stepped forward with a kind of blithe fearlessness, hands turned out at her sides. Kashar's eyes skipped across the audience, settling for a moment on Ashe, who hadn't backed away from the arena yet; Maleck tensed, hand dropping to his blade.

If the Prince showed a flicker of recognition, mission be damned, Maleck would see him pay for every blow he'd landed on Ashe's face.

Rozalie spared them once again, barreling forward to take Kashar's full attention, and the slam of flesh on flesh ripped through the low-roofed room. She brought her forearms together, fists up, and deflected a pair of strikes that might've stopped her heart if they'd landed. Her retaliatory jab passed over the hinge of Kashar's shoulder as he bobbed to one side, twirling behind her and tangling their feet. They both went down, Rozalie's blood slapping the sand when his elbow cracked her teeth.

Maleck slithered nearer to the edge of the arena. Off to his left, Ashe drew closer, too, watching Rozalie roll clear and stumble up. She spat more blood, wiped her chin, and plowed back in.

The cheers rose and fell with the pound of flying fists. The Prince and Rozalie slipped into a perfect match, block for block, blow for blow. She was mighty, dealing a blend of brawling hooks and uppercuts between lithe dodges and feints that looked as if they belonged on an elite's ballroom floor; but he was talented too, his quick hits like a serpent's strike, stinging and retreating, weakening her with blows to the nerves and hinges of her body.

No wonder Sacha thought they needed him. That sort of burning energy, turned against Jad, had the potential to consume his reign in a single stroke. But under Jad's control, Kashar was as deadly as a fire augment.

Rozalie fell back. Kashar darted in. They locked arms, hands to shoulders, grappling to flip each other; then Rozalie gathered her breath and swung up her knee, hooking out Kashar's legs. The Prince toppled, but he brought up his own leg as he did, flipping Rozalie over his head. She slammed down hard on her back, body arching as the air went out of her.

Ashe tensed. For a wild moment, Maleck considered interceding.

Kashar spun up to his feet, but Rozalie didn't rise, chest jerking up and down as she fought to catch her breath. Kashar loomed over her, planting a bare foot on her chest and bearing down, arms crossed on his cocked knee. "Nothing gives me quite as much joy as bringing Middle Kingdom dogs to heel. But you...I like you. Perhaps you can warm my bed once or twice before I send you to meet Dyalmun, *Raqian*."

Rozalie's hand flashed up, catching Kashar by the shoulder, and with the other she punched him straight in the throat. He staggered as she surged up, pushing off from the sand, hurling the Prince against the side of the pit and driving five punches into his thorax, then a kick to his ribs, then headbutting him.

Kashar's nose burst; he dug his fingers in like claws and wedged a knee between them, thrusting Rozalie backward. Then he planted his foot and swiveled in one vicious, circular kick, smashing her temple.

Maleck would never forget the sound when she struck the sand and lay unmoving. For a moment, his world went dark with shock. He couldn't hear the cheers, the screams from the Enforcers.

He couldn't see if Rozalie still breathed.

Then a voice pierced through: "A drink! A drink for the Prince!"

Maleck jolted, looking to the pit's edge where Kashar stretched up his hand, waiting for that drink from Ashe's platter, and his heart slammed in his chest. They would have to find a way to hustle him from the room before the ensorcellment broke, before every single Mahasari in this place turned against them and it became a fight with Ashe unarmed and Rozalie unconscious or far worse, the Enforcers dragging her limp body from the arena even now.

Ashe forced a smile when the Prince raised the cup in salute.

Then he doused himself in wine and shook his head, laughing as his men cheered. And Maleck watched in horror as the wine, and the antidote, dripped down the dark hair of his chest and thighs without a drop making it to his mouth.

Fury deadened his shock all at once.

If they could not save him, Maleck could still kill him.

He'd taken barely half a step when a hand seized his arm and Ashe spun him toward her. "Kiss me. Right now. Kiss me like I belong to you."

The words hardly registered over the cheering din. "But Kashar—"

"God's bones," Ashe cursed, and fastened his hand forcefully to the back of her neck, slamming her mouth upward to meet his.

The kiss obliterated his common sense, silenced the need for vengeance seething in his chest. His hand fisted in Ashe's hair by instinct, and he backed her against the nearest wooden support column. With both her hands, she swiveled his free one until it pinned her wrists above her head.

Raucous cheers broke out all around them, and at last he understood what she was doing. What this was.

He sank his teeth into her lip, her startled shout by no means part of the act. Then he jerked free and twisted her arms behind her back. "This one is mine," he growled to no one in particular, hauling her outside.

The cool wind struck his face like a slap the moment they set foot on the stoop, and he shook the last of the furious cobwebs from his eyes. "Forgive me, Asheila, I—"

"Don't apologize. I want to kill him, too." She shoved his shoulder with hers. "We need to get Roz."

The fighting pit was contained within a long wooden edifice off the center of Middleton—once a slaughterhouse and a tavern built into one. At the back of it, in the cattle pens, they'd dumped Rozalie out with the fighters she'd defeated earlier that night—one more amidst a heap of disappointments to the Mahasari game.

Ashe fell beside her friend, rasping her name, feeling the pulse at her neck.

"She's still breathing," she said, and only then did Maleck breathe deeply, too. "Help me, Mal. We need to get her away from here before Kashar decides to make good on his threats."

CHAPTER TWENTY-TWO

THE FIRE CRACKLED, warm and low in the center of their loft, but its heat was nothing against the inferno of guilt in Ashe's gut while she cradled Rozalie's head on her knees, waiting for her friend to wake.

It should have been me. The thought pulsed in time with her heart. *I survived the war against Valgard, Siralek, Apiriak, the Bloodwights...I should've taken that fight from her.*

Gold danced on the fringes of her vision. *EVERY WARRIOR NEEDS AN OPPORTUNITY TO PROVE HER METTLE.*

Ashe grimaced; she'd been so focused on Rozalie, watching her ribs rise and fall and searching for signs of consciousness, she hadn't realized she was starting to cleave. Now her friend vanished from view, blotted out by a dark sky full of stars. *She doesn't need to prove anything to anyone.*

BOLD WORDS, COMING FROM THE BEAST-SLAYER AND RAIN-DANCER. YOU HAD YOUR TIME IN THE REFINER'S FIRE. ALLOW ROZALIE HERS.

"What if it kills her?"

She didn't realize she'd spoken aloud until a heavy hand descended on her shoulder, bringing her vision back to the loft. Maleck crouched beside her with a damp rag in hand. "She will not die from this, Asheila."

Though he wasn't privy to the rest of the conversation, she didn't argue, taking the dripping rag to clean the thin seam of blood from Rozalie's bruised temple. Maleck settled beside her, taking Rozalie's slim hand in his. The tenderness with which he approached her—the same way he did Cistine—made Ashe's throat tight. The *valenar* mark on her palm twinged.

"I've never seen her fight like she did today," Ashe admitted. "I think Aden's been giving her lessons."

Maleck snorted. "Entirely possible. He flourishes when he has a student."

"If Rion had half a brain in his skull and took the shaft out of his ass, he'd have made *her* his second, not Viktor."

"Rion Bartos is not interested in cleverness or true strength, only in surrounding himself with people who blindly support his every belief."

She frowned. "Have you and Bres been discussing Rion behind my back?"

"His treatment of you might've arisen in conversation. Why?"

Ashe shrugged. "I just don't want you two picking up a burden I laid down a long time ago. I've accepted I'll never be Cadre again. Rion isn't our problem to solve."

"But if not us, then who, Asheila?"

Before she could answer, Rozalie twitched and stirred. Her limbs curled, and with a dull groan, she opened her eyes. "That bastard's feet are almost as annoying as his hands. And his gods-damned *mouth*."

"Welcome back," Ashe said wryly, and with a gentle squeeze, Maleck released Rozalie's hand. "How do you feel?"

"Sore. Concussed." Her tongue swiped her lips. "Thirsty."

Maleck retrieved a skin while Ashe helped her friend up. "That was a good fight, even if it ended with you drooling on the floor."

"I do not *drool*. Thank you," Rozalie added when Maleck passed her the skin. "Did it work? Where's Kashar?"

"Probably still pounding in faces. He decided to bathe in the wine instead of drinking it."

Rozalie's eyes widened, then slammed shut in a squint as if that hurt. "Damn."

"We wasted half our antidote," Maleck sighed.

"So we plan better next time," Ashe finished.

"I don't think there's going to be a next time," Rozalie mumbled. "Once a fighter's beaten, they're done. They don't want to watch the same show over and over. So unless Maleck fights him..."

"No," Ashe growled.

Maleck frowned. "Your confidence is noted."

"Don't twist my words."

"I don't recommend it, either," Rozalie said. "I just tasted the blood on that bastard's knuckles, and there's steel in it, Mal. You have strength, but it isn't worth wasting on this fight."

"And those were our two options," Ashe said. "Slip the antidote into his mouth after Rozalie knocked him senseless, or put it in his celebratory wine when *he* won."

"Well," Rozalie hedged, "a third option might've presented itself tonight."

Ashe shot her a narrow-eyed look.

"I knew I couldn't beat him," Rozalie said with the sort of frank honesty Ashe had never managed when she was Cadre. "Even before he landed that kick, I was flagging. But when he was making his taunts, I saw something...that necklace he wore. Did you notice it?"

Ashe glanced at Maleck. He nodded.

"I think it was a key," Rozalie explained. "Maybe even the key to a certain locked estate."

Ashe rocked back on her heels, the memory sweeping through her—Rozalie's hard, fast chop to Kashar's throat. "Roz, you clever little *fox*."

Her mouth slid into a grin, split lip puckering. From the pocket of her Talheimic fighting leathers, she drew a palm-sized, grooved disc on a heavy chain. Ashe stuck out her hand, and Rozalie coiled the key in it. "What do you think, Mal?"

He bent over Ashe's shoulder, examining the intricate circular design. "The make matches the lock on the estate's front door."

"Poor little Kashar, locked out in the cold." Ashe smirked. "He's going to want this back."

"I know." Rozalie's eyes gleamed. "And I'm going to give it to him."

Ashe's arm dipped. Her gaze leaped to her friend's bruised face. "I'm sorry, come again?"

She shrugged, wincing. "Sooner or later he's going to realize I have it, which means he'll tear this city apart hunting it down. Hunting *me* down. While we have the advantage, we should move in and take charge."

Ashe's fingers flexed around the key. "You're not saying what I think you are."

Rozalie opened her palm and curled her fingers twice. "I've got the key. Might as well walk in through the front door."

CHAPTER TWENTY-THREE

SOMETHING ABOUT DISTANT city lights always soothed Aden. He could still recall late nights perched with his father on the high wall that encompassed Stornhaz, learning to wayfind by the stars and mapping the districts and streets in his mind—streets he would one day race in augment-powered augwains with Maleck and feel the pressing weight to defend as High Tribune.

Talheim was not truly his responsibility, but it was beginning to feel that way, its intricacies entrusted to him by Cistine; its hive of avenues, its shops and homes all precious to his cousin—Thorne's duty by marriage and Aden's by blood relation to him. So many different obligations snarled up in his chest at once, he couldn't escape the weight anymore. Not even after he saw Nadeem safely to sleep, left him under the Queen's watchful eye, and retreated to one of the Citadel's balconies to think.

He'd discovered these places on another late-night wandering with the sleepless boy, where the spires and high towers gapped, and between them broad spans of white stone allowed a clear view of the city. These could only be accessed by winding staircases in odd corners of the Citadel or through locked rooms, and Aden wondered if they'd been built for rulers seeking escape from responsibility, kings and queens wishing to simply look at their city and think for a while.

It wasn't his city, but its quietude calmed him tonight, with the flares of ghostlight and the murmurs of those still awake in the warren of homes and shops below. He could've stayed all evening, alone, watching them.

But he wasn't alone anymore.

The glass door opened behind him, and Mira emerged onto the balcony. She'd abandoned her Valgardan threads for a Talheimic dress, bronze and loose-fitting, trailing behind her like a sandstorm as she came to the railing. Hair knotted in a mess of loose curls at the crown of her head, she bent her folded arms to the sleek stone.

"Just come back from the barracks?" Aden guessed.

She nodded. "Just finished with the council?"

"Hours ago. Nadeem is with the Queen...they tired one another out playing tonight."

"Hm." Mira's smile was genuine, but didn't quite reach her exhausted eyes. "They're good for one another, I think. Now that she may never have grandchildren..."

She trailed off from that thought. Silent for a time, they watched over a city that wasn't theirs to defend—but they did it all the same.

"Some of the Wardens are ensorcelled." Mira's frank statement broached the stillness like a cleaving blade. "How many and for how long, I can't say yet."

Aden's stomach plunged. "You're certain?"

"I'd stake my reputation on it, and you know I don't do that lightly." Mira's head sank beneath the line of her shoulders, a warrior's ferocity emerging through the calm counselor's mask. "That's why some of their tales have rung so familiar to me. Someone taught them to say these things."

"The question is *who*," Aden muttered. "And when. And why."

"Precisely." Mira's fingernails skimmed the rail. "Why send them out just to claim nothing happened on their patrols?"

Silence followed the question neither of them fully wanted to answer; then Aden turned, bracing his elbows back on the railing and watching the glass door. "Is it possible they brought down the missing patrols? Killed their own brothers and our augurs?"

"Stars, I wish that didn't make sense," Mira sighed. "But it's possible. Whittling the ranks from within would be the very strategy Solene used against Jad, turned on her people now."

Aden's molars ground together. "Clever *bandayo*."

"We need to find those missing patrols, even if we just unbury their bodies. But I'm reluctant to say who should be dispatched when any Warden or augur might be ensorcelled."

"Have you checked their eyes?"

"I'm not a fool, Aden," Mira reminded him...as if he would ever forget. "Whatever Sacha saw in them, I haven't spotted it yet. But this is an imprecise practice I'm still learning."

"Fair." Aden scratched his jaw. "It grows more dangerous here every day."

"True. But I'd be lying if I said there wasn't a thrill to it." Bracing her hands on the railing, she pushed back to meet his gaze. "I never dreamed of being a Tribune...that wasn't even possible before this past year. It's strange to think I could have been born suited to a future that didn't exist for most of my life."

Aden chuckled. "Well. Neither did help for the mind, not the way you do it. But here we are."

"Here we are."

The ghostlights of the half-asleep city played across Mira's brown skin, contoured her lips and high cheekbones in gold, and framed her dark hair in a palette of blue and red. Aden's throat went dry—not just at the sight of her, but at the thought of a lifetime as Tribunes dancing among the tapestry of laws together, heckling and bantering and helping their kingdom and its allies.

It made sense to him now why Thorne had fought so hard for this dream. Why he'd built a secret Court and risked his own skin, his own safety, everything he held dear for it. And why he and Cistine were so right for each other.

Mira broke his stare suddenly, diving into a pocket in the hidden folds of her dress and withdrawing a cloth-wrapped bundle. "I stopped by the kitchens on my way to find you. You haven't been eating as much these days, I notice."

"Am I so obvious?" Aden caught the muffin she tossed him, the buttery notes of banana and chocolate wafting into his nostrils. He beckoned with a tilt of his head, and they ducked beneath the eaves, stretching their legs out and staring through the railing at the distant Agerios where it crashed into the shore.

"You're like your cousin that way, you know. *And* your father." Mira smiled wryly. "You did it quite a bit back in Stornhaz as well."

"Ah. And is that why your guards plied me day and night with food?"

"Well, I couldn't have you fainting while carrying Nadeem." Mira winked, then grew serious again, face scrunching. "Do you want to tell me why you're up here at this disgusting hour instead of sleeping while the boy does?"

Aden ate half the muffin in one bite, then dissected the other and consumed it slowly while his mind trailed back through the events of yet another long and disastrous afternoon. "There was talk of surrender in the council meeting today."

Mira sucked in a hard breath. "*What?*"

"Mares and Brabec led the appeal. They believe if Talheim surrenders some of its southern lands to Mahasar, Jad will be appeased. They had Stannik half-swayed by the time the Queen called a recess."

Frowning, Mira took a piece of the muffin he offered her. "Mares and Brabec are northern lords."

"Precisely. Which makes it impossible to tell if this is the cowardice of those without a stake in the loss, or the indifference of the ensorcelled we're dealing with."

"Sorcel or not, it's troubling. The Queen needs the lords strong and supportive, not entertaining notions of surrender."

"I tried to argue that, but none would listen." Aden curled his lip. "They have no respect for a tamed Valgardan sitting at their table."

He didn't temper his tone in time, and Mira's eyes snapped to his face, reading the intention within the words. "What are you plotting?"

"I know what I promised the Queen." He drummed his fingers on the stone between them. "Quietly and diplomatically. But we've tried, and it hasn't succeeded. These spies grow emboldened in the King's absence. The disappearing patrols are being maneuvered into ambushes by their own superiors. This infestation stretches far and high, Mira. It's in the Wardens, in the lords, in our own ranks."

She propped her shoulder to the Citadel wall, angling toward him. "What are you going to do about it?"

The drumming stilled, his muscles slack with unease. "I know how to find the traitors. But to do it requires rousing a beast I've kept asleep for more than a year now."

Her knowing gaze searched his face. "The Hive Lord."

Aden nodded slowly. "I'm reluctant. After everything you did to drive that feralness from me..."

Mira laughed. "Aden, I didn't carve the Lord of the Hive out of you. No one ever could...being in that place made him a part of who you are. My methods were only to help you control the power the Hive had over you, not to erase your time there completely. I'm not a god."

He reclined, holding her gaze shrewdly. "Then you think I can do it?"

"Unleash the Hive Lord? Be ruthless and cunning? I do. But I'd counsel you not to think of him as a separate entity. You have gifts, Aden...some of them glowing, some of them dark. What you're learning now is how to use the darker side of your gifts for good."

He tilted his head. "And you don't think less of me for having those gifts...or for using them?"

Mira's hand snaked across the stone, stilling his drumming fingers; he hadn't noticed he'd begun to do it again. But he couldn't move—or breathe—when her fingers laced with his. "Nothing will ever make me think less of the man I see before me. Either you use your darkness, or it uses you. That's how people like Ariadne turn pain into power. It's also why, I gather, your friend Tatiana drank away her anguish for years and years."

Aden's gaze hitched on their twined hands. She withdrew swiftly, looking away from him, out over the city.

"Use your gift, Aden. Let's help save this kingdom."

Shadows clustered in the Citadel garden, low and dense, the moon framed by a thick fistful of clouds. Perfect cover for a meeting so clandestine.

Aden lounged in the shadows, arms crossed, chest rising and falling shallowly with every breath. It had been over a year since he'd made a choice as dangerous and reckless as this...putting his faith in a Talheimic he could hardly trust. Last time, it had led to a melee, to the Blood Hive's slow demise, and to Baba Kallah's death.

He could only pray it went in his favor now.

A flirt of blackness against blackness signaled he had company; then a brawny figure slipped through the hedge, a low curse lashing from him when his cloak ripped on a barbed branch. "You Valgardans are so gods-damned *dramatic*—"

Aden lunged, catching Viktor Pollack by the collar, spinning and slamming him against the garden wall so hard he lost his breath. Aden yanked down the man's hood and caught his chin, tilting his face to what little light seeped through the clouds.

"Get off of me!" Viktor broke Aden's hold with a sweep and kicked him away. "What in God's name is wrong with you? What sort of meeting *is* this, what are you—?"

"Looking to see if you're truly one of us." Aden stepped back, blocking any escape through the thick hedgerow. "Do you know what Sorcel is?"

Viktor's pale eyes narrowed. "Never heard of it."

Aden rapidly explained its properties and its source...everything Sacha had told them. By the end, Viktor leaned into the wall more heavily, rubbing a gloved hand over his mouth.

"God's bones," he breathed. "So *that's* how they're doing it. That's why you and that woman are spending so much time with our patrols. And you were checking my eyes—what, for a tell?"

Aden nodded curtly. "There's a certain gleam to the eyes of the ensorcelled at the proper angle. I haven't noticed it in anyone else...yet. No one has allowed me close enough."

Viktor's clear gaze settled on him then, the only glint within it one of dawning comprehension. "At the council meetings...you're looking for traitors."

"The Princess entrusted me with the task of rooting out Jad's ensorcelled sympathizers among them, yes. But it's proving easier said than done."

Viktor snorted. "I've noticed. You're not popular at the table."

"I don't need popularity, I need results. And I know how to obtain them, but it will require more than skill...it demands collaboration."

Now Viktor mirrored Aden's posture, arms folded. "I'm listening."

"How much do you love your kingdom, Pollack?"

"Enough to put up with your presence in it."

Aden loosed a feral smile. "Good. That proves you're a man who can go against his morals for Talheim's sake. And that's precisely what we need."

"*We?*"

"If you're willing to tolerate me, I trust you're willing to commit a bit of treason to keep Talheim from crumbling."

Viktor blinked slowly. "What did you have in mind?"

CHAPTER TWENTY-FOUR

Enforcer armor was thick, cumbersome, yet surprisingly breathable—a series of pleated leather parts with iron inlay and gold-trimmed floral motifs Tatiana had never noticed on the enemies she'd gotten close enough to kill during this stars-forsaken war.

"So this is where the stolen heirlooms are going." She followed a gold lotus whorl above her hip with her thumb. "Straight into the armor."

Quill swaggered up behind her, looping an arm around her waist. "Looks good on you."

She snapped a gentle elbow into his ribs. "You're forgetting I'm supposed to be a man."

"Well, you're the prettiest one I've ever seen, then. Don't tell Mal."

Snorting, Tatiana struggled to come to attention when Ariadne slipped inside their tent. The thick armor and helm, with a featherlight chain-link veil obscuring her features, made her so unrecognizable that for a moment Tatiana's hand surged to her nearest weapon.

"The caravan is departing soon for Ralathi Trench." At least Ariadne's voice was still distinguishable—which meant no speaking, for her or Tatiana, from Shinar to their destination.

"Good, I was getting restless." Quill cracked his knuckles and rolled his neck, then scooped up a helmet and passed it off to Tatiana. Its interior reeked of head-sweat and harsh soap from the newly-arrived Enforcers that she, Quill, and Ariadne had ambushed at their booth that morning, killed, and stolen this armor from.

Tatiana had despised doing it, knowing they were likely ensorcelled; but the risk was far too great of the men waking and alerting the entire oasis to their scheme. And with the decision already made that they'd linger another few days after they collapsed the Trench, keeping an ear open for rumors of retaliation and ensuring the blame wasn't meted out to the impoverished merches who called Shinar home, they couldn't gamble with those odds.

She despised Jad even more for making these kinds of deaths necessary.

A bellow ripped through Shinar, summoning all Enforcers back to the caravan, and Tatiana hastily fitted on her helmet and tucked her braid into her collar, safe from view. "Good?"

Quill's hands parted the chain-link veil, and he stole a swift kiss before she could protest. "Prettiest man in Mahasar."

She kicked his shin on the way out of the tent, but to his luck, she couldn't tell him where he could shove his compliments.

For now, she would be silent—playing the part of another ensorcelled Mahasari.

It was a long, uncomfortable, hot journey by covered wagon to the Trench, crammed onto a splinter-riddled bench with six Enforcers on one side and another six across from her. In the slam of bodies crowding into the wagons, she'd lost sight of Quill and Ariadne; all around her was a sea of the same armor, the same helmets, the same grim silence. Skin crawling, Tatiana wondered what these men could've possibly been like before the Sorcel stole their free will. Maybe she'd doubted its existence and power before she met Yasmin and Imane, but now...

Quill was right. This mission *was* personal.

The wagons finally shuddered to a halt where the reek of fumes was strongest. Tatiana bit back a gag when the wagon sides rolled up and a streak of nearly-identical bodies streamed past. Rough hands yanked her from the seat and shoved a heavy metal mask, slick with the last wearer's sweat, into her hands; then that man replaced her in the wagon bed, leaving Tatiana to swallow her last scrap of pride, turn away under the guise of checking the dragon lines leading into the Trench, and hastily fit the mask to her face before anyone saw her features with the chain veil tugged up.

The stench of barley beer and someone else's mouth filled her nostrils, and she took deep, measured breaths, arms folded, staring through the eye slits into the Trench. At least she couldn't smell the fumes anymore.

A shoulder knocked hers from behind—friendly, not rough. She knew it was Quill by nothing more than the way he held himself beside her, body angled like she was a lodestone drawing him inexorably closer.

She fought back a grin while they watched the dragons funnel down into the Trench, commanded by just one whip now—Vezzik's. Tatiana recognized that hoarse, vicious voice when he yelled at the beasts to keep moving. Maybe staying behind while the others changed shift was his punishment for losing Cistine...again. A slow death for his failure to play this game right, whatever it was.

It might even be a twisted sort of mercy, what they were doing today.

With a nudge to Quill's side, Tatiana fell in with the stream of Enforcers to report for duty. Her *valenar* lingered, watching the dragons disappear into the pit, scouting the danger they presented.

Tatiana's task was a simple one: tucked into a canyonside crevice, she and the men around her gathered the herbs harvested within the Trench itself, dried them by roaring firesides, powdered them, and funneled the contents into glass vials. These vials, she gathered, would be transported to Jad's alchemists in Arak Shehr and mixed into Sorcel—enslaved minds working to create and maintain more slaves.

Tatiana's hands itched for the augments buckled under her armor, ready to bring this place to ruin...but not yet. Ariadne hadn't given the signal, which meant she was still discerning patterns and threats and finding a way to convey them to Quill near the Trench.

They toiled through the day, Tatiana's nerves humming with every bundle of herbs she dried, crushed, and collected. These felt like traitor's hands doing Jad's work; if even one vial made it back to Arak Shehr, the lives it corrupted would rest with Tatiana. The families like Yasmin's it might coerce, the wealth it might strip from needy hands for the sake of a war against Cistine's kingdom...

Doubt banded her gut and made breathing even more difficult by the time Vezzik shouted an end to the day. And still no signal from Ariadne.

What in the stars is she doing?

Simmering, Tatiana joined the rest of the Enforcers in another cave for meals, this one broader and deeper, with only a single fire circle and a pot of stew bubbling above it. Tatiana's stomach dropped at the sight; she had no doubt its contents contained a general garnish of Sorcel. One bite, and who knew what she'd be talked into? It could be a thousand times worse than her worst binge of alcohol, when she'd nearly destroyed her friendship with Ariadne by making light of her past and pain.

But she played her part regardless, joining the line, sidling up for rations. The Enforcer behind her crowded so close she feared he'd feel the curves under her armor and realize she was a woman after all.

Then a hand clamped on her shoulder and squeezed. *Hard.*

Tatiana hissed, and that hand wrenched her back against another markedly female body. "Play along."

Ariadne twirled Tatiana on heel and punched her in the face.

It must've hurt her fist more than anything, metal gauntlet striking metal mask, but the vibration wrapping around her head sent Tatiana staggering. Shouts boomed from the other Enforcers as Ariadne's hands locked at the hinges of Tatiana's shoulders and they grappled, drawing more attention from their companions around the cavern. Men surged toward the soundless struggle, yanking at their arms, trying to wrench them apart In seconds, they were entrapped in a heave of bodies.

Through the eyehole slits, Tatiana beheld a flash of her friend's gaze—and knew.

She let go of Ariadne's shoulder, dove a hand into her own armor, and shattered a wind augment against her thigh.

Godlike power exploded from her body, throwing the Enforcers away. Some struck the cave walls at odd angles, dead before they crumbled to the floor; others floundered with broken limbs. Only a few staggered back to their feet, Vezzik among them, bellowing with rage. Tatiana drew the jewel-crusted Enforcer blade from her hip and launched into battle.

She and Ariadne whirled through the Enforcers together, spinning, carving, cleaving, and Tatiana hated every second of it, hated the blood on her hands, hated that while some of these men were Jad's through and through, others were like Yasmin's family...and she had no time to discover which was which if she wanted to keep herself and her friends alive.

A pained cry from Ariadne jerked her from the reverie of battle. Tatiana whirled, blade raised, just in time to catch Vezzik's blow. He'd streaked past Ariadne, sword ripping her armor, sending her down on one knee with an arm pressed to her side. His helm was gone, mask hanging askew, and one eye, wild with hate, blazed in the firelight as his scimitar pressed against Tatiana's dagger. "I know how you fight! You're the Princess's cabal!"

Tatiana broke contact with his blade, reared back, and slammed her foot into his gut, forcing him away.

Before they could come together again, a chain of wild, joyous bellows shook the cave walls, raining down stone dust, and Vezzik fell back, peering over his shoulder, teeth gritted. "*No!*"

He tore from the cave.

"Tati!" Ariadne stripped off her own helm, letting loose her dark hair, keeping the mask affixed to her face. "Go help Quill! *Go!*"

Leaping over fallen Enforcers—leaving the last two for Ariadne—she barreled out into dying daylight and black sweeps of shadows that at first made no more sense than the clamor of animal voices above. Squinting upward, Tatiana shaded her eyes against a cluster of sleek bodies and beating wings, and realized what was happening.

Her foolish, soft-hearted, justice-besotted *valenar* had slipped the dragons' chains. He'd set them free.

There was just one left, the piebald *Tayir* Vezzik had ridden out of

Talheim; Quill's *Svarkyst* sabers hacked at his restraints, and from behind, Vezzik hurtled toward them, feet noiseless on the sand—a silent death coming straight for Quill's back.

Tatiana was too far away. She screamed his name, but when his sabers contacted metal again, she didn't think he heard her.

Vezzik's sword slashed down, glistening in the daylight.

The dragon's serpentine tail snapped against Vezzik's face. Blood sprayed the sand and the Enforcer staggered, mask gone, clutching his broken jaw and rearing in agony. Without looking back, with a shout of triumph, Quill freed the dragon's leg, yanked a flagon from his pocket, and broke it in his fist. Whirling, he slammed his hand against the Trench's sharp edge.

A heave in the bowels of the earth sent Tatiana, Vezzik, and Quill all to their knees. The dragon thrashed, kicking at its restraints as Quill sent another bucking current of energy into the Trench. Then another. And another.

Tatiana started running when he cursed, pulling out a second flagon.

Vezzik regained his footing enough to lunge, abrupting Quill's next attack with a tackle. They rolled at the edge of the trench, fighting for control of the flagon, and Tatiana rallied the last burst of wind to blow the Enforcer off her *valenar's* back.

Cursing when Vezzik sailed away, Quill rolled and smashed the earth augment against the ground.

A blinding jolt of power surged through the canyon, and once again Tatiana tipped, slamming to her knees on the Trench's stone lip. Cracks and fractures spidered its edge like dried lips, and the dark maw began to collapse, starting at the farthest end.

Vezzik cried out in blind rage as his King's source of strength broke down before his very eyes. He scrabbled toward Quill, striking him a blow to the temple that Tatiana *felt*, though she couldn't hear it over the roar of collapsing rock.

Collapsing toward Quill.

She staggered up again, hurtling down the ledge as fast as she could, though more fractures and fissures bucking up under her feet made running almost impossible. Quill struggled, dazed, as Vezzik snapped him in a headlock and rolled onto his back, holding them both captive to the death splitting down the trench. The dragon bleated in pain and fear, kicking loose from its chains at last and coiling to launch skyward—

And the ledge gave out from under him. Under Quill and Vezzik, too.

Tatiana's heart stopped.

She'd watched Quill fall once before, through ice, nearly to his death. Never again.

Screaming in rage and desperation, she lunged into the shower of falling debris, breaking a flagon against her hip as she tumbled down into darkness, hand outstretched, reaching, grabbing, *praying*—

Familiar metal fingers, gloved, closed over hers.

The wind enveloped them just as the rocks did, spearing Quill and Tatiana into the heart of Ralathi Trench.

CHAPTER TWENTY-FIVE

$\mathbf{D}$RY LEATHER TAPPED her cheek, abrasive as the scrape of desert sand. "Tati." Quill's voice, brimming with worry. "Come back, Saddlebags. Show me those eyes."

Pain flickered along her ribs and wrists, and she was barely aware of the slide of power against her bones until it started to siphon off, tugged from her armor threads—

"Stop," she wheezed, and Quill froze. "Don't try to take it, you already wielded two augments. You'll wear yourself out."

"Not sure it matters anymore, but I'm glad you're awake enough to order me around."

Tatiana forced her eyes open to dimness, dank and thick, and faint curls of green mist floating far overhead.

Ralathi Trench.

They were buried alive.

Panic lanced through her chest, and she scrambled to sit up, then gripped her temple with a groan. Her fingers came away tacky with blood, and her stomach plunged deeper than the hole they'd landed in.

It's not Selv Torfjel, you're all right, it's all right...

"Tati." Quill gripped her chin, revolving her head toward him. "We're all right."

As if to prove him wrong, a grinding whine echoed in the dark. Tatiana stiffened. Quill's hand dropped away.

"It's not even *possible* Vezzik survived," Tatiana hissed. "That fall was over fifty feet."

But *something* was alive in the dark, letting out another pitiful, echoing moan.

Quill rose suddenly, brow furrowed. "Push the wind out."

"Quill..."

"Trust me."

Grimacing, she widened the bubble of clean air, the only thing keeping them from suffocating. Limping on his left side, Quill tracked a ways ahead of her, only the silver glint of his hair visible in the shadows.

Beyond him, at ground level, a curl of steam ignited. Bright ultramarine eyes flashed in the dark, crescent pupils waxing to full moons, and when her gaze adjusted to see patches of white, Tatiana knew.

That stars-damned dragon.

"Quill, get back here!" she hissed.

"He's pinned." His tone was strange, soft. "That foreleg looks mangled."

"*You're* going to be mangled if you don't get away from that thing!" Fear choked her, but Quill still didn't come back where it was safe. At the edge of the wind shell, he stopped, crouching.

"Faer used to look at me just like that," he said, raising his prosthetic hand. The *Tayir's* furious growl pitched down into an agonized huff so quickly, even Tatiana's core tightened.

Ever since they'd lost their child, sounds like that had a strange, visceral effect on her like they never had before.

Gritting her teeth, she shook her head, and pain jammed into her temple so fiercely she cried out. Quill cursed, falling back on his haunches as the augment sputtered and retracted. He whirled on her, eyes bright slices of fear in the dark. "What was that? Tati!"

She shivered, mouth full of metal, and spat blood; she'd bitten her tongue. "Leave that *stars-damned* dragon alone, Quill! We need to get out of here!"

He came back to her at last, kneeling swiftly, helping her lean back against the side of the Trench. "All right, I know. I know." He craned his head back, searching the blackness above. "Sealed up, but see those chinks where the light comes in? Can you push through, make us a path?"

"Not if you want to keep breathing *and* still have enough wind to lift us out of here."

"Right." A long, thoughtful pause. Then his fingers swiped the curls from her brow, his lips pressing to her forehead. "You're going to have to trust me on this." He stood and strode back to the edge of the wind bubble. "Widen it."

Tatiana stared at him so hard, her vision sizzled. "You've got to be *joking.*"

"We need enough wind to push through and still breathe. I'm finding us another way up and out." No trace of fear edged his words. "Widen it."

For a moment she weighed the odds of what she could do if that dragon was as vicious as its masters...whether she had enough clarity to lash out with the wind and put it down to save Quill's life.

But it didn't matter. She didn't have enough strength to save them anyway, not on her own.

Shooting up a silent prayer, she flexed her fingers and pushed the shell wider.

Quill limped forward, crouching just shy of those bright eyes, regarding the dragon at level. "I don't know how intelligent you are. At least, you're not half as mouthy as the dragon I usually spend time with. But you attacked Vezzik for me. The way I see it, that means we're in this Nimmus pit together. And I *never* leave anyone in the dark to rot alone. Understand?"

Another deep groan. It was probably Tatiana's own wishes that made it sound like *Get on with it, Featherbrain.*

"I'm going to push that stone off your leg," Quill went on, "but if you try to eat me, you see that woman back there? She'll snuff out your life faster than you can take a snap at me. So let's agree to work together, at least for now. All right?"

Those wide eyes blinked, falling to half-mast. Maybe a look of surrender, but Tatiana wasn't ready to trust it yet.

Quill straightened, rolling his shoulders. "All right. Here we go." He braced his back to the slab of rock Tatiana couldn't even see. A pained rasp shot from the dragon's throat, and Quill grimaced, tucking and curling, placing the muscled bulk of his spine to the rock. "On my count, you lift, I shove."

The dragon's shriek shook more dust and rock loose into the pit when he and Quill hurled their weight together. The slab shifted with a lung-shuddering groan, and the *Tayir* dragged itself forward, grunting and moaning, into the shield of clean air. Quill cursed and lurched away, the slab nearly clipping his heels when he fell to his hands and knees beside the beast—where he caught a tongue to the face, spreading saliva from his chin to his hairline.

Swearing, Quill wiped his jaw on his sleeve. "I could've lived without that."

The dragon collapsed, head on the floor, eyes falling shut.

Tatiana did the same.

An open palm patted her cheek, jolting her back. "Tati! Don't do that. *I'm* the one who just moved a boulder, if anyone should be fainting like a damsel, it's me."

"Thought that was Maleck's role," she slurred. The augment was proving harder to hold with every second, the power throbbing and shrinking in tune with the pulse ringing in her wounded temple. "Quill. We need to get *out* of here."

"I know." His hand squeezed her knee. "Look."

Tatiana pried her eyes open and followed his gaze up the dark spiral of the endless roof, to a thin gap shaken open by the dragon's roar.

"That's it," Quill breathed. "That's our way out."

Tatiana nearly shook her head, then thought better of it. "I don't know how long I can control this." The bubble of wind around them was weakening with her strength. In minutes at best, it would vanish.

Quill's fingers flexed on her knee; though he must be terrified, not just for her, but of this place, he was pushing it aside—concentrating for her.

He twisted to look at the dragon. "All right, we've got one chance at this. One punch to get out. We miss, we suffocate. We hit this wrong, the roof buries us with every other stinking dead thing down here. So, what do you say? Ready to push?"

The dragon blinked pain-flared eyes at him, then grunted.

"I'll take that as a yes." Quill's arm swooped around Tatiana's shoulders, bearing her up from the wall and bundling her into his arms. "What about you, Saddlebags? Got one last push?"

Dizziness pulsed through her head. "Maybe you'd better take it."

His gaze unbearably gentle, Quill locked his fingers through hers. "Let it go."

She did, keeping only a sliver of the power for herself. The protective bubble shrank to a thin film around her and Quill, the miasma outside pushing tangibly against it, heavy as a drenched blanket. She was so *tired...*

"Keep your eyes open, Dawnstar," Quill ordered, and almost against their will, her lids flipped wide. "You drop that wind, and I'm going to use my last breaths telling you what a pain in my ass you are." He beckoned with a jerk of his head, and the dragon crawled toward them, dripping blood where its belly scraped the floor. Tatiana wondered if it even had the strength to lift itself up, much less *them.*

We are in so much stars-damned trouble.

"All right." Quill rolled his head stiffly, windborne power flaring over his armor and inkings. "One punch."

He threw out his leg, and in a single powerful hop, they were on the dragon's back. Tatiana's stomach heaved, and she barely kept from vomiting on Quill's chest.

"Not bad for an eight-fingered augur," he praised himself quietly, adjusting his grip on her. "Almost there, Tati."

He'd better be right. The shield was slipping, tighter and tighter, weaker and weaker. Humid mist licked her armored legs.

Quill's knees tightened around the dragon, one arm closing around her, the other bracing against the creature's stout neck. She could *feel* him counting down. "Show us what you can do."

With a bellow of pain, the dragon *launched*, as deft a skyward thrust as an arrow loosed from its string. Tatiana screamed in terrified exhilaration as the green-tinged darkness swirled into an aurora beneath them, as they soared up toward that tiny seam they'd spotted above.

Four seconds, five, six, each one possibly their last—

With a roar, Quill released the dragon's scales and cut his arm upward. A vicious scythe of wind spewed from his armor, smashing into the cluster of rocks. Obsidian and shale hailed on them, slicing Tatiana's cheeks, jerking her and Quill backward on the dragon's sleek hide. But Quill's armored thighs caught and tightened, and he bent himself over her as they hurtled toward the gap, first widening, then shrinking—and burst through into clean air.

Quill whooped. The dragon shrieked triumphantly, a perfect harmony to match the whistling of fresh wind scouring Tatiana's ears.

She gripped her *valenar* by the collar, dragging his head down toward her. "Get us back to Shinar. Find the *almalij* tent. Ask for Yasmin."

The last drop of augmented power slid from her grasp. And with it, her consciousness.

CHAPTER TWENTY-SIX

THORNE AND CISTINE didn't speak a single word to one another after she left their grotto, and after only a few days, Thorne could hardly bear it. But he couldn't bring himself to apologize, either...not when the very friction between them felt like a testament to what he'd argued.

He couldn't be certain if it was a blessing or a taunt from the gods when, nearly a week after the feast, they found themselves ignoring each other at the same brazier on *Via Hosial's* edge at the very moment Sabir sauntered up and announced, "I'm looking for volunteers to run to the oasis."

Both their hands shot up.

It was inevitable they'd want a reprieve from dark tunnel depths and the persistent press of so many people; he'd never been fond of crowded places, and her even less so since the Deathmarch. Inevitable as well that they'd need to make the run far sooner than Esmail had threatened, with the addition of Suljafar's people.

"I see the tales of Talheimic fortitude are no myth!" Sabir laughed, clapping Thorne on the shoulder. "Mairin and I will lead the run. Nazir's coming, Sacha as well. I hope you're both feeling fit, because it's quite the journey."

"We'll manage," Thorne said, and with a nod the captain strolled off, whistling.

Cistine shifted closer to the brazier, holding her hands over it like she was staving off a bone-deep chill despite the tunnel's warmth. "It wouldn't hurt anyone to tell them you're Valgardan, not Talheimic."

Was that what she wanted—to set their differences apart? "I came here as your husband. That's all that matters."

Cistine muttered something under her breath and left the brazier, leaving *him* feeling more desolate than ever.

He hardly slept that night, thrashing and turning in the empty grotto, wondering yet again where Cistine had chosen to sleep and whether she was truly punishing herself or him. When Sabir came to fetch him in the morning, he was already armored, tugging on his boots; when the captain praised him for his punctuality, he couldn't muster even a smirk in return.

They didn't leave from the usual hole; instead they journeyed into the tunnel depths, into places where the darkness encroached so deeply it seemed moments away from snuffing the torches Thorne, Mairin, and Sacha carried. They walked for miles that way, Thorne listening for the pattern of Cistine's breathing in the dark. If it hitched even the slightest bit, he had a volley of questions assembled to distract her; and if she resented him for it, at least that would be a distraction, too.

But her breathing was even, never once changing rhythm, and that made him wonder if he truly knew his Wildheart's mind at all anymore.

At last, Sabir turned them into a narrow side hall that reminded him far too much of the claustrophobic Kosai Talis. Pulse rushing, he squeezed his wide shoulders through the gap until it widened and sloped up for another quarter-mile, and they emerged into blinding daylight from a dark gap in a rock wedged between the dunes. Tines of granite speared up from the tawny sand on every side, all leading to a dark-walled canyon in the east.

"Old bandit tunnels," Mairin explained at Thorne's questing glance. "They dug down for miles to lay siege to the supply lines traveling through *Via Hosial.*"

"We think they used to live in the oasis." Sabir adjusted the enormous waterskin pack slung over his shoulder. "Do you suppose that makes us bandits ourselves?"

"Makes us heroes." Nazir clapped him on the shoulder. "Are we going to stand about until the heat melts our brains? Come!"

Laughing, they set off toward the canyon. Thorne brought up the rear, casting a glance over his shoulder when they crested the dune. Masiya was no more than a winking jewel on the horizon, shimmering in the growing heat. He prayed it would remain quiet in their absence—that no cruel eyes would notice they'd gone.

It was hours more of walking, but Thorne didn't mind; hot as it was, the clean air soothed his lungs, and the conversations between the others grated on him far less than the constant hive of noise within *Via Hosial*. But no one invited him into the discourse. He may as well have been a shadow on their heels or a pack mule carrying their supplies.

Why are you here? The wind whispered, swirling lazily between the canyon walls. *What purpose are you serving if Cistine doesn't even need your support, when these people see you as nothing but a Talheimic Prince without claim to a throne?*

He grimaced, rubbing the exhaustion from his eyes.

The pass narrowed as they went, a thick fog rolling down its sides. Conversation tapered; up ahead, Sabir and Mairin laid their hands to their blades, gazes sweeping the dark stone walls with much more care.

Just as Thorne summoned the question to his lips, a dark shape flashed across the pass above. He halted, laying a hand to his own saber. "What was that?"

"What?" Sacha called over her shoulder.

Another skirl of movement, like smoke disturbed by a passing body. Thorne gestured. "*That.*"

Now everyone came to a stop. Cistine fell back two steps nearer to him, and despite the unease, his heart leaped in his chest.

For a long moment, everyone was silent.

Another flash of movement. The ticking of many vicious legs on rock all at once. Thorne's hair stood on end.

"*Mordo!*" Sacha cursed. "I thought you said you'd hunted them all out,

Sabir!"

"Well, apparently not!" he snapped.

"*Mordo?*" Cistine echoed shrilly. "What in God's name is that?"

"The blight of the Mahasari mountains," Mairin hissed. "Their poison will cause mad visions...waking terrors. Another of Jad's favored tools."

"The toxin secretes from the skin. If you see the *Mordo*, it has already poisoned you," Sacha added, gripping her provision pack tightly across her body. "Run straight through the pass to the oasis, as quickly as you can! They fear water, they will not follow us that far. Stop for nothing!"

Thorne looked at Cistine, terror striking bright as a flint in her eyes; but when their gazes met and held, she set her mouth firmly and gave him a grim nod. As one, they shot forward, the way painted by what little sunlight wriggled down through the high, close walls and stone arches that hemmed in the canyon. It was a wild run where the path sloped downward, boots skating on rock like thin ice, and Thorne's heart jammed into his throat as he pulled into the lead. He freed a saber and held it low at his hip, prepared for anything.

The mist congealed, and Thorne's lungs began to strain. He could no longer see any hint of an end to the canyon. He could see nothing but a dull gray veil.

He pushed himself harder, chest burning, eyes watering.

Cursing aloud, Sacha speared forward, dragging Mairin and Nazir by their hands. Sabir was right behind them, and Cistine winged around Thorne's side. "*Hurry,* Thorne! Put your sword away and just *run!*"

The fog swallowed her, too. The sunlight evaporated.

And his leg descended into a hole.

Bellowing, Thorne slammed on his hands and knees. If not for his armor, he would've gashed open both palms and his legs; as it was, he could already feel bruises forming, bones and joints straining at the impact with the black shale. He struggled up, reaching for the saber that had clattered from his reach...then faltered and broke down to a knee again. His ankle pulsed with pain when he put weight on it.

The mist danced ahead, calling his name.

Cistine. She'd come back for him.

Relief pierced the pain, and Thorne pushed himself up again, laying his shoulder to the pass's stone wall. A slurry of fog slithered over his armor, through his hair, whispering to him.

"*Thorne...*"

"Here!" he shouted. "I'm here, Cistine. I fell on my stars-damned ankle."

A beat, and the silence somehow felt condescending. "Of course you did, boy. Still such a disgrace, after all this time."

Thorne's shoulder slipped from the rock, shock mooring his unhurt leg as the mist parted like a veil and Chancellor Salvotor stepped through it, smile like ice and eyes like fire, scale-hardened face glinting.

"*No.*" Thorne stumbled back a step, hand skimming the wall. "Keep away from me. You're dead."

"Am I?" Salvotor folded his hands in the small of his back, strolling forward. "Or do I live on in every mistake you make? Every wound you deal to your *valenar's* heart?"

It was difficult not to fall back from that stare, and the mist made thinking difficult, made comprehending Salvotor's presence an effort. "You *are not* real."

"I'm as real as you make me." Salvotor paused, studying the saber at his feet. "I wouldn't be here if I wasn't summoned."

His foot contacted the blade, sending it clattering toward Thorne, and his mouth went bone-dry.

Tangible. *Real.*

"Do you see it now that you've tasted a season in power?" Salvotor's gaze leaped back up to him. "Do you realize how truly *alike* we are?"

Grief bladed through Thorne's chest, and the step he'd been about to take away faltered from more than his injured ankle. His father advanced, eyes flashing.

"That's the truth you're fleeing from, isn't it?" he purred. "Once I was gone, you lost your leverage. No longer could you blame your mistakes on me. *I* didn't put the Key's life before my kingdom's. *I* didn't let one of my own be taken by the Bloodwights. *I* didn't agree to the plan that allowed my *valenar* to nearly die on the Doors, then fail to fully restore her life and disgrace my blood oath vows *so badly* she was doomed to a mere shadow of existence. And it wasn't I who fled from the burden of being bound to her to sit on a stolen Judgement Seat and play Chancellor, was it? The one who felt *relief* at being apart from the woman he claims to love." Those glittering eyes fixed on him. "That was you, boy. Beginning to end."

Thorne shook his head, backing away another step, but his tongue felt as swollen as his ankle. No words would come.

"And, just like me," Salvotor added, "you put your own mother to death."

He closed the distance abruptly, adamant fingers catching Thorne by the throat and driving him against the canyon wall, knocking the breath from him. When he sucked it back in a panic-stricken gag, all he tasted was oily mist. His father's face shimmered before his eyes.

"How disappointed Kallah would be," Salvotor said. "Her soft prodigy murdering his own mother, failing to protect his *valenar*, lying to his blood-bonded family. What *do* you think Cyril Novacek will say when he learns you played into his daughter's defiance? Do you suppose he'll welcome you back with open arms...or cast you out into the cold where you belong?"

When he released his throat, Thorne doubled up, wheezing.

"They'll never trust you, boy." Stepping back, Salvotor dusted his hands on his fine robes. "You'll never truly be one of them. You'll always be the foreign Chancellor, the orphan boy...the man who let their daughter's life become forfeit."

"Her life isn't forfeit!" Thorne snarled, raising his eyes to his father's.

"Does *she* believe that?" Salvotor arched a brow. "Keep telling yourself the lies. Whatever you need to absolve your guilt. When you put her first, you failed your kingdom. When you put Valgard first, you destined her for Nimmus. You can't do anything right, can you?"

Anguish burned the back of Thorne's throat. "I tried, I *tried* so stars-damned hard to wake her before the battle, before—"

"Oh, enough. You know how I feel about your weeping theatrics."

Salvotor's hand cut through the air, and Thorne couldn't help his flinch. "Intentions matter little when you break everything you touch."

The argument faltered on his tongue; he remembered Cistine's heartbroken face at the feast, her rage and pain when she fled. "I love her."

"Love isn't enough!" Salvotor's shout swelled with the mist. "Better if she'd never met you, if she'd never come to Valgard...her kingdom is at war anyway, and for what? Because of you and this path you took together, now she has nothing, least of all hope—all because her *selvenar* is *precisely* like his father."

"No." The word ripped out of Thorne, half-broken.

Salvotor's merciless smile fixed on him. "You can't save her kingdom, Thorne. You can't save her family. You can't save *her*."

The pressure exploded from Thorne in a roar of fury. He lunged forward, drawing his second saber, blade biting through the mist toward his father's diamond-hard heart.

"*Thorne!*"

He heard her voice—but he could not stop.

Blade slammed against blade. The mist and his vision cleared, and he faced Cistine—his sword caught against Kaisill, an inch from her neck.

They stared at one another, Thorne bearing down, Cistine holding him at bay. Fear rippled in her eyes. Beside her, a creature lay dead, scorpion's tale cocked and lionlike maw agape, its glittering carapace pristine. Cistine's free hand was extended toward it, glove gone; and behind her, forming a wide-eyed falcate, the Mahasaris gaped at the pair locked blade-to-blade.

Thorne let go, sword clattering from his hand, his back striking the canyon wall. He tipped dizzily to the left, and a hand caught his shoulder—Sacha, appearing from nowhere, yanking his arm across her shoulders.

"We need to leave," she urged. "Quickly...we're nearly to the end!"

Thorne said nothing, merely watched Cistine hunt for and retrieve his other saber—precisely where it had fallen, not kicked by anyone.

But the trembling in his body, the ache in his chest...that was real.

Thorne's head throbbed and his feet dragged by the time they emerged from the canyon into the oasis, its waters clear and bright between white dunes tufted in hardy trees. In their shadow, Sacha finally let Thorne down. He hopped and hobbled to regain his balance, then crumbled to his seat. Every time he blinked, he saw his father's face again.

"We rest here for the night," Sacha announced. "It's too dangerous to face the *Mordo* again if any others still live, and we won't be able to flee from them in the dark."

Though he liked the idea of staying in the open no more than their grumbling companions, with weakness still gnawing at his limbs, Thorne didn't protest. They all shot him varying looks of resentment and irritation while they went to fill their waterskins and hunt.

Cistine knelt before him, face holding that familiar grim set it always did when she fought tears. She drew the same healing augment Thorne had used on her shoulder, uncorked it, and poured another kernel into her hand. The moment the power impacted, she caught her breath—a soft, pained sound, like pressing on a bruise. Thorne's eyes leaped to focus on her face. "What is it?"

"Nothing." Her voice trembled. "It just feels a little harder to wield today." She steadied her hand, then unleashed the drop of power into his body. It went to work at once, a soothing balm on his throbbing ankle and tracing along hurts he hadn't even realized were there—in his shoulders, in his back, in his pulsing temples. "Your head is bleeding. What happened?"

He frowned, touching his brow, and she gestured to the base of her own scalp.

So that was why his head hurt. He'd rammed it into the stone after all, running from the illusion of Salvotor.

When he didn't answer, Cistine stripped off her armored scarf and tipped some of her waterskin into it, then offered it out. Quietly, Thorne went about cleaning the blood from his hair. Cistine sat back on her heels, studying his face. "The *Mordo* was almost on top of you when we found you. Why weren't you fighting back?"

"I never even saw it. Not until you roused me." He swallowed against the dryness of his throat. "You touched it?"

"I had to. I needed to distract it and I didn't know where its armor was weakest." Cistine hugged her knees to her chest, a shocked, humorless puff of laughter escaping her lips. "Thorne, I've *never* seen you like that before. It was like you were facing a specter. What did you see?"

He debated whether it was wise to show this much weakness, to admit how taken in he'd been by a man he knew was dead. But he'd vowed to her, over and over again, to be nothing but honest. "It was my father."

Cistine's face paled. "You *saw* him."

"And felt him." Thorne grazed a hand over the back of his skull, and Cistine's lips pressed together. "Though I suppose that was just me, trying to get away."

"What did he do? What did he say to you?"

Here, speech utterly failed him, a thousand accusations clamoring in his wounded skull all at once. "Nothing I didn't already know," he murmured at last. Something shuttered in Cistine's face, as if she knew he wasn't telling her everything, and he hastened to add, "And you? Did you see anything?"

She was quiet for a long moment. Then she nodded. "I thought I heard the *Aeoprast's* voice. But it didn't matter, I didn't care. I just had to reach you."

"Cistine," he said when she rose. "Thank you for coming back for me. I'm sorry about..." He gestured to her neck, unable to fully form his regret.

Her flinty gaze softened. "No matter how much we argue, I'll never, *never* let anything hurt you."

Which made her a far better *valenar* than him. Stars, he didn't deserve her.

The others returned nearly an hour later, skins full and dragging nets full of fish. Cistine, who'd sat staring back at the canyon since she'd mended Thorne's leg, rose and crossed to them. "Here. Let me."

Mairin and Nazir dropped the net, watching carefully when Cistine knelt amid the fish, splaying her hands to touch them. It seemed to take longer than Thorne had ever seen for *Haval* to do its work; but perhaps that was because he was watching their faces instead, charting the shock and disbelief, his shoulders bristling at the flickers of revulsion in Mairin's eyes, in Nazir's quiet curse when their flopping catch finally stilled.

"So, this is the power Sacha spoke of," Sabir murmured. "The reason we're not to touch you. This is what you did to the *Mordo*?"

Cistine nodded slowly. "It's a curse. But against Jad, it could be a weapon."

"A powerful one," Sacha murmured, and Thorne's eyes wrenched to her. Something in her tone...

"I know how you've all struggled to reach him. That he's paranoid and well-prepared," Cistine went on. "But I have an advantage: he wants me, and he can't defend against this." The desperate, half-pleading lilt to her tone left no question of just how fiercely she ached for them to see this augment as power rather than something to be hated and feared.

His heart broke for her; but he couldn't bring himself to cajole them, to support this step toward enticing the *Alhuri* away from Esmail.

"Well, we're lucky to have you, aren't we?" Nazir said slowly, setting about skewering the fish. The others broke apart to help him, full of side-glances and murmurs, leaving Sacha, Cistine, and Thorne behind.

"Well done," the alchemist murmured, offering Cistine a crooked smile. "That is how you inspire people."

Cistine beamed, and Thorne's heart clenched painfully. He was resisting the very thing that brought her purpose—and when had it become him against Cistine's ambitions?

Stars, why was he even *here*?

CHAPTER TWENTY-SEVEN

IT ALWAYS SURPRISED Rozalie just how much a person could get away with in the right attire and enough authority in their stride.

Chain-veiled helmet affixed, Maleck's Mahasari armor belted on and stuffed into her boots and gloves, and swaggering like a man returning from conquest, she strutted straight up the hooped path before Lord Dorminger's estate, passed the guards, and unlocked the door.

By the time they realized she'd entered with the Prince's stolen key, she had already slammed the door in their horrified faces and tucked herself into a secret servant's closet she'd found during the peace talks with Jad.

She stayed there for half an hour, listening closely to the swells of disbelieving shouts and storming feet while Enforcers combed the estate in search of her. They might've been good at strong-arming into places they weren't welcome, but that didn't make them masters of these stolen locations the way Talheimics were.

Once the throbbing noise abated, the search fizzling, Rozalie slipped through the false wall at the back and into the estate's hidden passages.

Dorminger's ancestors had a streak of paranoia as vivid as their telltale red hair; these passages were how his daughters, Lucie and Alena, had escaped to bring word of Middleton's downfall to the King. The narrow, dark veins spidered between the walls where no one would notice unless they took time to realize not all the rooms in Dorminger's estate fit together the right way.

She found the proper passage after a hard, steep climb on shadow-soaked stairs and another pause to listen. Once she was certain the tromp of feet and clamor of angry voices didn't wait ahead, she pressed her shoulder gently to the wall and entered another musty closet, where Dorminger and his wife's clothing still hung from the racks, never to be touched again. Rozalie's heart panged for the vivacious Lord, dead long before his time, and for his orphaned daughters now begging every Talheimic and Valgardan in Astoria to teach them how to fight.

She knew what it was to be that helpless. Most recently, she owed that feeling to the man she'd come here to see.

With a steeling breath, she kicked open the door and strolled into Dorminger's old bedroom. It was darker than she'd expected, just one candle lit in a brass holder on the desk by the bed. The drapes were drawn, blocking out the moonlight, but by the guttering flame and a bold sliver of silver falling through the fabric seam, she found Prince Kashar posted at the desk, working over a sheet of paper—unarmored and utterly unaffected, it seemed, by the person sauntering from his closet.

"I was wondering how long it would take you to find me." He gestured to the chair across from him without looking up. "Come to sit, or to fight?" She bided her silence, knowing the moment she revealed herself as a woman, the game would change. With an irate sigh, the Prince looked up. "Let's not insult one another. My Enforcers reported someone came inside the estate using my lost key. Clearly it's me you're here for."

Rozalie stripped off her helm. "In a manner of speaking."

He reclined slowly in his chair, the only sign of surprise apart from the faintest hitch in his breath. "Well, well. I know that face. You're clever for a Talheimic, I'll give you that, *Raqian*."

"Are you going to tell me what that means?"

A taunting smile edged his lips. "Are you here to kill me?"

Oh, how she longed to. She came to the desk instead, dropping into the offered chair. "If I wanted you dead, you'd already be choking on my favorite dagger."

He poured himself a tumbler of a strong-smelling, brackish drink from the decanter at his elbow. "Please. If you could've beaten me, you would've done it in the pit."

Channeling some of the confident swagger she'd learned training under Ashe, Rozalie tossed her heels up on the desk. "What makes you think that fight didn't land me precisely where I want to be?"

Slowly, Kashar poured another glass and pushed it toward her. There was something far more thoughtful in the way he reclined now, the way his eyes traced her body. "And what could a woman possibly gain from veiling herself as one of my men?"

His attention made her skin crawl. She'd been paid that look more times than any person ought to, and all before she'd turned fourteen. "I want a rematch."

His brows rose. "You are beaten."

"I *was* beaten. *I'm* not beaten."

Kashar extended a hand across the desk, and she forced herself not to recoil when he seized her chin, thumb tracing her lower lip. "Why does it mean so much for you to win?"

"I don't care to win, I want to fight."

"And why do you fight?"

"Because it's all that matters." She hoped that sounded like something an ensorcelled Talheimic fighter would say. "It's all I can think of."

"Wearying, isn't it?" Kashar released her, sitting back. "When winning doesn't matter. When it's all about the game."

Rozalie fought not to show a flicker of recognition. Hadn't Cistine mentioned a game, down in the dungeon after they met Sacha? "Fight me," she said.

He canted his head, and for a moment where the light caught them, his eyes glinted a strange silver. "Drink with me."

She doubted anyone truly ensorcelled would ignore the suggestion, so she took the cup and swigged. It burned like absolute *fire*, harsher and hotter than any Talheimic drink, leaving a scalding cinnamon aftertaste she all but spat out. Kashar chuckled, rocking back in his seat.

"God's bones, what *is* that?" Rozalie cursed.

"*Ivrran sahlah.* Shadow-killer. A drink from *my* kingdom. Talheimic ale is not strong enough to silence the *ivrrans* in..." He prodded a finger at his temple.

"*Ivrrans?*"

"The shadows that stalk the desert. Some say they're real, but do you know what I think? They're *memories.*" He sipped, lips curling back from the burn of the drink. "Memories of your sister's knife in your chest, her last screams, her blood on your hands while you choke the life from her..."

Every instinct in Rozalie's body raged to get away from this murderer. Instead, she made herself lean toward him. "We all have our shadows to slay, don't we?"

His eyes sharpened on her like a blade to the throat. "What shadows do you drink away?"

Damn. She'd walked right into that one.

"Tell me." His tone was lazy but fierce, used to being given whatever he wished thanks to Sorcel's chokehold on this city. How many men and women had he violated with that power, forcing their secrets from them?

She fixed on a smile. "The brothel."

He blinked. She stared at him, transfixed, heart pounding. She'd meant to lie, but the words had just tumbled out—

The drink. *The gods-damned drink had Sorcel in it.*

Panic squeezed her throat. She had to get out of here, had to get back to Ashe and Maleck before—before—

"Slavery or choice?" Kashar asked.

"Slavery." She slammed down the cup, started to rise, then hesitated as a thought winnowed into her mind.

The fight. She *needed* that fight.

Every muscle bunched, she bent forward against the desk, letting her breath waft in his face. "So. About that rematch."

His gaze trailed down to her lips, then floated back to her eyes. "What did you have in mind?"

Likely nothing he did, judging by that husky tone. "We spar at the lakeside. No Enforcers, no audience."

"Then no one will see if you win."

"They won't see if *you* lose, either."

His tongue swiped his lips. "Shall we make a wager? If you win, you may ask one favor of me. Anything in the world, for the woman who could defeat the Shadow-Slayer."

"And if *you* win?"

"*When* I win," he said smoothly, "you will owe *me* a favor."

She didn't want to know what he was scheming that was so nefarious he wouldn't simply demand it of her now, with Sorcel beating through her body. Or maybe he needed time to dream up a punishment fit for the woman who'd slipped past his guard and threatened his honor.

"The lake," Kashar added. "In three days."

"Three days it is."

"And what shall I call you when I see you there?"

"Whatever you want, as long as you fight me."

"*Raqian* it is, then."

Cocky Mahasari bastard. She curled her lip. "If you bring a single Enforcer, I'll spread reputation of your cowardice throughout this city."

"And when you lose, I'll spread *yours*."

Dangerous, given what her loose tongue had revealed tonight. But she merely flashed him a sultry smile. "Until then."

"*Raqi?*" His voice, almost playful, halted her at the closet door. "My key?"

Looking back, she found him with elbow propped up and hand outstretched. He wiggled his fingers. Clutching the key tight in her fist, she shook her head. "Consider it collateral. What if I want to see you on my own terms again?"

"I'll give the Enforcers orders to let you through."

"Then it's not on my terms, is it?"

His brow ruffled. "You're all about that, aren't you? Being in control."

Rozalie swallowed a curse. "I'll see you at the rematch, Prince."

She ducked into the closet before his confusion could turn to sense—before he could order her to hand him the key and force her to choose between her cover or her control.

Donning her helmet, Rozalie fled.

Her head felt funny, like an overfull skin swishing with wine, by the time she crawled into the loft. Maleck and Ashe, dressed for training, sat against the wall, him working the kinks from her shoulders while she polished her sword. They both looked up when Rozalie tumbled inside and crawled straight for their rations.

"I need..." The words were an effort. "I need the antidote."

Ashe shot to her feet. "Roz, what did you *do*?"

"Had a drink." She pulled a face. "Hurry, give it to me!"

She sat against the support column, clutching her whirling head in her hands, and didn't look up until Maleck's heavy hand touched her shoulder. "Drink, *malat*."

She snatched the skin from him and gulped down two hungry swallows, ignoring Ashe's quiet curse. She knew it was more than her ration of water for the day, but what else could she do?

Afterward, she sat quietly, waiting for the lightheadedness to pass; neither Ashe nor Maleck spoke, but she felt them on either side of her, concern and anger radiating from their warm bodies. When she opened her eyes at last, Ashe was glaring at her. "You had a *drink* with him?"

"Pretending to be ensorcelled." A crooked smile twinged across her mouth. "Ironic, isn't it?"

Ashe groaned. "I knew this was a bad idea."

"Maybe not." Rozalie pushed herself up against the post. "We're having a rematch at the lake."

Ashe stared at her, the steel in her blue-and-green eyes shifting to surprise. "*Outside* the city walls?"

"Without Enforcers."

"How in the stars did you manage that?" Maleck had never sounded more bewildered.

Rozalie shrugged. "I gained his trust, then challenged his pride."

Ashe dropped her gaze to the vial of antidote in her hand. There was pitifully little of it left...a single dose, if that. "I just hope we have enough."

Rozalie squeezed Ashe's knee. "So do I." She couldn't have the ensorcelled Prince, still his uncle's puppet, running around with the truth she'd given him tonight. And yet some part of her, stirred by the poisoned drink, wasn't as eager to see him dead as when she'd walked into the estate tonight.

She needed to end this. Three days couldn't pass quickly enough.

CHAPTER TWENTY-EIGHT

TATIANA WOKE, NOT to the sight of Quill's concerned face, not to his whispered promises and fears in another war camp vigil, but instead to quiet prayers from a familiar mouth.

She stifled a groan. "It must be bad if you're praying for me."

The break in the mantra lasted a beat too long. "I always pray for you, Tatiana."

She opened her eyes to tangerine-striped fabric and the rich smells of sage, lavender, and poppyseed. Pain thumped dully in her left temple, and her skin prickled at the rub of a coarse blanket. Ariadne sat beside her, legs and arms crossed. Thick bandages peeped from under a thin cardigan and linen shirt carelessly tossed on—neither of them hers.

Tatiana frowned. "Where are we?"

"The *almalij* tent." Ariadne's eyes flashed. "That girl Yasmin...she and her mentor are talented and generous. They saw to us right away."

Tatiana fought off a wince. She would have some explaining to do when Yasmin joined them, but at least for now, things were quiet. The broad, sunset-hued tent was empty apart from her and Ariadne. "Where's Quill?"

Some nameless emotion flickered in Ariadne's gaze. "You wouldn't believe me if I told you."

"It had better be somewhere good, if he's not fretting at my sickbed."

Tatiana pushed herself up, bracing a hand to her head. It hurt less now, and unlike the last time she'd woken in medico's quarters, that world-ending emptiness didn't rip through her. Still, a dull throb of memory brought her hand to her middle and her eyes to Ariadne's face. "He's all right? *You're* all right?"

"Yes, aside from these ribs."

Guilt hammered at her injured head. "I shouldn't have left you."

"No, what you should *not* have done was bury yourselves alive in the Trench. I thought you were both lost. No victory was worth that."

"Victory?" Tatiana echoed. "So it's really done?"

Ariadne nodded. "The gap sealed itself behind you. Ralathi Trench is no more than a scar on Mahasar's skin now."

A swift, victorious breath flew from her lips. "*Excellent.*"

Ariadne reached over slowly—the only indication of how much her side truly pained her—and clasped Tatiana's forearm. "And I thought we took the safest mission." They both laughed, and she added ruefully, "As for Quill, he was out of this tent the moment he could be."

Tatiana grimaced. She would have to find him and talk to him. Soon.

The tentflap rustled, and Yasmin entered, hands laden with a mortar and pestle and two clay cups. When her eyes met Tatiana's, relief lit through her gaze, a kind of happiness Tatiana didn't quite feel worthy of. "Thank Dyalmun you're awake!" She shuffled to join them, laying out the cups. "That was a nasty concussion, Tati."

"I've had worse." Likely true, though that did nothing for her headache. "Thank you for putting us back together."

"I'm honored to, though I hardly knew what to make of the state of you." She brought a kettle from a hot rock over a bed of coals in the corner, and Tatiana's dry mouth watered. "Your friends said it was a hunting accident?"

"Like I've said, trade is scarce."

"Hmm." Yasmin poured steaming cups of tea. "You'll have to forgive the vessels...I had a lovely chalice a nomad traded me, but when the Enforcers left, they took it along with everything else."

Ariadne regarded the drink Yasmin offered her like a biting adder, but Tatiana wasn't afraid to take hers and cradle it, at least. The steam helped ease the pain in her head.

"Is anyone looking for us?" Ariadne asked.

"Not that I overheard. Not by name, anyway." Yasmin settled in with them. "Why do you ask?"

"No reason."

But the girl wasn't fooled. Her eyes swept between them, brow knitted with doubt. "My brothers used to hunt when we still had our own lands. I helped *Umma* stitch their hurts more times than I could count." She gestured to Ariadne's side. "That is a blade slice, and that," she pointed to Tatiana's temple, "was from falling rock."

None of them spoke for a tense moment.

"We heard the booms all the way here in Shinar," Yasmin added at length, "like the pillars of the world falling in. I've never heard *Umma* pray so hard. Not an hour later, you all come staggering out of the desert, bloody and begging for help."

Ariadne's fingers closed tighter around her cup. Absurdly, Tatiana fought the urge to smile.

"You collapsed Ralathi Trench, didn't you?"

Ariadne's breath hitched, fighting not to rush out. Tatiana lost any inclination to grin, and simply held Yasmin's gaze.

This girl was just as sharp as she'd guessed when they met. Even muddled from a head wound, Tatiana had known it was a risk when she begged Quill to bring them here. But she didn't want to lie to her...the Taia family had been lied to enough.

When Tatiana nodded, Yasmin's eyes gleamed with glee. "I *knew* it. I knew you were one of them the day we met! No wonder you're going to Masiya!"

Tatiana glanced at Ariadne, and though they were used to conveying their thoughts in silence, this girl was clever enough to notice that, too.

Yasmin faltered, excitement fading from her face. "Oh. Or...perhaps I was mistaken."

She snatched for cleaning bowls and tincture bottles, and with some effort, Tatiana caught her wrist. "What else do you think is in Masiya?"

No answer.

"Yasmin?" she repeated sharply. "What *else* is in Masiya?"

Flighty hands froze, then skimmed a lock of hair around the shell of her ear. "A band of rebels. *Alhuru en-Asgaid*. The Free People. They're like me, they..."

She trailed off, that unspoken truth hanging in the air.

Ariadne's eyes softened. "How long have you been...awake?"

The girl tensed as if she would bolt from the tent, then sagged all the way back to the floor. "A few months. We ran low on rations once. I left the water skins and food for my family and drank from the oasis, though they said it was poisoned. I didn't care, I was so thirsty. By the time the caravans returned, my eyes were opened...I saw what the King was doing, how he lies and steals and deceives Mahasar, how we only need the riches he promises we'll find in defeating Talheim because he's stolen what was already ours to make war against them." She smoothed the rugs crisscrossing the tent floor. "He makes us poor for his war, then promises victory will make us rich again."

Tatiana scooted closer, pressing her shoulder to the girl's. "What about your family? Are they pretending, too?"

Yasmin shook her head. "I tried once to wake them, but when *Aba* and *Umma* realized that they'd given up our family's home and all our heirlooms for nothing, they were so distraught they went back to the caravan rations. They chose to be numb."

Indignation fisted Tatiana's guts, and she wrapped an arm around Yasmin's back. "I can't imagine what it's like, trying to pretend you still serve the man who's stolen everything from you."

Yasmin wiped her nose on her arm. "I'm just glad you came here. As horrible as this must be for you, it's nice to have someone else who knows."

Tatiana arched a brow. "You knew I was awake the first time we met, didn't you?"

She nodded. "I suspected you were *Alhuri*. But you don't know them?"

Tatiana hesitated. "Actually, we *were* sent by one of them. Someone we need to go and find now that the Trench is sealed."

"You're leaving again?"

"Soon," Ariadne said, "but not yet. We don't want to arouse suspicion by fleeing outright."

Yasmin nodded vigorously. "That's wise. It will be four days before the Enforcers return. Stay for three, then go."

Something harsh twisted in Tatiana's stomach, but it was Ariadne who answered. "We appreciate your generosity and welcome the opportunity to recover."

A voice called out from the other side of the tent flap, a spate of Mahasari syllables with Yasmin's name peppered throughout. She hopped up, smoothing her light top and loose pants, her eyes shining. "Even if you are not *Alhuri*, I'm thankful for you. I know what they were doing in that Trench, and none of us could stop it. I'm glad Dyalmun sent you."

Ariadne smiled. "So he did."

When Yasmin ducked outside, firing back a retort in her native tongue at whoever had summoned her, Tatiana grabbed the tent post and wobbled to her feet. Though her head still ached, it felt good to be standing; she hated lying down for days at a time.

"Off to find Quill?" Ariadne asked.

"Aren't I always?"

She laughed. "He went south. Walk straight, you won't miss him."

An oddly-confident statement given the span of the desert, but Tatiana just said, "You'll be all right here by yourself?"

Ariadne waved a hand. "Something tells me I can trust this new friend you've made. And I have more praying to do."

Grinning so wide her cheeks ached, Tatiana hurried out into the blinding early-morning sun.

⌒〜〜⌒

Ariadne was right, Quill *was* impossible to miss; or, more accurately, his companion was.

Tatiana walked nearly a mile south of Shinar, wishing every step for a healing augment, before a sound reached her and wiped her mind utterly blank.

It wasn't possible, she assured herself. Not even Quill was that brash, that *reckless*.

But when she crested a ridge of sand dunes at a staggering jog and came to a halt, she saw he was *exactly* that brash and reckless.

Her *valenar* was down in the valley below, coiled up like a race-runner, bent on one knee with hands braced on the sand. And beside him, crouched and ready to explode forward in an instant, was that piebald *Tayir*.

"Ready?" Quill's voice carried thinly on the hot wind. "And..."

The dragon slapped its tail into the sand, arcing it across Quill's face, and while he staggered sideways the creature was off, bounding toward a black spear of rock jutting from the opposite side of the valley.

Laughing, Quill bolted after him. There was really no hope he'd win when his opponent had at least three sturdy legs bred for desert terrain, but in a purely selfish way, Tatiana enjoyed watching him try. She'd spied on him training plenty of times, with sober excuses and drunken abandon, but it never really got old. He was built for physicality; if anyone besides Ashe might have outrun a dragon, it would've been her Nightwing.

The *Tayir* lunged over the last stretch, banked off the rock spear, and landed facing Quill. He coughed out a sound almost like a laugh as Quill skidded to a halt before him, hands on knees, panting. "And the *cheater* wins! *Shocking!*"

The dragon butted its forehead into Quill's chest, knocking him to his seat, and instinct propelled Tatiana into the valley, a warning shout barking from her chest. The *Tayir* recoiled and Quill spun to his feet, stumbling on the shifting sand, his eyes wide.

The way he breathed her name...it was like he saw a specter. And when he shot toward the base of the dune, caught her in his arms, and crushed her to his chest, her irritation at waking to find him gone melted away.

Now that she saw the look on his face, she was beginning to grasp what this was all about.

"Thank the stars," he breathed into her hair, confirming her suspicions—then pushed her out at arm's length. "That medico, what did she say about your head?"

"I'm fine, Quill." Tatiana gentled the last of her annoyance, gripping his wrist and peering past him. "I see you made a friend."

Laughter burst from him, shaky and apologetic. "Not my idea. I thought he'd go with his kind after we landed, but he keeps creeping up on the oasis. Ari's worried he's going to ruin our alibi."

Of course. Because who could've collapsed the Trench but the man with a dragon scurrying after him?

"He seems...attached to you," Tatiana remarked as Quill circled her to examine her from every angle, the *Tayir* shadowing him effortlessly. "How did that happen?"

"Maybe because I stopped Vezzik whipping him that night in Talheim? Or maybe because I cut him loose—*twice*."

Tatiana took his hand as he came back around to face her, satisfied she wasn't breaking into bleeds anywhere. "Why *did* you stop to save him?"

"I don't know, maybe he reminds me of Faer. Still miss that bag of feathers."

When Tatiana arched a brow, Quill sighed, then tugged her over to sit in the shadow of the rock. The *Tayir* trotted after them, settling some distance off, keeping those bright eyes on Quill.

"Same reason I wasn't in that tent for most of the last day," he admitted once they'd gotten comfortable in the shade, side-by-side. "You know...I don't blame Cistine for this, but ever since she came along, I've almost lost you more times than in all the years we were running from Salvotor."

Tatiana winced at the slew of memories—cold lakes and icy logging fields, dark mountains and battlegrounds. "I've almost lost you, too."

"Right. That's my point." Quill scooped up a handful of sand and let it run through his fist. "I'm tired, Tati...more tired than I was even during Salvotor's trial. I agreed to find a house, settle in with you and Pip somewhere in Blaykrone back then because it's what *you* wanted. I figured

I'd find a way to want it, too, if it made you happy." Fist empty, he squinted across the valley. "This time, it's me. I'm done, I'm just tired. Tired of seeing you hurt and wondering if it's the last time I get you back. Tired of killing Vassora and *mirothadt* and Enforcers. Back at the Trench, all I could think about was how those people weren't much different from the dragons…they were slaves, but to free a lot more people, we had to kill them like they were there by choice."

Tatiana's chest twisted into a painful knot. "We did what we had to."

"*That's* what I'm tired of. Being the ones to choose which sacrifice is worthwhile. Like Faer choosing to get between Pippet and the *Aeoprast*. Or Cistine choosing the Death augment. That wasn't fair, and she shouldn't have had to make that choice, but she made it anyway. For us. Just like we chose *Selv Torjjel* for her. We lost our *child* that day. What if next time, we lose each other?" When she didn't answer, he shook his head. "Two wars is enough for me. I'm done. I don't care if there's no house waiting for us when we go back to Valgard…I just want to live peaceful. And I want us both there for it."

Tatiana squeezed his hand and didn't mind the harsh press of his metal fingers squeezing back. "So you set them free because you didn't want to take more innocent life. That's all right, Quill. It's what you had to do."

"Right." They watched the *Tayir* leap up, suddenly on alert, just to gambol into the middle of the valley and chase an iridescent dragonfly. "But what do we do with *him*?"

Tatiana studied the dragon, far smaller than Bresnyar's four horse-lengths, but easily large enough to carry two or three at a time. "Well, I just used most of our wind augments in the Trench. Maybe the gods are answering one of Ariadne's prayers, sending us a mount that can ride the breeze."

She hadn't realized how much Quill's withdrawn face made her ache until the misery evaporated, replaced by that mischievous grin she adored. "So you're saying we can keep him."

"I'm saying *I'm* not going to be the one trying to chase him off! I don't want to lose an arm." She jabbed a finger into his bicep. "But if you start doing that thing Ashe does, *cleaving* or whatever she calls it, you're sleeping on the couch in whatever house we *do* find."

"No cleaving," Quill chuckled, catching her hand and kissing her fingertips, one by one. But even then, his eyes were on the *Tayir*. "I don't think that's possible, anyway. He's...different from Bresnyar. He doesn't talk. I think he understands me, mostly, because any time I mention the Trench..."

The dragon whipped toward them at the word, croaking deep in his chest, eyes wide.

"He does that," Quill finished wryly. "I don't know if they keep their dragons simple here, or if that's just how his kind are, but this isn't like Shei and Bres."

"Well, good." Tatiana flipped his hand over and kissed the *valenar* scar across his palm. "Because I'm not eager to share any of this space with a dragon's rune."

Chuckling, Quill slid an arm around her waist, tucking her close to his side and leaning them back against the stone.

And though they were in enemy land, her head aching, his heart half-broken, they had peace watching a dragon flirt with a dragonfly.

Quill's chin brushed the back of her head, and he kissed her hair. "I'm glad you're all right, Tati."

She squeezed his bent knee. "You, too. But leave a note next time."

His laugh ruffled her ringlets. "I'll do that."

For a time, they were silent again, watching the *Tayir* play on the sand. Then Tatiana ventured, "So, what should we call—?"

"Shrike." Quill shrugged when she twisted forward to give him a raised-brow look. "He's already responding to it."

"I was never really going to have a say in this, was I?"

"You're the one who's afraid for her arms!"

Rolling her eyes, Tatiana elbowed him and settled back into his grip. Luckily for them both, this wasn't a battle she minded losing.

CHAPTER TWENTY-NINE

THORNE WAS QUIETER after they returned from the oasis, the poisoned vision the *Mordo* had shown him of his father haunting the depths of his eyes.

It haunted Cistine, too—the memory of racing through the fog to find that strange creature looming before him, vicious tail cocked to strike; of how it had bucked and writhed at her touch, nearly spinning in time to snap at her with its lion's maw before death had finally pierced its thick shell. And how Thorne's eyes had focused on her, so full of revulsion that she had utterly dropped her guard while his sword swung toward her neck in a brutal arc, just like the first night they met.

What if she hadn't reached him in time? What if she'd found him impaled on that creature's barb, and this time the gods had sent no messenger to redeem his life?

The journey along that path of thought was exhausting, yet she wandered down it night after night when sleep eluded her. She was up early each day, judging by the burning wick of her private alcove's time-telling candle, hammering punches and kicks on sandsack dummies and practicing with Kaisill and Nail until her arms felt like lead.

All the while, Thorne's doubts circled in her mind, as they had ever since the feast.

Had she invoked the Rite for just reasons? Was she grasping at leadership for unattainable salvation? What if she ascended all the way to the ivory throne and found *nothing* filled the gaping hole ripped into her chest?

Whenever those thoughts came, she fought harder and faster. This was not about her; it was about freeing the ensorcelled Mahasaris, unbalancing Jad's game, ending this war. If Thorne refused to see that...perhaps it would've been better if she'd brought someone else along and never put him in the path of these people, against Jad, against that *Mordo*.

All these notions made her feel half-mad herself, reckless and uneasy the day Sacha found her training in the dark hours of the morning and invited her for an escort mission.

"Where are we going, exactly?" Cistine asked when they slid from the grate beside the aqueduct. Sacha swung out behind her, and Shathen, a young *Alhuri* boy from the Tribe of Red Shadows who'd begged to come along, fitted the stone back into place. Cistine would've preferred to have Thorne at her side despite the tension between them, but urgency had kept her from hunting him down.

"Alchemy supplies." Sacha grinned, furrowing the scars around her mouth. "I wouldn't risk showing our faces for anything less. But this is good for you, too, Cistine...it shows the *Alhuri* you aren't content to crouch in the tunnels like Esmail. First the supply run, now this. You fight your own battles, and that is noble."

Heat crept across Cistine's cheeks. "I only came because you asked me to."

"But you could've said no. And that matters, too."

Cistine almost wished she had; the memory of Jad lurked around every corner of the city, as if he might still be waiting for her. Nevermind that he had a war to oversee, Magnates to tax, and people to steal from; she still watched for obsidian armor and clawed gauntlets in the shadows.

They reached the central market, the tea vendor's stall conspicuously deserted this time, and Sacha glanced at Shathen. "You brought food?"

He patted his satchel. "Plenty."

"Good. You two, keep watch and feed yourselves. Meet me back here in a quarter-hour."

Cistine shot a nervous look at Shathen, but judging by that beaming face, he was not afraid to leave Sacha on her own while they filled their stomachs. Reluctantly, Cistine followed him up to an awning above the market for breakfast.

The boy had brought quite the spread—honey-buttered biscuits, a flask of tea, and meat skewers. They ate and observed, tucked back into the shadows atop the awning, waiting for Sacha to emerge from an herbalist's stall across the way.

"So, what's it like," Cistine asked when the silence grew too thick, "being part of the *Alhuri?*"

"It's perfect!" Shathen grinned. "We have *purpose*, we have...well, you know."

"Do I?" Cistine laughed despite herself, plucking meat from her skewer.

"You're practically one of us, Nazir says! You're going to lead us when Esmail's gone."

The laughter died in her throat. "Esmail isn't *going* anywhere. I'll defeat him in *Bar Resam*, but I still hope he'll fight with us after."

"Well, however it goes, you'll win."

"Do you think so?"

Shathen shrugged. "You're Talheimic, you can do anything. Your people burned Khorraris, and that was a stronghold for centuries."

Sacha's reappearance saved her having to answer. With a swift jerk of the head, she ducked into a side alley; Cistine and Shathen rose, dusted crumbs from their clothes, and climbed down into the market. Harried shoppers scurried around them, some clutching and weighing coinpurses anxiously, others creeping up bare-handed to stalls.

Cistine slowed, then halted in the alley mouth, looking more closely at them.

She wasn't imagining it; the air in the market was different this time. Vendors were turning prospects away; men and women with empty hands and empty pockets stood helplessly in the midst of the open district, eyes simmering wetly with distress.

"Sacha," she spoke without turning, "what happened to these people?"

"According to the herbalist, regulations have worsened over the past week," Sacha explained. "The Magnate raised taxes twofold. Most households are tightening their belts now."

Because of them. Jad was putting pressure to the people to draw her and the *Alhuri* into the open. Cistine laid a hand to her churning stomach, guilt souring her throat. "Isn't there anything we can do to help?"

"Of course we can, we're going to free them!" Shathen boasted with all the confidence of youth. "That's why Sacha started *Alhuru en-Asgaid* in the first place."

"*Ay, duin du fahi!*" Sacha popped the boy on the back of the head, and he yelped, rubbing his hair.

Cistine whirled on her, shock pulsing in her temples. "I didn't know *you* built the rebelliom!"

"You be quiet, too!" Sacha shot a glare down both sides of the alley. "It doesn't matter where it began or by whose hands. What matters is where it's going and who will lead it there. And *yes*, Cistine, we are doing something...you're going to take control of the *Alhuri* and end this war, once and for all."

She stalked toward the alley mouth, Shathen scurrying sheepishly after her. Cistine watched them go, a twinge of unease snarling in her gut. She supposed that was all true, but why had Sacha never disclosed the origins of the free forces before? And why had she made Esmail leader, knowing the sort of man he was, when *Alhuru en-Asgaid* was her own creation?

They emerged into the neighboring avenue to find it deserted, nothing stirring but a faint puff of sand on the cobblestones where wind sighed between the tall buildings. Lonely laundry banners hung across open windows above, casting shadows on their path.

Shathen shivered. "Something doesn't feel right."

Cistine sensed it, too.

No sooner had her hand descended to Kaisill than doors whispered open up and down the street, Enforcers stepping into view.

Cistine expected to feel fear at the sight of their veiled faces, but a strange calm punched through her instead. She'd been anticipating this all morning, though Jad wasn't with them, and it was an odd relief when they emerged. Better an enemy she could see than one she assumed.

"Princess," one Enforcer crooned. "Your presence is required at the Palace of the Sun in Arak Shehr."

And *there* was the fear, quickening in her throat. She spun, placing her back toward Sacha and Shathen, but that felt little safer. A boy of thirteen and a peaceful alchemist—how long could they hold ground against more than a dozen Enforcers?

Sacha shifted, balancing her weight squarely on both feet. "Give me one of your blades."

Cistine darted a look at her. "But you don't—"

"Do as I say!"

Cistine flipped Nail and offered her the hilt backward. The moment it struck Sacha's palm, the Enforcers broke forward, all converging on them at once. Shathen raised his blade to charge, but before he could even take a step, Sacha's hand clapped to his head, shoving it down. She made a deft sweep, dropping one Enforcer to the ground with blood spurting from his arm. Her hand slid down to Shathen's shoulder and she vaulted up and slid across his back, slamming her feet into another man's chest. Nail reared in her hand, clashing with Enforcer scimitars, and the familiar clang of colliding steel rattled Cistine's molars.

Fight! The urge roared through her, and she lunged into combat beside Sacha and Shathen, Kaisill singing.

The boy was quick but unsteady, jabbing in and ducking out of reach, while the alchemist moved in a dervish of bloodspattered skirts, severing heel tendons and crippling fighting hands; she took a gash to the cheek like it was nothing, giving not even a cry to gratify her attacker's blow, then stuck her knife through his eye, dropped his body, and leaped on an Enforcer who swarmed up on Cistine's left with twin daggers flashing. They fell to the ground, kicking and stabbing.

Shathen's terrified cry had Cistine spinning in the fray. An Enforcer had disarmed the boy and backed him against the wall, scimitar cleaving toward his exposed chest.

Dropping Kaisill, Cistine lunged, swept the Enforcer's legs out with a kick, and gripped him by the throat from behind, jerking him backward to the cobblestones. Heat sprang along her body everywhere it contacted his; the man thrashed and fought, but Cistine locked her limbs around him until he stopped kicking and death buckled him limply against her. Then she shoved him off and scrambled up, shouting at Shathen to hide. Wide-eyed and slack-jawed, he darted into a nearby doorway.

Cistine yelled for Sacha, and they lunged together, backs close but not touching, their blades a gleaming wheel of metal blocking the rest of the Enforcers. Light scattered from their weapons, every blow forcing the men back, and through the mist of blood and sweat they began to pull away, dragging their wounded into the gaps between buildings.

As quickly as it had first dissolved into chaos, the street fell silent once more—which made the roaring of her pulse all the louder in Cistine's ears. She couldn't tear her eyes from the Enforcer she'd brought down with her touch.

Sacha dropped Nail and called for Shathen, her voice cracking a bit around his name. He reappeared in a heartbeat, clutching one bleeding arm, eyes bright with fear—and also glee. "Did you see me fight, Sacha?"

"I saw everything." Sacha took his arm and peeled back the sleeve, cursing quietly at the gash beneath. Her gaze leaped to Cistine. "Thank you for interceding."

"Of course." Even if her hands felt filthy for it, at least there was only a dead Enforcer—not a dead child. "You've trained in the sword?"

Tearing off a hank of her skirt, Sacha bound Shathen's wound. "That, or I was just possessed by Dyalmun's breath for a few moments, wasn't I?"

"Who taught you?"

"Anyone I could convince to school a poor girl in the art of the sword." Her eyes blazed on Cistine. "I still don't kill."

"I saw." A tentative smile tugged her mouth. "That's a true testament of your skill...it takes more talent to cut without killing than to slash at the most vulnerable parts in battle."

Those words—*Quill's* words—made her heart pinch desperately for missing him. But Sacha only shrugged, then turned Shathen up the alley. "We go back *now*. Quickly."

They hurried through dark furrows between the buildings, Sacha leading them along switchbacks to avoid pursuit. They'd walked nearly a half-hour, looking constantly over their shoulders, before she beckoned Cistine to fall into step with her.

"I grew up in slums," she explained. "For many years, to fight was the only way to survive. I had no choice except to learn to defend myself, but this...I *despise* this part of myself." The last words emerged hoarse, furious. "Fighting is something I *can* do, not something I *want*."

"Can I ask why not?"

"Because the moment you pick up a blade in someone else's war, you give them power to tell you who the enemy is. And the moment you give up the right to choose that for yourself, you become guilty."

"But this *is* your war. You started the *Alhuri!*"

"My war is against Sorcel, not against people. That's why I have faith Prince Kashar can be saved." Sacha squinted ahead. "That's a lesson you must learn well as leader, Cistine. If you tell someone else to pick up their blade in your name, you had best be certain the person they're swinging against is truly an enemy."

A storm of questions greeted their return near sunset, when Sacha at last deemed it safe to descend below the aqueduct. Shathen led the procession with a glorified and exaggerated tale of the alleyway scuffle, while Cistine hung back and waited for the crowd to disperse—and searched its ranks for Thorne.

She caught his gaze at the edge at last, relief breaking through his tense features when he spotted her, and her breath tumbled out in response. For the first time in days, her irritation evaporated. All she wanted was to be near him, to tell him what had transpired and what she'd learned about Sacha's past.

"We would be dead and this place discovered if not for Cistine," Sacha's call rose above the storm of voices and Shathen's story. "She risked her own life saving Shathen's. Saving *mine*."

Cistine caught a protest on the tip of her tongue; it wasn't really a surprise that Sacha kept her own part in the fight secret, that she lauded Cistine's part higher than her own. For there, lurking on the fringes, was Esmail. And beneath the fury in his eyes—

Fear.

The people were looking at her differently now. Shouts of gratitude washed through their midst. A teary-eyed woman with Shathen's same broad nose and wide eyes dipped her head to Cistine, a gesture of unspoken gratitude from a relieved mother as she bundled her son away to tend his wounded arm.

Her chest swelled with pride—and for a brief moment, happiness. She'd saved one of their own. Protected their hideaway. Gained their love.

She could *do* this.

The crowd dispersed, some pestering Shathen for more details, others following Sacha. Cistine made her way toward Thorne, a stone in the sea of moving bodies; but Esmail slipped rapidly through the throng, blocking her path. "What were you doing above? Wasn't it you who claimed we shouldn't go into the streets?"

"Sacha needed herbs for the antidote."

"We have runners who are trained for that. Sacha knows this! You willfully endangered a *child* just to prove your own strength!"

Cistine faltered, holding his furious gaze; then the acrid bite of indignation surged in her throat. "Maybe Sacha doesn't trust your runners to do their duty anymore, knowing they're led by a coward."

She brushed past him, ducking into the central tunnel to meet Thorne.

"I wondered where you were today." His gaze skipped to the *Alhuri,* then back. "Are you all right? What did Esmail want?"

"I'm fine. It was just more posturing with him." Cistine rubbed her face with both hands. "Jad did more than search for me here. He has his Magnate over Masiya levying more taxes. Everything is changing...we need to move against Jad as soon as possible."

Thorne's eyes narrowed. "Sacha told you this?"

"Well, the herbalist told her, and she told me. Why? What does it matter where I heard it, I also saw it for myself!"

"I know you did." Thorne dragged a hand back through his hair, holding it from his eyes while they tracked after Sacha. "I'm not certain..."

When he trailed off, she scowled. "Whatever you're thinking, just tell me, will you?"

His focus slid back to her. "I wish you hadn't gone today."

Cistine's fingers curled into fists. "I helped route the Enforcers, I saved a child's *life* today, and all you can say is you wish I hadn't gone? You know, you're starting to sound like Julian."

Pain flashed through his wide eyes. "Wild—"

"Don't," she cut him off. "Not today."

She stormed past him, everything so hopelessly snarled in her chest, she couldn't pluck apart the rage from the doubt, the hurt, the grief.

All she could think to do was train. Train for the day, nearer now than ever, that she would fight for the right to lead these people to their freedom.

CHAPTER THIRTY

THE TAVERN SWEATED with ale and anxiety, their humid, tangible weight pressing down on Aden where he sat across from Pollack at the corner table. Uneasy silence hung between them, crowded with memories of far too many encounters for this tenuous alliance to erase. But they'd plotted for days now, and they would see this through...whatever the cost.

Exhaustion thrummed behind Aden's eyes. He and Pollack had spent too many late nights conspiring, shifting all the necessary pieces into place, while during the day they kept up appearances in council meetings with the Queen. It wasn't ideal, going into this so tired and with alcohol in their bodies to keep up appearances. But once again, all necessary.

Eyes shifting from the taverngoers to the door over Aden's shoulder, Pollack adjusted his casual lounge, one hand propped on his thigh, the other spinning his half-empty tankard. "So. What's your story, augur?"

Aden arched a brow. "I don't recall sharing our lives being part of the plan."

"Whatever you say. Just making conversation." They lapsed into silence again, sipping their drinks. Then Pollack added, "You were in that arena with Kovar, weren't you? That Blood Hive."

"I'm surprised you can remember one of its many names."

Pollack snorted. "Well, I've heard more than a few whispers about it since you and your kind came here. Seems like a brutal place."

"Like nowhere you'll ever see, if the gods love you enough."

He cocked his head. "So how do you do it? How do you sit at the council table like some well-mannered nobleman when you've got all..." he gestured with a sweep of his hand up Aden's length, "*that* living under your skin?"

Aden shrugged. "I've had help. Friends, family. A woman who helped me overcome the shadows I carried from the Hive."

"If only it were that easy," Pollack snorted. "Shadows don't just go."

"They do if you're willing to face them."

"*Watch* yourself." Pollack bent forward, jabbing a thumb into his chest. "I know how to face shadows, all right? You try growing up without a father, with an uncle who likes to take his fists to you and your mother on bad days, who looks at your little sisters too closely when he's got enough drink in him. You'll learn fast how to stand up to *those* shadows." He sank back with a shake of his head, swigging ale. "Think you're better than us because you wrestled wildcats in a desert pit? I make the shadows afraid of *me*. That's what it means, being Cadre."

Aden studied his surly companion. Between Ashe, Rozalie, and now Pollack, an image was beginning to form in his mind, not just of the Cadre itself, but of the sort of people Rion Bartos liked to recruit. Orphans, waifs, and outcasts, youths without parents or with poor excuses for them; malleable children in need of love who would believe they'd found it at the ends of his fists on the training grounds because they knew no better. "How do *you* sit at the table?"

Pollack banged down the tankard and shot him a wicked smile. "By knowing I could break their skulls like I did my uncle's if they try to come after me."

And that was the difference between a leader and a warrior, Aden mused. It was where they drew their sense of power from.

Pollack stiffened suddenly and gave a subtle chin nod to the door. "Here they are."

Aden didn't have to look; he could all but smell the change in the air when men of obvious wealth, if not recognizable countenance, stepped into the dimly-lit room. A rapid exchange of muttered syllables came from the bar counter to their left; then Moravec's deep voice, recognizable only by the hours they'd spent with him in council: "I'm not waiting about in this squalid pit for an overpriced informant. If he can't bother to be timely for a sum of fifty zaltos, his information's rubbish to begin with."

The western Lord stormed from the tavern as swiftly as he had arrived, leading his companions back out, and with a subtle exchange of glances Aden and Pollack were up, abandoning their table and stealing out into the night after them.

They'd taken a carriage from the Citadel, as Aden had suspected they would, saving themselves the hour's walk Aden and Pollack had spent; but when they emerged into the street, the carriage was gone, nothing but thin curls of mist lingering where it had let them off.

Moravec swore, coming to a halt. "What *is* this?"

With a grim nod at Pollack, Aden unleashed his sabers.

On the rooftops framing the street, shadows rose: six hooded and cloaked figures to the four lords in the street all whirling with their backs pressed together now, weapons drawn. They laid eyes on Aden and Pollack, also hooded, and little to Aden's surprise, two of them broke rank and fled. They made it only to the next cross-street, where an innocuous cart shot out from the darkness, blocking their way.

The figures above descended like ravens on carrion, and the street erupted into fighting.

It was an utterly one-sided battle, the lords aiming to wound or kill, Aden and Pollack's people charged only to subdue. Blades clashed, shouts riddling the damp air, and Aden gritted his teeth when steel bounced off his armor. A wind augment would've solved all of this in a heartbeat, but he couldn't risk wounding the lords. He leaned back into his Hive training instead, the slam of muscle and bone, the unforgiving clash of weapons. He and the rest were made one by it, a cleaving force under which the lords— softer and unprepared for this fight—quickly buckled. By the time Moravec and Mares retreated as well, Brabec and Stannik were a heap in the back of the wagon blocking the way; and when the six gave chase, Aden and Pollack at the head, there was nowhere for them to run.

The lords cried out when rough hands caught and shoved them into the iron-banded prison box, but before they could recover enough to turn for the door, Aden slammed it shut and Pollack banged down the metal crossbeam.

Shouts and threats, kicks and punches rattled the wooden slats, but the cage held.

Wardens and augurs slashed back their hoods to swap smiles. Aden, panting, faced Pollack, who bled from a shallow cut across his left arm. But in those pale eyes, for the first time he found commonality—a brother in arms. And perhaps Pollack saw it, too; though he shifted his feet uncomfortably, he still managed a terse, "Not bad for a pit-fighting rat-romper."

Aden arched a brow. "Not bad yourself, for an uncle-thrashing *bandayo*."

They swapped grim smiles; then Pollack whistled, and the Wardens driving the cart sent it off with a snap of the reins, trundling down the cold cobblestone avenue.

Aden turned to his augurs. "Their carriage?"

"Waiting to return you two to the Citadel." Liv, a brawny Yager archer, picked beneath her nails and shot him a coy smile. "Really, High Tribune, I expected a *challenge* when you suggested capturing Talheimic lords."

"They put up plenty of fight," Pollack snapped, turning to his Wardens.

Liv caught Aden's gaze and rolled her eyes. Some things, like Talheimic pride, would never change.

"Take your sisters back to the Citadel," he ordered, and Liv nodded, mustering Ingrid and Vatalie, her fellow archers. By the time they disappeared into the shadows, Pollack's three Wardens were gone as well, leaving just the two men in the street when the Talheimic carriage trundled back into view around the tavern's side, its pair of drivers—one Warden, one augur—flashing innocent grins at their commanders.

They had argued endlessly about this—ten was a broad pool for a mission so clandestine, Aden felt. But if the rest of it went this well, he was prepared to humbly admit he had been wrong. Pollack might have a knack for strategy, after all.

They entered the carriage's plush interior, and Aden melted onto the velvet seat. Exhaustion crept over the corners of his eyes the moment he turned them to the curtained window, and his lashes scraped together while he fought desperately not to fall asleep.

On the opposite bench, Pollack cursed, and Aden rolled his eyes open with some effort. The Warden clutched his arm and leaned his head back against the headrest, staring at the lacquered roof. "What if there was Sorcel on their blades?"

"I doubt that's possible."

"If it is, I might turn on my kingdom. Just like one of them."

His tone simmered with contempt, for once not directed at Aden and his people, but at his own kin who'd compromised Talheim's safety against their will.

Swallowing a sigh, Aden yanked off the armored scarf around his throat and tossed it to Pollack. "If that seems to be the case, I'll take the pleasure of imprisoning you myself."

He let his eyes sink shut again, and almost missed the scuff of cloth tying around a wound and Pollack's grudgingly quiet, yet sincere reply: "Thank you."

They abandoned the carriage across the southern bridge and stole into the Citadel on light feet, parting ways indoors. Come morning, Aden and Pollack would be contemptuous rivals again; but for tonight they shared nods of respect and a brief smirk over a task done well before Pollack retreated for the Warden barracks and Aden wove through the halls toward his quarters.

No one paid him a second glance, being up this late—or early, judging by the glints of first light flirting along the eastern horizon. They'd grown used to his strange hours, usually with Nadeem in his arms. Small favors, he supposed, though with his eyes so heavy everything felt like a curse. The climb up the broad staircase to their floor was pure torture; by the time he slipped inside, his whole body ached, and not just from the skirmish with the lords.

He shut the door and halted, rubbing his eyes. If he could just make it to his cot for an hour or so before the next council meeting at sunrise...

"Aden?"

Cursing, he dropped his hands and squinted across the room. Mira sat on the bed, rocking Nadeem. Her head was tilted at a strange angle, twists of her hair caught in plump infant fists, and Aden realized he was tired enough to be delirious. Because the emotion that swept through him at the sight of them safe and warm and waiting for him was so powerful, and so forbidden, it nearly knocked him to his knees.

"Did you *just* return from meeting with Viktor?" Mira's harsh whisper jerked him away from that feeling. "It's nearly sunrise!"

"I know. Bed. I was on my way to—"

"For how long?"

"I have a meeting at dawn."

"Aden. When did you last *sleep?*"

"I sleep every day. I'd be dead otherwise, you know that."

She arched a brow. "When did you last sleep for more than an hour or two at a time?"

Spine sagging to the door, he shrugged. "I have responsibilities."

"*You* have a death wish. Come here." Her tone brooked no argument.

Aden came to the bed. "Do you want me to take him?"

"Aden, Nimmus' teeth!" Mira gripped his arm and yanked so hard his knees hit the mattress at her side. "Lie *down*, will you?"

A thousand protests crowded on his tongue, but he was too weary to voice any of them. Still, he kept a respectable distance on the broad bed, arms folded and back propped to the pillows. "I can sleep perfectly well on my cot."

"You mean you can slip away unnoticed the moment my back is

turned." Mira fluffed a corner of the blanket over his knees. "You are going to *rest*, Aden Bloodsinger. As your friend, I'm warning you not to argue with me about this."

"The council—"

"*Hush.*" She punched his arm. "*Sleep.*"

Huffing, he let his eyes fall shut. "Wake me in two hours."

Her noncommittal hum drifted off into a lullaby for Nadeem—a Valgardan song as old as time itself, one Aden's own mother had sung over his cradle, and he'd sung Thorne, Quill, and Tatiana to sleep with, and then Pippet after her nightmares of the last war.

A slow smile pulled at his mouth, and his head fell back into the crevice of pillows. He could spare an hour for this. For them.

It was the last thought to cross his mind before darkness claimed him.

CHAPTER THIRTY-ONE

NADEEM'S WHIMPERING STIRRED Aden from slumber. Strong daylight poured across his face, and in half a thought he was out of his bed and across the apartment, the murmurs of city life greeting him through the open window when he stood beside the bassinet, peering down into that crying face.

"Nadeem." He scooped the boy up into the cradle of his arms. "You have to stop this. Sleep isn't something to be feared."

Arms circled his waist from behind, lissome and strong, and a chin descended on his shoulder. "Tell that to his mother."

Aden frowned at her over his shoulder. "Another nightmare?"

Mira hummed low in her throat. "The usual one." The warmth of her arms vanished. "Bring him to bed."

They were already settled in the sheets together before he blinked, Nadeem resting in the crook of his arm, Mira's head on his shoulder. Aden's thumb stroked the boy's dark hair, fuller than the day he was born, and he couldn't look away from that peaceful, sleeping face.

"He's so calm whenever you or your father hold him," Mira laughed. "A warrior to his very blood, to be so comforted in the arms of the Hive Lord."

"I'm certain he'd be just as comforted in yours."

"Perhaps. But I like seeing you both this way."

Aden glanced at her sharply. "Do you? Why?"

Mischief danced in her eyes, and her lips brushed his jaw, light as sand carried on the wind. "Don't you know?"

Stars, he did. He *did*. He'd known since the day he'd helped bring her child into the world, when neither of them had any strength left and they leaned so much into each other, he forgot where he ended and she began.

Aden twisted his head, Mira pushed up sharply from the pillows, and their mouths collided with painful force.

All else faded, the golden world and the sounds of life. The child was gone from his arms as he gripped Mira's shoulders and turned them both, mouths unbreaking, his knees pressing on either side of her hips, hands settling her gently against the pillows. The *valenar* scar on his palm roughed along her bare arm and the taste of her mouth filled his head with wonder, with relief and desire—

That scar.

Not the *valenar* mark. A blood oath.

Sander. This was *Sander's valenar*, this was *Mira* beneath him.

Aden jerked back, the breath pushing out of him in a rush, his horrified gaze meeting her sensuous dark eyes. He shouldn't be here. Shouldn't be with her now, shouldn't be with her like *this*—

"Aden, you've never had to hide from me." Her hand cradled his jaw. "I feel it, too."

A pattern of sharp, impatient knocks woke Aden suddenly, violently, Mira's body vanishing from under his knees. Jolting awake in a disoriented mess, for a moment he couldn't begin to fathom where he was—the bed too soft and high to be his cot, the scent of vanilla soap and spice filling his nostrils. He thrashed upright and only stilled when his bare feet brushed the floor and the walls swam into view—white accents stroked in strong midday sun, the duvet piled in his lap a rich crimson. And Mira, sprawled asleep on the other pillow, Nadeem beside her, between the place where she lay and the impression Aden's body had left. Mother and son dozed with his small fingers wrapped around one of hers, their mouths forming the same gentle oval while they breathed.

Something unbearably soft lodged in Aden's throat, and a strange feeling pinched his stomach, the remnants of that dream refusing to be forgotten. Carefully, dangerously, he reached over to shift a wayward strand of hair from Mira's face, letting his fingertips graze the round of her cheek.

Another knock, louder and firmer, sent him up from the bed and out of his daze. Thank the stars he was still dressed; he crossed the room in three long strides, wrenched open the door, and forced himself out into the hall, nearly bowling over the Queen.

"Mira and the boy are sleeping," he growled. "Let's keep this outside."

"If you wish." Solene's arms were a hard cross, her gaze smoldering green fire. "You weren't present for today's council."

"I was sleeping. Medico's orders." And he felt better for it, though still a bit groggy and ruffled by that dream.

"I see. And would you like to tell me why four of my lords have gone missing after an altercation with you?"

He blinked at her. "Who said I altercated with anyone?"

"The barkeeper at the tavern where I tracked their movements after they failed to make today's council session. Apparently, they came to meet with a man claiming to have information about the missing patrols...a man named Sander?"

Aden grimaced. Perhaps he should have given a different alias for that part of the ruse. He folded his arms as well and reclined against the wall, giving the Hive Lord's leash a bit of slack. "They're alive, I assure you."

"I am not asking for your assurances, High Tribune. I want to know where they are and why. Or would you prefer to be removed from my council and banished from Astoria?"

Aden flexed his fists in the cross of his arms. The wild posed no imminent threat to him, but the thought of leaving this city while it was under Mahasari oppression—leaving his augurs, leaving Mira and Nadeem... "They're in your dungeon."

With a curse, she tossed up her hands. "Of all of the *places*, Aden—!"

"You said you trusted me as Cistine does."

"To politick with us, yes! I don't recall ascribing you the power to imprison my people!"

"This is no flex of Valgardan might. You wanted the ensorcelled found. I've placed the likeliest culprits in the one place they're unable to find the drug."

Solene's arms dropped. For a long moment, she gazed at him, her expression inscrutable. "You've left them there to sober up."

Aden shrugged. "They're being seen to by my most trusted augurs. Pollack's men are collaborating. We're giving them special rations to ensure none of *them* can be ensorcelled, either. I'm confident that in time, your lords will remember themselves, remember where their loyalties lie, and confess. Or else we'll know it's not them, and that narrows the pool of suspects among the council."

Solene's face shifted at last into a smile so cunning it nearly made his hair stand on end. "I can see why Thorne made you High Tribune. Clever indeed, and well done. How can I help?"

He tried to let out his held breath silently. "An excuse for their absence to the rest of the lords would be strategic. If there are others ensorcelled, we don't want to alarm them before they're caught."

"Certainly not." Solene winked. "I think I can manage something. I'll leave the rest to you...and you *will* inform me as soon as any of them confess."

Aden dipped his head. "At once."

"Good." Solene laughed under her breath. "Now go back to bed, will you? The circles below your eyes are making *me* feel exhausted." With a matronly squeeze to his arm, she strode down the hall.

Tossing up a silent prayer of relief, Aden slipped back into the room. To his disappointment, Mira was awake already, feeding Nadeem at the table where she poured herself a cup of cold tea. Her eyes found him with a strange mixture of humor and sadness. "You gave them Sander's name?"

A pang of shame pierced his chest. "It was the first that came to mind."

"I'm glad it was." Mira nudged out the other chair with her foot and poured tea for him as well. "He would've loved this scheme of yours. He would've played the informant until every lord in this Citadel truly believed he was an ensorcelled Mahasari."

"And I would've preferred his help over Pollack's." Aden slid into the offered seat, running his thumb over the knotted scar inside his palm. "I miss him."

"So do I. Every day." Mira adjusted her grip on Nadeem. "But I like to think the best of everything he was lives on in Nadeem. And I know all the precious things he left behind are in good hands, just as wonderful in their own way."

They shared a glance across the table, the fire in her gaze so like what he'd beheld in that dream he should never have had—this night or any of the uncountable ones before it.

Shame and desire spiked through him, jamming into his throat like a spear. Downing his tea in one swallow, Aden lurched to his feet. "I should check the watch on the dungeons."

"Aden, wait a moment," Mira said, and her tone pierced him with pure panic.

Like she *knew*.

"I'm sorry. I don't have the time." Pressing his scar until it ached, he escaped the room before he could make another mistake—one that might undo all the peace the precious hours of sleep had brought him. One that might make good on that traitorous dream that made the truth impossible to deny.

He loved that woman sitting across the table from him. He'd loved her for months now, if not longer.

And that love could never be. Not when he was the reason she was alone in this world.

CHAPTER THIRTY-TWO

ANOTHER SLEEPLESS NIGHT of tossing and turning ended this time with Thorne at the mouth of Sacha's private grotto, head swirling, body bristling for confrontation.

He should've felt tired, but his mind sparked like struck flintrock, and this conversation would no longer wait. Not after what Sacha and Cistine and Shathen had encountered in the streets the day before.

This room was different from all the others in *Via Hosial*, deeper and broader and absolutely cluttered, its worktables full of flagons—though not like the ones used to bottle augments. Some were beaked and wide-mouthed, some squat and narrow, some large and some small. Clusters of herbs hung from the ceiling and a pot bubbled over a stone firepit on one wall, filling the room with sweating humidity that glossed the stones. Sacha twisted her hair off her neck as she stirred the pot with her free hand.

Thorne cleared his throat, but his words still emerged as a growl. "We need to talk."

"I wondered when we might." She didn't turn from the pot. "Your eyes were burning holes in me during the evening meal."

He'd been watching her far longer than that, puzzling her out since the disastrous supply run. It was only over the past night, while the *Alhuri* had celebrated Cistine's apparent triumph over the Enforcers, that a disturbing possibility had fully annealed at last in his mind.

Stepping into her grotto, he folded his arms and leaned against the wall. "What are you doing with Cistine?"

"Unless you believe I'm cooking her down in this pot, I don't know what you mean."

"I think you do." Thorne forced his voice to hold calm. "I know my *valenar*. I know precisely what she's capable of, how mighty she is...and where her weaknesses lie. She wouldn't kill a dozen Enforcers with the power in her hands, and she couldn't match that many with a blade. She brought no augments with her when you went to the streets, which means either Shathen is lying about how many he killed in this battle he can't stop boasting about...or you are."

Sacha's stirring stopped.

Rage strummed the cords of Thorne's throat. "I don't believe it's coincidence that anywhere Cistine goes with you, trouble follows. First the *Mordo*, now these Enforcers. And each time, she slides deeper into the Free People's favor."

"You think she's undeserving of favor?"

"I believe it's false praise, but she's too wounded to see that. And I can think of only one person who has both the wherewithal and the motivation to take advantage of her damaged heart."

Sacha turned, mirroring his posture with folded arms and steely eyes. "If you've come to accuse me, I suggest you get it over with."

"Gladly," Thorne snarled. "You didn't bring Cistine here to make rousing speeches. You've been watching Talheim for as long as these kingdoms have been at war, learning its royalty from afar. You knew Cyril would refuse to come himself. You knew she would come in his stead because she's desperate to prove the sort of ruler she can be. And you knew Esmail would reject her, and when she saw the sort of man *he* is, she'd choose to remove him from power by any means necessary."

Sacha said nothing, leaving herself open to his final blow.

"You don't just want her to defeat him, you want her to *kill* him in the Rite. That's why you plotted all this." He shrugged up from the wall, carried on the wave of his own anger. "You knew there was still a *Mordo* living, you knew the Enforcers were in the city, and you brought her to those places so her renown would spread. You're putting her life in danger to rid yourself of Esmail az-Lochan and put someone in power who *you* can control."

The faintest cock of her head. Silent admission.

Thorne shot forward, slamming his hand against the wall next to her head. "This ends *now*. Tell Cistine what you've done, and if you're so fed up with Esmail, fight him *yourself!* You clearly have the skill for it!"

"I don't kill."

"And my *valenar* is not a murderer!"

"Evidence would suggest otherwise. The Rite was her idea, not mine."

"She would never have chosen it if she knew you were manipulating her. Why won't you just take control of the *Alhuri* yourself?"

"Because I'm not fit to lead. Cistine is born for it."

"She is *Talheim's* princess, not your people's savior!"

"There's no reason she can't be both. I don't want to *control* her, I simply recognize the need for a leader who is not cowardly, stubborn, and immune to reason."

"You're already trying to control her, and either you're lying again, or neither of you can see it. Tell her what you've done, or I will."

Sacha straightened, shoulders bobbing. "Do what you must. But will she even believe you anymore?"

Thorne hated himself for the doubt that cracked in his chest. "What exists between Cistine and me goes beyond petty arguments."

"Is that all this is?" Sacha's eyes narrowed. "You know she feels burdened by you. Helping the *Alhuri* gives her purpose...you're a shackle around her leg reminding her of a past she can never go back to."

A smile jerked across Thorne's mouth. "You can't wound me deeply enough that I'll leave her side. Nothing can."

"Not even if *she* tells you to go?"

His molars clicked together so hard, his ears pinged. "Don't act like you know Cistine better than I. *No one does.*"

"I suppose time will tell." Sacha brushed past him and returned to the vat, taking up the spoon again. Thorne turned after her, rage sweating in his palms.

"You took a heartbroken, desperate princess and twisted her into your perfect conqueror. How are you any better than Jad?"

He was on his back before he realized what had happened, before it fully registered that Sacha had swept his legs and thrown him down in one smooth, powerful thrust. Now she knelt on him, knee jammed into his groin, hands fisted in his collar. "Don't you ever, *ever* compare me to that *ivrran*! I am not a shadow, I am not a creature like him!"

"Then why are you manipulating these people the way he does his entire kingdom?" Thorne rasped. "Why won't you step into the light and face your specters yourself rather than hiding behind anyone and anything you can control?"

Sacha's grip on his collar loosened and she stared down at him, eyes wide and overbright in the gloom.

Footsteps scuffed on rock. Cistine's voice floated from the darkness. "Thorne? Sacha? Is that you?"

"It is!" Sacha let him up when Cistine ducked inside. "Thorne was just teaching me how to disarm an Enforcer. Apparently he was concerned for my safety when he realized I would've been dead in that alleyway if not for you." Smile plastered in place, she swung toward Cistine—and swore. "What happened to your hand?"

Cistine tucked her bleeding fist behind her back. "I had a little accident during training. I was wondering if you had a poultice?"

Sacha rolled her eyes. "I just gave my last jar to Sabir yesterday. Let me see if he has any left." She cast a parting look at Thorne, full of challenge, then hurried down the tunnel.

Thorne levered himself up, stomach aching with fury. Cistine frowned. "You really wanted to teach her?"

He opened his mouth and shut it, gaze drawn irresistibly to her bloody knuckles. He knew those wounds well, the result of a volley of blows landed too quickly, too fiercely, without proper wrappings and fed by anger and desperation.

"No," he said, and Cistine's head tipped slightly. "I confronted her about her behavior with you."

"What behavior?"

He heaved a sigh. "It was a trick, Cistine. None of this was ever about giving speeches or sowing hope. She's always wanted you to take Esmail's place and lead. She believes she can manipulate you more easily than him."

Cistine's jaw firmed. "You think *this* is how you're going to discourage me? *I* chose the Rite, and I did it for my *own* reasons—because these people need our help!"

"Maybe they need to help themselves. Maybe Esmail needs encouragement, inspiration to become the leader he was meant to be...the things you came here to offer before Sacha planted these notions of taking power in your head."

A strange look passed through her face; then she shook it forcefully away. "Thorne, why are you even here anymore? Just to argue with me? Just to make me doubt myself?" There was no malice in her voice, only exhaustion. "I can't fight with you *and* Esmail. Maybe it's better if you just go home. Leave the *Alhuri* to me and go help Aden find the traitors, since that seems to be all you want to look for...people to accuse for not measuring up to your standards."

"No." He stepped toward her. "I swore I was with you, and I meant it."

Cistine shot him a smile, void except for a thin trace of sadness. "Maybe *I'm* not the one who can't stand to be happy, then. We both know you're miserable here."

"I'm not miserable with *you*," he said when she turned toward the tunnel.

She halted, gathering her breath, and he knew she was about to swing a blow. But he couldn't brace properly for the parting words she cast without a backward glance: "You're not with me, Thorne. Not anymore."

CHAPTER
THIRTY-THREE

WITHIN TWO DAYS, the last of Tatiana's headaches cooled. She was almost sad to return to their booth, leaving behind the secret smiles Yasmin flashed whenever the head *almalij* was around. She'd miss being in the company of a Mahasari who knew and understood what they were truly fighting for.

The Enforcers' return—and the time of their departure—loomed nearer. And every night, Tatiana fell asleep with a weight on her shoulders and woke with a heart twice as heavy.

The day before they were set to leave, she snuck away from Shinar before dawn while Quill and Ariadne still slept, just to think. Hands stuffed in the pockets of a thick wool cardigan she'd traded one of her trinkets for, she wandered up and down dunes kissed golden-pink by daybreak, her stomach a weighted coil and her back slumped.

She didn't see Shrike until she nearly ran into him.

"Stars!" she cursed at the assault of a stone-rough dragon tongue swiping her left side. "Why can't you just *eat people* like normal dragons?"

The *Tayir* cast her a look of vague affront, then coiled around her and trotted at her side while she stalked deeper into the dunes.

"He's not coming," she snapped. "He's actually *sleeping*, like I *should* be doing...except I can't, because I can't stop thinking about what's happening in this stars-damned *oasis!*"

She flopped on top of the next dune, cradling her head in her hands, and Shrike lowered to his haunches beside her. He could be remarkably quiet when he wanted, unlike the warrior he'd bonded with.

Sighing, Tatiana kneaded her temples. "A little over a year ago, something terrible happened to our friends. I decided the safest thing for me was to shut them all out, but someone convinced me that wasn't the best choice. I *know* she was right, but it seems like I just keep falling into problem after problem ever since. Right now, I don't know what to do about the one in front of me."

Shrike nudged her arm, and she dropped her hands to find him watching her, eyes wide and earnest—almost sympathetic.

"We could just leave," she muttered, testing out the words. "Disappear like specters. Let them sort out the Enforcers and the Trench themselves."

She yelped in shock when Shrike lunged suddenly, catching her arm gently in his mouth. His dagger-tipped teeth didn't even prick the skin, but his fixed gaze was trying to convey *something.*

"Ah, there you two are."

Tatiana swiveled, oddly guilt-stricken for fraternizing with her *valenar's* dragon; but Quill was grinning when he sauntered up the dune. Ariadne shadowed him, hand to her blade, smiling cautiously at Shrike.

"Nice to see you're bonding," Quill remarked, halting beside them, and Shrike spat out Tatiana's arm with a frustrated huff. "I wouldn't want your *only* thing in common being deep, undying devotion to me."

Ariadne kicked his haunch in passing, and Quill laughed; Tatiana didn't feel like laughing, and she knew they saw it. Ariadne beckoned Shrike away to examine his mending foreleg while Quill lingered with Tatiana, his gaze on her face. "Something on your mind, Saddlebags?"

"Nothing new, just..." She glanced over her shoulder toward Shinar. "We're still set to leave tomorrow?"

Quill said nothing for a time. When he did speak, his voice was soft. "You don't want to make them face the Enforcers alone."

Ariadne's eyes swung to them, missing nothing even from a stone's throw away.

"I know we have a job to do," Tatiana muttered, meeting neither of their gazes. "We're supposed to find the others. But these people...they're like Blaykrone refugees. They're the Village of the Moon. They need us."

Quill conferred with Ariadne in silence; and then, it seemed, with Shrike. "All right. How do you want to dance this?"

The moment he asked, the ideas came to her like they'd been knocking at the door of her heart while she held them at bay. Taking his hand, Tatiana swung to her feet. "I want to do the last possible thing anyone expects of us. How much do you trust that dragon, Quill?"

He cast another glance at Shrike, belly-up and thrashing while Ariadne tried hopelessly to examine his leg. "I'm starting to. Why?"

"Because we're going to need him to stage a rescue."

The interior of the *almalij* tent was dimmer than usual when Tatiana sought Yasmin out during the sacred hour when she was alone, grinding herbs—not for Shinar's people, but for the Enforcers. In her short time recovering here, Tatiana had learned they took more than gold or precious artifacts; they took herbs to soothe their lungs at the Trench and some sort of spicy chew that gave them energy for hours. Yasmin was hard at work preparing it, for which she'd never see a morsel of payment. Tatiana couldn't imagine how much worse it was for her than the other merches, knowing full well her work was thankless and unjust.

She must've made some sound from her place at the tentflap, because Yasmin looked up, her smile lacking its usual fervor. "Tomorrow's the day?"

"That's right." Tatiana settled on the rug-covered floor.

Yasmin went on grinding, eyes fixed on the mortar and pestle. "I'm going to miss you, Tati ra-Nova. Promise you won't forget me?"

Tatiana's throat tightened. "How could I? You saved my life and showed me there's good in this kingdom worth fighting for."

A sheen of tears stained Yasmin's eyes. "Well, then all this suffering hasn't been for waste, has it?"

It was the first time she'd admitted aloud that she suffered, but nothing could've solidified Tatiana's resolve more fiercely today, like new steel plunged into water.

She reached over, took away the stone bowl, and clasped Yasmin's hand, turning the girl to face her. "I'm leaving tomorrow, but not in the way you think. Whatever you see happening, I need you to understand two things: the first is that I'm doing it for you, for your family, and everyone else here. The second is that you *can't interfere*, no matter what."

Yasmin's eyes widened. "Why not?"

"Because if they suspect you're not ensorcelled, they'll force the drug back into you. And I don't want to lose you like that, do you understand? You *can't* go back under their control. Not for me."

Yasmin squeezed her hand so tightly the bones ached. "Tati, you're frightening me. What are you going to do?"

"You'll see tomorrow. But I need your reaction to be real...no one can know we spoke like this. Just promise me, whatever you see, you'll remember."

Yasmin's chin quivered like she might burst into tears. "I will."

Tatiana folded her into an embrace that smelled of herbs and hot sand. "Don't give up hope, Yasmin. Mahasar *will* be free again." With one last quick squeeze, she set the girl back at arm's length. "There's something I need from you and your *Umma*, if you're willing."

Yasmin wiped hastily beneath her eyes. "Anything."

Tatiana grinned. "I need clothes."

CHAPTER THIRTY-FOUR

THE DAY OF the rematch dawned bleak and cold, precisely how Ashe's insides felt while she dressed in the dim loft. She and Maleck slipped out before dawn to make their way to the lake, hastening through a burrow wyrm tunnel out of Middleton. Ashe's paranoia turned the walls humid with ill intent, the anticipation of the day giving everything a slick, dark feeling, as if evil had gone running down the way before them. She was grateful to emerge on the plains and circle the pike wall to the lakeshore, ducking in where the foliage hid them; there she could remove her suffocating helmet and loosen the tight straps of her stolen Mahasari armor.

"I haven't seen you this tense since you faced Rion Bartos during the peace talks." Humor laced Maleck's deep voice as he watched her settle across the narrow, well-concealed hedge—her back to one tree, his against another, their feet tangled comfortably in the space between them.

Ashe glared over her shoulder toward the mist-veiled lake. "I don't like this."

Maleck's smile softened. "Regardless of any title given to you, you always carry the weight of the kingdoms on your shoulders. Let Rozalie help shoulder the burden."

Ashe opened her mouth to answer, then hesitated, scalp prickling, skin tingling. Hushing Maleck with a cut of her hand, she rocked to her knees, peering at the lake.

Through the mist, he appeared.

God's bones, she hated that face. It brought all the memories surging back: pain and false friendship and lies spun in the dark, cold rain on her face and how hard she'd fought the Mahasaris, nearly flung to her death by their ruthless hands before Bresnyar interceded.

With a shimmer of gold, the lake turned to a sea and a low growl rattled inside her skull. *THAT RUTTING, YELLOW-BELLIED—*

Ashe severed the connection. She needed to focus.

Kashar seemed to be alone, though that meant nothing; to his perception, Rozalie would be alone, too. While he limbered up with a series of shirtless stretches and exercises that bared the white scars down his tawny chest and torso, Ashe scouted the shore behind and around him for any trace of Enforcers who might be lurking nearby to ensure he didn't gain any more marks today.

Maleck pressed closer, hand on her back. "He puts on quite the show for being alone."

"Jealous, Mal?"

"That entirely depends on what you're looking at."

She shot him a grin. "Don't worry. Watching you train takes all the excitement out of other men for me."

Footsteps padded nearby, and Maleck drew away as Rozalie strode into view. She tossed her belongings carelessly by the hedge—a cloak, a knife belt, the key to Dorminger's estate, and a waterskin. For a brief moment, through the foliage, her gaze met Ashe's.

Trust me, Rozalie mouthed.

And Ashe did. But that made it no simpler to watch a friend stride down the shore to face Kashar az-Kyrian for the second time, her face still riddled with bruises from the first.

"You're late, *Raqian*," he remarked.

"*Dawn* is a broad term." She raised her voice a bit, masking the rustle when Ashe drew the waterskin into the bushes and tipped the rest of the antidote inside—their last chance to put a Mahasari who might be less of a bastard than the current King on the throne.

Shooting up a prayer, she capped the skin.

"That it is." There was no telling if the amusement in Kashar's voice was genuine or indulgent, but Ashe was willing to bet on the latter. "Are you ready to be truly beaten?"

"Are *you*?"

That was all the warning they gave one another; then they were fighting again.

Ashe had fought her share of battles—bloody wars and tavern brawls, sparring matches against fellow Wardens, and Blood Hive duels. She knew the look of a creature unleashed, of a tether snapped, and there was no denying what was happening on this shore. Kashar and Rozalie had just been toying with each other in that pit match, both putting on their own kind of show; now they fought in earnest, every blow contacting with sickening crunches and shouts of pain. They whirled and blocked and spun, using fists and feet and heads and teeth.

She bloodied his nose; he smashed her jaw. She kneed his groin, he bruised her kidney. She slung him to the shore and tackled him, and he flipped them, pinning her down with his hands around her throat. But then he recoiled of his own accord, jerking back with wide eyes, and Rozalie plowed upward, bucking him off. She jammed both heels into his abdomen and handsprang over his side, snapping a kick into his spine for good measure. Even then, by the time she whirled he was up again, fists raised.

There was a lethality to him Ashe hadn't seen before. He was dangerous underneath the lies and bluster, like a pretty snake with fatal venom. And that was cleverness, not just cockiness, in his eyes.

Maybe they *could* make something useful of him.

She nudged the waterskin back out into the pile of Rozalie's belongings, the sound muffled by a sharp *crack* and a cry of pain. Ashe's heart stopped, then kicked into a wild race as her friend went down on elbows and knees, gripping her ribs. Fractured, certainly, maybe even broken.

Ashe started to rise, but Maleck caught her arm, warning her back with a shake of his head.

"Still a bit soft under all that armor?" Kashar spread his stance over Rozalie, bending to grip a fistful of her hair. "Beaten yet?"

With a furious shout, she seized his wrist and pitched her whole body to one side, tangling her limbs with his and bringing him down hard on one knee. She gripped him by the groin, twisted, and shoved him up and off—straight into the lake shallows. With a wildcat's ferocity, she landed on the Prince's shoulders, shoving his head under the water.

A flicker of blackness in the foliage to their right. Ashe cut a look at Maleck, but he was already gone—her death-god, a silent and mortal shadow, Stormfury a scythe of vengeance in his hand. By the time Rozalie let Kashar's head up enough for him to plead mercy, Maleck was back, wiping Enforcer blood from his blade. He sheathed it and crouched beside Ashe to watch the rest of their plan unfold.

Coughing, Rozalie triumphantly dragged Kashar out of the shallows by his collar and flung him onto the shore. "Beaten."

The Prince slung water off his jaw with his equally-wet wrist, panting up at her. "You Talheimic women fight dirtier than your men."

Rozalie sketched a vicious bow. "I can't say the same for Mahasari women, seeing as I've never met one in your ranks."

"If it was one of our women you faced, you would not have won this duel. You have my uncle to thank for that."

A brief, frigid pause; then Kashar stretched out a hand, and Rozalie, after a moment's hesitation, accepted it. The Prince shook all over like a dog when he straightened, spreading his arms. "Well, it seems I am yours to do with as you please. What favor do you wish, *Raqi*?"

Her gaze skimmed over him, the perfect blend of resentment and appreciation. Ashe wondered with a pang of unease how much of *that* was an act. "Have a drink with me."

Kashar cocked a brow. "Really?"

"I know something that will erase *all* the shadows from your mind. A Talheimic drink no one's ever offered you before." With an alluring flirt of her lashes, she swaggered over to the hedge. Kashar trailed, scooping up his linen tunic to mop his soaked face, and the way he admired Rozalie from behind made Ashe reconsider the brief thoughts she'd entertained of his usefulness.

Rozalie scooped up the waterskin and tossed it to him. Arms crossed, she shrugged back against a tree woven into the hedge's greedy arms. "No bathing in it this time," she warned when Kashar uncapped the skin. "I paid good coin for that."

He blinked at her. "You know of that?"

Rozalie's head tilted. "You didn't think I'd come walking into your estate without being certain of exactly what sort of man you are?"

"You know nothing of the man I truly am."

The smile hung evident in Rozalie's voice, though Ashe couldn't see it. "We're about to find out."

Galled by something in those falsely-playful words, Kashar brought the skin to his lips and drank in two deep, loud draws. Then he offered it out to her, smacking his lips. "It tastes like..."

"Licorice?" She didn't take the skin. "I know, doesn't it?"

Ashe and Maleck burst out of the hedge, laying hands on Kashar's shoulders before he even had a chance to drop the skin. They heaved together, slamming him on his back and knocking the wind from him. Maleck jammed a boot into his throat, and Ashe drew her dagger from its sheath, resting it against his thumping pulse. His eyes locked onto hers, widening with horrified recognition. "*You.*"

Rozalie smiled grimly. "Sweet dreams, Prince."

She drove her foot into his temple, knocking him unconscious.

CHAPTER THIRTY-FIVE

ROUGH BARK PINCHED Maleck's seat as he adjusted his perch on an overturned tree, tossing a knife to himself, watching Mahasar's Shadow-Slayer in unconscious slumber.

Despite what his own kingdom believed of him, Maleck Darkwind was not a violent man. He had killed when necessary, carried out missions to stop Salvotor and the Bloodwights and now these Mahasaris, but he was never one to sit and contemplate violence with what little spare time he had.

Not until Kashar az-Kyrian.

Ensorcelled or not, this man's crimes stacked a stairwell down to Nimmus in Maleck's mind. Foremost was what he and his men had done to Ashe while Maleck rotted in the dungeon below Middleton, wearing his soles bloody with pacing and his throat raw with prayers for her. An alliance with this Prince, however necessary, felt like betraying every vow he'd made to guard Ashe's back and uphold her honor over his own; and if acting would not have been an equal betrayal to Talheim, to Cistine, he might've slit the man's throat and been done with it.

Across the camp, a quiet, pained sigh stirred him from his thoughts, his gaze leaping from their prisoner to Rozalie. She'd been reserved while Kashar slumbered, watching him often and rubbing her shoulder; Maleck had reset it after they'd dragged him into the trees, then pitched a fire and splinted her injured ribs. Until then, none of them had realized her arm was dislocated, even Rozalie herself. Maleck had to admire that tenacity, though the faraway look in her eyes unsettled him.

It was just them in the camp now, Ashe away hunting for the evening meal. Maleck sheathed his knife and cleared his throat, drawing Rozalie's eye. "What troubles you?"

"Just hoping we had enough antidote left." She bent forward, hands trapped palm-to-palm between her knees. "And hoping he's not as disgusting without Sorcel as with it."

Maleck fought back a smile. "In my experience, every one of us has darkness we hold at bay. Kashar lost the inhibitions that tamed his."

"That Sorcel..." Rozalie shuddered. "It's powerful, Mal. Like being drunk, only cleaner. Freer. By the time I made it back to the loft that night, I could've danced on tavern tables or let a man's hands all over me, even his, and I wouldn't have minded."

Maleck frowned. "You felt suggestible."

Rozalie's cheek indented where she gnawed on it. "I felt like nothing I did had any consequences at all. Like I was dreaming, maybe...you know how sometimes when you dream, you'll kiss people you wouldn't usually, or rob a treasury because you know you won't have to pay any of it back?"

His lips twitched. How often his dreams had been the stage for a red-haired woman with a fiery mouth and a deadly gaze to toy with him, long before she was his to hold or love. "I do."

"Well, it was like that, but about everything." She shook her head. "Jad's going about this the wrong way. If he wanted, he could poison every ruler in the kingdoms and tell them to do what he wants. He wouldn't have to go to war with Cyril, just slip him a dose."

Maleck frowned. "And yet he hasn't. One wonders why."

The conversation halted at the rustle of foliage. Ashe slipped into the camp, twigs and leaves woven into her hair, a scowl in her eyes but her mouth held captive to a firm line—a war not to show any emotion when her gaze fell on Kashar. "Lazy bastard."

"I wonder if that's the antidote or the kick to the head." Rozalie caught the brace of squirrels Ashe slung at her. "My turn to cook?"

"I hunted." Ashe dropped onto the ground before the fallen tree, draping her arms over Maleck's spread knees and wiggling back into the open space between his legs. "Middleton's still quiet, strangely enough. You'd think they'd be in more of an uproar with their leader missing for a full day."

Maleck shared a glance with Rozalie across the camp, fighting a rumble of unease in his gut.

As if stirred by the mention of the conquered city, Kashar shifted—a flutter of lashes, a quickening of breaths toward waking. Maleck stood at once, swinging one leg around Ashe and offering his hand to help her up. They joined Rozalie near their prisoner, whose wrists flexed against his bonds and eyes finally slid open. Rozalie knelt beside him, gripping his chin and wrenching his head toward her. "Look at me. Do you know me?"

His tongue swiped his lips. "*Raqian.*"

Her jaw tightened, and she forced his head up, examining his eyes from a few angles. Then she released him. "The gleam is gone. It worked. He's free."

Kashar's gaze elucidated with several blinks, finding Ashe next, and a curse slid from his lips at the glint of her steel drawing. He dug his heels into the soil, flipping over with surprising alacrity, but he could only scuttle so far before he struck the hard tangle of foliage in the lakeside grove and came to a halt, panting.

Ashe's voice was hair-raisingly calm. "You know who I am."

Kashar rolled onto his shoulder to face them, those harsh, frantic breaths petering out. "I...yes. As if from a dream."

"More of a nightmare. Do you know where you are?"

The words escaped him as a breath. "Tal...Talheim. For the game."

A rain-wrapped echo of familiar words and Cistine's fear traced Maleck's spine. He stepped nearer, a hand to Stormfury. "What game?"

"The one my uncle is playing. The one we are all part of. He used to tell us bedtime stories of it...how old were we then? Ten years old? Eleven? How long has it been?"

"Over twenty years since Khorraris burned," Ashe said.

"*Twenty?*" Kashar burst into stunned laughter. "Twenty *years?* I remember *weeks!* What—*how*—?"

"Because you were ensorcelled," Rozalie said. "Does that sound familiar, *Prince?*"

Kashar's gaze skipped to her, and Maleck didn't know what to make of the expression darting through those dark eyes. Relief, like he knew her; horror, like he remembered why. And then a desperation as if he might tell her anything in penitence. "He learned how to brew it?"

"And fed it to you," Maleck said.

"Of course he did, that wretched—!" Kashar wrenched against his bonds like he might rise, then slammed himself back against the tree, turning his head aside and taking a moment to gather his breath. "Ever since he took us off the streets, he would tell us we were the first gamepieces, my sister and I—" He broke off with a throaty gasp, bringing his bound hands to his mouth. "*Tirzah.* Dyalmun's *breath*, her face...I remember putting my hands around her throat..." A tear snaked to his jaw. "*What did I do?*"

"You killed her," Ashe said bluntly, "like you killed my people and tried to kill me. You took possession of the city of Middleton in your uncle's stead."

"*Why?*" Kashar roared, and Rozalie's hand flexed on her knife.

"That's what *we* want to know," she said. "Tell us more about this game."

"I remember pieces. All of it is hazy." Kashar squinted. "War councils. The Enforcers. He told us to taint the headwaters flowing near Arak Shehr and the Haqat Uise. He sent us to villages to take the men and boys, and they all came meekly, it was as if...as if they had no will of their own." His eyes blinked wide again. "How did you wake me?"

"With an antidote from Mahasar's Free People," Rozalie said.

Kashar blinked. "*Alhuru en-Asgaid*...they did this? Is *that* why he's been hunting them so fiercely?"

"Most likely. And I'm glad it works, although I'd still love an excuse to beat your face in," Ashe muttered. "What about this game of his?"

"It's something to do with the Talheimic royal family." Kashar shook his head as if to clear it, and sympathy twinged unbidden through Maleck's chest; he knew that feeling all too well, a distant shadow of strangled consumption when augments had been all he cared for.

Then all at once Kashar was on his feet, with a bend of his knees and an upward thrust. They all surged back, then rushed in; Maleck with a blade to the man's liver, Ashe's knee trapping his legs to the tree, and Rozalie behind it, hand fisted in Kashar's short, dark hair, locking his head back against the narrow trunk with her knife to his throat.

"How long have we been here?" Kashar demanded, as if he thought nothing of their weapons trapping him. "How long have I been asleep?"

"A day," Ashe spat. "And unless you want us to leave you bleeding here when we go, I'd suggest avoiding sudden movements."

"A day." The strength went out of Kashar so fiercely he dipped against their weapons. Maleck winced at the sound of fabric fraying, the rip of his hairs coming out in Rozalie's hand. She released his head and gripped him by the jaw instead, thumb digging into the hinge, guiding him back upright.

"Why does that matter?" she demanded.

"We had an understanding, my Enforcers and I. If anything were to happen to me, if I was captured or killed, they must move the game into its final stages."

A chill tumbled down Maleck's back. He glanced at Ashe and found his horror reflected in her tight-jawed face.

"What *plan*?" Rozalie snapped.

"We have a spy," Kashar rasped, "a powerful one within your Citadel. That's how we've managed to hold Middleton so long. Any scheme to retake it was fed to us weeks in advance. I don't know how you managed to keep her from knowing your strategy, but you're the first to have come close."

"You Mahasaris love your spies," Ashe growled. "She's one of you?"

"No! One of *you*." Desperation raised Kashar's voice to a shout. "And if it's been a day, my men are on their way to her. When they arrive, the game enters its conclusion."

"What's the goal?" Ashe shouted, pressing him back against the tree again. "What does he *want* with the royal family?"

"I don't know!" Kashar snarled. "He never told us the outcome, only the steps to reach it. But without me in Middleton, the end has already begun."

Ashe whipped back, gold already flickering over her gaze. "We go. We go *right now*."

"Wait!" Kashar shot forward, and Rozalie tightened her hold, wrenching him back against the tree. "Let me accompany you!"

"Give me one reason why we should," Rozalie hissed, "after *everything*."

"Because I remember wrapping my hands around Tirzah's throat. I remember my knife slashing her face to ribbons. I remember the light going out of her eyes. The most important...the *only* person I have ever loved. Jad didn't just take my sister from me, he made me kill her myself. So long as you wish *that ivrran* dead, consider us allies."

Rozalie let out a short, audible breath. Maleck held Ashe's gaze, letting the hunt be hers. After a long moment, she flicked her hand, gave the choice up to him, and stalked away, gripping her temples in her fingertips.

It was the first time in nearly a year Maleck had seen her struggle to cleave.

"Kick out the fire, Rozalie," he requested, and she loosed Kashar to stalk away. The Prince's eyes followed her to the task until Maleck slit his bonds, gripped his throat, and slammed him up against the tree. "Your death is the first in my long life that would bring me true pleasure. I do not like you. I do not *trust* you. I will arm you only because to do otherwise would sentence you to death at a hand besides mine, but make no mistake...if you harm us, if you touch Asheila *or* Rozalie, you will face a slow, painful demise. You may be a better brawler than most, but you are not a better swordsman than me."

Kashar flashed both palms beside his head. "Understood. And...who are you, again? You'll forgive me if—"

Maleck tightened his grip on the prince's neck, wrenching a groan from him. His dark eyes met Maleck's, what little bravado remained in them dissipating to darkened embers.

"Listen to me. I have no intention of putting a knife in your back," the Prince growled. "I'm saving it for my uncle's. I take it you don't know what it is to be controlled against your will, but it rather puts the rest of these petty squabbles to rest."

"I do, in fact." Maleck stepped back and drew his dagger Remany, offering its hilt to Kashar. "Which is the only reason I offer you the chance to prove your true self, as it was once offered to me."

CHAPTER THIRTY-SIX

THE REPORT CAME to Aden at supper in the Citadel's dining hall three nights after his mission in the tavern, delivered by a servant who bowed and cast him a shy smile before she scurried away, stumbling over the address of *Lord High Tribune* in parting.

Smiling to himself in her absence, Aden reclined and tore open the envelope, shaking out a note in Pollack's crisp, militant scrawl. He read it three times before the words fully sank in; then he was up with a bark of relief that turned heads throughout the room. The moment he escaped into the halls, he broke into a run.

Faces flashed by him, Wardens he hardly knew watching him go with quizzical eyes. For once, he didn't care what they thought of him, whether he seemed as noble and composed as his title demanded. He ran without stopping across the Citadel's breadth and up the looming flights of stairs to Mira's room, knocking only once before he strode inside. She was at the table, reports of ensorcelled augurs spread out around her, chin on her fist; when he entered, her head shot up, eyes wide. "Aden! What brings you here?"

He bit back a grimace that was nearly the death of his joy; it was the first time he'd sought her out since sharing her bed, the first time he'd seen her apart from passing Nadeem back and forth. It would be a lie to say he hadn't planned it that way—the snarl of emotions at the sight of her, the memory of that damning dream, and their conversation about Sander too much to grapple with amidst the chaos of the ensorcelled lords—but with this note clutched in his fist, its words pronouncing the beginning of the end, there was no one else he'd rather share this victory with in the stars-damned world.

He crossed the room and caught her up in an embrace, and she laughed when he spun her away from the table, her hands fastening to his arms. "Hush, you'll wake Nadeem!" She pushed back from him, laying a finger to her lips, but her eyes shone. "I take it your trick played out?"

"It was Stannik and Mares." Aden flicked the note into her waiting hands. "Once they dried off from the Sorcel, they confessed everything...sending the patrols into ambushes, ensorcelling Wardens and augurs, all of it."

Mira gripped the note with both hands, giving it a sharp shake. "This is precisely what we need! They can name which people are ensorcelled, and we can isolate them, let them dry off for themselves." Her eyes shot back to him, full of excitement. "Well done, Aden."

There was something in the way she was looking at him now that he'd been running from ever since they'd arrived at the Citadel—perhaps even longer. But this time he didn't move away when she stepped nearer, taking his face in both hands, the letter fluttering from her grasp.

"I am so *proud* of you." Her tone was low and fierce with passion. "What you've done for Kanslar as High Tribune, and for Talheim, though it's not your kingdom...you're a good man. The kind I hope Nadeem will learn to be as he grows."

Aden cleared his throat. "He has all the example he needs in you."

"I know I'm a good mother, but I can't fill the hole that the lack of a father's love will leave in his life." Her gaze dipped from his eyes. "I'm glad it's you. I hope it will always be you."

Aden's hands ached to grip her hips, her shoulders, her face in turn; so instead he curled them into fists at his sides when she inclined, angling her head, her breath brushing his lips. The blood-oath scar throbbed, and he jerked back. "Mira. I can't."

She fell on her heels, but her hands still held his face; her gaze searched his, shifting from earnest to inquisitive. "Can't, or won't?"

"I *won't* betray you like this."

"Betray me?" Shocked laughter burst from her lips. "How is this in any way a betrayal? Did I not *just* make my opinions on the matter perfectly clear?"

He held her gaze, tongue as knotted as the scar across his palm. He couldn't bring himself to do anything but press on that self-inflicted wound to remind himself all the reasons this was wrong. Why it was a cruelty to both of them.

Mira's gaze dropped to his fisted hand, and for the first time since they were adolescents teasing one another in the schools of Stornhaz, true rage bloomed in her eyes.

"Look at me!" Releasing him and stepping back, Mira drove a finger into her chest. "At *me*, Aden! I don't want you to see Sander when you look into my eyes. I don't want to be your penance, I want...." She broke off, shaking her head. "I know you came for him, but I thought you stayed for *me*. How could I have misjudged you so much?"

Aden stepped forward, gripping her shoulders. "Mirassah—"

She shrugged off his hands and backed away again, flashing her palms in warning. "*No.* I am not searching for another person to look at me and see an illness or a grief-stricken widow—a woman who needs *fixing*. And I have no time for someone who clings to me out of guilt and grief. You choose who you're truly here for. His memory, or a future with us?"

Aden's mouth crowded with the answers he wanted to give—the lies that were easy, the truths that felt like betrayal.

When he didn't speak, Mira's eyes leaped back down to his scarred hand, a deprecating smile slashing across her mouth. "I think it's best if you stay in a different room from now on."

He wondered if the sound of his heart cracking open in his chest was audible to her. "Mira, wait—"

Her wide-eyed gaze stopped his breath.

A second *crack* split the air, this time with a concussion that sent them staggering against one another. He caught her around the waist by instinct, and when she tore free and ran to the window, he followed her. Together they towed apart the heavy drapes—and looked out to a city burning.

Those streets they'd observed from the roof, the ones Aden had sworn in his spirit to defend, were alive with fire. Screams shredded the columns of smoke, and on the bridges below, a swarm of black-clad bodies carved their way into the Citadel—and carved out, as Wardens and augurs set upon each other from behind.

"What is *happening*?" Mira shouted.

"Get the boy," Aden growled, but she was already at the bassinet, swooping Nadeem up in her arms. "Get him to safety and meet me in the central ballroom!"

With a deft nod, Mira ran for the door. Aden ripped his sword harness from the back of the dining chair, slung it on over his armor, and bolted out into a wave of fleeing servants and running warriors, everyone stampeding as chaos descended.

At the mouth of the corridor, a Warden turned on the servant girl who'd delivered Aden the letter of victory—and slit her throat.

Roaring in blind fury, Aden Bloodsinger descended into combat.

The glass ballroom had always struck Aden as magnificent and mysterious, a place where he'd often spotted Cistine sitting in rapt silence when she needed a moment alone. He couldn't count the times he'd stood guard outside its grand doors, turning away wanderers when she didn't even know he was there; so he also knew it was one of the largest and most defensible rooms in the Citadel. Two doors in and out, and one to the balcony. With the bridges fallen, Pollack would gather the innocent there.

Somehow, Mira arrived ahead of him—he'd lost more time cutting down enemies than he thought. She led a brigade barring the balcony when he darted between the augurs holding the outer doors. He shouted her name, and she cut him a look equal parts irritation and relief as he ran to lend his shoulder, barring the glass while servants and warriors piled tables and chairs against the door. "Nadeem?"

"With the wet nurses, sealed in the siege rooms. He'll be cared for." Her tone was hard, as if she'd placed Nadeem utterly in their care and now removed him from her mind for the task at hand.

Pollack joined them, jamming a table against the balcony door. "They've already breached the Citadel. They were inside before we even realized there was a siege."

"Enforcers?" Aden demanded, and Pollack nodded grimly.

"*How?*" Mira shouted. "Mares and Stannik are imprisoned, how could they manage this?"

"It must've been a contingency for if we broke them," Pollack snapped. "It's like a wound that won't stop bleeding, we can't begin to say where they've come from. They caught us completely exposed."

"Tell me you saw the bridges," Aden growled.

"I saw." Pain flashed in Pollack's eyes. "Those bastards are wearing our uniforms, cutting down *our* people. I don't know how they crossed the trench..."

Mira's eyes widened. Her hands dropped to her sides, tremoring. "Oh, stars, they weren't ensorcelled Wardens and augurs at all. They were *Enforcers*. We brought them straight into the city."

"Wearing the armor they stole from the murdered patrols," Aden finished bleakly. "Using stolen augments to cross the trench and bring their brothers in."

Pollack utterly paled. "I assumed the ones I didn't recognize in the ranks were your augurs!"

"I assumed they were your Wardens," Aden admitted.

Their gazes met, a shared burden of guilt and shame singing between them. In that moment, they were no longer rivals of different kingdoms; they were leaders who'd failed, letting the enemy's weapon jab past their guard.

"It still shouldn't have happened!" Pollack roared, jamming another chair against the door. "Those men were all quarantined, waiting to be questioned and released. They never should've been in rotation tonight!"

"Then who gave the order?" Mira asked. "Who changed the guard without alerting anyone?"

"I don't know! The only ones with that power are Lord Rion and the royal family!"

Aden's heart stumbled, stopped, then started again, but not at its normal pace. Dread and shock and *heartbreak* crashed through him like when he'd watched Rakel turn away from his father...like he'd been betrayed by his own flesh and blood.

"Where is the Queen?" The words emerged guttural. "Why isn't she with her people?"

"She and Lady Eboni went to her study," Pollack said. "Something about royal papers she didn't want the Enforcers to find. They took an escort—where are you going?" he bellowed when Aden spun away. "She doesn't need an augur's protection, she has our best Wardens with her!"

"Your Wardens are already dead!"

"Aden!" Mira shouted, and his heels dug in, spinning him back to face her. "Be swift. Be *safe*."

With a deft nod, he tore from the ballroom through the opposite door. It swung shut behind him; on the other side, he heard the iron bar slam down.

He kept running, praying to all the gods his intuition was wrong.

CHAPTER THIRTY-SEVEN

Every step between the ballroom and the Queen's study hammered against Aden's ears. Small moments tumbled through his mind, the past weeks repeating in a torrent, clarity bouncing in blinding lines off every one—a torn skirt and muddied flats, a smirk in the dark, a faith too deep to be real.

He'd been so trusting, so naïve. He'd never looked twice for the enemy hidden behind the face of their truest friend.

Sabers leading, he forced his way through Enforcers garbed in Mahasari armor, Cadre uniforms, and Valgardan threads. Anyone who made to kill him, he brought them down first, clearing a path with the haste of a man with moments left to live.

He burst into the large, windowed parlor outside the Queen's study and slid to a halt, curses rising and faltering on his lips.

The exterior was strewn with bodies, each one brought down by a precise arrow to the heart. Quick, calculated deaths, made with almost Hive-like precision. And there, lying before the half-open study door, was a body not of a Warden or an augur.

Heart hanging heavier with every beat, Aden crossed the parlor on soundless feet and knelt beside Eboni Bartos, touching two fingers under her jaw. No pulse greeted his touch; her head was bent at a grotesque angle, neck clearly snapped. A quicker, painless death. Yet it was still a betrayal.

Rising to his feet, Aden gripped the half-open door and swung it wide—then jerked aside as an arrow thudded into the frame beside his head.

Spinning, he placed his back to the outer wall. "*Solene?*"

"You should not have come here, Aden." Her voice was strange in its calmness, so matter-of-fact they might have been discussing harvests or patrols over breakfast. But her arrows jutted from the hearts of her fallen guards, and he had no doubt who had snapped Eboni's neck.

His throat burned. "Don't do this, Your Majesty."

"I must. I am going to Mahasar now." His skin crawled at her unaffected tone. "They tried to tell me I mustn't go. But I will."

Aden cursed silently. "What about your husband? Cistine?"

"Why do you think I sent him away to the southern forts? He's too keen, I never could've managed everything with him here. And Cistine...she had to go eventually. Why not now? It's all part of the game."

Rocking his head against the wall, Aden swallowed a swell of panic. "Stannik and Mares were never ensorcelled, were they? Not until you brought the drugs to them in the dungeon and ordered them to confess to these crimes." He gritted his teeth around the next words. "*Your* crimes."

"It had to be done. I must go to Mahasar at any cost."

Aden did not need to see her eyes to know.

She was ensorcelled. Perhaps she had been all along. The traitor they'd sought among their ranks was the King's own bride turned against him, against them all. The perfect vengeance after she'd brought about the burning of Jad's city two decades ago.

He had to get her out of there, wrest the bow from her hands and bundle her into the dungeons. He would stand guard over her himself, fight off any Enforcers who came—because they were here for her, he had no doubt now. They'd stormed the city to take the Queen.

But they would have to kill him first.

Carefully, Aden unbuckled his bracer and slid it from his right arm. "What happens when you go to Mahasar?"

"The game ends as it was meant to."

"Not if we have any say in it."

He kicked the door shut and flung his gauntlet across the room, knocking a vase from its perch to the floor. Solene's booted feet slammed against stone; the door sailed open again, and her bow jutted out, leading with arrow nocked, aiming toward the vase. Aden hurled his weight, slamming her into the doorframe; she cried out and dropped her bow, slithering rapidly back into the study. Yanking the door wide, Aden dove inside after her—and froze.

A pulsing green jar rolled in the Queen's palm, held aloft in threat. His fingers fell from the hilt of his offhanded dagger. "Solene. *No.*"

"I'm going to Mahasar," she hissed. "Anyone who tries to stop me dies."

"That won't kill me, it will destroy *you.*"

Her lips tipped in a savage smile. "I know precisely what happens if I break this flagon. I've seen Cyril and Cistine use them. But I'll do it if I must. I will go to Mahasar at any cost."

"I can't let you." Aden drew his dagger. "I swore an oath to Thorne and Cistine that I would not let this kingdom fall. And I will keep that vow."

Solene tipped her head. A strange glint of grimy silver flashed across her eyes. "You will die trying."

"We'll see."

He hurled his dagger toward the arm that held the flagon and lunged at the same moment, hand outstretched toward her. Solene twisted aside, wrist skimmed by the blade but hand unharmed, and crushed the flagon against her thigh.

Aden's shout faded in the roar of power bursting from the Queen's palm. It utterly consumed her—dress turned to ash, pieces crumbling and floating away on the wind—baring the Valgardan battle armor below.

Aden slammed into her, driving them both to the floor, but for just a moment the shock of her battle threads left him speechless.

Solene huffed with maddened laughter. "I have no death wish. I must go to Mahasar. But as for you, Aden...you have served your use."

Her palms slammed into the stone floor, and the world exploded around him.

CHAPTER THIRTY-EIGHT

THE JOURNEY FROM Middleton to Astoria was a black-edged blur of night lit with gold from Bresnyar's scales, but for once even his presence didn't soothe Ashe. Her mind was chaos, a battlefield already.

I should have known, I should have known.

Of course Jad had a contingency if his only heir fell into enemy hands. Of course there was a spy.

And that spy, Kashar had told them while they waited for Bresnyar to arrive, was Queen Solene.

The royal family itself infiltrated, Cyril's most trusted advisor whispering Jad's intentions into his ear. How long had Solene been a puppet of the enemy? How long had Jad *dreamed* of turning the woman who'd burned his last city into a weapon against her own kingdom, her own family?

She bent her face to Bresnyar's arched neck. "Faster, Scales."

He grunted, shooting forward with a pump of his wings. The clouds mushroomed ahead, thick and damp, the current of a storm moving beneath them. Dim strokes of lightning discharged over Talheim. A final early-winter storm—the perfect night for a Mahasari siege.

Ashe shuddered, then relaxed at the heat of Maleck's hand against her back. "Focus, *Mereszar*." His voice was night itself, gentle, dark, and firm. "We will reach her."

Ashe nodded, gulping wind like water, bringing in the briny smell of the Agerios Sea. "It's time. Brace yourselves." She laid her hand on her dragon's shoulder. "Bres, dive."

He tucked his wings and fell in a fast spiral through clouds so thick Ashe could hardly breathe. The drum of rain filled her ears, blotting out everything else. Then they burst into the open, Bresnyar pulling out of the plunge over a city aflame. Ashe's heart still fell even as they leveled out and shot toward the Citadel's pale fang gnawing through the torrents of smoke.

The Enforcers had turned her home to a burning forge. Though the streets below hung empty, the echo of clashing weapons from the Citadel itself tore at her ears.

Solene hadn't merely been taken, the enemy had carved their way to her. They were *still* carving.

Bresnyar alighted on one of the bridges, blasting down a flock of Enforcers with his fiery breath. Ashe led the others in a leap down from his back, sliding her hand to her dragon's cheek and taking his broad face in both hands. "Get to the southern barracks and find Cyril. Bring him home. This was a trap. It's all been a trap." *And I didn't see it in time.*

Bresnyar's glowing eyes held hers a moment, missing nothing. His mighty head tilted deeper into her hands. "This is not your burden alone to bear, *Ilyanak*."

"I know." She pressed her brow to his muzzle, then released him. "Get to the King!"

Bresnyar bounded down the bridge and leaped skyward. Ashe drew Starfall and her offhanded dagger, looking between her three companions. Mistrust still shook her when she met Kashar's gaze, but she'd know soon enough the kind of man he was. No better proving ground than in battle against his own people. "Get to the Queen. Rozalie, watch the Prince."

One quick nod, and they bolted for the doors, bursting into the Citadel's western wing. The sounds of combat greeted them like an oven torn open: the humidity of spilled blood and sweat, the bubbling shouts of Wardens and augurs locked in battle against Enforcers. Ashe, Kashar, Rozalie, and Maleck plowed in, weapons singing.

Kashar locked Remany at the hilt with an Enforcer aiming to jab a Warden through the neck. "As your Prince, I order you to cease this assault!"

The Enforcer gave no reply; he socked Kashar straight in the mouth, then broke blades with him and lashed out for his neck. Rozalie blocked the scimitar overhead and backhanded, snapping her heel into the Enforcer's groin. He doubled up, freeing a serpentine dagger at his side and aiming for her unguarded spine, but before Ashe could shout a warning Kashar pivoted around Rozalie and removed the man's head.

Through the crowd of dueling bodies, Ashe locked eyes with Viktor Pollack, dueling across the entry room. Blood dripped into his panting mouth and battle blazed in his face. He looked as feral as any Valgardan.

"They're here for the Queen!" Ashe shouted.

Viktor shot an arm toward the door at the end of the hall, telling her where to go just as it burst open and augurs poured inside, augments blistering, weapons drawn, and leaped into combat beside their Talheimic allies. Ashe and her friends escaped the hall and flew for the grand staircase at the center of the entry parlor, dashing up two flights before Rozalie slammed to a halt.

"Petra?" Her shout drew Ashe's attention to another Warden sprawled at the top of the steps, a blade wedged deep into her shoulder but her chest still rising and falling in rapid breaths. Not far from her lay Njal, one of Thorne's Tribunes, blood pouring down his side.

"We can't leave them!" Rozalie barked. "Kashar, help me!"

Perhaps in penance for his many crimes, the Prince didn't protest; he swung Njal up with surprising ease while Rozalie hoisted Petra's arm across her shoulders.

"The infirmary is half the Citadel away," Ashe growled. "We can make it if—"

"No!" Petra choked, gripping the blade in her shoulder to stop it wobbling. "Infirmary's full...they're bringing the wounded into the ballrooms!"

Ashe met Maleck's eyes bleakly, wondering just how far this siege stretched. Then she banished that thought, swinging Starfall to loosen her wrist. "Ballroom it is."

She and Maleck led the charge, hewing through any resistance that arose, though the Enforcer ranks were already dwindling when they neared those familiar doors. More than a year ago, nobles and commoners alike had poured through them to celebrate Cistine's coming-of-age birthday; now they were guarded by a blockade of Wardens who squinted through bloodied faces, recognized Ashe and Rozalie, and grabbed for the doors, towing them open. They stepped into a damp triage chamber, the glass dome above fogged with the echoes of pained shouts. Countless tables were erected for surgeries done behind thin curtains; augurs and Wardens peppered makeshift cots or lay in blanket nests on the floor, no longer distinguishable in their bloodied armor. Their wounds made them one.

Kashar breathed something in Mahasari, gaze raking the room, and there was no way to know what thoughts might be racing through his mind.

Ashe almost spat that this was his doing—his people's fault. But she couldn't, knowing her queen suffered the same affliction.

The absence of Solene was a wound ripped through the room; she and Eboni should've been there, aiding and offering comfort, strategizing as they had during that first siege the day the cabal had brought aid from the north. But Ashe saw nothing of them, or of Aden and Mira, as Rozalie dragged Petra to a free cot and lowered her there. She summoned a physician while Kashar did the same for Njal; then she spun on the Prince, gripping his collar and dragging him into the corner.

Grimacing, Ashe squeezed Maleck's arm. "Go find Aden."

She hurried after them just as Rozalie spun Kashar and smashed him against the wall. "Why aren't your own men *listening* to you? What kind of Prince do they think you are?"

"I don't know!" Kashar dragged a hand through his short hair, frustration sparking in his eyes. "Perhaps my uncle gave them an order I knew nothing about...that if I stopped following his plans, they must treat me as an enemy."

"So you're useless to us!"

"Useless?" He jabbed a finger in her face. "Was I useless to you when I saved your *life* just now? I killed my own people tonight for you, *Raqian!*"

"Both of you, enough!" Ashe stepped between them, shoving them apart. "Roz, as long as we're here, don't call him Mahasari. We don't have time to explain that he's on our side." She spun on Kashar. "You, tell me exactly why our Wardens and augurs are fighting their own."

He hauled in a deep breath, then loosed it in a rush of words. "They are not your people. We took their weapons and armor, to infiltrate. To bring down the Citadel and ensure we could take the Queen when the time was right. A scale perfectly balanced for Khorraris."

Exactly what they'd done to breach Middleton—how had she not predicted Mahasar would do the same to them?

"We'll go back out there," Rozalie said. "Kashar, every Enforcer you recognize wearing our people's armor, we'll bring them down."

Ashe waited for an excuse to knock Kashar's teeth down his throat, but he simply nodded and followed Rozalie out.

Dragging her hand down her face and settling it against her mouth, Ashe held her place a heartbeat longer. Cyril wasn't here; Rion wasn't here. Neither was Cistine, and they couldn't trust Solene. There was someone in this Citadel who was in charge now, but she didn't know where they were or what state they were in. She needed a High Tribune's help restoring order.

"Ashe!"

She whirled toward the sound of a vaguely-familiar voice and caught sight of Mira; hair knotted at the top of her head, sleeveless dress billowing and arms whorled to the elbows in blood, she looked like a Vassoran guard on the battlefield. Fire blazed in her eyes as she strode toward Ashe.

"Thank the stars you're here. We've been trying to hold them at bay, but the injuries..." Mira's bleak gaze swept the glass-domed ballroom with as much pain as if these were all her people.

Ashe seized her elbow. "They had help. Solene is ensorcelled, we need to get to her before they do. Where's Aden?"

Mira's tawny complexion paled. "He's *with* her. He went to find her when we realized..." She trailed off sharply, hand locking to her brow. "Stars, that was so long ago."

Ashe's stomach fell. Cursing, she dropped Mira's arm, screamed for Maleck, and tore back out into the fighting with him at her heels.

The path between the ballroom and Solene's private study was so familiar Ashe could've walked it in her sleep. She would have felt better if she and Maleck faced a tide of opposition on the way, but only a handful of Enforcers darted past, all moving in the same direction—the doors. The bridges.

They were leaving. Which could only mean...

Aden and Solene's names drummed in Ashe's head in tune with her footfalls, thudding up the steps to the parlor outside the Queen's study, some half-formed prayer living in her chest and nothing more. She skidded inside and nearly came neck-to-blade with an Enforcer's scimitar, dropping to her knees at the last instant to slide under his blow; his weapon clashed against Maleck's instead, and her *valenar* decapitated him in a deft pirouette, pulled her up from her knees, and kept running to the Queen's study, the doorway in absolute rubble, white stone spewing from within like shattered teeth kicked from a fighter's mouth.

Half-buried under rubble lay Eboni Bartos, broken in so many ways Ashe's knees nearly gave out at the sight of her.

"*Gods, no,*" she seethed, gripping the frame and lunging over Eboni, up on top of the heap of caved-in stone. The roof was gone, the sky an open black globe above them crawling with clouds and lightning. Rain turned the stones slick as she gazed down into the cratered pit.

Aden would not have done this, would never have dared endanger Solene this way. Which meant...

"No, no, no, please..." she chanted, gaze sweeping the ruin frantically.

The gods revealed it in a flash of lightning: blood sprayed from beneath the stones, running off in the rain. So much gods-forsaken blood.

Ashe's knees hit the stone and the world tilted wildly around her. She barely heard Maleck's roar, feral, distraught as he gripped her shoulder and hurtled past her, sliding down into the pit of Solene's study. He stumbled at the bottom of the slope and crashed to his knees, grabbing blocks of rock and heaving them away from where the blood ran, crying out with the strain of it.

Her head told her to go to him, but her heart failed. Her courage failed. She did not want to move those rocks, to peel them back and see what lay below. What Solene had done.

Gods help her, she had endured so much in the past year, *so much*, but this...this was going to break her.

"Aden!" Maleck shouted, still tearing stone heaps away. "Hold on, *Allet*, I'm going to save you, I'll save you, I'm coming, just—"

He broke into a shattered whoop of triumph when an arm lolled free of the wreckage, pale and blood-striped. Ashe buckled forward, clutching the stone with numb fingers as Maleck dove halfway into the cave of unstable stone, wiggling up to his hips inside. His words were no longer discernable over the blur of rain and thunder, but he never stopped talking to his friend—and Ashe didn't start breathing until Maleck planted his heels to the rock and heaved backward, sliding first himself from the rubble and then...

"Aden!" Ashe finally moved, skidding down the slope, ungloved hands tearing on the rock and smearing blood all the way down. She reached them just as Maleck toppled back against the slope of stone, Aden sprawled in his grip, head lolling limp against Maleck's shoulder. His eyes were shut, rain and blood slicking his clothes close to his body.

"Check him!" Maleck's voice broke. "*Check him, Asheila!*"

She knelt in the bend of their tangled legs, sweeping the hair from Aden's neck and feeling for a pulse. "Please don't do this to me, you stupid Valgardan *bastard*, not this, *not this*..."

Too many seconds of stillness, of silence apart from noiseless, thready sobs jerking Maleck's breath out of him. Then Aden's pulse rose to meet her fingertips, the quietest, most hopeful *hello* she'd ever heard.

Once, Ashe might've tried to hide how much that meant, but no more. Shoving the hair from his temples, she pressed her lips to Aden's brow, then her forehead to his. She clutched his head to her collar and looked at Maleck over his bloodsoaked hair. "We need a healing augment."

It was a silent, brief war of wills, an unspoken decision of which of them could bear to be gone if Aden breathed his last while the other raced to save his life.

Then the decision was made for them in the pound of slippered feet, in the cut of skin and fabric down the slope. Mira splashed into the shallow pool gathering in the divot of what had once been Solene's private chamber, flagon in hand, and froze at the sight of Aden pressed between them, his blood swirling into the water. Ashe knew exactly what she saw—the same nightmare Ashe had faced for weeks after the Deathmarch.

Sander's death played out before their eyes.

"*No.*" From Mira, it was not a plea; it was an order against the Undertaker making its way through the storm to lay hands on Aden. Then she was there, crouching swiftly beside them, shoving the augment into Ashe's grip. "Heal him. *Now.*"

Ashe forced her fingers to let go of Aden, to let Maleck bear him fully, and she broke the healing augment and shoved with all her might. She didn't want a drop of it for her skinned palms, her blade wounds, her bruises and aches. All that mattered was him.

Silver power spidered through Aden's body, sinking into his Atrasat inkings. The seconds thundered on, gobbled by flickers of lightning and the pouring rain. Mira took Aden's hand and gripped it so tightly Ashe couldn't see where one ended and the other began. Maleck pressed his face into Aden's hair and shook with weeping.

All at once Aden gasped in air, feet slamming the rock on either side of Ashe, body arching as the power of the gods knitted what was broken inside him. Ashe cursed in shock, falling back, but Mira twisted forward instead. She gripped Aden's face in both hands and pulled his head down from its rigor until his wide eyes, dilated to pinpoints, found hers.

"Look at me, Aden Bloodsinger!" Hers was the voice of a Tribune, harsh with power. "*Look at me.* You do not leave me, do you understand? I forbid you to go!"

Ashe gripped Aden's leg, stomach churning when she felt the bones knit back together beneath her hand. Aden's gaze was locked on Mira, no thought, no reason in those gray eyes. Just a well of pain that went so deep, it seemed unlikely anyone could reach him at the bottom.

But Mira did not let go. She held his face, held his void stare. "Remember your oaths. You *do not leave me.*"

Aden's breaths ripped out, every one threatening to drop his chest and never lift it again. Ashe grabbed for his hand, laced her fingers with his, and held on.

And then, just when she thought the rigor might snap his spine, that his body might break under the war between his mortal injuries and the power of the gods coursing through him, his jaw flickered. His eyelids fluttered, breaking that death stare for an instant. His fingernails dug into Maleck's leg. His hand squeezed Ashe's. Then he crumbled, slack in Maleck's arms, and a sound came from Ashe's *valenar* she'd never heard before—like all the wind kicked out of him at once, a prayer and a shout and a sob spun together. He struggled to pull Aden back up, adjusting his grip while his brother's hand traveled weakly to Mira's back, stroking a trail along the notches of her spine with the fabric plastered to her body by the frigid rain.

"Solene," he rasped.

"We know," Ashe said. "We're managing it. You just..."

Live. She couldn't force out the word. *You live, and that's enough.*

A long breath shuddered out of Mira as Aden's hand found the back of her head, resting in the tangle of her hair. No words passed between them, but Ashe wondered how much Aden had heard; how much he saw, looking into Mira's eyes.

His hand guided her face down to rest against his bloodied shirt. She clutched it in both fists, and maybe she wept; Ashe didn't care if she did. Maybe they were all crying as she edged closer, wrapping her arms around them from one way, Maleck from the other. The sky sobbed with them for the devastation across the Citadel, for the lives lost tonight. For the ones saved. And for the fragments of hope, however small and jagged, they clung to as the storm deepened and the night darkened around them.

CHAPTER THIRTY-NINE

THE ENFORCERS CAME to Shinar at sunrise, their black-fletched wagons like a ribbon of old blood cutting through the sunlit sand.

Tatiana watched them spill out to collect tribute while she and Quill hid in the shadows of their makeshift tent, strapping on their disguises. Imane had done fine work; not a peek of their Valgardan armor showed through the silk wrappings. They wouldn't be exposed for who they truly were unless someone shredded their clothing meticulously.

She didn't intend to let it get that far.

Quill fumbled with the thick Mahasari sash, cursing, and with a playful roll of her eyes Tatiana batted his hands away. "*Here*, let me." She knelt, threading the belt through the thin hoops, and Quill quietly watched her work. The heat of his stare against her curls, at this angle, warmed the back of her neck.

"You know what no elite ever saw in you back in Stornhaz, but I always did?" His question came so suddenly, she could think of no reply, witty or honest. "Nobility. The way you shared even the little bit you had with the others in your district while people like my parents clutched their jewels and looked down on you for it. Most would've left Shinar the second their concussion healed, but not you. You're putting yourself in danger for strangers in a kingdom we're at war with."

Tatiana shrugged, knotting the belt. "It's the right thing to do."

"I know that, but not everyone does." He took her hand and guided her up. "You know, in another life, you would've made a damned good princess yourself."

She tipped her head left and right, considering. "Too strict. Not enough card games. Though the wardrobe would be tempting."

Laughing, Quill spun her toward the tent flap and clapped her on the backside, pushing her out just in time to see an Enforcer grab someone's booth and hurl it over, breaking it at every corner.

With one swift glance between them, Tatiana and Quill broke cover and ran for the edge of the spring.

"Where are they?" the Enforcer shouted at the merches emerging from their tents. "Where are our brothers?"

"Late, perhaps?" A man stood with his hand on the frame of Imane's wheeled chair, and even never having laid eyes on him before, Tatiana recognized him as Imane's husband and Yasmin's father, Kadeen az-Taia; he had his daughter's wily brows and plump cheeks under his thick beard. "There was a sandstorm to the north last night."

"They have come through worse!" the Enforcer roared. "They are never late! *Where are they?*"

Kadeen looked helplessly at the growing crowd. A furrow moved through their midst, and Yasmin burst to the front, ducking under her father's arm. Six smaller children swarmed around them—her brothers and sisters, all of whom had helped fix silk over Quill and Tatiana's Valgardan armor in the rush of the last two days.

Tatiana wanted to move right then, but they had to wait. Still, her gaze darted to the north. *Where are you, Ari?*

Drawing a knife, the Enforcer stepped toward the Taia family. "You were quick to speak a moment ago. No more *insight* to offer?"

Kadeen angled himself, spreading his arms before Imane and Yasmin. "Please. We know nothing. We serve the King in Dyalmun's name."

That eerie mantra rippled across the watching crowd. Tatiana fought back a shiver.

The Enforcer's gaze raked over Kadeen and his family. "I've seen you before, metallurgist. You do good work." He gestured with the tip of his knife. "But I think you could spare a son or daughter, hm? So I will take them, one by one, and I will slit their little throats until someone tells me where my men are. You will allow this, because King Jad demands it, and you serve the King in Dyalmun's name."

Kadeen's horrified expression slackened. Tatiana met Yasmin's gaze and decided right then, plan be damned, if that Enforcer took one step closer to their family—

"Is *this* who you're looking for?"

Tatiana's breath rushed out in a prayer of relief as Ariadne's shout stilled the Enforcer's hand. She swaggered from around the caravan of carts at Shinar's northern edge and hurled an Enforcer's severed head, four days bloated and discolored, at the man's feet.

Shocked cries rose, and Tatiana stepped to the spring's edge, grinning, raising her saber. "*Tawal marsinn Alhuru en-Asgaid!*"

She'd practiced the words enough with Yasmin that they rolled effortlessly from her tongue, accented in all the right places. Quill was right; she probably could've been a great princess, but it would never be quite as fun as seeing the shocked faces when she cheated, like the Enforcers when they spun toward her and Quill, who raised a silk-wrapped fist high, taking up the shout. By the wagons, Ariadne did the same. And when they turned to bolt, the Enforcers were already on them, ruthless hands seizing silk and armor, dragging them back toward the spring.

"Do you know these people?" The lead Enforcer gave Tatiana a rough shake. "*Do you?*"

She met Yasmin's eyes as a bluster of shocked murmurs rose from the crowd, naming them as merches and wanderers, a handful of Mahasari words sprinkled in between.

The Enforcer towed Tatiana close to his chest. "They are your enemy. *Alhuri* are all enemies. They did this, they betrayed our King. You agree they must be punished."

"We agree." The words wove like a grisly echo from the merches. "They must be punished. We serve the King in Dyalmun's name."

Yasmin's eyes gleamed with tears, but true to her promise, she mouthed the words along with her ensorcelled family while the Enforcers dragged Tatiana, Quill, and Ariadne away.

They traveled deep into the desert, over two miles—far from where any merch might hear what passed between them. They weren't bound, which came as no surprise; what did sixteen Enforcers think they had to fear from three people willing to die for a cause?

That was the trick, of course…Tatiana Dawnstar wasn't ready to die. But the Enforcers had to believe she was.

They came to a halt on yet another dune, and the Enforcers cast them to their knees. On every side, blades cocked from their sheaths; and, far more worrisome, thick black bows and fletched arrows slid from shoulders.

Tatiana stiffened, and Quill's hand found her knee, digging in against her armor.

"I will make this plain for you," the lead Enforcer said. "Tell us where your friends hide in Masiya, and we will let you go free."

Quill scoffed. "You think we'd sacrifice all of us to save a few of us?"

"Three of us destroyed your Trench," Ariadne added. "*Three.* Imagine what ten of us could do."

The Enforcer barked something in Mahasari, and the man to his right strung his bow and notched an arrow, aiming at Tatiana's chest. Her pulse stuttered, and Quill shifted, shoulder blocking her front. "Perhaps while one dies writhing in the sand, the others will not be so confident."

"Wait!" Ariadne cried, and the men looked to her.

Tatiana dipped her hand into her pocket and jutted her chin, meeting the Enforcer's gaze when it jumped back to her. Quill let out a long, fluting whistle, and the man's arm cut down. The arrow flew.

Tatiana slammed her palm into the sand.

The fire flagon erupted, turning the arrow to powder; drawing the power back into her grasp, Tatiana whirled to her feet, silk burning away in shrouds, and passed the rest of the augment to Quill. The Enforcers scattered with cries of "*Ivrran!*" and orders of "*Sah ris!*".

Whatever that meant, they primed those thick, wicked bows, taking aim at Quill's back.

They never managed a single shot.

The fire augment caught against an explosion of fetid breath pluming over the dunes, forging a wall of heat that forced the men back. Shrike dove from the clouds in a snakelike spiral, landing between Quill and the Enforcers, hackles raised, snarling.

"Go, go!" Tatiana shoved Ariadne toward Shrike and Quill, then backed up to them herself, casting out another spray of sand to blind the Enforcers. "Tell your Poisoner King *Alhuru en-Asgaid* has friends in powerful places...friends who are coming to take his kingdom from him. The Trench was just the start! *Tawal marsinn Alhuru en-Asgaid!*"

Long live the Free People.

Quill and Ariadne took up the cry as they swung onto Shrike's back and the *Tayir* streaked across the dunes; unlike Bresnyar, he needed a good path to make his leap into flight.

"They're pursuing," Ariadne called above the rush of wind in their ears.

"Good!" Quill cast a handful of fire back at their enemies. "They make this almost too easy!"

With a powerful leap, Shrike crested the dunes. Piebald wings snapped out, gathering wind, and when the twang of bowstrings followed them Ariadne drew the daggers from her boots and twisted back; she cleaved two apart, and Quill's fire dealt with the rest. Tatiana, heart soaring, looked back only once to see the Enforcers charting their course toward Masiya.

The band of tension loosened from Tatiana's middle; Yasmin's family and the rest of the innocents in Shinar would be safe. Already the Enforcers were running back for their wagons to give chase.

"To Masiya," Ariadne said after a moment.

Quill grazed a hand over Shrike's side. "You heard her."

With a roar of delight, Shrike leveled out and tore through the sky, barreling toward the Trade Haven where their Chancellor and Princess awaited.

THE
KING

OF

HONOR AND
SACRIFICE

CHAPTER FORTY

Hands shaking, Rozalie plucked through the rubble of what was once her room.

It had been a favor from Cistine at the beginning of this war not to have to dwell among so many men and women in the close-quarters barracks anymore, where the stink of sweat and the crude banter occasionally dredged up memories from a life better left forgotten—something Rion had always thought she'd overcome with enough exposure, but the Princess felt differently.

Over the past few months, Rozalie had started to accumulate the kind of trinkets few veteran Wardens kept for fear a new initiate would steal them on a dare: teardrop bottles, silk chemises, jeweled knives with molten swirls in their blades. It was the sort of superfluous finery no farmgirl or brothel worker would ever expect to own, things Rozalie loved, all sealed safely behind a door—until tonight.

Now the weapons were gone, the slips shredded, the glass broken by whoever had started their raid on this level. Kneeling by the remnants of what had once been her favorite vase, she stared blankly at the windowless walls. Light fell past her through the open door, illuminating the massacre—then abruptly went dark.

"What a dismal little hole."

She turned on her heels, frowning up at Kashar. He sloped in her doorway, looking for all the world like he belonged there. "What are you doing? Where's your guard?"

He arched a brow. "*You're* my guard, if I recall correctly." He shrugged off the stone arch to enter her room. "Who lived in this ghastly place?"

"I did."

"Ah." Glass splintered under his boot, and she winced. "In my kingdom, that which is of most beauty lives in the grandest halls."

"This is not the time for flirting."

"Is that not what you were doing when you had me by the throat back there?"

She couldn't even muster a scowl when he knelt at her side. "Our Queen is gone."

"So I heard."

"It's our fault. Wardens are meant to protect the royal family. We...*I* failed her."

"Word about Mahasar is that Queen Solene's quite the wildcat. Are you certain you're not better off without her?" Rozalie shot him a look of such venom, he held up both hands. "Then again, I suppose not." Under his breath, he added, "It must be a common trait of Talheimic women."

A smile flitted over her lips, but it was short-lived. Everything they'd done in Middleton had amounted to nothing, even her bruised face and this Mahasari shadowing her. They'd entirely missed Jad's crippling blow. Now Aden was injured, the Queen gone, the King on his way home, and when he and Rion arrived and learned what had become of Solene, of *Eboni*...

"I should've been here."

Kashar turned over glass fragments with his fingertips. "As the man these Enforcers once answered to, I believe I'm in a privileged position to say that had you been here, you would've been buried like that man your friends dug out and carried off to the upper wing."

"I could've stopped the Queen from going."

"You could've died with an arrow in your throat." She scowled, looking away from him. "Your kingdom's better off with you alive to fight, you proved as much tonight. War isn't a martyr's requiem, it's a survivor's game. Which part would you rather play?"

Rozalie rocked back on her haunches. "I'm tired of playing games."

"Aren't we all?" He shifted the last bit of glass, then leaned away; the light splashed past him onto the floor, turning the stained-glass fragments to a dancing northern aurora dazzling on the walls.

Throat tight, Rozalie stared at the multifaceted splashes. "I left you unbound and unsupervised. Why didn't you run?"

He mirrored her posture, enough distance between them to keep the lights shining. "Please, *Raqi*, I could never leave without saying goodbye to you." At her snort, he sighed and added, "Pure stupidity, I'm sure. A touch of arrogance. And the simple fact that if I return home now, knowing what I know, I'll march my wretched hide straight to my uncle's parlor and try to stick a blade in him. I'd be swinging from the city gates before another day passed, and we wouldn't want that, would we?"

Rozalie grunted. "I might not want it as much as I used to."

"Ah, violence and bare tolerance. My favorite traits in a woman."

He was determined to eke a smile out of her, this Mahasari. She offered him another glare instead. "Why did you come to find *me?*"

His grip around his knees tightened a bit. "It's recently come to my attention that every person I ever knew or trusted was likely either a liar or a victim. You, on the other hand...your temper is as honest as your passion for this miserable kingdom, and as honest as your hatred of me. I know precisely where I stand with you. That makes you, astonishingly, the person I trust most in the world at this moment."

Swallowing, she reached for the glass, turning the pattern with the tilt of a shattered blue vase. "It's not quite hatred."

"Oh? That's a pleasant surprise."

"Hatred is too invested. Like you said...violence and tolerance."

He stuck out his hand. "Barely-abided accomplices, then?"

She eyed the offering with some reservation. Who knew what striking bargains with this Mahasari Prince would lead to? But a part of her, wrecked and ravaged by this horrible night, was too tired and heartbroken in the

Queen's absence to hold onto another enemy when she could have an ally instead.

She clasped his hand. "Until the violence takes over."

"I look forward to that day, *Raqi*." Eyes glinting, he pulled them both up in one surge. "Would you like some help dealing with this mess, then?"

Despite herself, Rozalie decided she did.

CHAPTER FORTY-ONE

ASTORIA STILL SMOLDERED, but the siege was over. Everywhere Maleck looked, Citadel halls wore stripes of blood. Battle cries gave way to weeping; weary Wardens and augurs, indistinguishable in their tattered clothing and haggard faces, tallied the dead or slipped into Nimmus side-by-side. In glittering ballrooms, medicos and physicians toiled to save whomever they could.

Maleck ached from numerous wounds blunted by his faithful armor, and his eyelids hung heavy. He'd spent the better part of the night on patrol, scouring every avenue with Kashar, Rozalie, and even Viktor's aid, but to no avail; the Queen had long fled. The only mercy was that no one in the Citadel seemed to know it—or else true pandemonium might've descended, and he wasn't certain anyone could bear another crisis.

With daylight painted in strong splashes against the marred white walls, Maleck trudged to Aden's door. Outside, he paused a moment, listening to the murmuring within; two voices pitched low, the sound of their banter a soothing balm to his troubled heart and weary mind.

Silent as a shadow, he opened the door.

The curtains were thrown wide, ushering in the light. Aden was awake, to Maleck's eternal relief, and sitting up in bed, though pale enough to still be of some concern. Ashe sat against the footboard, boots kicked across his legs, and with a sweep of her arms she regaled him with an account of Middleton. Aden listened intently, nodding, even chuckling when she reached the part where Rozalie thrashed Kashar at the lakeside.

Maleck lingered in the doorway, head and shoulder bent to the stone arch, his body torn in half between the grief of the night and the joy of this moment—the two most precious people in his life, still breathing, their lives priceless gifts from the gods.

He longed for the day when war was just a memory, and it no longer felt like the world was trying to take them away from him.

Aden's gaze leaped past Ashe to Maleck, and at once he tried to throw the covers off and rise. Ashe jammed her heel into his groin, twisting around on the bed, ignoring Aden's bark of pain. "I thought that was you breathing back there. Any sign of the Queen?"

Maleck shook his head. "Gone."

Ashe's mouth firmed. "You stay with him. I'm going to look, and you're not stopping me this time."

"Ashe," Maleck and Aden sighed.

"I know some tunnels the rest of the Wardens don't. Maybe they're holed up in one of them, waiting for things to settle above—"

"Asheila." Maleck caught her arm when she brushed past him, and her gaze locked with his, blazing with hurt and defiance. He released her after a moment. "Go carefully."

She kissed his jaw, gave Aden a two-fingered salute, and slipped out into the hall. Aden slumped back against the pillow, turning a glower on the window. "This is ridiculous. I don't need nannying."

Maleck shrugged out of the doorframe and went to the bed, leaning his crossed arms on the iron rail. "You know I've never been one to doubt your strength, but you did have a *building* collapse on you."

"I know, I know." Aden's fists warped the blanket into knots. "Mira?"

"Resting. She had a small fit. Nothing serious," he added when Aden's stormy gaze jumped to his face. "I was with her through it. She has Nadeem now, and the nursemaids are keeping watch over them both. She's already talked of returning to the ballroom to aid the injured."

"That woman." Aden shook his head, then changed the subject. "I tried, Mal. The Queen, the lords...I tried to defend this city. I was blind until the very end."

"Any of us would've been. In what world would we ever suspect Cistine's own mother of betrayal?"

"*I* should have suspected. I was with her every day."

"Judging by the circles under your eyes, those were not your easiest days." Maleck raised a brow at the dry glare Aden shot him. "You overlooked something. It's been known to happen, that makes you no less a worthy High Tribune. What matters is you gave everything, even nearly your own life, to make it right. The mark of a leader is not that they never fall, but that they rise again."

Aden's mouth jerked into a smile. "When did you become the wise one?"

"One learns much in the presence of Chancellors and princesses."

"True." Aden frowned. "And our Chancellor may be in more danger than we know. We can safely assume Jad is aware of his and Cistine's presence in Mahasar, and that with the Queen gone, he'll move against them next."

Before Maleck could reply, a commotion reached his ears: shouts in the hall, Ashe's among them. Aden gripped the blankets again, and Maleck straightened, flashing up a hand. "I'll deal with this. You rest. I shudder to think what Mira will do to you if you dash off into another battle before she's even had a chance to visit."

Aden's cheek ticked. "You're a filthy fighter, has anyone ever told you that?"

"Asheila has, plenty." Maleck clapped a hand on Aden's foot, held his gaze for a moment in silent warning, then hurried from the room.

Ashe had not escaped to search the tunnels; her way was blocked by a furious King Cyril and a glowering Rion Bartos, both windswept from the flight on Bresnyar's back. Behind them, panting as if they'd chased on their heels, were Rozalie and Kashar.

"Where is my wife?" Cyril growled. "Where is *Cistine*?"

"I'm trying to tell you, if you'd just let me *speak!*" Maleck had never heard Ashe take such an abrupt, harsh tone with the King. "I can only tell you one thing at a time!"

"Then start with why the Citadel is going up in smoke!" Rion snarled.

"Mahasar attacked. They had help from inside our walls."

Cyril stiffened. "The Mahasari girl—"

"Hasn't been in the dungeons in weeks." Ashe shook her head when the King opened his mouth again. "It was Solene. She's been ensorcelled, likely for months now."

Cyril's hand clapped to his mouth. He fell back a pace, shaking his head, eyes scrunched in the first blows of disbelief.

"What *happened?*" Rion demanded.

Ashe's gaze swung to him, full of something Maleck himself could never muster on behalf of *Meszaros* of Cerne Mosiar: pity. "She was determined to go to Mahasar. That was the lie the drug made her believe. She killed her personal guard, nearly Aden too. And..." Her gaze cut away from Rion, the only ground she dared give.

Cyril's eyes squeezed shut and he buried his forehead in one hand. But Rion went on staring at Ashe, dragging breaths deep down into himself, each one wetter and shakier than the last. "*Where is Eboni,*" he seethed at last, and Rozalie winced.

"There was nothing we could do," Maleck said when Ashe didn't reply. "She was fallen long before we uncovered her body from the rubble."

Roaring with atavistic rage, Rion lunged at him; but Cyril intercepted, catching him by the arms and yanking him around. The Commander fell against his King and wept: great, heartbroken, heaving sobs, arms slung around Cyril's shoulders like a lifeline in raging seas. Cyril held him tightly, tears tracking his own face. "Where is Solene now?"

"On her way to Arak Shehr," Kashar said. "It's where the game ends."

"What game?" Cyril released Rion, who stumbled off to the side, clinging to the wall to keep himself upright. "Who *are* you?"

"Prince Kashar az-Kyrian." The Prince sketched an arrogant bow. "And the game is Jad's strategy enacted against Talheim...against your family."

Cyril blinked rapidly, then whirled on Ashe again. "Where *is* Cistine?"

Ashe swallowed, grimacing. Maleck, too, found the words impossible to summon.

Cyril's eyes narrowed dangerously. "Where is my *daughter?*"

"Mahasar," Rozalie said. "Inspiring the Free People to stand with us against Jad."

Half-mad laughter burst from Cyril's lips, but there was no humor in his face or the wild shake of his head. "That girl...that *girl*..." He swung around, slammed his fist into the wall, then strode away from them. "Summon your dragon, Asheila. You are going to take me wherever she's gone, *right now*."

Rion, shoulder slumped to the wall, trailed after him, disappearing around the bend in the hall with a muffled curse.

Maleck winced. Rozalie blew out a breath. But Kashar said, "All things considered, that could've gone worse. He hardly seemed to notice me."

"That's what I'm afraid of," Ashe muttered. "He's furious. Distracted. And that's exactly how Jad wants him."

Her gaze held Maleck's, and guilt jammed through his middle. Some of that distraction was, without question, their doing for how they'd deceived him. And whatever happened in this fight as a result of the King's blind fury would be their doing as well.

CHAPTER FORTY-TWO

CISTINE SAW NOTHING of Thorne or Sacha for many days. She kept to herself, sequestered in her grotto with only a satchel of orange tea to drink, blades to sharpen, and hours between bouts of swordplay and sparring against the sandsack to chase her thoughts in circles.

A strange calm had entered her after that argument with Thorne; not pleasure, not pain, but a comfortable numbness that carried her through the days. He did not come for her, and she no longer looked for him at meals. She had plenty to keep her occupied with the *Alhuri* asking questions about her, about Talheim, about the skirmish with the Enforcers.

But she knew it wasn't right. None of this was. Not after the questions raised in their last conversation; not when his doubts fed her own.

He had vowed never to lie to her, and beneath her exhaustion, her frustration, she didn't believe he'd lied about Sacha. There was something more at work here, a thread she tugged during those long, lonely hours in her grotto, weaving an impossible tapestry that left her lying awake in wild thought when she should be asleep.

Finally, the night before her duel with Esmail, she couldn't bear it anymore. She couldn't go into battle until her speculations were laid to rest, either proven right or wrong. Just like the cabal had taught her—she must go into a fight clear-minded, or not at all.

So she steeled her nerves, left her grotto at last, and went to find Sacha.

It proved more difficult than she expected. The alchemist wasn't in her workshop, and Sabir, Mairin, and Suljafar hadn't seen her in days. Cistine wondered if Thorne was to blame for that.

It took the better part of the evening to track her down, and then she was not in *Via Hosial* at all; Shathen had seen her slip outside earlier that evening, and an *Alhuri* fighter on the street by the aqueduct directed Cistine to a nearby rooftop. Sacha sat atop it, wrapped in silks and skirts, gazing up at the stars. Her calm face registered no surprise when Cistine clambered onto the roof beside her. "Shouldn't you be preparing for tomorrow?"

"Actually, that's why I'm here," Cistine confessed. "Do you mind if I sit?"

"It's the right of all free people."

She lowered herself cross-legged at Sacha's side. "I haven't seen you for days."

"I've been avoiding you."

"I thought so." Cistine hooked her hair behind her ear. "I know you had an argument with Thorne."

"So, he did tell you." She shook her head. "That man is desperately loyal. He would be a good member of the *Alhuri* if he wasn't already sworn to two other kingdoms."

"He is loyal, isn't he?" Cistine played with the finger loops of her armor. "I hurt him after you two fought...on purpose this time. We haven't spoken since."

"I'm sorry," Sacha said, and sounded like she meant it; but Cistine wasn't sure she could trust that anymore.

She twisted toward Sacha, resting her weight back on one hand. "Was he right about you?"

Her throat bobbed, her gaze never leaving the stars. "Yes and no. You would do better to make amends with him than me. I'm not certain I'm worth your time."

"Well, *I* say you are." Nevermind that this conversation would be a thousand times easier than the apologies she owed to Thorne. "I can see you're hurting. Let me help you."

"I don't deserve that help."

"That's not true—"

"It isn't your place to say, Princess! You don't know what I am!" Sacha snapped, then bent forward, resting her brow on her fist. "What I have *done...*"

"Tell me," Cistine urged. "If you let it fester, it will kill you."

Sacha shook her head, but it was a slow wag, resigned. After a moment, she loosed a dry, hopeless laugh. "This was bound to happen the moment I chose to fight the Enforcers with you. I thought I could keep ahead of it until you completed the Rite, but I should've known better. I broke my oath to Dyalmun. This is how he punishes me."

"What oath did you break?"

"That I would never take another life. Not a beast, not a man...no more killing. I've killed enough." She rubbed her wrists as if invisible shackles chafed there. "But Thorne was right. He's been right from the start."

"He has an infuriating habit of that." Cistine smiled faintly. "What did he say to you?"

"That I was like Jad. And it's true. I may not have killed for some time, but I'm still the same manipulative *hasac* I've always been. I've used people for years...I used *you*, your pain, your promise to help, and I'm sorry. I'm so sorry, Cistine. Everything about me is a lie."

Cistine's pulse thundered in her throat. "What do you mean?"

"I'm not who the *Alhuri* think I am. Sacha ra-Fyra does not exist." She cradled her head in her hands. "I am Tirzah ra-Kyrian. I'm the King's Shadow, the assassin Princess."

For a long moment, Cistine didn't speak. She let the words hang there and weighed what she ought to do with them. How much she could say.

At last, she chose honesty. "I knew it was something like that."

Sacha stiffened. "*What?* How? Who told you?"

"No one. It was just...the way you talked about her, even back in the Citadel dungeon. Like you hated and admired her. It makes sense." Cistine stared down at her cursed hands. "I feel the same way about the girl I used to be. I've been acting like she died on the battlefield so I could live with how different we are...with everything she had that I don't anymore." Swallowing against a hitch in her voice, she glanced at Sacha. "And then when we fought the Enforcers together, I really meant it...the only way to not kill people in a battle like that is to know exactly *how* to kill. You couldn't just be good at it. You had to be one of the best."

Sacha said nothing, merely stared at the stars.

"Can I guess about what happened?" When Sacha didn't protest, Cistine went on, "You really did grow up on the streets...but then Jad took you in. You and Kashar loved each other until Sorcel took that away, and he didn't fight back when Jad ordered him to kill you. That's when your ensorcellment broke. You ran away, and Suljafar and the others took you in and helped you discover the antidote. That's when you realized you could redeem yourself."

"Go on," Sacha whispered.

Cistine pressed her lips together, considering. "You built *Alhuru en-Asgaid* out of people you hurt serving Jad...people like Esmail. That's how you used them, isn't it? You only knew to recruit them because *you* hurt them in the first place. But you wanted to make Sacha everything Tirzah wasn't...that's why you never kill, why you don't want to lead."

Scoffing quietly, Sacha thumbed her eyes. "All true. And yet, she's always part of me. I manipulated you and your family. I placed Esmail in power, underestimated his pride and fear, and now I've tried to remove him at the tip of another's sword. I've gained loyalty from people who hate the woman I was, who would kill me if they ever knew the truth. And I know when Kashar returns, clear-minded, he'll recognize me...I intended to flee the moment the antidote was finished and Esmail brought down."

Cistine's heart skipped. "You were going to leave? Let me lead *Alhuru en-Asgaid alone?*"

"I've had my satchel packed for weeks." A hard smile twisted Sacha's mouth. "You see how wretched I am? Dyalmun's name...you must *hate* me."

Cistine tugged at the tangled knot of emotion in her chest for several minutes before she answered. "Maybe I should. I'm certainly not happy about any of this. But I didn't come here with the best intentions, either. I've been desperate, I've been looking for *anything* that would make me feel alive again. I shouldn't have been this easy to manipulate, after everything I've learned and seen, but...here we are."

"Here we are," Sacha echoed. "And where do we go now?"

"I wish I knew." Cistine buried her face in her hands. "I have to apologize to Thorne. And I think...I think I have to stop the Rite. I can't do this for you. Not if it's going to cost me everything I am."

"I was afraid of that. I don't know where it leaves me."

"You should stop running." Cistine let her arms fall limp at her sides. "We both should. We have to face what we've done and who we are....and what made us this way. Standing up to the shadows is the only way we escape them. I'd almost forgotten that, but I think it's time. For both of us."

Sacha eyed her shrewdly. "Are you truly ready for that?"

Before Cistine could answer, a faint scuffle caught her ears. Boots thumped stone and fists crunched flesh. A muffled cry cut short. With a swift glance, Cistine and Sacha were at the roof's edge, looking down at a dark-clad figure stealing through the streets toward the aqueduct, leaving the guard either unconscious or dead in his wake. He had a man's height and build, and he prowled like a thief searching for something hidden.

Heart in her throat, Cistine lunged from the rooftop, slid down the awning, and tucked into a roll in the street. With Sacha trailing silently behind her, she darted after the man.

"Stop!" she hissed, drawing Nail when only a few meters separated them. "Who are you and what do you want?" He whirled, hands tipping back his hood, and Nail winked when her knife arm dipped in shock. "*Papa?* Papa, what are you doing here, what's—?"

The words floundered in her throat. Cyril had never looked at her this way before—with despair and rage and betrayal, like she'd put Nail in his gut. "Is Thorne with you?"

No inflection. No greeting. No warmth.

Cistine's guts shriveled into a knot. "He's here, but—"

"Get him and come straight back. We are going to have a *talk*."

CHAPTER FORTY-THREE

THE JOURNEY TO retrieve Thorne was excruciating, but the silence after was far worse—as terrible as the look on his face when she found him in his grotto and her first words to him in days were that her father was here in Masiya.

While Sacha stayed in *Via Hosial*, Cistine and Thorne followed Cyril away from the aqueduct into the black, twisting streets. Every step hammered fresh fear into Cistine; beside her, Thorne was tense as well, eyes bearing the same stoicism as the first time she'd ever seen him face Salvotor, in the Chancellor's sanctum when he'd come to her rescue.

Cyril chose their stopping place in the darkness between one street mouth and the next, pivoting on them with rage kindling in his eyes. "How dare you. How dare *either* of you?"

"Papa, let me explain," Cistine began.

"This requires no explanation! You defied my direct order! When I left for the southern forts, I expected you, of all people, to heed my word. Instead I return to find the Citadel besieged, some of its best defenders gone for *weeks*, and your mother..."

He broke off, hand shading his mouth, and the world pulsed and tipped around Cistine. She staggered a step closer to him. "What about her? *Papa?*"

Harrowed eyes locked on hers. "She was ensorcelled. She fled the

Citadel with Jad's Enforcers, killed Eboni, and nearly killed Aden when he tried to stop her."

A groan ripped from Thorne, his hand slamming against the stone building to his right to keep his feet beneath him. But Cistine had nothing to grip onto; her knees struck the ground, and she stared up at her father, ears ringing, chest stuck between breaths.

This couldn't be happening. The traitor, Jad's spy, it couldn't be her own *mother*—

But why not? Wasn't that a perfect angle to the game? Hadn't she even told Tatiana how easy it had been to leave the Citadel with the Queen's blessing? Solene wasn't dull; she'd known all along. She'd *let* Cistine come here, had sent Cyril away to the southern forts despite the threat of ensorcelled spies within Talheim, all for the game.

Tears slipped over her lashes. "We have to get her back."

"Not *we*," Cyril growled. "You two are going straight home."

Cistine surged upright, fists flexing. "Papa, *no*, that's not—"

"Do you *really* want to defy me again?" The cold question stopped her argument swifter than a slap. "I can't trust you, Cistine. Gods, I can hardly look at you. After everything you've done, everything you've learned, *this* is what you chose…to betray me like this."

Shame rived through her body. She couldn't even hold his gaze.

"She was doing what she thought was best for her kingdom. For all the kingdoms." Thorne's voice was hoarse from lack of use. "She should be honored for that."

"There is something you need to learn about loyalty and love," Cyril retorted. "They do not amount to supporting every decision someone makes. You should never have gone along with this."

Thorne's jaw feathered with tension. "I was trying to be a worthy *valenar*."

"And I was trying to be the queen Talheim will need," Cistine added, desperate to remove Thorne from under the scrutiny of an angry father. "I thought I could help lead the *Alhuri* against Jad—"

"And that is precisely why you're *not* ready," Cyril snapped. "Seeing war does not make you fit to lead."

"How can you say that? Look at what happened to you!"

"That is *exactly why* I'm saying it! Gods, the mistakes I made as King...the secrets I kept from you..." Cyril shook his head, raking a hand over his bearded mouth again. "The greatest gift I *ever* hoped to give you was that you wouldn't have to inherit the throne by my premature death. Leading before your time, before you've even lived a sliver of your life, is a greater curse than the death you hold in your hands."

Cistine's mind struggled to make sense of the raw honesty and anguish in his voice. "I don't understand...you *love* being King."

"I do. But if I could've raised you as a Prince myself, without the burden of a kingdom's worth of lives on my shoulders, maybe I would've made fewer mistakes. Maybe I would've been a better husband, a better father." All at once, the anger was gone; there was only weariness in Cyril's face. "I am going to Arak Shehr to finish this. The augurs and Wardens who can still fight are coming behind us. But I want you back at the Citadel."

"Papa, *please*," Cistine begged, "I made a mistake, I know that now! But I can help, I—"

His eyes held hers with an unspoken agony that took her breath away; and at last she saw that this was not only about her betrayal.

He was preserving the royal line.

"*No*." The word rolled out as a sob.

"You were eager to play at being Queen before your time. Now you have no choice." Cyril's tone was adamant again. "You go home and keep the throne. And you go with her," he added to Thorne, whose heels clipped sharply together. "Whatever happens to me, you keep her alive. The royal line *does not fall*, do you understand?"

Thorne dipped his head, and Cistine's heart cracked in two. She should've saved all her defiance, all her betrayals for this moment—to keep her father from walking into battle against Jad without her. But there was no time for arguments, for justifying herself. The Mad King had her mother. The only penance left to offer was her silence, to let him go before it was too late for Solene.

"Your people brought wind augments," Cyril went on to Thorne. "They made me swear to send you to them on the southern outskirts of the city. Say your farewells and go. I leave for Arak Shehr at dawn. You go home tonight." He strode toward them, though Cistine didn't know where he intended to go—whether he would appeal to the *Alhuri* or if he was going to walk the city and gather his wits tonight for the battle tomorrow.

"I'm sorry," Thorne said quietly when the King was abreast of him. "I hoped to be a good man. The *valenar* Cistine deserves."

Something ripped in Cistine's middle, a harsh and wild pain. Cyril raised his hand, and Thorne, twice his girth and matched in height, flinched so sharply it was nearly a sidestep. But the King's hand merely descended on his shoulder. "You know what it is to be Chancellor, but you are still learning what it means to be part of a family. In *this* family, we don't keep secrets anymore. And we don't let one another fall by the poor choices we make, even if it puts us at odds."

His eyes flashed to Cistine with a last stroke of reproach—then softened in a way that was somehow worse than if he'd walked away unspeaking.

"I love you," he said, and another sob hitched in her throat. "Remember that. No matter what comes, I do all of this because I *love* you."

Then he was gone.

A throbbing, muffled silence descended. Cistine swiped both hands down her wet cheeks, looking up at Thorne as he stared after Cyril, heartbreak twisting his features. "I'm sorry," Cistine whispered. "This is all my fault."

"No, it's also mine. I was so afraid to lose your love and respect, I lost myself instead." Thorne shook his head. "Let's go home."

She nodded. "I'll get my things. Meet me at the city's edge?"

Dipping his head, Thorne vanished into the darkness; Cistine returned to *Via Hosial* alone, numb to the shouts and questions that greeted her, the eager anticipation of the Rite tomorrow.

She would have to forfeit before she left, and she'd never be able to show her face in Mahasar again even if she wanted to. Sacha—Tirzah—

would confront the uncertain future without anyone who knew the truth of her origins, the depth of her remorse. And the *Alhuri* would cower under these streets while Talheim and Valgard marched on Arak Shehr, where her mother was being kept. Where her father...

The grotto blurred before Cistine's eyes when she entered, falling to her knees by her bedroll. She gripped Kaisill and the tea satchel, but didn't lift them. Her hands felt like lead. Then she hurled both into the corner, fell back on her heels, and wept.

She'd made so many mistakes; coming to this place, invoking the Rite, forcing Thorne away, grasping for leadership and usefulness so obstinately it had clouded everything else. Now her mother was Jad's captive again, Aden nearly killed, the King forced to finish this game—all because she'd been seeking a sense of purpose in the strange tides her life had become.

Her father was right...she wasn't fit to be Queen yet. But because of her poor choices, she might become one anyway.

Cistine curled forward, buried her face in her hands, and tried to pray, but the divine remained a chasm within her. No words would come.

She was still on her knees, sobs ripping through her, when the first explosion rocked the street above.

CHAPTER FORTY-FOUR

WHAT DO YOU think Cyril Novacek will say when he learns you played into his daughter's defiance? Do you suppose he'll welcome you back with open arms...or cast you out into the cold where you belong?

His father's words haunted Thorne every step after he left Cistine in that dark alley, like specters he couldn't outrun. The edge of the city was a target in motion, and by the time he crested the sand dunes at Masiya's southern edge and caught a distant glimpse of gold dragon scales, his chest was too tight for words.

They all came to attention when he appeared: Ashe straightening from Bresnyar's side, Rozalie leaping up from her cross-legged seat by the dragon's tail. A dark-haired, tawny-skinned stranger beside her eyed Thorne with cautious interest; next to him, blade drawn, Rion Bartos turned his attention from the stranger to Thorne, loathing holding steady in his gaze.

Then Maleck reached him, clapping him in an embrace, and Thorne nearly broke down right there in front of them all.

His father was right. Cyril was right. Most days, he didn't know how to lead, how to serve, how to be the man his people needed him to be. He didn't truly know what it was to be part of a blood-forged family; but when he was with his cabal, it all made a little more sense.

"It's good to see you," Maleck said quietly, pushing him out at arm's length.

Thorne bore down on the inside of his cheek, the pain snapping him back to composure. "Aden?"

"Still in Astoria." Ashe shouldered forward to clap him on the arm. "He'll be all right, he just needs more rest."

Good. He and Cistine wouldn't be holding the city alone, then.

"Where's Cistine?" Ashe added. "Is she all right?"

Humiliation colored Thorne's neck. He didn't even know the answer to that question. "She's on her way." He gave a chin nod over Maleck's shoulder. "I take it this is Prince Kashar?"

"In the flesh." Ashe's tone was flat with dislike. "He helped us hold the Citadel. He's here to overthrow his uncle."

Dully, Thorne wondered if Kashar ought to invoke the Rite and lead the *Alhuri* instead; if perhaps they should've put more of their effort behind winning favor to his name rather than their own.

Stars, why was he only thinking of this *now*?

"I know that look," Maleck said. "What's the matter, *Allet*?"

His answer was lost in a distant concussion, a plume of smoke, the sound of screaming. Bresnyar's head shot up from the sand. "*Again?*"

Rion, Rozalie, and Kashar were at the top of the dune around them in a heartbeat, hands to their weapons; below, back in the city, a second burst of fire lit the sky.

"Blasting powders," Kashar hissed. "This is Enforcer work, the same as in your Citadel."

"Jad." Thorne unsheathed his sabers.

Kashar cursed in Mahasari, kneading his temple. "I remember this! Toppling Masiya was a last resort if the *Alhuri* still stood when Jad held the Talheimic royal family under his control. He's ready to end it."

"Good," Rion snarled, drawing his sword. "So are we."

"Not at the cost of innocent lives!" Rozalie snapped. "Those people below are as much his victims as anyone. They need our help."

"She's right," Kashar urged. "I know Enforcer patterns, I know how they fight. We can push them out if you let me lead."

"Not in this life," Rion scoffed.

But Thorne held Kashar's gaze—one born leader to another. "You hold the line. I'll muster the *Alhuri*."

Kashar dipped his chin, and at Ashe's whistle, Bresnyar cleared the dune in a leap; Ashe swung onto his back, Maleck behind her, and Rozalie towed Kashar up after them. With a blast of the dragon's wings, they arrowed out over the city.

Rion's hand clamped on Thorne's shoulder, spinning him around. "Have you lost your mind? Did you ever *have* one? That bastard is Mahasari to his core, his people helped murder my wife!"

Thorne's stomach twisted, heart dropping at the thought of Eboni, kind and quiet and eternally wounded, yet another victim of this war. But even so, Rion's prejudices could not become his. "Kashar is not responsible for his people's actions."

Rion's fingers twisted in his collar, hauling him close. "No one, *no one* harms my family and lives."

Thorne broke his hold with a shove, sending him staggering back on his heels. "Kashar is not your enemy tonight, the Enforcers are! They're here for Cistine and Cyril. Help me defend them, and let that be vengeance enough!"

Rion heaved and glared at Thorne. After a long moment, he grunted, "Lead on, then, *Chancellor*."

Gripping his sabers, Thorne turned back to the city, glowing in dragonfire and Enforcer flames, an inexorable fate marching toward *Via Hosial*.

His family was down there.

I'm coming, Wildheart. The words were a prayer left unspoken as he launched himself down the dune, Rion at his side, and shot toward the city where Jad's wrath bore down like the Undertaker's scythe.

Already, smoke choked the avenues; the people foolish enough to be out in the streets broke before Thorne and Rion's reckless charge from the outskirts, their sobs and screams riddling the air. It reminded Thorne far too much of their siege to retake Stornhaz, a battle where he'd nearly lost

Ariadne, *had* lost Cistine for a time—and truly, the last few moments he'd seen her as she used to be, brilliant, fierce, framed in fire, marching to war afraid but confident in her schemes.

He had to put himself between her and Jad's endgame, whatever the cost.

They were more than a mile from the aqueduct when he realized the *Alhuri* were already in motion; whether Cistine had taken charge or Esmail had shown spine at last, the Free People rushed into the streets, parting to protect their ensorcelled kin. Some held a line through the middle of the city, others hurtled straight toward the thickest of the fire and fighting, where draconian bellows shattered the night.

Fear pulsed in the base of Thorne's throat; he slowed his stride, gripping Rion's arm to halt him as well. "The King is out there somewhere. He was moving toward the market when we last saw him."

"And you let him go off *alone*?" Rion snarled under his breath. "You Valgardans—"

"Enough! I'm not having this argument with you. Get to Cyril, I'll find Cistine!"

Swearing, Rion peeled off. Blades drawn, Thorne turned down a narrow side street and shimmied through, emerging alongside the aqueduct where he broke into a run again. Murky water churned to his left; fire breathed at his back. His eyes stung with smoke, and every step thudded in tempo to prayers tumbling through his head.

Let him be in time. Let the King be safe. Let his cabal hold the line. Let this city be saved. Let his Wildheart be all right.

He heard no pursuing shouts; nor did he feel pain when an arrowhead seared through the flesh of his arm. He only knew he'd been attacked when the projectile clattered past him, rolling down the dip in the walkway nearly to the stone that hid *Via Hosial.* Someone had left it open, the dark maw exposed below.

Cursing, Thorne planted his feet and whirled back. Six Enforcers framed the street behind him; one had already nocked another arrow.

Now he felt the dull seepage of blood from the wound across his upper arm. Teeth gritted, he flexed his grip on his right-handed saber; still steady, though thin jolts of pain fluttered in his muscles. He would have to end this fight quickly and seal that hole before more Enforcers arrived.

These six moved with predatory grace, half-encircling him. Nothing he hadn't faced before and emerged victorious. He was not afraid; he was furious, and not just at them. A night, a week, half a month's worth of anger or more churned in his gut, anchoring his stance.

He loosened his wrists with a twist of the hands, blades singing. "If you want her, you'll have to cut me down."

The bowman tipped his head. "Who said we came for the princess?"

No sooner did the words leave his mouth than the blow came, a solid strike to the base of Thorne's skull that turned the world to a dull white roar. He barely felt his knees crack the stone or the hands that seized his arms, wrenching the sabers from his grasp. He couldn't breathe, couldn't hear, couldn't *think*. Dimly, eyes watering, he saw a shadow move; on the rooftops above the aqueduct, Rion crouched, hand to his sword, muscles coiled to leap.

Then their gazes met. And slowly, the Commander pulled back his hand, turned, and vanished from the rooftop.

It was the last thing Thorne saw before the dark burlap sack closed over his addled head.

CHAPTER FORTY-FIVE

THE TRADE HAVEN was under attack.

Tatiana knew it before they even crossed the horizon, Shrike's slender body heaving to cross the distance with three people on his back. They'd already stopped twice for hours at a time to let him rest; but when those first black plumes of smoke appeared over the horizon, there was no longer any hope of a leisurely flight.

Quill laid low on the dragon's neck. "Let's *move!*"

Gathering his breath, Shrike streaked forward, flanks shuddering between Tatiana's knees. Her concern for the dragon's wellbeing was only dimly eclipsed by her concern for Cistine and Thorne in the city that smoldered with battle above the dunes.

"Oh, stars," Ariadne breathed, catching sight of Masiya's stricken expanse, burning in whips of flame. Tatiana's heart plummeted.

A piercing roar split the sky, and something slammed against them from the left, hotter than forge-fire and heavier than a Mahasari catapult launch. Shrieking, Shrike dropped, tucking at the last second to land on his shoulder in the sand and avoid crushing them. Before Tatiana could shake the panicked grip of near-death from her head, the world blazed gold, flame and fury sparking in the night.

"Bres, *stop!*" Quill kicked free of Shrike's weight and staggered to his feet. "*Stop,* it's us! He's with *us!*"

Bresnyar crashed down beside them, nostrils steaming, gullet glowing. "This pitiful lizard is *yours?*"

"Seems that way." Quill laid a hand on Shrike's head. "Stand down."

Swallowing his fire, Bresnyar stalked toward them. When Tatiana wriggled free and tugged Ariadne to her feet, the dragon planted a taloned foot on Shrike's shoulder and thrust him into his back, exposing his vulnerable belly, freckled in black ticking. After a long moment gazing down at the smaller dragon, Bresnyar scoffed. "You match." Then he swung back toward the city. "There's a battle afoot. We need all the help we can muster."

"You don't say," Tatiana muttered, unsheathing her sabers.

"What happened?" Ariadne demanded.

"I'll explain later. For now, up on my back!"

With a parting glance at Quill, who'd already mounted Shrike again, Tatiana and Ariadne obeyed. Bresnyar launched skyward and streaked back toward the city, dropping into the infernal heat at its heart.

Tatiana could hardly discern friend from foe through the smoke. Enforcers were barely distinguishable by their chained veils, but some who guarded their backs were dressed in merch clothing. And those they fought—

Augurs. Wardens. What were they doing here?

There was no time to ask. The moment Bresnyar landed, Tatiana and Ariadne plunged into the fray, sabers singing.

It was more difficult not to kill anyone here than in the oasis. In the utter bedlam, no one pulled a single blow, and it wasn't entirely clear what they were fighting for, or why. Tatiana only knew Thorne and Cistine were somewhere in this city, and now Ashe and Maleck, at least; and that was enough to keep her swinging even when the weariness of fighting these ensorcelled enemies choked her limbs.

Stars, what was Jad making of them? There was no end to the killing.

A familiar shout rived the smoke-clotted air, and Tatiana and Ariadne spun together to catch sight of Rozalie Dohnal darting into the marketplace, leaping onto Bresnyar's back. A cut across her cheekbone wept freely, and the inferno among the market stalls reflected in her eyes. "We need augurs in the western district! Water augments—start putting out the fires!"

"On our way!" Tatiana shouted back.

With a blink of recognition, Rozalie nodded. Then she and Bresnyar took flight, and Tatiana and Ariadne broke from the marketplace, racing west.

This, she was happy to do—putting out fires, saving homes, making sure there was still a glorious Trade Haven left for people like Yasmin to visit once Jad's grip broke. She didn't even mind using all her augments for the task.

⌒∿⌒

Masiya fell into a nearly-even divide between battle and recovery; while dragonfire and smoke lit the sky to the south and east, Tatiana and Ariadne mustered the augurs and swept down from the northwest, blotting out fires, dragging dazed merches and wide-eyed families from the rubble. Help came in numerous hands and feet, faces of every color, bodies of every build, all in the same dusty, ragged attire; they climbed over wreckages, carried out weeping children, and supported stunned men and women. Tatiana had no doubt this was *Alhuru en-Asgaid*, the Free People Yasmin revered; they crawled out of Masiya's cracks to lend aid, district by district, until the raging cries of battle at their backs started to fade.

"Retreat?" Tatiana panted while she and Ariadne maneuvered an elderly man from the ruins of his home.

"At best." But the clever strategist didn't look convinced.

"Tati? Ari!"

"Cistine!" Tatiana nearly dropped the old man at the sight of the Princess racing toward them through the smoke and steam. Her face was a mess of soot, silver hair tossed wildly around her shoulders, eyes wide—the look she always gave right before throwing her arms around them.

"I've been looking everywhere for you!" Cistine's voice cracked between gratitude and desperation as she halted a safe distance away. "I'm so glad

294

you're here…the northwest?"

"Extinguished." Ariadne lowered the old man gently to the ground. "And it's good to see you, too, *Logandir*."

"I'm sorry, I just…" Cistine waved a hand. "I feel like I haven't stopped to breathe since I heard that first attack! We need to get to the others. Where's Thorne?"

Tatiana shrugged. "Probably with the others."

Ariadne beckoned a Warden to care for the old man, then jerked her head. "Lead on, Cistine."

They raced through still-smoldering streets, the augurs making slow but effective work toward snuffing out the few remaining pockets of flame. The dragons had gone silent, thank the stars; if Bresnyar wasn't roaring and Shrike wasn't shrieking, it meant there was no one left to intimidate.

Tatiana breathed easier when they came into the open near a gushing channel and found a cluster of familiar faces; Ashe and Maleck, smoke-scoured, standing near Quill, whose wild gestures seemed to be in mid-recount of their first meeting with Shrike. His dragon sprawled on the dusty road, sides heaving; Bresnyar, perched on a corner rooftop above, eyed him with disdain. Nearby, Rozalie spoke to a cluster of Wardens and *Alhuri* with a stranger who nodded along grave-faced to everything she said. Tatiana had a feeling that was Kashar az-Kyrian, and if so, they were all about to owe the war's ending to Sacha—who was just now heaving herself out of a hole in the path, hands freckled with blood, eyes wide and solemn.

Cistine's breath hitched at the sight of her. The man beside Rozalie followed her gaze and stiffened. A wild, charged energy flickered between him and Sacha, raising the hair on Tatiana's arms. He stepped away from Rozalie's side with dazed slowness, chest rising in fast, labored breaths. "You—you can't…"

"I am Sacha ra-Fyra," she interrupted. "It's good to finally meet you, Prince Kashar."

He shook his head. "No. I know that face."

Sacha was stiff all over. "I'm Sacha ra-Fyra, alchemist of *Alhuru*—"

"Stop saying that! It's not your name. I *know your name*." Kashar halted before her, and they stared at one another.

When Sacha spoke again, the power had gone from her voice. "If you *ever* loved me, you will not say that name."

So many emotions broke through the Prince's face, Tatiana felt them like blades in her own heart. The back of his knuckles brushed Sacha's scarred cheek. "I did this. I thought...I *remember* doing far worse."

"Dyalmun was not finished with us. Perhaps he spared me so I might save you before I went to face his judgement."

His eyes blew wide. "*Save* me?"

"Who do you think manufactured the antidote these people used to free you?" She jerked her chin at Rozalie. "From the moment I woke, I was looking for a way to wake you, too. The little boy who toddled after me through every dangerous path in Arak Shehr...how could I leave him in that madman's clutches?"

Kashar's hand grazed his stubbled mouth. "*You* made the cure?"

"For you. All of it for you, *brashiq.*"

With a strangled choke, Kashar brought her to him, arms wound around her back. Sacha's gaze gleamed, too, when she held him, her eyes flitting to Cistine.

Thank you, she mouthed, and the princess ducked her head.

Tatiana would have to ask her about that—but later.

They had company.

"Mahasari forces are routed," Rion Bartos announced in that despicably smug voice, always sounding just enough like his son to make Tatiana taste a twinge of regret as well as annoyance. "They fled north, tails tucked."

"Are you all right?" Cyril Novacek directed the brittle question at Cistine. Judging by the way she avoided his eyes when she nodded, this was not their first—or their happiest—reunion.

Tatiana's scalp prickled with a spike of dread; she glanced at Quill, finding her concern reflected in his eyes.

There were too many allies here. Something was wrong.

Sacha and Kashar drew apart, wiping their eyes, and Cyril's eyes narrowed at the alchemist. "Somehow I'm not surprised to find you here with my runaway daughter when I last saw you in my dungeon. You haven't behaved like a friend to Talheim."

"I'm aware," she said. "Forgive me. And I beg you, forgive Cistine. Her presence here was my doing, I—"

"No, it was my fault," Cistine interrupted sharply. "Thorne and I knew exactly what we were doing. We chose to come." She blinked suddenly, then turned a full circle, looking around at the cabal, the Wardens, the *Alhuri*. "Where *is* he?" she muttered, then raised her voice. "*Thorne!*"

"We saw him just before this started." Ashe gestured at the city behind them. "He went to find you."

"Perhaps below?" Maleck nodded to the hole.

"The only ones left inside are mothers and children," Sacha said. "Everyone else went to fight."

"Rion." Rozalie's eyes were fixed on her commander, and he didn't meet her gaze. He scowled past them into the shadows.

Slowly, Cistine revolved to face him. "Rion, where is he?" When his jaw only shifted, Cistine shrieked, "*Where is my husband?*"

"There was nothing I could do," Rion grunted. "It was too late, there were too many of them..."

Tatiana's heart pounded so loud, his words had to force their way into her ears. Cistine fell back a step, face scrunching to fight off tears, head flinging. "No, no, *no*...where is he? Where did you see him *exactly?*"

"Here." Rion spanned an arm at the street. "This was where he made his final stand."

Ariadne pressed a hand over her throat. Quill swore so colorfully, Shrike raised his head, wings ruffling in concern. Tatiana nearly reached for Cistine when the princess wobbled, crumbling back another step. "No, *no*, he's not—he *can't* be—"

"He isn't dead," Cyril said with calm, chilling confidence. "If he was, the body would have been left as a taunt. Jad's taken him, too."

Cistine stopped breathing altogether. Rion blanched. "Cyril, if there was *any* chance, I would have..."

"You would have *what?*" Ashe snarled. "I thought there was nothing you *could* do."

Rion fixed her with a glare. "I would have brought *word* of it."

"I know Jad. He's captured Solene already," Cyril said, and Tatiana's stomach turned over at the idea of the fierce, sweet-spirited Queen taken prisoner by the madman they fought to dethrone. "Now he has Thorne as well...to lure us to him."

"A final confrontation," Maleck murmured, "on his terms."

Kashar dragged a hand through his hair. "It's the culmination of the game."

Cistine's eyes widened; without a word, she turned and dashed down the street.

Cursing, Quill gave chase. "Stranger, get back here!"

"Let them go!" Cyril barked when Rion took a step after them. "We see to our wounded. We craft a plan. That's two members of the royal family he's taken. We'll pay that back in blood."

Tatiana could hardly focus, the world pulsing and blurring around her. This was just like Salvotor all over again, the night he'd plucked up her cabal one by one and forced them to face their worst fears, their grimmest fates, while she was powerless to stop it.

Ashe's hand descended on her shoulder. "We'll get them back."

Tatiana forced a smile. "I never thought I'd say it, but I preferred falling into a poisonous trench over this."

Shrike bounded up at her side, a low, huffing cackle in his chest, and clamped his teeth lightly over her arm. Ashe jerked back, swearing, but Tatiana just glared at him. "Would you *stop* that?"

"Biter?" Ashe asked cautiously, hand still on Starfall.

"I don't know what's the matter with him. He does this *every* time we mention Ralathi—" His teeth pushed harder against her armor, and she winced. "*Trench.*"

"Hold a moment." Bresnyar slithered down from his perch and stalked toward Shrike. A pattern of sound fell from his lips—not exactly like the *Tayir's* guttural babble, but close enough that it sounded like a conversation going back and forth when Shrike released her to chatter back. And it was a testament to how unprecedented the past year had been that a conversation between dragons didn't astonish Tatiana at all.

Bresnyar's wings flattened suddenly to his flanks. He growled deep in his throat and barked his next retort. Shrike's shoulders bobbed in what nearly passed for an apologetic shrug.

"What is it?" Ashe demanded. "What's he trying to say?"

"Oh, skin me alive." Bresnyar stared at Shrike for a long moment, then swiveled his fiery eyes to Ashe. "There is another Trench. He claims its contents are worse, somehow. Quicker, more poisonous. And I cannot find a word for the rest of it, but it involves the air."

"Air," Tatiana hissed. "*Shrike,* is Jad manufacturing Sorcel that can be *inhaled* instead of ingested?"

Bresnyar jabbered at the other dragon in their shared tongue; Shrike's wings fanned in a nervous shiver, and he barked back.

"Yes," Bresnyar said bleakly. "This trench has harvested a different strain. Its particles travel on the wind."

Tatiana exchanged a horrified glance with Ashe. Sorcel in water or food was terrible enough, but this…there would be no escaping it. The winds themselves would become an enemy.

She cursed aloud. "We need to close that second trench."

CHAPTER FORTY-SIX

CISTINE FLED UNTIL her legs refused to carry her and the streets alongside the aqueduct were little more than black ribbons beneath a smoke-mottled sky. When she crashed to her knees, her stomach heaved, threatening to spew bile; but she lacked the strength even for that.

Thorne was in Jad's hands. Believing she was furious with him. Perhaps even believing she hated him.

If it becomes a choice whether you return or I do, I will choose you.

He'd warned her, all the way back in the Citadel—why hadn't she heeded that more closely?

Panting breaths and jogging footfalls broke the stillness, and Quill's voice rang from the dark. "I'm right here, Stranger."

That calm, even voice gave her permission to fall apart.

Curling up on the night-chilled street, Cistine burst into sobs.

Quill's silent presence kneeling somewhere behind her was a different support altogether. A quiet energy breathed between them, the same as that day in Villmark more than a year ago when he'd taken her blows after her first fight with Julian—the same steady absorption of her rage and agony, the rock-solidness she'd come to rely on so much.

She'd pulled away so much, but he'd never left. None of them had.

It was some time before she could bear to move, more than an hour curled up with Quill beside her, her gaze fixed across the churning aqueduct while her mind crawled through thick darkness, a memory around every edge—her mother over these past months, her smiles and laughter, her steady wisdom and clever counsel hiding Jad's insidious workings below; Thorne's warmth and life, their arguments these past weeks that suddenly seemed so foolish and infantile.

She had to find them. She *had* to.

But not alone. She'd tried carrying the weight that way, and it had cost her far too much.

At long last, the grief and terror waned, and a plan took shape in their place. When she finally struggled up, Quill rose swiftly beside her. "What do you need from me?"

"There's someone I have to face." Her voice was hoarse from crying. "Will you come with me?"

His gaze softened. "As far as you go, for as long as it takes."

The burden in her chest felt a bit lighter on the long walk back to *Via Hosial*. While dragons stood watch on the rooftops above, Cistine and Quill slipped below the aqueduct to find their cabal at the tunnel mouth, distributing bandages and salves, treating wounds with grim efficiency. Cistine's heart throbbed to see even her father among them, sleeves rolled up, putting pressure on a gaping slash in Shathen's arm while Maleck's quick, steady fingers stitched another on the boy's leg.

All this pain, all this fear...she'd led it straight to their door. Yet here they all were, working together. *Helping* one another.

Half-blinded by tears, she looked up at Quill. "Can you clear us a path?"

With a sharp whistle, he parted the people, and Cistine moved swiftly on his heels. The throng closed back together behind them, a few voices raised in terse recognition of her silver-streaked hair and swift stride. Questions followed her, but she didn't answer any. These people were not hers to soothe and encourage; she left that daunting task to Kashar and Sacha, buried in the ranks together while she and Quill slipped into the heart of *Via Hosial*.

The mothers and children had emerged from the hiding places they'd retreated to when Cistine had left for the fight. Some cried; others stared blankly at the dim braziers. Suljafar's Tribe clustered around him like limp petals on a dying rose, the elderly man's countenance barren with grief.

"Stars, I hoped we were done seeing faces like that," Quill muttered, sliding a cinnamon stick between his teeth.

Outside the familiar chamber, Cistine halted, motioning him back. "I have to do this part alone."

Though his eyes narrowed, he merely said, "Here if you need me, Stranger."

With a parting nod, she made her way down the short hall to Esmail's private grotto.

She found him sitting at the map table, as still as he'd ever been, bloody hands folded and pressed to his lips. He didn't raise his head at her appearance—but nor did he send her away.

"Twenty-three," he said while she stood in the doorway, trying to summon the courage to speak. "That's how many people I lost tonight. Nazir was one of them."

Cistine's heart twisted at the thought of Suljafar's smiling, enthusiastic son, of his wife now a widow and the half-orphaned children sprawled in Suljafar's lap. "I'm so sorry, Esmail."

"As am I." A bleak smile turned his mouth. "Have you come to gloat? To tell me battle was always going to find us, no matter how I resisted?"

Her throat was too tight to answer.

"I know what you think of me," he added. "Esmail the coward, Esmail the arrogant, Esmail the selfish. But what I am, Princess, is a failure."

That stirred her feet. Cautiously, she slid into the chair across from him. "How do you mean?"

A dull scoff scraped from his throat. "I was the one who encouraged my father and brothers not to let Jad take our possessions and land. I was the youngest, the boldest, the most foolish. I whipped them into a frenzy to stand against him. And then the King's Shadow came."

Cistine shuddered at the specters dancing in his eyes, Sacha herself clearest of them all—and Esmail didn't even know it.

"They hid me in the cellar because I was the youngest, though I was already halfway to being a man," he went on. "Once she finished with them, she left, though I know she was told precisely how many children of Lochan there were. I spent years after that playing the part of the glory-jackal, hungry for vengeance and victory, telling anyone who would listen that I'd take the King's Shadow and anyone else I could with my bare hands. And I have wanted that. But once Sacha found me and placed me in power, do you know what I realized?" When she held her silence, he shot her a rueful smile. "It's all the same. It's the land and possessions all over again. It's the power of control in another person's life, and you're ordering them to die for the cause *you* believe in. Do you understand the weight of that when they fall for *your* ideals?"

Cistine's vision swam. "I'm beginning to."

"Then perhaps you understand why I now play the coward's part." Esmail reclined in his seat. "It's one thing to dream of having the power to destroy the King's Shadow. It's another entirely to have that power and realize you've killed with it before…killed everyone you loved." His narrow eyes traced her face. "I saw you, you know. The moment you walked into my chamber that first day. I still see the angry child looking out of those eyes, ready to fight and fall for anything. You think you could lead better than I, but we're no different, Princess."

"I know." Tears streaked down her cheeks, plopping against her hands. "I *have* been arrogant, and proud, and I've wanted glory, too, because I thought it would fix things—fix *me*. But none of that matters now. The King has my mother and Thorne, and I have to get them back. I need *Alhuru en-Asgaid* to help me do it."

He tilted his head. "Come to finish the Rite?"

"To Nimmus with the Rite!" Cistine shouted, and his eyes went wide. "I came to ask you for help…as a fellow leader, as someone who's lost everything to Jad. Help me, *please*. If Talheim, Mahasar, and Valgard stand together, maybe we stand a chance. We can avenge your family. We can save mine."

Esmail drummed his fingers on the desk. "*Alhuru en-Asgaid* has only survived this long by not confronting the King outright."

"There's more to this life than just surviving. There's *living*, Ez. There's thriving. I *know* you want better for your people...so do I. Together, we can do this. If you love them, *lead them*. You can give them more than spare rations in a tunnel under the world. You can give them a better future...the future you wanted for your family."

Minutes ticked by. He stared at her, stared at the wall, tapped his fingers. Pondered. Then he said, "What did you have in mind?"

The cabal had all gathered outside the chamber by the time Cistine and Esmail emerged, side-by-side; each face held equal parts concern and exhaustion, shadows stamped beneath their eyes. Cistine slowed at the sight of them, heart clenching with dread. Her father was there, too, jaw wired tight, Shathen's blood on his hands. The weariness in his gaze matched hers.

"I'm staying," Cistine said, and when his mouth opened, she added quickly, "just as a warrior, as an augur. I'll go wherever you send me, Papa, I'll fight however you think is best. But I can't go home. Not when he has Mama and *Thorne*." Her voice cracked around his name, and Cyril's cool gaze thawed slightly.

"Well, I for one am glad. We're going to need all the help we can get," Tatiana muttered. "There's another trench, *Yani*. Even Sacha didn't know about it. And the Sorcel they're harvesting from it is worse...it's a powder than can be inhaled, not just ingested."

Cold dread spilled down Cistine's back. "Where is he mining it?"

"North of Arak Shehr, in the foothills." Quill folded his hands around his nape, scowling across *Via Hosial*. "That's why Jad collapsed the stars-damned roads to the coast. He sealed the way to the trench, made it more defensible."

"A failsafe in case anyone did precisely what we've done," Ariadne added. "He knew Ralathi wouldn't hold forever as the *Alhuri* grew."

"The only way in and out is by dragonback," Ashe said. "Or by wind augment, if you've got them."

Cistine flattened her back to the wall, looking around at their harried faces, then at Esmail.

She knew what most would counsel her to do—step away, regroup, assess all these changes and revelations before she struck out to save her family.

A queen did not put her own heart first, after all. A queen did not think of her own needs before her people.

But she was not yet a queen.

"We're getting Thorne and Mama back," she said, and the others broke into grim smiles—even Esmail. Even her father. "Let's sack Arak-Shehr."

CHAPTER FORTY-SEVEN

ESMAIL'S WAR ROOM wasn't meant for this many bodies, but there was no helping it; everyone wanted to know what Talheim's King and Princess, a band of powerful augurs, and *Alhuru en-Asgaid* would drum up together.

Ashe was fortunate to claim a spot standing at the map table before the room packed in; augurs, Wardens, and *Alhuri* jostled for position as far back as the corridor mouth leading out to *Via Hosial.* Anyone with strength to lift a sword and half a reason to care was here; the only small gap was a crescent around Cistine. That was where Ashe stood, faithfully at her princess's side, listening to debate rage across the table.

"A direct siege on Arak Shehr would never work," Esmail argued with Rion, and Kashar nodded vehemently. "It's built in tiers from the destitute Lower Quarter all the way to Jad's Palace of the Sun."

"He made it his capital after Khorraris fell for a reason," Kashar added. "From the upper heights, he would be aware of any assault moving up through the city. By the time you reach the Palace, every trap and fortification will be ready for you."

"Is that where he'll keep Solene and Thorne?" Cyril demanded.

A look passed between Kashar and Sacha that told Ashe enough. Cistine had beckoned her aside while this council assembled and explained in a whisper that the scarred alchemist was the sister Kashar believed he'd killed—and after the shock of that realization had worn off, it made sense. Tirzah, the King's Shadow, wouldn't die easily; and Sacha ra-Fyra held her silence now because she wasn't meant to know the finer points about Arak Shehr. But in that one glance, Ashe saw a lifetime's history.

"Most likely." Kashar tore his eyes from his hidden sister at last. "He'll want them nearby. The endgame is meant to be played close to the chest."

Cistine bent against the table, fingertips tracing the Palace where her mother and husband were being kept. "How long do you think we have?"

"Before he escalates the game again?" Kashar shrugged. "Days, at the very best. Dyalmun only knows what *that* would entail."

"I have my suspicions." Cyril's gaze flitted to Cistine, then back to the map. "We won't let it go that far."

"We do have some advantages," Ashe said. "Dragons, for one."

"True. But two dragons can't besiege a Palace alone," Esmail said. "We need Jad distracted enough that he isn't able to muster his forces when we sweep in."

Kashar cleared his throat. "I might have an idea for that."

Rion scoffed under his breath. "And once again, I ask why we're meant to trust the bastard who captured and tortured one of our own during the peace talks between our kingdoms."

Maleck shifted, and Ashe rolled her eyes. Of course Rion would drum up her ordeal with Kashar when it suited him, as if he'd truly cared what became of her back then—or even cared now.

"You are not the only one who's lost much to this madman." Kashar's gaze skipped to Sacha once more. "Years of life I can never reclaim, crimes I've committed against my own people...we have all been made pieces in his game. But we can finish this and free our kingdoms if we put aside our contempt and fight together."

Ashe hated how noble that sounded—how much this prince she despised managed to sound like a worthy king when the need called for it.

"He's right," Cyril said. "We're already in this, Rion. I'm willing to have a bit of faith." When the Commander scoffed, Cyril gripped him by the shoulder. "For Eboni. For Solene."

Rion's jaw held fast, but his eyes silvered with tears. "For love, Brother."

With a shaky smile, Cyril nodded to Kashar. "Tell us your plan."

Kashar tapped the map over the Palace. "I deliver you straight to the throne room."

A cacophony of protests broke around the table, Quill shaking his head, Cistine gripping her neck with both hands, eyes wide, the augurs and Wardens all arguing at once.

"*Be quiet!*" Rozalie barked, and dead silence fell. "Have any of you been to Arak Shehr? Fought Jad before? No? Then *hold your tongues* and let him speak!"

When no one else argued, she dipped her head to Kashar. Mouth twitching, he went on, "If I act as if I'm still ensorcelled, just another player eager to finish the game, I can bring you and the Commander directly to Jad."

"One man, alone, capturing a King *and* his Commander?" Rion scoffed. "It would never work."

"Oh, I won't be alone." Kashar flashed a smirk at Rozalie. "I will require an ensorcelled assistant."

"Why me?" she snapped.

"Because you have rank and title within the Wardens—the highest of those present besides your Commander. It will raise no brows if I claim to have ensorcelled you to take the Commander while I took the King myself."

Ashe grimaced. Much as she hated the way Kashar seemed to have taken an interest in Rozalie, it was a good plan. Perhaps better than he realized. "You've tasted Sorcel before, Roz. Can you play the part?"

Her cheek sucked in, her gaze fixed on the map. "Most likely."

"He'll hardly look at her," Kashar vowed. "It's just a matter of holding the ruse long enough for the King to reach Jad. After that..."

"The game ends," Cyril said grimly. "We'll do it."

"What about me?" Cistine asked. "Jad will want me there, too. I'm part of his game."

"I know. Which is precisely why you won't be anywhere near that Palace." Cyril skimmed his finger along the map. "This second trench Bresnyar told us about, we need to collapse it. No one here has greater stamina with as many augments as you."

Though distress flickered in her gaze, she nodded. "Leave it to me."

"I'll go with her," Ashe added. "Bres and I can fight off anyone or anything that attacks her."

Rion frowned, but Cyril's nod was quick and unquestioning; it was simply instinct for him to trust his daughter's life in her hands. He gestured across the table at one of the Wardens—the third highest in rank below Rion and Rozalie, though that was by quite a large margin. At least, it had been when Ashe was part of the Cadre. "Farrah, Esmail, and Maleck, you're our coalition of leaders for the three armies on the battleground. While Rion, Rozalie, and I are in the Palace, you strike the city itself."

Pride swelled in Ashe's chest when her *valenar* bent his spread hands to the table. "We'll need a signal."

Quill smirked. "You'll get it. Shrike and I will watch from the skies."

"Divide to your groups," Cyril ordered. "Today and tomorrow, we strategize. Then we take that city."

There was little Ashe and Cistine needed to do to prepare; just a quiet conversation and an inventory taken of their weapons and augments before they settled against *Via Hosial's* curved wall, heads leaned back, watching the vaulted ceiling far, far above.

"You're ready for this?" Ashe asked. "All right with not being part of the final siege?"

Cistine shivered. "I don't need to be the one who faces Jad. I don't need another nightmare after all of this. Besides, this is what's best for Mama...for Thorne. Jad can't use me against them if I'm not there." She shifted her seat, head grinding sharply against the wall. "I still can't believe Jad has him. I can't believe the last thing we did was *fight*."

Ashe chuckled ruefully. "I know what you mean. Before Kashar captured me, that was the last thing Maleck and I did, too...argued like we never had before."

"How did you come back from that?"

"We talked. Did our fair share of apologizing. And afterward, we never took each other for granted again." She shrugged. "Crisis has a way of putting everything into perspective...what you can live without and what you really can't. It happened again at Braggos when we forged the bond." She flexed her hand against the *valenar* mark crossing her palm.

"I thought I was finished taking anyone or *anything* for granted after the Deathmarch. It turns out I've been doing it all year, and I never even saw it."

Ashe snorted. "Doesn't your friend Mira have a saying—something about healing not happening in a straight line?"

Cistine threw up her hands. "But the people around me can't afford to keep hurting while I find out how not to be broken!"

Ashe settled forward, arms crossed on her knees. "Listen to me. If we couldn't afford it, we wouldn't still be here. After all this time, I think I finally know my own value. And my limits. I would've walked away if it was too much...if *you* were too much. But I'm in this, as long as you need me, while you find your way back to being whole."

Cistine cleaned her face on her sleeve and offered a wobbly smile. "I'll always need you, Ashe."

Warm to her core, Ashe rested her chin on her folded arms and stared across the shadowy tunnel.

"I said so many cruel things to him," Cistine added after a time. "He was right about so much, and I punished him for it."

"Well, you'll have your chance to make amends. I'll make sure of that."

Cistine blew out a trembling breath. "I'm glad you're going with me to the trench."

"There's nowhere else I'd go." And it was true; though much had changed between them, though Cistine no longer required a Warden guarding her every step, in moments like these that old strength and love still echoed between them. There was a part of her life that would always make the most sense when Cistine was in it; not as the coming-of-age princess who needed defending, but as the friend who knew Ashe better than almost anyone, whose heart was tuned to hers in perfect harmony.

Cistine gathered her limbs close, chin on her knees. "Do you think I'll be a good queen, Ashe?"

The question was so utterly unexpected, it took her a moment to gather her thoughts around it. "When the time comes, I'm sure you will be. But if I were you, I'd spend less time thinking about being a great queen now and more time being grateful you don't have to be."

Her back rose and fell in a shuddering breath. "Because if I'm Queen now, it means Papa is gone."

A cold chill skittered down Ashe's spine. "Exactly."

They didn't speak again after that; gradually Cistine's posture loosened, and Ashe scooted sideways when she slid down to the tunnel floor, deeply asleep. Looking down at that face, pinched even in slumber, she wished she could offer more comfort than just her presence a safe distance away.

Footsteps padded down the tunnel to join them, and with a gentle *snap*, the first blanket fluffed out, draping over Ashe's shoulders. She pinned it at her throat and offered Maleck a smile when he knelt, fanning the second around Cistine. "Long night."

"Much to discuss." His tone was heavy, but his eyes gleamed. "Esmail is a clever but wary man, and Farrah is an unparalleled Warden. Another of your students?"

"One of Rion's, actually," Ashe admitted. "He didn't churn out all hopeless causes, I suppose."

"I've known that for some time." With a gentle smile, Maleck slid down at her side, and Ashe flung out the blanket to welcome him in. It didn't quite cover his bulk and her brawn, but leaning against his side discouraged even the memory of cold. "How is she?"

Ashe sighed. "Scared. Guilt-stricken. She and Thorne had a fight, apparently. Or...several."

"I can hardly imagine what that feels like."

Ashe jabbed him in the ribs. "Hilarious. You know, there's talk in the Citadel of resurrecting the court jester's position. You should take it."

"And deprive Quill of his life's calling?"

She rolled her eyes. "He's never held a candle to you, you beautiful, braided bastard."

"Indeed." Maleck's gaze fell past Ashe, on Cistine again. "She's fortunate to have you."

Ashe glanced up at him. "Depending on what happens in Arak Shehr, with the King…"

"I know," he murmured. "Wherever you choose to go after this war, I follow you. I haven't forgotten my promise from the Deathmarch."

"Good. Gods, I'm fortunate to have *you*." Ashe let her head fall on his shoulder, a yawn ripping her jaw wide. "There's never been a better pillow in all Three Kingdoms."

His answering chuckle was like a lullaby, and she was on the cusp of sleep when feet brushed stone. Across the way, two familiar voices wove in quiet argument: Kashar and Rozalie.

It was difficult to tell what they were discussing, but it sounded like it had something to do with their part in the plan. Bodies impacted stone, one after the other, and the unmistakable sound of whetstone against blade filled Ashe's ears.

Typical Warden behavior: when in doubt or on edge, there were always weapons to sharpen.

"If you don't think it will work, why did you even suggest it?" Rozalie snapped after a moment.

"Keep your voice down, will you?" Kashar retorted. "I'm not saying it won't work, only that Jad is cunning and mad. What would fool a clear-headed man might not fool him…his thoughts have never run fully on the track of sanity. Does that make sense to you?"

"All I hear you saying is *this plan is a terrible idea, and no wonder, because it's my idea.*"

"It very well may be. But for those few moments we hold the element of surprise, we command the room. And that may be our only chance to ensure Talheim's royal family survives."

"I *know*," Rozalie hissed in tandem with the whetstone's drag. "Why do you think I agreed to it?"

A beat of silence. "You're a decent Warden. Loyal well beyond a fault."

"Oh, and you're awfully observant, aren't you?"

Ashe bit down a laugh that would've given her eavesdropping away. She was beginning to understand why Cistine struggled so hard not to gossip.

"I know I lost our rematch by the lake, but I would still beg of you one favor," Kashar added.

Rozalie kept sharpening. "I'm listening."

"Kill me."

Ashe's breath caught despite her best efforts. Rozalie's blade slid off the whetstone and did not return. Silence, heavy and hard, descended on their stretch of the tunnel.

"If it seems he's won the day," Kashar went on, "or if it seems he might overpower me and turn me back into that *ivrran* I was before...do not let me become that creature again. His monster."

"Why me?"

"Because you possess the dislike of me to do it cleanly, but the sound-mindedness not to remove my head too soon if there's any hope I can be saved." A note of jest slid into his voice, then faded. "And because you have beaten me before."

The quiet stretched on, and Ashe's heart twisted—not for him, but for Rozalie. Who else knew better what it was to be forced into something against her will, violated and desperate never to return to that place?

"All right," Rozalie said at last. "I give you my word."

CHAPTER FORTY-EIGHT

THE HALLS BENEATH Arak Shehr were low and curved, stinking of urine—or at least he assumed they still were. All Thorne could smell now was his own blood and sweat as he swayed forward against the whipping post while the Enforcers gathered the lash for another strike.

They'd tried to make him count them, but he'd refused. He would not give an inch of ground to servants of the King who had dragged his *selvenar* and her family down this path to war. So when his mind caved, begging to give them the count so the pain would stop, he brought Cistine's face to his mind—her laughter on their wedding day, the way she'd spun in her dress, the way her body had felt under his hands, the way she'd looked at him when he'd found the cabal on that ledge in the Calaluns...before everything had become so tangled between them.

He clung to those memories when the next lash struck. Then the next. Then the next. Blood slapped the stone tiles and the tinny echo of his father's cruel laughter rang in his ears.

He rested his forehead on the splintered wood, soaked with the blood of men and women before him, and struggled to breathe through gritted teeth. Every wet gasp pushed back out in a huff, but he couldn't seem to fill his lungs all the way. His body throbbed from the soles of his feet to the top of his head. He squeezed his eyes shut and chanted the Names of his cabal in his mind, bringing their light into the darkness with him.

Darkwind, Dawnstar, Nightwing, Lightfall, Bloodsinger, Dragonfire, Wildheart. Each one an anchor mooring his feet to the floor, lending him the strength of the warrior who carried that Name. *Wildheart, Wildheart...*

"I think that's enough, the balance is reclaimed," a pitchy voice echoed along the hall. "Get him down."

The Enforcers took his bound hands and lifted them off the whipping-post hook. Thorne lurched backward on his heels, knees like water, calves trembling. He shuddered at the sensation of blood slipping down his flanks as the men marched him across the dark chamber toward a figure reclining in its only doorway, passing a wineskin from hand to hand.

Thorne had grown tall and strong and fearless in the company of Chancellors, little less than kings; he knew a ruler when he saw one. This was Jad az-Rashar, stiff-spined and wild-eyed, wearing plainly the madness Cistine had told tales of in the Izten Torkat more than a year ago.

"So, this is the man who bedded Talheim's princess and found his way into Cyril's precious family," Jad said. "You know, that was my plan, too! Marry the princess, make Cyril suffer that way. Clever you, getting in ahead of me. Though I don't think she's quite as much the prize anymore, what with that..." he flaked his fingers in the air, "*killing* power about her."

Thorne gritted his teeth against a retort. Jad's frenzied smile grew at the silence, and he shrugged up from the arch.

"You have her to thank for those stripes on your back. She set the game out of balance when she came to Masiya ahead of schedule. You see, I was meant to take you first, and *then* she came, so I had to set it right. The simple laws of gameplay. And now, now that things are as they should be..."

He uncorked the flask.

"Put him on his knees."

Thorne's struggles were useless, all his strength giving way to pain. He crashed down to the floor with the Enforcers' hands on his elbows and shoulders, twisting his arms behind him, just like back in Masiya's streets. One of them caught a fistful of his hair and wrenched his head back. Jad loomed above, clawed glove stroking the arch of Thorne's throat, drawing thin streaks of blood.

"It's better you married her than I. One more blade to slide between Cyril's ribs. Cut, cut, cut." He jabbed Thorne's ribcage with each word. "Son takes daughter...poetic, yes? Like brother takes sister. That was another of my favorite games. Pity it ended so quickly."

Go to Nimmus, Thorne wanted to spit, but his tongue was clotted up with blood.

"It's time to have a taste...yes, yes, just a little one," Jad clutched Thorne's chin in that taloned hand when he reeled backward in the Enforcers' iron grip. "And then, and then, and *then*, my dear, let's have a different game when your little piece of Talheimic flesh comes for you, yes?" He dug his fingertips into Thorne's cheeks. "You can *smell* her like Cyril *smelled* Solene in that tower where I locked her away, can't you? Oh, I should have had her, too, but then, but *then* there would be no game, would there? No game at all for us to play."

Thorne forced the words out around his swollen tongue. "You're a dead man."

"Someday, someday, like my father!" Jad sang, raising the wineskin in a shaking hand. "But *first*, the game. This is how you break a kingdom, this is how you break your foes...first you take his love, everything he knows..."

"No," Thorne croaked. "I won't drink your poison."

"Who said anything about a drink?" His grin bobbing madly, Jad tossed back a gulp of wine, hurled the skin away, then dipped into his pocket and pulled out a fistful of black powder. Cackling, he blew it across Thorne's face.

It stung like hot sand and tasted of ash crawling down his throat. He coughed and sputtered as Jad's men released him, and the madman himself stroked Thorne's jaw like a loving parasite. He jerked away, but could go no farther; his vision shivered, turning silver at the corners. The light spread in lilypad dapples, eclipsing the whole room. Paralysis took hold, and Thorne heard his own breaths, distant, echoing, a tide speeding and slowing...

No. No. Darkwind, Dawnstar, Nightwing, Light...Light...

He was forgetting. It was all slipping away.

Cistine, Cistine, Cistine.

A flash of augment-shocked hair, her face smudged with dirt, her smile bright, shining, full of love...

Slipping away.

Darkness, fetid and damp, unspooled around him.

He woke on his knees, head raised, looking out from a new form. Before him, a craggy, smiling face and dancing eyes. This man was Lord, Master, King, Creator, Maker and Unmaker.

Gamemaster.

"There you are, welcome!" the Mad King said. "We're going to play a game now. Let's confirm a rumor my lovely spy whispered to me and set the last piece on the gameboard." He bent forward, hands resting lightly on his knees. "Tell me what happened on the plains of Eben outside Jovadalsa the day you went to confront your father."

CHAPTER FORTY-NINE

H E WAS FINISHED lying in bed, waiting for the world to end.

It took him two days to rise, and weakness still riddled his limbs when he moved; but Aden Bloodsinger, son of the Lion, son of the Storm, would not be bedbound while his cabal went into another battle without him. He would not leave Solene in a madman's hands while servants tended him night and day.

He was tugging on his boots when the voice came from his doorway. "I'm surprised it took you this long."

Letting his foot slide to the floor, Aden turned his eyes on Mira. She had a Vassoran guard's bearing today, arms crossed, posture firm between him and escape, but exhaustion and sorrow stamped her face.

It was the first time he'd seen her since that flooded, broken chamber where she'd called him back from the Sable Gates. He didn't expect the ferocity of his emotions at the sight of her wan countenance and weary eyes.

"I'm surprised it took *you* this long to visit." He rose, sweeping his hair back with one hand and knotting a leather cord around it.

"Can you blame me?" A harsh, breathy laugh. "What company do you need from a hypocrite and a coward?"

Sword harness in hand, Aden swung sharply toward her. "You are *neither* of those things."

"Please, Aden, spare us both. I of all people can't flee from the workings of my mind." With a deprecating smile, she stepped inside his room. "After how cruelly I dealt with you over your penance, about what you see when you look at me, do you know what *I* saw that night—why I've avoided you since?"

It served neither of them to tell her just how much he'd turned that question over in his mind, waiting two days for a visit that never came. "It doesn't—"

"I saw Sander." Her voice dipped around his name. "I saw what it must've been like for him at the end. I saw myself losing you as I lost him."

A hundred replies danced on the tip of his tongue, and he spoke none of them, merely shrugged into his sword harness and belted on his knives.

Mira's hands caught his. She had moved into his breathing space so swiftly, he had no time to put distance between them. "You shouldn't go. You're still injured."

"I'm healed enough, thanks to you and that augment."

She shook her head. "This Citadel is full of terrified people without a king, a queen, or a princess to soothe them. They need a leader. They need *you.*"

"It's you they need." Aden gently freed his hands. "You have wisdom, strength, and cleverness to spare. My *cabal* needs me. I can't let them fight this battle alone when it might decide the future of all the kingdoms. I must *finish* this." He stepped past her, snatching up his armored cape and casting it over his shoulders, then striding for the door. "I'll return in a few days."

"I've heard that before."

Aden halted at the crack in her tone, head bent, shoulders sagging under the burden. With his hand to the door, the forbidden words escaped his mouth at last. "I'm not him."

Mira's breath audibly hitched.

Run, his mind begged. *Do not pursue this.*

But he wasn't fleeing this time. He was looking back, still holding to the knob. "I am not him," he repeated softly. "I *will* come back."

Mira stood by the bed, one hand covering the hollow of her throat, her sternum—protecting the heart that had endured more suffering than it ought to, been broken in ways he would never understand. "He said the same thing. It was the *last* thing he said before he left Holmlond."

Aden swallowed a curse and let go of the door, turning back to face her. "If you ask me to stay, I will. For you. Not for myself, not for this Citadel, but for *you,* Mirassah Brighteyes."

She blinked. "Aden—"

"Ask me to stay."

She held his gaze for so long his courage failed, and he wondered if he really could stay and keep the peace beside her while his brothers and sisters bled and fought, perhaps even died, to bring the peace they all longed for.

He didn't know if he could. But he would try until he cut his teeth on the impossibility and bled, just to say he'd given her what no one else had been able to: the choice between her heart and the war.

Mira blinked several times. Then she drew the dagger belted at her waist, striped it lightly against her palm, and stepped toward him, the hilt extended, a clear challenge in her eyes. "I know now how fiercely you keep your oaths. Swear it to me. Swear it and come home."

Aden took the blade, and the sacred trust that came with it, and made a light slash crossing the vow he'd made at Sander's death. Blood welled up like a memory of holding his friend's dying body in his grip, a reminder of the promise forged then.

This oath was not so different...yet infinitely more sacred.

He clasped Mira's hand, blood to blood, and held her stare. "I will come home to you and Nadeem. I swear it."

Her mouth twitched into the most unsteady smile he'd ever seen, freeing a single tear to travel down her cheek. "And I will watch for you. Don't keep me waiting long."

CHAPTER FIFTY

ROZALIE ENTERED THE city of Arak Shehr with an augur's threads on her body, a fire augment hidden in the seams, a blade in her hand, and a heart pounding fit to burst.

She'd almost let down her guard at the sight of the plain outside the city, a fertile land where the harsh dunes gave way to hard soil, hardy trees and stones, and stunted grass pushing up all the way to the fortressed outer wall. Pilgrims streamed in and out, likely bringing tithes and deeds and other treasures for Jad. The Enforcers at the wall had hardly even looked twice when they'd slipped in among the stream.

She wished anyone besides Kashar was with her...some friend she could truly trust. But this was all they had: a brief plan, a tide of cowled allies slipping inside with the pilgrims to await the signal, and this unreliable Prince to whom she owed her head at least once.

She tried to focus on other things—the crunch of packed sand beneath her feet, the height of the city ahead, the destitute quarter around her. Arak Shehr might've been lovely in the hands of any other ruler, but from Kashar's stories over the past two days, she knew rot festered in its heart; and now she saw it with her own eyes.

The homes and bazaars and shops grew upward on tiers of foothills from the mountains behind the city, the architecture itself all uniform sandstone and brown-brick buildings trimmed in scarlet. The occasional tower rose above the flat rooftops, tipped in golden onion domes that inferred some importance. But the people who whispered in the markets where Kashar and Rozalie passed, marching Talheim's King and the Cadre Commander in rope bonds, all had suspicious gazes and angry mouths. A few Enforcers, recognizing the prisoners, spat and laughed.

Rozalie's nerves jangled, but it wasn't wild fright; it was practiced fear, honed like a blade, pressed to the edge of the Novacek name. She was party to whatever came next, leading her own King to the throne of a madman. If danger or harm befell him, it would be on her shoulders.

Kashar turned his hooded head. "I feel like I haven't seen this city in years. Look at it."

Rozalie followed his gaze to a line of slaves being sold from an auction stand; her stomach flipped nauseatingly with the memory of how being bought and sold felt, the back-bending weight of the degradation and shame. "It wasn't always like this?"

Kashar angled between her and the block. "When I was a boy, no one sold flesh in the streets. Mahasaris looked out for one another. If your neighbor was hungry, you fed him. If a field needed plowing or a vineyard tending, people came together to do it. That was how Tir—Sacha and I survived. Those who had nothing still gave us a bit to fill our hungry bellies."

Rion snorted under his breath, but Cyril's head angled slightly, like he was really listening.

"Did I not realize how bad it became?" Kashar muttered, half to himself. "Or did I just not care?"

"You care now," Rozalie grunted. "That's what matters."

"I just hope it will be enough." Kashar shaded his eyes, peering up at the spires and gold minarets high above the Lower District, a structure at the city's apex like a glistering jewel smoldering in early-morning light. "There it is. The Palace of the Sun."

Rozalie eyed him shrewdly. "It almost seems like you miss it."

He shrugged. "It was my home for decades. Why shouldn't I miss the way its halls gleamed when dawn struck over the mountains, how its corners turned every hall to a prism?"

"You make it sound like a dream."

"To the bastard son of the King's half-brother raised in the streets most of his life, it was."

There was so much to unravel in that reply, Rozalie answered nothing.

Kashar marched their small entourage up endless flights of stairs along the tiers, past checkpoint after checkpoint, each one a bricked arch and a wall tipped in fatal finials, dripping with Enforcers. Dread pooled in Rozalie's core, nudging at the edges of her anger, but none of Jad's men remarked on Kashar's return; they let him pass and watched him go with beady, dark gazes.

Rozalie didn't envy Maleck, Esmail, or Farrah. They would have their battle carved out for them with these ones.

It was midday, the sun burning their scalps and the stone blistering under their feet, when they at last reached the Palace of the Sun perched at the upper tier. Its walls were plated in pure filigree that dazzled in the daylight, the dome sizzling like fire. Scaffolding clung to its eastern edge, where Jad seemed to be expanding an entire wall outward in the shape of a man's face gazing over the city. Notes of deep lavender and white-gold glinted where the walls met, both beside the keyhole-shaped doorway and along the Palace's reflective walkway. Smoke wafted in sensuous curls from broad bronze basins near where Enforcers stood guard, carrying wicked pikes.

"More for the harem?" one sneered.

"Even better." A sharp tug on the rope brought Cyril forward at Kashar's side. "I bring a prize for my uncle: King Cyril Novacek and his Commander, captured while plotting a siege to rescue the Queen."

The second guard scoffed. "A siege? What do they think this is, Khorraris?"

"Who's the *basac*?" the first demanded.

Though Kashar had called her the same thing when they first fought, his spine straightened sharply now. "Another Talheimic prize."

"A poor one, by the look of her. He won't like you bringing a woman as a guard."

"I'm sure he's going to care when she's helping me march his greatest adversary to his doorstep," Kashar sneered. "Let me through, I'm in a bit of a hurry."

"His Eminence is in the Parlor of Winds." The Enforcers stepped aside and pushed open the door.

The Palace itself was grand, Rozalie had to admit, with floor-to-ceiling windows playing daylight over low wading pools and potted ferns in the foyer. People lounged on the edges and drank wine, laughing and chattering. Kashar, Rozalie, and their captives swiftly left them behind, hurrying down great halls with high rafters and bronze chandeliers glittering in candlelight, past doors of deep brown wood so polished, she saw her reflection when they passed. One was open, and Rozalie caught a glimpse down a short hall toward so much lush greenery, she slowed and stared.

Kashar nodded past her. "That is the *garriqah,* our oasis. We cultivate things there that can't grow in Mahasar...well, except for deep in the mountains. It was my favorite place when my uncle first brought us here. I'd wander the rows sometimes and pretend I was in another land—"

"Now isn't the time," Rozalie hissed, but she regretted interrupting his one good memory of this place almost as much as she regretted the traitorous part that could've kept listening while he painted a vision of this kingdom he once knew before Sorcel stole him away.

They left that hall and mounted grand, serpentine staircases, flight after flight through domes dripping in cushions and blown-glass ornaments and down long halls full of gossamer curtains in every color, where ensorcelled visitors and Jad's harem were tended by blank-eyed servants moving like puppets on their strings. At last, they exited a great half-circle hall onto a terrace and climbed a steep set of outdoor steps to a broad ledge and an open-sided parlor, so perfectly round and high it had to be directly beneath the Palace dome. The scaffolding was at their height now, jutting out to the right on the other side of the sheer curtains that framed every open archway in the room.

With a last nod to Rozalie, Kashar led them beyond the veils.

The room was cooler than she expected with only the thin fabric blocking the sun. Enforcers stood on silent watch at the stone arches, motionless as the potted plants beside them. A long scarlet rug spread like blood to a serrated throne of volcanic glass at the back of the parlor.

On that throne, King Jad. And at his feet, the Queen.

Rage scalded Rozalie's throat at the sight of Solene Novacek, shackled and slumped against the razor-edged seat, face marked as if by wildcat talons—or those clawed gauntlets of Jad's. Angry and inflamed where tears ran into them, the marks stood out stark against her pale face, but she didn't seem aware of them, staring dully at her hands; possibly ensorcelled, but more likely defeated. Rozalie had seen that look on her fellow brothel girls so many times, had felt it looking from behind her own eyes when the drugs had run their course and she'd realized what they'd done to her, what she'd been made to do.

Broken. Solene looked so *broken*.

Cyril choked, bearing forward. Jad raised his head at the sound, then bolted to his feet, gripping the armrests of his throne. "*Cyril.*"

Solene's heavy gaze followed Jad's, and every last lick of color slid from her features. Open-mouthed, her breaths staggered in and out. The King shifted forward again, the line of his shoulders tensing.

"Greetings, Uncle." That smooth, ensorcelled tone was back in Kashar's voice, adopted so perfectly even Rozalie believed it for a moment. "I'm told by the Enforcers you thought me taken or killed. That's a pity."

Jad's face twisted with suspicion. "You broke the rules. You were meant to stay in Middleton until I had the Prince-Consort in hand."

"Yes, well, I had a bit of trouble with the pair from those sham talks." Kashar strolled forward, and Rozalie followed him, pushing Rion along and fighting not to bristle when the Enforcers enclosed them from behind. "I had to let them defeat me, play prisoner, then turn on them when the time was right."

"Is that so."

"How else do you think I captured such a prize?"

Jad's dilated gaze leaped from Kashar to Rozalie. "And who is *this* helping you? I know that face..."

"One of their prized Wardens. She helped me lure and capture the King." Kashar rolled his eyes. "Really, I don't know why they let women into their guard. A few drinks and she was suggestible enough."

Rozalie barely kept herself from glaring at him. He was too right—a mistake she'd never make again.

"Well, we are *quite* the persuasive family, aren't we?" With a demented giggle, Jad drove his foot into Solene's back, knocking her forward on her knees. Rozalie almost lost her grip on Rion when he flexed against his bonds; beside him, Cyril breathed his wife's name.

"Cyril," the Queen sobbed in reply, "no, *no*...why are you *here?*"

"Isn't it obvious?" His voice cracked around a laugh. "I always find you. I *always* come for you."

Solene wept in earnest now, shifting forward on her knees. "I'm sorry, Cyril. Oh, gods, I remember everything I did..."

"I know, my love. I know."

"Ah...*no*," Jad laughed. "I don't think you do know. Not really, not yet, not *everything*." He slid two fingers into his mouth and whistled so shrilly, Solene and Kashar both flinched. Still, it took a moment for Jad's newest puppet to arrive, as if he knew the grand entrance his master wanted him to make.

Rozalie had never truly feared Thorne; she'd known him too early as the man who held Cistine's heart. But seeing him in battle armor, swords drawn, and that dullness in his eyes beneath an ensorcelled silver sheen, like the very spirit had been torn from him...all of it together made her guts shiver with dread.

This was not like when Kashar was ensorcelled. This was something far worse.

"It's quite interesting, the effects of this new plaything I've discovered," Jad mused. "You know there are drugs that can twist the mind, yes, Kashar? Open it up to suggestion? I used to tell you and your sister stories of that, didn't I? But it can take years and years and *years* to achieve. What if we could have it from the start? Make weapons of our enemies with a single breath?"

"I'm listening." A streak of nervousness ran through Kashar's tone.

Giggling, Jad beckoned Thorne closer. "Put your throat in my hand."

Thorne shoved his neck against Jad's gauntlet so hard, his skin opened and bled. Cyril jerked forward, and Kashar towed him sharply back.

"Fascinating," he said, but the belligerence in his tone was barely-contained.

Rozalie's pulse thundered. This must be the new Sorcel from the second trench, so absolute in its effect she didn't even see a flicker of the Thorne she knew.

Solene's voice cracked out suddenly, raw with grief. "Let go of him!"

Jad pushed Thorne away. He didn't even move to press his own wounds, bleeding freely in thin trickles down the sides of his neck. "Isn't this delightful!" Jad crowed, clapping his hands with a sound like ringing blades. "All that's missing is..." he trailed off, scouting the Parlor entryway, then glancing between Cyril, Rion, Solene, and Thorne, then back to Cyril. "Where's the rest of it?"

Kashar's grin froze. "The rest?"

"Where is *Cistine*?"

Brow creasing faintly, Thorne raised a hand to graze the bleeding rivulets on his neck.

Somehow, Kashar's frown seemed genuinely confused. "The Princess? I heard she was here, why should I have her?"

"No, she was with *him*! The Enforcers told me! Didn't you see her in Masiya?" Jad gripped fistfuls of his hair near his temples. "*No!* This is not how the game is meant to be played! *Princess* comes to rescue Prince, Princess kills Queen, Prince kills Princess, Commander kills Prince, King kills Commander! And *I kill the King*!" He drove his foot into a potted fern at the foot of the dais, toppling it with a tremendous crash; everyone except Thorne flinched at the sound. "This is *all wrong*! You unbalanced the game!"

"I am not here to play your game," Cyril snarled. "I am here for my wife and son. And for your head."

"No, you *are* here to play the game! But then you *broke* it! Where is your pretty daughter, Cyril? *Where is that scheming little whore?*"

Solene and Cyril both tensed, but Cyril recovered first, smiling viciously. "Somewhere you'll never reach her."

Jad's lips fumbled over half-numb words. "You set the game out of balance...there's too many and not enough..." His voice rose suddenly, its pitch and volume so high Rozalie's eardrums throbbed. "*Very well!* We will have our *glorious* ending, but your allies will take no part in it, to set the balance!"

An Enforcer's boot slammed into Rozalie's back. Her knees pounded the stone floor, and Kashar's gaze shot to her, then back to his uncle. "What are you doing?" There was a flicker of panic in his voice, too invested—too *real*. "This is *my* spy! I need her to keep these men subdued!"

"Not anymore!" Jad stomped forward, fingers weaving into Rozalie's hair, and before she could think of a reason to dodge him without breaking the ruse, he dragged her to the foot of the dais and flung her down. His boot landed on her chest like an anvil, and panic flooded her straining lungs. "Too many Talheimics, not the right ones, we end this *now*..."

His blade snapped from its sheath, sailing for her throat.

"*STOP!*"

Kashar's shout roared on the heat-spiced wind snapping the drapes along the Parlor edges.

The knife froze an inch from Rozalie's neck. Slowly, Jad's head revolved toward his nephew. "What did you say? *What did you say to me?*"

Kashar's dark eyes were bleak. He knew precisely what he'd done.

Slowly, Jad straightened. "You...you want to *spare* this delicate Talheimic flower?"

Kashar gave no answer, not even a twitch of muscle.

Jad curled a taloned finger. "Come here."

Rozalie didn't understand why he submitted so willingly at first, without an explanation or a lie; then she realized Rion and Cyril were playing with their bonds while everyone else watched Kashar. He halted before his uncle, almost within reach of Rozalie's fingers. Her field of vision pulsed with every breath, Jad's weight bearing down on her chest.

"Kneel," Jad ordered, and Kashar did.

Cyril's breathing shifted. Rozalie forced her head aside and caught his subtle nod.

Jad gripped his nephew's chin, tilting his face up to the sun—examining his eyes. Then he shrieked, talons piercing Kashar's jaw so hard he groaned. "I *knew* it!"

Rozalie curled up both feet and slammed them into Jad's gut; the Mad King howled in rage, hand diving into his pocket for another weapon, and Kashar bowled into Rozalie, knocking her out of the way.

Dark dust fumed from Jad's hand and dashed across Kashar's face when he spun back to confront his uncle.

For an instant, no one moved. No one breathed but Kashar, gasping and choking, pawing black sand from his eyes. Then Jad looked down at him, gaze coldly insane, and said, "Remove yourself from the game."

Cyril and Rion moved without warning, hurling back into the Enforcers, sweeping their legs, then smashing their heads to the floor. They took up the dazed men's scimitars and lunged at Jad, swords clashing his in a hail of wild sparks.

By the time Rozalie recovered from her shock, Kashar had drawn the dagger at his hip and aimed it toward his own chest.

"No!" Rozalie lunged, gripping his hands and staying the knife. They tussled for it a moment, then Kashar flipped them the same way she had when they'd fought by the lake. All at once the knife wasn't aimed for his chest anymore—it bore down toward hers.

Panic yanked his name from her mouth. "*Kashar!*"

The knife's tip froze an inch from her sternum. Dark eyes widened. Light popped in them, then fizzled out.

"*Raqi.*"

He dropped the knife and swung off her, scooting away on his haunches, hand clapped to his nose and mouth where the bitter brew had entered his body. Horror flooded his once-arrogant face.

"Kill me!" he shouted over the cacophony of blades. "Kill me *now!*"

Was he pleading of his own accord, or because Jad demanded it?

"Kill me, *Raqian*! You gave me your word!"

Rozalie lurched onto her knees again, taking his cheeks in her hands. "Look at me, Kashar! Don't let him do this. We don't let our abusers win. We fight back!"

His betrayed gaze fixed on her, hands clenching for a knife that was no longer in reach. "*You gave me your word.*"

"Now I'm giving you a different one! I'm saving you so you can become the King you were born to be. Nothing we're doing matters if you're not alive to lead your kingdom. Tell me you understand that!"

A beat. Then, "I understand."

His voice was monotone, but a fire struggled in his eyes, flickering through the core darkness. Fighting to make the words mean something.

"Good. You stay alive," Rozalie ordered. "Then I'll consider our match complete."

She snatched up the dagger and struck him hard over the skull. His head fell limp in her hands, eyes rolling up, and she winced, laying him out on the floor. "You can thank me later."

She struggled to her feet, the room in chaos around her: Thorne was up on the dais, holding Solene with a blade to her neck; Rion and Cyril had Jad backed to the foot of it, but the Mad King didn't look defeated. On the contrary, he was laughing as he faced their upraised blades.

"Well, we can do it this way, if it pleases you!" he cried. "We'll finish this part, then put the game back in balance, very *well*. Once Commander takes Prince, then we're restored to only the Novaceks by blood in the last glorious altercation!"

"You're a fool," Rion hissed. "I won't lay hands on a member of the royal family."

"No? Not for anything at all? Not even for the delicious story my spy learned about the history between you from her gossiping little daughter?" Ignoring Solene's furious shout, Jad beckoned his newest ensorcelled warrior. "Thorne, tell Rion what happened on Eben's plains last year."

Thorne slowly released Solene's arm and gazed at the Commander with pitiless, empty eyes.

"I lied to my cabal," he said. "I went to Jovadalsa to confront my father. Cistine and Julian followed me."

Rion's gloves creaked as he fisted his hands. "What?"

"I went out of selfishness," Thorne continued. "A battle ensued. I was wounded, unable to escape alone. And when Julian went back for Cistine..."

"Thorne!" Cyril barked. "Don't—"

"My father destroyed him with a lightning augment," Thorne finished. "He made him suffer agony in his last moments because I was where I should never have been."

For a moment there was no sound in the Parlor but Rion's ragged breaths, trying for calm—and failing.

Then he lunged at Thorne.

"Rion, no—stand down!" Cyril shouted; but not even the King's command was enough to stop an incensed father taking vengeance for his child.

So when Rion and Thorne met each other, blade for blade, Cyril shot forward, swung Solene behind him, and attacked the perpetrator who'd set all this in motion: Jad, cackling like the madman he truly was, plucking a second concealed sword from the arm of the throne to parry Cyril's strike.

Cursing, Rozalie leaped over Kashar's inert form and raced back out onto the terrace. The distant waft of screams rose from below with plumes of smoke and the sizzle of faraway augments.

The plan was in motion, the tiers falling in blade and fire.

Rozalie plunged a hand into the hidden seam of her jacket, fingering the augment Maleck had given her.

It was time to make use of Valgard's power.

CHAPTER FIFTY-ONE

BACK PROPPED TO the hot stones of a Lower District bakery, Maleck traded his attention from the high clouds above to the prowling opportunists looking for someone to rob. He wasn't concerned with them, only with how they could impede the mission if they attacked the wrong person at the wrong time.

Everyone was moving into position: three city districts on three tiers, one for each army. But to hold them, they must first reach them, and now Maleck waited for the signal to begin the siege. He shifted against the bakery's fragrant stones and glanced at Ariadne, paring an apple with a knife beside him, the picture of casual grace.

He wished he felt so at ease.

"You don't need to burn a hole in the Palace with your eyes," she said wryly, offering him an apple wedge. "We won't miss Quill's signal."

"Thorne is up there somewhere." He had tried to keep himself calm, composed, to not think of his friend and brother, his *Chancellor*, captive of the madman who struck such fear into Cistine's heart. Yet whenever he closed his eyes, he saw the Poisoner King's insidious delight the night Maleck had accused him of abducting Ashe. That evening was a black blur of blood and disarray ending in the dungeon, but he would never forget the look in Jad's eyes. And that man, no longer constrained by the farce of peace talks, held Thorne captive now.

Ariadne sighed. "I know, Mal. But we *will* reach him. This ends today."

As if summoned by that notion, Esmail passed by in a casual cloak and cowl, pausing to peruse the baker's window. His lips hardly moved when he breathed, "*Alhuru en-Asgaid* is in position." Then he moved on, vanishing into the packed Lower market.

Minutes later, Farrah Burrian, black-skinned and nearly Maleck's height, strode by. Unlike Esmail, she didn't speak, but the cut of her eyes beneath her hood said enough: the Cadre was in position.

Maleck's heart began to pound.

Sacha and Tatiana slipped from the market and into the alley around the corner from Maleck and Ariadne; with his arms folded and shoulder tilted, he could nearly feel the brush of Tatiana's elbow to his around the side. "Augurs are in place."

Maleck dipped his head, fixing his eyes across the market at the stone arch through which Kashar and Rozalie had led their prisoners—the first checkpoint. "You know your task."

"Get Sacha up to the Palace, find the Queen, rescue Thorne."

And then, fight. Fight with everything they had to liberate this city.

Maleck's blood buzzed with the impending hunt. It was so different from fighting against his brothers and their godlike schemes, the burden of guilt no longer a distraction. Before him was a path straight to his Chancellor, to Cistine's family...to finishing this conflict that had first brought the princess to them.

All his life, Maleck had fled from notions of destiny, believing his could only end in dark temple halls and animal-skull masks. But perhaps the gods had always intended him for something better, something truer...a purpose born with a simple scouting mission to Veran and a raid on the Vingete Vey.

What if this is all there is? Quill had asked him that night in Veran, the night he'd gone away to drink and returned with slaver blood on his hands—though Maleck had not known it for what it was then. *Just this, for the rest of our lives?*

He hadn't had a true answer then. Hadn't known how empty that life was—or how full it could become. How much he could have to fight for.

He gripped Remany's hilt, breathing deep and wishing Ashe stood at his side, and Aden—but those were selfish desires. What they had already was far more than he'd ever imagined: the Three Kingdoms unified, augurs, Wardens, and the *Alhuri* aligned to their marks. All were warriors, visionaries like Sillakove Court, who dreamed of a better life than the one they lived and were willing to fight and bleed for it. He was honored to have been chosen to lead this arm of that revolution.

It felt like grace, like forgiveness. Like redemption.

High above the Palace's golden onion dome, a puff of *Tayir* smoke turned the clouds miasma-green, and Maleck's racing heart halted altogether.

They'd reached the Parlor. It was time.

At his nod, Ariadne shrugged up from the stones and crossed the market, hood towed up to hide her face from the two Enforcers at the checkpoint arch. Maleck gripped Remany tighter and started after her. He didn't have to look back to know that on a count of five, Tatiana and Sacha did the same.

With every footfall puffing sand from the stone path, every stride bearing him closer and closer to that arch, the world fell away. A strange, heavy calm settled over him, like the humidity before a storm.

This was it. Their last stand, the final charge...their greatest hope to end this war and free the kingdoms.

He breathed in deeply, time shrinking to the space between heartbeats.

One prayer. One hope. *Just one more step.*

Ariadne's blade slashed the first Enforcer's chest, drawing blood. Before his companion could whirl on her, Maleck swept his legs and bashed his head into the arch, knocking him unconscious. Ariadne kicked the first man, rendering him senseless as well. Screaming broke out, not just from the market behind them, but across the Lower District's rim as the *Alhuri* and the Cadre repeated this assault at every arch, against every Enforcer.

The plan was simple: break down the checkpoints and move up the tiers, taking them one by one, each army dispatching the Enforcers that defended their level; then hold the line until Kashar brought Jad's head to call a halt to the fighting.

But now time moved against them. Esmail, Kashar, and Sacha had estimated precisely thirty seconds for the Enforcers at the next checkpoint to take up arms and ring the warning bells attached to their arch.

Three armies. Thirty seconds. Now twenty.

"*Go!*" Maleck bellowed, and all across the market augurs whipped off their cloaks and shattered their flagons, preparing to hold the broadest tier with their best weapons. Pops of lightning, tines of ice, and curls of shadow burst on the edge of his vision as he pounded up the steps, Ariadne beside him, Tatiana guarding Sacha a pace behind. The steps snaked between homes and shops on the steep incline, then veered; he caught a glimpse of the next arch across a broad ledge just as the Enforcer at the bell caught sight of *him.*

The man's hand was still raised to grip the rope when a throwing knife slammed straight through his palm, nailing it to the bricks. Maleck whirled to catch sight of Esmail, already on the ledge, offering a deft nod before he attacked his own Enforcers—and those were already occupied by a Warden who broke rank to come to the Mahasari's aid.

It was happening everywhere; augurs shielding Wardens, Wardens intervening for the *Alhuri*, the *Alhuri* defending augurs. Warriors from three kingdoms fought at Maleck's back, and though no one army stayed with the tiers as they were meant to, that was not a failure; Maleck's heart practically sang when they cleared the second tier, leaving the Cadre on guard against any Enforcers who slipped past the augurs or emerged from the buildings stacked across the steep slope. The *Alhuri* raced with the cabal and a handful of Wardens in ever-tightening circles toward the latter checkpoints—the last line to hold.

And then, with a crackle and a fuming flash, a fire augment broke open at the edge of the Palace above. Maleck's feet nearly stopped, his chest aching.

Rozalie's alarm. Something was wrong.

CHAPTER FIFTY-TWO

THE FIRE AUGMENT was a wild, angry beast barely tamed between Rozalie's shaking hands. The few times Aden had taught her to wield this power, she'd nearly passed out; but this time she didn't try to hold it. Desperate and gasping, she sent the fire up and out, and from the cloudbank above an owl-like warble replied. Shrike plummeted over the city, shooting toward its southern edge.

Rozalie's knees wobbled as the fire sputtered in a hail of flagrant drops. Warning bells rose from the uppermost tier; below it, blades stormed and more augments flared. This beautiful, broken city was alive with fighting, and at the base of the terrace's steep staircase, the drum of many armored feet raised the hair on Rozalie's neck.

Another whistling shriek, and Shrike ascended the sweep of the steps, stirring sand by the powerful gust of his wings. He crashed into the bronze bowl on the edge and shook all over as Quill cursed him soundly and Maleck slid from his back, hair windblown and eyes locked on her. "The cabal are on their way. What happened?"

"The game changed," was all she could offer.

With a deft nod, Maleck drew Stormfury. "Then we change it again. Quill, get below...bring the warriors up the steps and hold the line. No one else comes or goes until Jad is dead. Kashar?"

Rozalie shook her head. "Jad ensorcelled him with the new drug.

Thorne, too, I think."

Horror streaked through Maleck's gaze. "Sacha is coming. The antidote—"

"It won't matter if Rion kills him first!" Rozalie shouted. "Come on!"

They burst back into the Parlor of Winds where the battle still raged; Rion against Thorne, Cyril against Jad, the Queen fighting with a pin from her hair to pick her bonds loose, and Kashar still dazed on the floor.

Maleck shot straight toward Rion and Thorne, their blades blurring as they fought, but before he reached them the Commander kicked Thorne against the nearest pillar, his head cracking the stone. He crumbled to the floor, and Rion drew back for a mortal double-handed strike—only for his sword to clash against Stormfury when Maleck lunged between them.

"Get out of my way, augur!" Rion howled. "You're defending a murderer!"

"I'm defending my *Chancellor*—your Prince!"

"I will never serve the bastard who killed my *son!*" Rion broke blades with Maleck and whirled away, gesturing at him with the tip of the sword. "Step aside, or I'll finish what I began with your *face* as a boy."

Maleck's shoulders relaxed, as if a tether had been cut...as if he'd been *waiting* for this fight. "You may try, *Meszaros*."

They came together in a storm of blows, steel ringing while Thorne struggled to rise.

Pain slammed through Rozalie's side, sending her staggering. Distracted by her commander and Maleck fighting like sworn foes, she'd missed the Enforcers the King and Rion had knocked unconscious rallying at last. One of them had struck her; another darted toward Jad and Cyril.

Spinning to clash blades with the man at her back, Rozalie cried out in warning, and Cyril whirled, catching the second Enforcer's blade; but Jad seized the opening, boot drilling into Cyril's abdomen and flinging him straight into a pillar, stone bursting with a horrendous crack all around him.

Solene surged up with a furious cry, hands still bound, the chain linked between them becoming a weapon. She lunged on the Enforcer and brought him down, legs wrapping his waist, metal bonds around his throat, strangling him. Rozalie clashed with her opponent wildly, once, twice, three times, then broke his guard and his leg in the same deft sweep. She brought him down, bashing his head into the floor and laying him out limp.

By the time she whirled back to the dais, Cyril had struggled up, wiping blood from his lip and pulling his blade back to himself. Jad laughed as the King attacked, blades slamming again and again, toying with him, *enjoying* this demented charade.

"Maleck, behind you!" Solene cried, struggling out from under the Enforcer.

The strike of Thorne's blade on Maleck's, pivoting him away from Rion, rattled the backs of Rozalie's teeth. The Chancellor bore down hard on his friend, knowing nothing but battle and Jad's orders. But he was winded, wobbling, and when Maleck heaved him backward with all his weight he stumbled to his seat and was much slower to rise.

Rion wasn't. He moved quick as a biting adder, slamming the butt of his blade into Maleck's skull.

Something cracked—not in Maleck, but in Rozalie's chest. Rage poured into her with a ferocity she didn't know she was capable of as her friend buckled to the stones and Rion leaped over him, moving toward Thorne.

Solene screamed, "Don't touch him! That is an order from your *Queen!*"

"And it's one I can't obey! Julian must be avenged."

Rozalie skimmed over Maleck's senseless form, slamming both feet into Rion's side and hurling him against the wall. Boots planted, she stood over Thorne. "You heard your Queen. *Stand down.*"

Rion, gripping his ribs, straightened and glared at her. "Out of my way, Dohnal."

"You'll have to kill me."

The notion did not frighten her. *He* didn't frighten her. He was just another abuser who used power to break others to his will. She didn't know why she hadn't seen it before, seen *him* for who he truly was—a bully and a bruiser. But his pain and sorrow gave him no right to be ruthless. And it did not excuse murder.

Eyes narrowed, Rion watched these thoughts play across her features. "You forget your place."

"No. This has *always* been my place—between the royal family and their enemies."

Without another word, Rion attacked.

Rozalie had never fought her Commander with his full might unleashed. She'd always been glad he was on their side, but in the brawn of his strikes, the deft might of his attacks, she understood why he alone was Cyril's choice for Commander. Why he had been so irreplaceable for seven long years. Rion Bartos unleashed could bring any warrior to their knees.

He was going to kill her; there was no mercy, no remorse in his eyes. Eboni was gone, Julian gone, every tether cut free, with nothing to lose and no one he truly cared for alive to suffer the consequences of his betrayal. He assailed her with blow after blow, while behind her Thorne began to stir again, to rise. If he attacked, it would be at Jad's behest; she would be caught between two of the most powerful warriors she'd ever known, and there was no one who could come to her aid.

Rozalie Dohnal was staring death in the face. Yet she felt no fear.

It was odd, the calm that washed through her. Outside, the sounds of fighting swelled; within the Parlor, they grew strangely dim. If she could just win enough time for Sacha to arrive with the antidote, if she could just keep Rion occupied long enough for Cyril to kill Jad and call his friend off...

It would all be worth it. If the King and Queen survived. If the Prince and Princess did.

Her life was of value beyond measure; she'd decided that long ago. But she would gladly lay it down if it meant keeping Talheim safe, the royal family alive.

This was what it was to be Cadre.

Rion's blade skipped suddenly past her guard; the serrated tip caught against hers, and with a complicated swivel, he ripped the sword from her hands and sent it skidding across the floor. Chest shaking with a cry of fury, he swooped in, so fast she had no time to block, to pivot, to defend. His blade sang for her chest—

And caught against another Valgardan saber.

Rozalie hadn't felt the wind come in through the drapes; they were still upraised, not yet settled from the current of power passing between them. That was how fast he arrived; fast enough that his blade wedged between Rion's sword and her neck, abrupting that fatal blow.

With a deft spin, Aden broke Rion's guard, hurled him against the pillars, and rendered him unconscious with a ringing blow to the head. Then he whirled, caught Thorne by the arm, kicked him onto his chest, and pinned him down.

"Check Maleck!" he shouted.

Still dazed by his abrupt arrival, Rozalie could only obey, dropping to feel Maleck's neck; his pulse thrummed, but his eyelids didn't flicker at her touch.

"We have to get them out of here," she said.

Aden's gaze shot to Cyril at the next ring of clashing blades. The two Kings were stalemated, swords locked at the hilt, faces inches apart; in the shadow of the throne, Solene fumbled at her bonds again.

"Look at what's become of us!" Jad chortled. "Such a perfect crescendo. Vengeance and hatred and death, isn't it glorious? Can't you hear it, Cyril, the world is *singing!*"

"All I see is chaos you created to sate your own gods-damned appetites!" Cyril snarled. "When does it end?"

"When you have lost *everything*, just as everything was lost in Khorraris! When the world is in balance again, *then* it stops. There is just *one last small inconvenience* to right, to set everything even again. Tell me where your daughter is!"

Cyril kicked him back; Jad howled with laughter and lunged for the Queen, towing her tightly against his chest.

Aden drew his blade and shot forward; Rozalie gathered herself to bolt after him. But Cyril hurled up his hands. "Aden, stop! Jad—*enough!*"

The High Tribune slid to a halt. Rozalie froze. For a moment, the room hung suspended on the King's word.

"Tell me where you've stashed your daughter, Cyril," Jad taunted, "before you watch Solene's blood pave my stones."

Cyril held Solene's gaze. Between them hovered an understanding, fierce and deep and true, that had made them such strong rulers for two decades; that had made Rozalie want to serve them, even to her last breath.

The pause hung suspended for a lifetime while the King looked at his Queen, the clawed fingertips of Jad's gloves beginning to pierce into her neck, making plain the impossible decision before him: his daughter or his wife.

One would die today.

And then, like a dark wind moving through their midst, a challenger stole their focus.

Sacha ra-Fyra stepped into the Parlor, dark hair undone, a vial in one hand and a blade in the other. Her gaze cast over Kashar, unconscious on the floor, then over Thorne, pinned beneath Aden's knee, and Maleck unconscious in Rozalie's grip.

Then she looked at the dais with a face Rozalie had seen in the mirror so many times: a woman facing the unspeakable horrors of her past.

The vial tumbled from her hand. Aden barely caught it before it shattered. And while he whirled back on his maddened cousin, Sacha said, "Enough, Uncle."

Jad's head whipped aside, manic eyes black as twin graves. Grimacing, Rozalie released Maleck and scrambled up, taking hold of her own blade again as foul intent filled the chamber.

"*Tirzah*," Jad breathed. "No, this is not...the game doesn't allow for the *dead*."

"I was never dead...only fleeing from you and every shadow you made in me." She stepped forward, mouth twitching in a grim smile. "But I am done running. And I will take you with me before I ever let you learn where to find Cistine Novacek."

The blade flipped and she was up the dais steps quicker than Rozalie had ever seen a person move, slamming into Jad with one arm and ripping Solene from his grasp with the other. Tucking low, she rolled them down to the floor, out of reach. The Mad King whirled as Cyril cut in, swinging to cover their escape; Sacha shoved the Queen into Aden's arms and whirled back on Jad just as he kicked Cyril off the tip of his own blade where he'd impaled him through the shoulder.

Solene screamed as her husband staggered backward off the dais and collapsed to his seat, and Sacha surged between him and Jad, blade laid back against her arm.

"Not another step." Her tone didn't belong to an alchemist in danger; it belonged to a warrior on familiar battlegrounds. "I won't let you finish the game. I've let it go on too long already."

Jad's lips fluttered with a sickening giggle. "I seem to be seeing shadows. So, *you* know where the Princess is?"

"Where all the lost things go." Sacha tipped her head. "Far beyond your grasp."

"Where you came back from to kill me?"

"I'm not here to kill you. I'm here to save *them*."

"Pity. Your loss."

Jad reared back to strike, and a blur of black and silver shot from the floor at Rozalie's side; she barely had time to shout a warning to Sacha before Thorne mounted the dais steps, stepped up to her side—and drove his blade through the meat of Jad's abdomen.

The breath poured from Rozalie's throat in a battered prayer.

Gasping and bleeding, Cyril croaked Thorne's name.

Jad did nothing to remove himself from the blade. His gaze flashed from Thorne to Sacha and back again. A single word slid with a plop of blood from his lips: "*How.*"

Sacha's smile was feral. "I know your secret. I know how to defeat even your strongest poison. You no longer have power in this kingdom...and none left over me. You made me this way, but my steps are no longer yours to command. You've *lost*, Uncle, your game is finished. You've ensorcelled your last victims."

Jad staggered, panting up at her and Thorne.

And in the horrific turn of that moment, something shifted.

His gaze adopted a horrific, deadly calm, as if the madness itself had fractured…or else become so whole, so complete, it no longer showed flickers of sanity at the edges. "So. That's where she is. The second trench."

And before Sacha could do more than suck in a breath, the Poisoner King kicked Thorne away, ripped the blade from his own flesh, and slammed it straight through Sacha's middle.

Shock and rage punched twin cries from Rozalie and Solene as the alchemist seized up, wide-eyed, doubling backward down the steps. Thorne lunged up to catch her, bringing her down in a heap against him, out of Jad's path; and as Aden leaped to disarm the Mad King, Cyril staggering up at his side, Rozalie and Solene scrambled to Thorne and Sacha.

Even before she saw the extent of the wound, Rozalie knew; she'd faced battle enough to name mortality when it glided among them. But still Thorne croaked, "Keep your eyes open, Sacha. A healing augment—"

"No." Sacha shook her head, freeing anguished tears from the corner of her eyes. "I've been running from this death so long, it…it seems more like a friend. Just tell Cistine I'm sorry, and…that she was right. You were both right." Her head lolled to the side, finding Kashar's stricken form. Another tear slipped away. "Tell him I loved him. I never stopped…I never will. And I will always be watching over him as I did in the…the streets."

For a single second, Rozalie's mind drifted somewhere she had no business going…back to a farmhouse filled with sunshine and wild laughter, two golden-haired shadows always on her heels.

Thorne's gaze, wild with unnamable emotion, held Rozalie's for a moment, dragging her from the clutches of a sister's grief. He smoothed the hair from Sacha's brow. "He'll always know."

Her chest shuddered up, then dropped all at once. And just like that, it was over.

On the dais above them, Jad barked with rage, and Rozalie spun on her knees to see the King and Aden weren't the only ones holding him at bay. Shadows had poured into the Parlor: Quill, Tatiana, and a bristling Shrike from the balcony, Ariadne from the Parlor entrance. Thorne laid out Sacha, still and lifeless, and rose beside Aden and the King, and Rozalie pushed herself up beside them while Solene fell back beside Maleck, lifting his head into her lap, tugging Remany from his sheath with her shackled hands.

The cabal surrounded Jad—trapping him, his gauntleted hand pressed over his bloodied gut.

"The game," the Mad King hissed, "it doesn't end like this."

"Maybe not," Quill drawled, "but *you* do."

He and Tatiana were the first to lunge, sabers drawn; but Jad ducked between them, nimble like he felt no pain from that weeping slit in his side.

Ducking their blades, he opened his palm and blew the last of the Sorcel powder straight into Shrike's nostrils.

Quill's enraged bellow twisted up with the Mad King's laughter. Shrike stumbled sideways, head wagging wildly, and Jad caught him by the lower lip and swung onto his back. "Take me to the western mountains, *now!*"

Not even Quill's cry was enough to stop Shrike; the ensorcelled dragon vaulted from the Parlor, lurched onto the railing, and took to the air. With a snap of his wings, he shot toward the west—toward the second trench, toward their princess and Ashe, utterly oblivious that death and chaos and the end of the game were coming for them on piebald wings.

CHAPTER FIFTY-THREE

GRITTY DESERT WIND scraped Cistine's cheeks above her armored scarf while she and Ashe perched on a high mountain ledge half a mile from the trench—a brief span of open sand with a chasm torn down its middle. Bresnyar, tucked over them against the dark stone, snorted. "Those fumes *reek*. No wonder the *Tayir* are the only creatures who can stomach it."

"Are *you* all right?" Ashe asked.

"I will be, so long as we end this swiftly."

"We will." Cistine touched the augment pouch lashed to her hip and tried desperately not to think of her family in that golden city they'd passed over this morning, now far at their backs—of whether her father had already saved Solene and Thorne, or whether she would be the last of the Novacek line alive at the end of this day.

If she'd remembered how to pray, she would've done it right then.

"There are at least a dozen dragons here," Bresnyar said. "Three times as many men."

"Jad must be trying to make up for what he lost in Ralathi." Ashe drew Starfall. "How long do you need, Cistine?"

She measured the abyss with her eyes, dread tightening her chest. "I don't know. As much time as you can give me. Wielding augments has been...difficult lately."

"*Now* you're telling us this?"

"I can still do it...maybe not as quickly as on the Deathmarch, but I just need time."

Grimacing, Ashe leaped onto Bresnyar's back. They sprang from the ledge, and Cistine slid down after them, limbs spread to slow her descent, the power thrumming in her augment pouch bringing new sparks of life to her fingertips.

She didn't need accolades or titles or an army to lead today. She just needed to fight, to help set the Three Kingdoms free. That would be enough.

Her boots slammed on the sand the same moment Bresnyar's roar and Ashe's battle cry erupted along the canyon walls. Then Cistine ran for her life, for all the lives depending on her—straight to the trench.

Most of the Enforcers were already consumed with the dragon and his Wingmaiden descending like the shadow of death from above; but two whirled to greet Cistine's charge, and she was ready, Kaisill already in hand. She parried one strike, blocked the next, then ducked and swiveled away from the men so their swords clashed against each other. In the confusion, she reached into her augment pouch and broke an earth flagon, crouching and slamming her hand into the ground.

The first concussion sent the Enforcers staggering away; the next brought them to their knees. The third pitched their heads together, and they crumbled in a heap. Whirling, Cistine directed the power down the trench where Ashe and Bresnyar fought; and with a mighty cry, she began to collapse it.

She'd never faced a foe like this before. The ground itself bucked to meet her fingers, a tangible weight to it, like yanking wet clumps of sand up from the hard-packed shore just to hurl them back into the ocean. Gradually, the edge of rock and sand crumbled inward, sending Enforcers dancing to safety or tumbling to their deaths.

Her heart ached for those who didn't escape, but she couldn't stop if she wanted to keep more from dying.

Piece by piece, the trench broke into itself, burying Jad's last weapon and ending his planned game of ensorcelling people by the very air they breathed. Stone dust and sand joined the sickly fumes on the air, scabbing over the wound of that open chasm from which the nightmare of a fresh, horrifying Sorcel escaped.

Then the pain came, with the second flagon's breaking—a rip across her middle so fierce Cistine looked down to see if she'd been stabbed in the same place where Grimmaul had impaled her, long ago in Kalt Hasa.

There was nothing. No wound. But the pain built and built with the power pumping out of her until she had to bite her lips to hold back a scream, the hearing going out from her ears, her chest struggling to rise and fall. She couldn't distract Ashe and Bresnyar—but she couldn't breathe, couldn't form a rational thought, could barely cling to the augments and her consciousness at the same time.

Her knees struck sand. The roar in her senses braided into the roar of breaking earth, and tears soaked her cheeks. Gasping and retching, she clung to awareness, vision dappled with purple and green, the augment still flooding out of her even when her lungs shrank to pinpoints and her head filled with a dull shriek.

It felt like pieces of her were coming undone—so much worse than when she'd healed Thorne, when she'd fled from Jad.

But she couldn't stop. They needed her not to stop.

She was not a queen today, she was a woman fighting for her people, for *all* people. And if that was all she had to give, she would continue pouring out until there was nothing left within her.

Let this be her duty. Her honor. Her sacrifice.

Through watering eyes, she squinted at the trench, only a few feet of its jagged edges left to bring down. She reached out a trembling arm to meet it, begging the augment to peel free of her, to finish this—

A strange, hooting screech broke on the sultry wind. Arm dipping, augments fizzling, Cistine glanced over her shoulder to the east, where a dark shape barreled through the clouds, racing their way.

By the time Cistine's exhausted gaze registered it was Shrike, Quill's dragon, bucking and bawling toward her, it was already too late.

A shadow—not Quill—descended from his back, smashing into her, knocking her off her knees.

Cistine and King Jad rolled in a tangle toward the trench's narrow maw.

Screaming at long last, all the agony and shock pouring out of her at once, Cistine thrashed, limbs digging into the sand. She managed to halt her head-over-heels tumble, feet near the edge, lungs searing. She pawed backward from that fatal drop, and Jad dragged himself upright beside her, wheezing with hate, his blood speckling the sand.

It didn't matter how he'd found her. He was here, this killer, this Poisoner King, the madman who'd stolen her mother, stolen *Thorne*. She'd kept her word and stayed away, and *still* he'd found her, just like in her nightmares ever since that war council more than a year ago.

It was time to end this. The game was over.

Cistine hurled herself at Jad, tackling him back down into the sand with her hands around his throat, squeezing, choking. She reached into the hollowness of herself, into the black pit in her middle, pulling on whatever flickers of energy and power remained—and shoving them all at once into him.

Inside her throbbing head, she screamed for the Death augment to come, like any other augment in her control. She ordered it out from her hands, into his body...ordered it to snuff his life.

His clawed gauntlets raked her sides, raked her face. Anguish burst through her, no sharper or kinder than the pain of wielding those augments today. She dug her fingernails into the sides of Jad's neck, drawing blood, willing death to leave her.

Come! she roared at *Havel*, shutting her eyes. *Come and take him, give him the end he deserves!*

His body went slack. Cistine opened her eyes, squinting down at him.

He was staring up at her, mouth curled in a cruel, vicious smile.

He was not dead. The augment had not finished him.

"The world is out of balance." His voice was soft. "Everything must be put right again."

His claws hooked around her throat, and he lifted her as he stood—

lifted her straight into the air, talons sinking into her, blood bursting, her vision staining scarlet.

Dragonfire scythed through the air, blasting Cistine and Jad apart. She plowed into the ground, and glossy white power impacted her body.

Bresnyar and Ashe, with a healing augment.

Her staggering pulse evened, the pain in her throat vanished, the red across her vision cleared just as Jad lunged toward her again—and Cyril descended in a mighty gust of wind from above, plowing into him with a father's endless strength and rage. They rolled and tussled, grappling across the sand, heedless in their wild descent down the slope.

And before Cistine's horrified eyes, the Poisoner King and the King of Talheim fell over the chasm's edge.

CHAPTER FIFTY-FOUR

THORNE WOULD NEVER forget the sound of his *valenar's* scream when her father dropped into the trench, taking Jad with him; or how his own lungs caught against his ribs, how his heart utterly stopped.

He stumbled from the wind augment's embrace and hit the sand on his knees. The others dropped around him; Quill was up at once, sprinting toward the piebald dragon Jad had ensorcelled, his hands up, shouting at it to heed him. Thorne and the others sprinted toward Cistine, who stumbled upright and hurled herself toward the chasm like she'd leap in after the kings.

The cabal reached her first; not their hands, but their power.

A cord of fire shot from Tatiana, wrapping around Cistine's armored wrist, yanking her back. "*Yani, no!* You can't!"

The Key's might snapped against the augment, ripping it from Tatiana's grasp; but Ariadne was ready, lightning piercing the sand in a dancing glaze to block Cistine's path. Tatiana broke open more fire, creating a shield, and at Cistine's feet the sand turned to mire where Aden dropped, breaking open an earth augment and rooting her in place.

Trapped. They'd *trapped* her.

Thorne knew why; if he wasn't still addled from the black powder Sacha's antidote was chasing from his blood, he might've joined in. But he could only stand and stare, Cistine's heartbroken screams ringing in his ears. She was too drained to take in their augments, too weak to truly fight back; but still she flung herself against the power, fighting to get to the place where her father had fallen.

"*Please!*" she sobbed. "Let me *go*, it's not too late, I can get to him, I can still reach him—!"

"He's gone, Cistine!" Rozalie's voice cracked as she approached, both hands bared—the only one reasoning, not holding her in place. "No one could survive that fall."

Maybe. *Maybe…*

"I have a wind augment!" Cistine shrieked. "I can check him, I can—"

But she couldn't. She couldn't carry him out if a flicker of life remained, or *Haval* would snuff it out. And if the fall had indeed killed him…

If it had taken her father's life, she would be forced to carry his corpse out of the trench with her own two hands.

Heart racing, every inch of him feeling useless, worthless, *helpless*, Thorne stared at his *valenar*, at his cabal, the anguish in all their eyes the same, their bars of flame and lightning holding steady while she hurled herself against them, frustrated sobs ripping from her chest. They were all fixated on her because she was the desperate one. His reckless, loyal wife, who would fall or rise as many times as needed for the ones she loved. For her kingdom. Her *family*.

Maybe he didn't know what that meant—hadn't had the chance to learn as a boy, as a young man. But he'd known reckless and wild and impossible. He'd learned them when he'd heard his grandmother's leg shatter under her son's cudgel. Her screams, like Cistine's now, echoed in his ears.

He could not do what his *valenar* could—he could not wield wind and bring healing all at once. But he could risk, and he could dare, and he could *fight*, as he'd fought for Baba Kallah against his father, and his cabal against the world.

No one paid a scrap of attention to him, not even when he approached them; not when his fingers, featherlight, lifted an augment from Aden's pouch. No one looked, even when Thorne lurched around and broke into a run, whistling with two fingers in his mouth; or when Quill's dragon snapped around Bresnyar's guard and bounded to meet him, taking Thorne's leap onto his back in stride. He knew he'd been spotted only when Quill shouted his name and Cistine's sobs turned to furious screams of denial.

But it was too late to stop him and the dragon from leaping straight into the chasm.

They spiraled down into deep darkness. Thorne didn't know if the creature obeyed him of its own will or because of the Sorcel still coursing through its body, and he hated to take advantage of the latter, but there was no other choice. Despite the armored scarf over his nose and mouth, his throat already burned. Noxious clouds plumed past them, and the beast gave a low, uneasy huff that Thorne's spirit echoed.

But it was too late to turn back now. Nor would he, even if it wasn't.

Thin beams of sunlight still spiraled into the trench. Far below, the shadows swallowed it, swallowed it—and then something gleamed.

A wild curse of relief ripped from his chest, and the next inhalation burned like fire. Coughing and choking, Thorne urged the dragon down to a narrow ledge jutting from the chasm where Cyril lay sprawled, a broken heap of Valgardan battle armor pooled in blood; but when Thorne slid from the dragon's back and stumbled toward him, the King's back fluttered in faint, weak breaths.

Those would not last long. He needed to *move*—but every motion felt like slogging through mud.

Thorne dropped to his knees and crawled the last inches to Cyril's side. He didn't dare touch him in this state; instead, he broke the healing augment he'd stolen from Aden and laid his hands on Cyril's body. The power was a struggle, every drop forced out of him rather than flowing freely; it wanted to stay, wanted to heal *him*, but he refused its pull.

A dull wheeze began in his lungs. His throat felt tight, his head too muddled to drum up a single prayer while he spooled the augment out of himself and into Cyril's broken body. At last, with a wet, rattling gasp, the King stirred, eyes sliding open to find Thorne's face in the barely-broken dark. "Thorne. What are you...*doing?*"

"Saving my father."

He'd never tested any words like those before, but spoken to Cyril Novacek, they felt right. Everything about this felt right, even if it was killing him.

"No...no, go back," Cyril wheezed. "Cistine can't lose us both."

"She's not losing either of us!" Thorne willed the augment to slither faster from his hands. "I may have more to learn, but I know we don't leave one another behind. *I* don't...I fight for my family. And I need you here to teach me everything else."

Cyril's half-conscious eyes struggled to find him, then gave up, shutting again.

Cursing, Thorne abandoned the augment, swung Cyril's arm around his shoulders, and dragged him toward Quill's dragon.

Two steps away, a low, pitiful moan echoed in the dark. "*This is not over.*"

Thorne hesitated, looking back.

Broken, bleeding among the shadows, Jad az-Rashar dragged himself toward them. One side of his face was dented, one half of his body useless, but he didn't seem to feel the pain at all. He clawed forward, inch by inch, blood streaking from his broken, clenched teeth.

"As long as a drop of Sorcel remains in the world, as long as anyone breathes my name, the Novaceks will never be free of this," he croaked. "What I began today will curse them for the rest of their lives. They will always have enemies carrying my shadow! The game is not over...it's just beginning."

Thorne stared down at him—this shriveled Poisoner King, the madman whose shadow Cistine had fought in since she'd first traveled to Valgard, the enemy she had stood against as long as he'd known her; now he was just a weak, writhing, broken gamemaster with nothing left to give but threats and fury.

Still. Thorne owed him for lashes, for corruption, for his own free will stolen right out of his hands. And he owed him for every threat against the Novaceks. For Solene and Cyril. For Cistine.

Arms shaking, he heaved Cyril onto the dragon's spine, then drew the King's sword and stalked to Jad. "You're right: there will always be shadows. But not yours. Not anymore."

He brought the blade down in an arc like a falling star, severing Jad's head from his neck.

The world was a tipsy, vibrating blur when the dragon bore them up from the trench, Cyril an unconscious heap on his spine, Thorne pinning the King in place with the last of his strength. Dimly, he was aware of screams and shouts growing nearer, many voices raised together in terrified rage—then in shocked relief.

Sand whirled up toward his face, a copper-colored blur. Jad's severed head tumbled from his grasp. He barely realized he'd impacted the ground until his forearms started to burn from the hot grains. There were hands on him, people shouting his name, Cyril's name. Someone snatched up the Mad King's head he'd carried back with him, and bore it away.

But all he could see were green eyes and silver hair filling his whole world.

Cistine sprawled on her stomach before him, mirroring his posture with folded arms, her face inches from his—the nearest she'd come of her own volition since the Deathmarch. "I can't believe you did that, I can't *believe*...are you all right? Thorne, look at me! Are you *all right?*"

He raised his head to catch her gaze, shining with tears, her chin on her wrist. Her whole body shook in harmony with his, quivering with the ache to touch one another. To feel for themselves that the other was alive.

He forced a smile, tired as he was, tight though his chest felt. "I'll be fine, *Logandir*."

Then he fell unconscious.

CHAPTER FIFTY-FIVE

ARAK SHEHR STILL smoldered when the cabal crashed back into it—two dragons alighting in an inner courtyard, a wind augment depositing Cistine in a sprawl behind them. Heart in her throat, she flung herself up and sprinted toward a cluster of *Alhuri* near a keyhole-shaped doorway, screaming for the familiar, dark-haired man in their midst.

"Sabir!" His head jerked at the sound of his name. "We need your help!"

He shouldered free of the crowd, striding to meet her. "What happened, Princess? Is Jad—?"

"Dead," she panted. "But my father—*Thorne*—"

She couldn't choke out the explanation for their reckless, selfless bravery. All she managed was a wave of her arm toward her friends dismounting from the dragons: Ashe and Rozalie bearing Cyril between them, Quill and Aden with Thorne.

In undulating Mahasari, Sabir called to a pair of *Alhuri* and dispatched them through the doorway; then he beckoned with a jerk of his head. Cistine let the cabal go ahead of her, traitorous hands clenched at her sides—hands that had failed to kill Jad quickly enough; hands that, if they had, would've prevented all of this. Her father would never have gone into the trench. Thorne wouldn't have gone after him.

If one of them died—if she lost them *both*—

She had believed she was willing to pay any price to end the war. But not this. *Never* this.

Silent, hot tears coursed down her sunburned face as she stumbled after them through Jad's Palace, overrun with Wardens, augurs, and *Alhuri* marching shackled Enforcers away. Servants gaped wide-eyed through doorways, watching their strange procession all the way to what must've been an infirmary, an open-aired room full of tall windows, sheer curtains, and sunlight. A place too fine to stink of this much death.

Cistine's heart jolted at the familiar sight of Rion's body, limp on one of the beds. Three down from him was Maleck, head settled back against the pillows, eyes shut. And sitting at his side, head in her hands...

"*Mama!*"

Maleck flinched, eyes cracking open at Cistine's scream. Solene's head jerked up, the breath gusting from her. "Oh, Cistine..." She stumbled to her feet, took a handful of steps, then froze again when she caught sight of who Ashe and Rozalie carried. Her face blanched, contorting with dread, with terror, then with grief. "No. Oh, no, *Cyril*..."

"He lives." Aden stepped into her path, flashing both hands. "But barely. Let the medicos see to him."

Solene retreated a single step, then broke down on the floor. Cistine did as well, crawling to her mother's side, and if she could've touched her, she would've laid in her lap and sobbed while physicians rushed from every corner of the room to attend the dying King and the unconscious Prince.

The hours that followed were a horrific blur, among the worst in Cistine's life.

She gathered from clusters of conversation traded by passing mouths that they'd secured the city; Prince Kashar, soon to be called King, was somewhere in the Middle District, putting out fires both literally and figuratively, but the fighting was winding to a halt. Most remaining Enforcers had surrendered or fled. All that remained were angry, curious, or frightened people, the kind that needed her help.

But she couldn't raise her voice for them, couldn't muster a single word for anyone. All she could do was stare at the faces of her beloved, injured family on their sickbeds.

At sunset, they carried Cyril to his own room, where the air was fresher and he could be cared for away from the turmoil of the infirmary. And though it absolutely broke Cistine's heart, she left Thorne under the cabal's watch and accompanied her mother up to the private chamber where they brought the King.

While Mahasari physicians dashed in and out, bringing brews and drinks and pillows, Cistine sat on a sofa beside the Queen. She couldn't bring herself to move away, even when her skin prickled at Solene's closeness. In tense quiet, they watched Cyril's shallow breaths come and go, halting every so often. Neither of them breathed again until he did.

"I can't believe this is happening," Solene croaked when they had a moment of solitude, the last physician scuttling out before the others returned. "I don't even remember...so much of these last months is a blur..."

"Do you know who fed you the Sorcel?" Cistine asked hesitantly. What might the council, Viktor, and Mira be dealing with back in Astoria?

A heartbroken smile laced the Queen's face. "It was Eboni, I think. Not maliciously, but because she was the only one I ever trusted to bring me tea. And who gave it to her, I don't know. She was too absent to check for those sorts of things, and I loved her too much to send her away. In the end, they found that chink in our guard and exploited it perfectly."

Jagged rage spiked through Cistine's chest, then abated. For the first time in over a year, she had no one alive to direct her anger toward. Jad, Salvotor, the Bloodwights...all gone. Her rage was an arrow with no target; it bowed from the air and plunged into a yawning abyss, and all that was left was sorrow. "I don't want to remember Aunt Eboni that way. I just want to remember her smiling."

"So do I, Cistine." Solene's voice cracked. "But I'll never forget what I did to her. To Aden, to our *kingdom*."

"It wasn't you, Mama."

"It was enough of me to have them all fooled." She buried her face in her hands. "Gods, I wish it had been enough of me to *resist*."

Cistine had nothing to say to that. She and her mother had both brought about pain, but at least the Queen had the excuse of Sorcel; Cistine had lashed out in her own hurt, let Jad's appearance in Masiya push her over a moral line and drive a blade between her and Thorne.

Solene was right...the Mad King had plotted this perfectly. He'd taken the Queen by Eboni's hand and Eboni by the Queen's, stolen Thorne and pitted the royal family against one another. She knew from Rozalie's account in the infirmary that Rion was aware of the truth Cistine had never wanted him to know: how Julian's death had come about.

Now her father was dying, perhaps Thorne too, and she and her mother were helpless to do anything for the men they loved. Worse than the rest of it, Jad had made them all responsible for one another's pain, so they could never look into each other's faces again without thinking of him.

The room darkened inch by inch, the physicians rotating in and out while shadows crept lower on the walls. When they'd been gone for some time, Solene went to Cyril's bed and climbed into it. She lay with her head over his heart, her body curled tight around him just like he had with her after her pregnancies had ended so tragically.

Once again, Cistine had no part in their pain; she couldn't go to them, lie with them, hold them or be held. She was a silent guard—nothing more.

When the moon rose and Solene's snores braided into her husband's faint breaths, Cistine rose stiffly and stumbled into the adjacent bathing chamber. She found a copper basin already full of water and splashed it on her face, hissing through gritted teeth when the tepid drops found every scrape and rash stamped into her skin from the fight at the trench. But she endured, scrubbing and washing, removing blood and sweat from her hands. She didn't even know whose blood it was. Jad's? Hers?

Why didn't my touch kill him?

She raised her eyes to the windowsill where moonlight scattered around a tall, potted orchid. Hesitant, Cistine walked to it, examining its blush-red-and-gold blossoms; then she buried her fingers in the soil and waited.

And waited.

It happened so slowly, nearly a full two minutes...far longer than she'd held onto Jad. But then the rot crept up the stalk, and the orchid wilted, blossoms flaking off.

Cursing, Cistine swept the pot from the windowsill, shattering it on the floor; then she slumped to the wall and cradled her face in her hands, choking back her tears to listen for any stirring from the other room.

Nothing. Her mother snored on.

"And the last enemy to be defeated is the nefarious orchid."

Wiping her eyes, Cistine looked toward the hall's entry where Kashar stepped over the broken pot and shut the door. The moonlight gave her a good look at the man who would succeed Jad—the one who captured Ashe and nearly thwarted the peace talks in Middleton. And the one who had risked facing his torturous uncle to buy her family time to save each other; to ensure her mother and Thorne walked away with their lives.

A fellow ruler now, just like the Chancellors; and one she might need as an ally, sooner than later, if her father did not recover.

"I'm sorry," Cistine croaked. "I'll clean it up."

"No need. I came to see how your family is, but I suppose this is answer enough." Kashar gestured to the carnage of potting soil and air roots. "He hasn't woken?"

Cistine shook her head, rubbing a chill from her arms. "Has Thorne?"

"Haven't been to the infirmary to check. There's too much else to do. Enforcers to catch, people to calm, antidote to manufacture..." A shadow flitted through his eyes, almost like grief. "After I set aside the portion for your kingdom, of course."

Of course. Because that was why she'd come to speak to the *Alhuri* in the first place. How could she have lost sight of that in the mess of what leading meant to *her*? "We're going to need it. My mother doesn't know exactly how the Sorcel reached her, but there are still Talheimics loyal to the memory of Jad."

"I'll give you plenty. It's the very least I can do after all this."

His pained eyes darted past her, and sympathy and sadness scorched her throat. "Rozalie told me about Sacha. I'm so sorry. She was a good woman."

Kashar snorted. "In fact, she was a mortal terror and an absolute master of manipulation, but I appreciate the sentiment." He scratched the back of his neck. "She left the *Alhuri* with the recipe for her antidote. I wonder if she knew...and what in Dyalmun's name possessed her to face Jad? She had to know he wouldn't rest until she was truly dead."

Cistine gnawed the inside of her cheek. "I think...she was ready to stop running. Whatever that cost her."

"No more running from our *ivrrans*. That's a thought." Kashar dropped his hand and swallowed. "At least she died true to herself. Not a drop of blood spilled from him, even when she could've cast the killing blow."

That was how Cistine wanted to remember her, the way Rozalie had described her last minutes: freeing Solene, saving Thorne and Kashar, and stepping between Jad and Cyril. Not just an alchemist, not just the King's Shadow, but her own woman made of her own choices, to the very last of them.

"I already have a contingent preparing to travel to your kingdom," Kashar added when Cistine didn't speak. "I'm planning to send Esmail— and Mairin, as it's come to my attention on *numerous* occasions the sort of sway women have in Talheim. Sabir I'll keep here, to help quash any rebellion that arises on our own sands. Assuming you're agreeable to having *Alhuri* rounding up their kinsmen within your borders?"

She wet her dry lips at his official tone, one leader speaking to another. "We'll allow it, so long as they report to our Wardens in Astoria and work with them."

"Best to send a few augurs along as well, then. With the right armor, they could travel more quickly."

She nodded. "I'll see what we can spare."

"Thank you." Kashar dragged a hand through his hair. "I assume the trench is dealt with?"

Cistine nodded. "Quill, Tati, and Ariadne collapsed the rest of it as soon as my father and Thorne were free." His name sent a pang of longing through her. With her parents both resting, she wasn't needed here anymore; it was him she wanted to be with, waiting at his side for him to wake so she could apologize the moment he did. "I should go see my husband."

"I'll make certain there's a watch on this door, day and night. They'll inform you if anything changes." Kashar scratched his jaw. "And if you would...deliver a message for me?"

Halfway to the door, a word of thanks grazing her tongue, Cistine paused and looked back at the new King.

"Would you tell Rozalie Dohnal that Mahasar owes her its King's life...and no more favors. She may visit whenever she likes."

The old gossip in Cistine began to stir, but she pushed it down. "Of course. I'll tell her."

Then she slipped out, shut the door, and dashed for the infirmary.

CHAPTER FIFTY-SIX

IT WAS WELL into the night when Cistine joined them, ashen and quiet as a specter. The cabal, gathered on various couches and seats around Thorne's bed, all brightened when she ducked through the gossamer veil that separated his space from the other injured. Though Tatiana ached from the day's fighting, she forced herself up from her sprawl in her armchair and nodded to the princess. Cistine nodded back and whispered, "How is he?"

"Still breathing," Quill said with so little tact Tatiana would've flung something at him if there was anything in reach besides Quill himself.

"His lungs aren't as badly off as your father's," Maleck added, still looking faintly dazed from the blow Rion had struck him, but abandoning his own bed for Thorne's bedside. "The medicos believe he simply needs to rest and recover his strength."

"The healing augment helped," Ariadne added. "He'll be all right, *Logandir*."

She collapsed in the chair they'd left vacant for her, nearest to Thorne's head. Her hand crept onto the pillow, inches from his cheek. "He was so brave."

"Stupid, more like," Tatiana muttered, pulse clamoring while she relived the moment her Chancellor and Quill's dragon had leaped over the chasm's edge. She would've dived in after them if holding onto Cistine hadn't been an effort requiring all their strength.

"Foolish and brave." Cistine's smile was lopsided, unsteady. "That's our Thorne."

Tatiana folded her arms over her abdomen, holding the Princess's damp gaze. "I'm sorry for what we did with the augments. We—*I* panicked."

"You did exactly the right thing," Cistine assured her. "I wasn't thinking…I panicked, too. I've been making plenty of decisions lately that haven't been the right ones, and love doesn't always look like supporting those decisions." Cistine's gaze fastened to Tatiana's so fiercely, her stomach dropped. "If you hadn't done that, I would've jumped in after my father. Even with a wind augment, I don't think I would've been able to get out. And I couldn't have brought him with me even if I did."

Thorne had realized all that in a matter of heartbeats. And he'd reacted, trusting them to protect his *selvenar* while he tried to save her father.

Overcome with emotion and desperate not to let it burst from her control, Tatiana reached for the pulley bell beside the bed. "Well! As long as we're all stuck waiting for Thorne to stop being lazy, why don't we have something to eat?"

"Is it safe?" Cistine asked.

"The *Alhuri* have been out hunting in the foothills," Ashe said. "I'm sure we can convince them to spare a ration."

There wasn't much to go around—some ram's meat skewers, a handful of dates, almonds, and olives each, and waterskins filled from the clean mountain streams—but Tatiana had never tasted a feast so sweet. Between mouthfuls, Aden regaled them with his hunt through council sessions and public forums, in dark alleys and dungeon depths, for the ensorcelled in Astoria. Rozalie broke in, waving him off and making him repeat himself when he said Viktor Pollack, of all people, had been his accomplice; when Ashe asked him to repeat it twice, he flicked his last date into her hair.

Quill, Tatiana, and Ariadne went next, telling their story of golden sands, shadowy chasms, a glittering oasis, and a glimpse into Mahasar's true heart. Tatiana couldn't help smiling when she told them of the Taia family and Yasmin, who would have plenty of time and help to heal now that Jad was gone.

Then Maleck, Ashe, and Rozalie took up the tale, theirs a mess of sweating halls and fighting pits, a musty attic and a lakeside duel. Tatiana noticed how often Rozalie glanced at the door during that story, and made a note to tease her about it later.

Cistine told her story quietly, arms folded on the edge of Thorne's bed, eyes on his face. It was a memory of arguments and darkness and sorrow, but also of dancing and training and the beauty of Masiya. No one laughed or interrupted; they simply listened, solemn in their silent support.

"I'm sorry I've been such an awful friend to all of you." Tears traced Cistine's cheeks when she finally lifted her head from her arms, looking around at them. "I've been rude and selfish and *cruel*, not just to Thorne…I haven't been the person or the princess I wanted to be ever since the Deathmarch, and you didn't deserve any of that. You've stayed with me through everything. I should've fought harder to stay with *you*."

Quill shifted, clearing his throat. "I'm just glad you're here now, Stranger."

"That goes for all of us." Tatiana flung her feet across her armrest, into his lap. "Anyway, a reckless, wise, precious little princess taught me once that we stay together and fix things. So we weren't going anywhere."

"That's why we're *all* here," Aden added, and Maleck shot him a crooked smile from the divan he and Ashe shared by the wall, her back and head propped to his side, his arm flung around her waist.

"And I'm glad you are." Cistine wiped her cheeks. "Gods, I'm *sick* of crying."

"Unsurprising," Ariadne said. "You do it quite a bit."

Cistine threw a date at her this time. It flopped, rather disgracefully, onto the bed by Thorne's leg.

"I thought I taught you to throw better than that!" Quill complained.

Tatiana cackled. "I knew you taught her to throw *punches*—when did you teach her to throw food?"

"Same day you learned good insults. So, *never*."

They all laughed, and a deep warmth settled in Tatiana's chest. These were the moments she lived for, after the fighting and killing and bleeding were over—a glimmer of normalcy, a flicker of happiness at the end of a long, painful road.

"We did it." Cistine sat up swiftly, and the laughter faded. "Jad is *dead*."

Tatiana's happiness cooled into caution. She grazed her palms down her armored legs, straightening again as well, following that cord of dread in Cistine's gaze. "So...everything that brought us together is over."

Ashe dragged herself upright by the seatback, still leaning into Maleck. Rozalie rocked her shoulders back, frowning. They all looked around at one another, a year of heavy memories settling between them; battles fought, specters conquered, friends made and lost. Some they might still lose, if the King wasn't as strong as his daughter.

Then Cistine murmured, "What now?"

"Now, nothing." Quill folded his arms behind his head and stretched out with that lazy cocksurety Tatiana had always loved. "We still have the treaty. Our kingdoms are still joined by marriage. And this...what's happening here, now?" He spun a hand at all of them. "Nothing breaks that."

Ashe laced her fingers with Maleck's. "Nothing ever will."

A broken laugh slid from Cistine's mouth. "Gods, I'm so thankful for all of you."

Quiet swelled in the wake of her words, full of understanding and a love so deep, Tatiana felt like she'd spent her whole life craving it. She sank into its warmth now, so content she almost didn't notice the flicker of movement outside the thin curtain. But then the hair on her nape rose, the way only one person ever really made it.

Stooped from the blow dealt him by Aden, Rion Bartos hovered outside the veil.

Tatiana doubted the others noticed him; he was only really in her periphery, and even Quill, absorbed with tossing olives into his mouth, didn't seem aware of that lurking specter beyond the curtain. He didn't move, just stayed there, like he was listening in on their joy...or waiting for the right moment to encroach on it.

Then, swifter than a man with a head wound from the former Hive Lord had any right to be, he was gone.

Tatiana started up from her seat, and the others all looked at her when she went to the veil and twitched it aside, glancing toward the infirmary door. It whispered shut—the only sign he'd been there at all.

"What is it?" Cistine demanded. "What did you see?"

"I wish I knew," Tatiana muttered.

The silence was different this time, fraught and uneasy. She wondered if they would need a guard on Thorne's bed.

Ashe winced suddenly, grinding the heel of her hand against her temple. "Oh, God's bones...Quill, Bresnyar says your dragon chased his own tail and now he's bleeding."

"Stars *damn* it!" Quill lurched up from the chair. "This is just like Pippet all over again."

"Pippet bit herself?"

"Hilarious." He shrugged into his sword harness. "Where are they?"

"Out on the plain. I'm coming with you," Ashe sighed, swinging to her feet. "You're going to need help...bandaging dragon wounds takes getting used to."

"Admit it, Shei, you've wanted to be better than me at *something* ever since I started training Cistine."

Ashe cocked a brow. "Actually, I've been waiting since the first time you swaggered out of that alley in Veran."

They were still throwing verbal jabs when the door shut behind them.

"I'll go look in on the King and Queen," Rozalie offered. "We can trade shifts if you want, Princess."

"I'd like that." Cistine's chin drooped onto the bed. "Come find me if anything changes."

Tatiana dropped into Rozalie's vacant seat next to Cistine. "Ready to sleep?"

"Yes, but I'm not leaving him. If I close my eyes, will you keep watch?"

"Absolutely." It wasn't like she'd be resting herself, knowing Rion

Bartos was prowling the Palace halls now.

Cistine shot her a grateful smile, curled up in the chair, and leaned her temple on the edge of Thorne's bed. In a minute, she was snoring.

Slowly, the others broke apart; Ariadne first, taking Aden with her to look in on the augurs arrayed through the city, still patrolling for rogue Enforcers; then Maleck, vowing a report on the state of the city after he slept off the last of his headache.

It would be like that from now on, Tatiana knew; lines had been drawn, decisions made that hadn't yet come to fruition. Some would stay and some would go, and Sillakove Court would never be again what it had been at its largest and boldest—a cabal of visionaries sharing every dinner around the same table, laughing and scheming of a better future.

But they could always come back to that. To nights like these, like the one they'd spent in Aden's old home on Darlaska before the Bloodwights returned, drinking and dining and dreaming together.

No matter how far they went, no matter where their journeys took them, they could still come home.

CHAPTER FIFTY-SEVEN

THE WORLD WAS dim when Thorne returned to it from a sleep so deep he had no concept of passing time.

His chest hurt. He lay on his back, simply breathing, watching the dance of wind-ruffled cloth around his bed, the ceiling arching grand and dark above him. His senses stretched in fingerlengths beyond the friction in his lungs, burning like two blades rubbing together, and he became aware of the breeze kissing his bare chest. Someone had removed his armored shirt, and for once he was grateful of that; he couldn't imagine breathing under its tight confines.

A second wind brushed his bare arm. Someone breathing in tandem with him.

He turned his head, chest seizing, heart plummeting and soaring again at the sight of Cistine. She slumped against the bed from the edge of her chair, the only one occupied of more than a half-dozen bunched inside that gossamer veil. Her hair fell across a forehead flushed with emotion and sunburn, cheeks blotchy from crying, silver streaks stirred by her deep snores. Thorne burned with yearning to tuck that hair behind her ear and kiss every track where the tears had dried while she'd slept. Who knew how long she'd been here—how long he'd been asleep, how much she'd worried?

Shifting onto his side, Thorne breathed her name so near the word stirred her hair. She was slow to wake even then, days—weeks—*months* of exhaustion dragging her eyelids down. When they slid up at last, her clouded gaze finding his, Thorne's pulse clattered out of control. He truly hoped she'd never stop having that effect on him.

"You're awake." Though groggy, her tone tilted up with relief; and to his surprise, she didn't withdraw, though their noses were as close as that day beside the trench. "Good morning, you."

"Is it morning?"

"I really don't know." She scratched the back of her head, leaving her chin balanced on one arm. "It's been three days at least. How do you feel?"

"Sore. Like my chest was trampled by a horse." He raised one shoulder in a shrug. "Little different than after most fights."

Cistine snorted quietly and finally straightened, taking a piece of his heart with her. "We closed the trench. It's over." Her gaze fixed on him, full of a fathomless emotion. "Kashar showed Jad's head to the people."

"Have they resisted his ascent?"

"Some have. But the antidote helps with that." She chewed the corner of her lip. "I'm sorry my touch didn't kill him. If I'd been enough..."

"What have I told you, *Logandir*?" Slowly, Thorne eased onto his stomach, folding his arms beneath his head. "You are *more* than enough."

He didn't realize his mistake until Cistine's countenance crumbled, her hand flying to her mouth as her gaze snagged on his back—on the new whip-marks there. "Oh, Thorne, *no*..."

"It's all right," he said quickly. "These are nothing."

"How can you say that? Why do you *always* say that? This isn't all right, he *whipped* you!"

"But I didn't break. I fought for my family with everything in me, and I have never regretted a single scar gained for that." He slid his hand nearer to hers on the edge of the bed. "Enough about me. Your father?"

Her lips trembled, eyes darting from his back to his face. He saw the effort it cost her to ignore those wounds and come back to this moment—to him. "Alive. Still breathing, thanks to you. Thorne, when you jumped into that trench..."

"It was certainly a day full of surprises." He shifted, seeking a more comfortable position on the bed. "Aden came for us, Jad survived your touch...Quill has a dragon now? A raven before wasn't enough?"

"This isn't funny."

A contrary smile tugged at his lips, then slid away. "I know. But I had faith in myself when I jumped—the same faith you've always had in me. How could I fail, given that?"

She bit her lips together, shaking her head. "After *everything*, you still believe in me. After how we fought, how I treated you...I chose *Sacha* over you."

"True. That did sting."

Her eyes glossed with tears. "Did you know she was Tirzah?"

Though the words blew through him so swiftly he grunted, reawakening the memory of the alchemist's blood on his hands and her last apology... "No. But it does explain the ease with which she manipulated those around her. And why she hated to be told she's like Jad."

"I hate myself for being so taken in. Everything I did, especially to you..."

"I wasn't entirely without blame, either. Besides, I knew precisely what I was getting into that day in Hellidom. You warned me yourself, even before we swore our oaths, that you would be furious and terrified and make mistakes. I've never been afraid of that...I know who I married."

Her top lip slid free, teeth grinding along that lower slip of blush-pink that made him wish all over again he could touch her. Then she rose abruptly, kicking back her chair. "Move over."

Frowning, Thorne raised his head. "What?"

"You heard me." She kneed the bed until he obliged, dragging himself to the far side. She climbed in with him and pressed her back against the opposite edge, facing him.

And just like that, for the first time in nearly a year, they were sharing a bed.

"What are you doing, *Logandir*?" he asked.

"I'm going to do one terrifying thing every day from now on, one thing I absolutely don't want to do, until fear stops controlling me. Now hand me a pillow." He pushed one to her, and she bunched it under her head, then pulled the linens up tight around Thorne's throat. "There. Now you have some protection in case I have nightmares and start kicking and screaming."

"Have you had those often since the trench?"

Cistine nodded, a movement almost heartbreakingly vulnerable in her curled posture, arm crumbling the pillow under her ear.

"Do you want to talk about them?"

A hesitant beat.

Then it all began to pour out of her—the fear, the anguish, the pain of wondering if Cyril would ever wake, how until minutes ago she'd feared the same for him. And though his body hummed with pain and he suspected she talked only to keep herself from falling asleep with him, he listened to every word—and felt the wound through the center of their blended hearts beginning to mend, easing back toward a pulse that felt familiar. Safe.

Like coming back to the truth of who they were.

CHAPTER FIFTY-EIGHT

AFTER ONLY A few days—and most them spent marshalling and dispatching the augurs while Thorne grew stronger—Aden was restless. This Palace was beautiful, he had to admit; the servants were kind, the people bewildered, but cautiously welcoming of their new King— particularly when one of his first decrees was to empty the royal treasury, returning all the heirlooms, artifacts, and deeds Jad had hoarded for his war. It seemed Sacha had been right about the nature of the man beneath the Sorcel, and Aden prayed it would stay that way.

The cabal was never without something to do, assembling patrols or taking rounds themselves. Quill, Tatiana, and Ashe trained that piebald dragon, and Rozalie kept watch on Cyril's door whenever Cistine was with Thorne. Aden tried to join her on guard once, but the heaviness of Solene's look the moment he entered, her grief-riddled smile and the way she avoided his eyes, made it clear that while he might be welcomed, his presence was not helpful.

There was still much to say, much healing to be done. And she wasn't ready yet, so he let her be.

Maleck was on watch at the infirmary. Rion Bartos hadn't been seen but in snatches since he'd escaped the physicians, walking the city occasionally, speaking to his Wardens, lurking down the hall from the King's room but never entering. Aden kept guard, too, just in case the

Commander's vengeance decided to enact itself against a still-weakened Thorne; but day after day, Bartos remained little more than a specter roaming Arak Shehr or flitting around the wing of the Palace where the *Alhuri* were hard at work on the antidote. Aden himself had visited the alchemy chamber and found it as glittering and grand as everywhere else.

A fine, gilded cage, this entire place. He was ready to be rid of it.

He made his choice a week after Thorne rallied—when he himself woke yet again without any duties prompting him or cries from a child needling into his dreams, and dressed and ate at a leisurely pace, not in the least rushed, not juggling a small body in one arm while he spooned porridge in with another...and he realized every moment how much he missed those things.

It was finally time.

He made his rounds to the infirmary after he saw to the augurs, and there he found Thorne finally moving, perched on the edge of his bed, toes feeling out the warm, dark floor.

Aden raised a brow. "Should you be up?"

"I assume if I wasn't, someone would've come to stop me by now, with how long this is taking." His cousin shot him a mischievous half-smile, which faltered at whatever look Aden was too slow to hide. "What is it?"

He examined Thorne, a hundred thoughts tumbling through his head. "Did anyone ever tell you that you took your first steps without me?"

Thorne snorted. "Salvotor and Rakel didn't frequently reminisce about my childhood achievements, no."

"Fair enough. I thought maybe Kallah mentioned it. We'd been waiting weeks for the moment, she claimed you were close...and then you did it while I was in school." Aden chuckled, shaking his head. "Here you are, doing it again."

"If getting out of bed is such a monumental feat, we'll need to alert the rest of the Chancellors when we return home."

Home. The word sang in Aden's chest. Why did it feel so much nearer today than it had any right to? "It's not the rising, it's the walking. You've never needed me to walk, *mavbrat.* Sometimes I forget just what you're capable of on your own."

Thorne frowned. Sinking the heels of his palms into the bed, he lurched upright, stumbling slightly. It was instinct that brought Aden to him, propping him up with a hand on the hinge of his shoulder; Thorne gripped his wrist in turn, straightening with a winded, genuine smile. "I've always needed you. And I always will."

They embraced, and Aden knew Thorne could feel it—the farewell in the gesture, the faith he had that his cousin could lead the augurs in this city without him.

They broke apart, and Aden smirked. "I'll see you soon."

"As soon as we can."

They bumped brows, and Aden left Thorne to find his own way from the infirmary; he went out into halls streaked in amber light, signaling sundown, and with joy finally burning in his heart again, he burst into a jog toward the outer terraces. A gust of wind greeted him despite the encroaching evening, a slap from the hot desert breeze that reminded him far too much of Nordbran. He was ready for damp, cool winters, a chill that went right down to his bones; for firesides and pelt rugs and balcony conversations, and so much more.

He halted on the edge of the scaffolding outside the empty Parlor where he'd saved Rozalie and Thorne. He'd done what he came to do— fought with his cabal, saved his family. And now, hand wrapped around the wind augment in his pouch...

"Were you really going to leave without saying goodbye?"

Aden froze, fingers springing open, and glanced back.

Ashe had arrived silent as a shadow, her dragon a golden blur on the terrace behind her as she swaggered in to join him. A smile framed her mouth, but sorrow seethed in her gaze.

Aden stepped back off the scaffolding to face her. "It's only for now."

"It always is. Until it's not." Ashe moved to his side, and together they gazed over the great city to the desert stretching endlessly beyond, bruise-purple in the gathering dusk. "Somehow, I knew you'd leave first."

He glanced down at her, those blue-and-green eyes somber despite her joking tone. She must've known all this time how he ached to go; little about him had ever escaped her attention. "But I stayed for you, too," he said. "Not just for her, or for Maleck. I heard you first. I held on for *you*."

A glint slid into the edge of her eye. She blinked it away and tossed him a small burlap satchel. "Here. Antidote from the *Alhuri*. If you're going to run off on us, you might as well get to work setting Talheim free."

Aden strung it from his belt. "I'll see to it immediately."

"You know, I actually trust that more than I would from most people," Ashe scoffed under her breath. "We've come a long way, haven't we, High Tribune?"

"Indeed we have, *Mereszar*."

Back to looking at the desert, so like the one that had brought them together in the Nimmus-pit of Siralek.

"I owe you," Ashe said quietly. "I'm not sure if anyone else has said it yet, but Rozalie told me what you did here...how you came at the end and put Rion on his knees." She cast a glance back into the room where Aden had been drawn to the thickest of the fighting, to an innate sense of where Thorne and Maleck were—as if the gods themselves had led him here. "If you hadn't come when you did, my *valenar* and one of my closest friends would be dead at the Butcher's hands. Thorne, too. As dark as things are now, they could've been so much gods-damned worse. I can't thank you enough for that."

"It was my pleasure. I've wanted the excuse to put Rion Bartos in his place from the moment you introduced us."

Ashe rolled her eyes. "I'm serious, Aden. I'm not sure I *ever* thanked you...for helping me see Valgard differently. For never giving up on me completely in the Hive, no matter how badly I betrayed you. Most people would've, but you didn't. Everything I get to call my own now, I owe at least a part of it to you."

"You love my brother." Aden shrugged. "I consider us even."

"Not quite." Ashe draped an arm over his shoulders and nodded north. "But we will be once you go home."

Home. Again, it rung like a strummed instrument in his chest, and

Ashe's smirk was infuriatingly all-knowing. Aden sighed. "How long have you suspected?"

"Only since the first time I saw you two in the Citadel together." She peered sidelong at him. "I know you're hating yourself for this. Don't. If it couldn't be him, Sander would want it to be you. Besides, it's time for *you* to find something to call your own." She gave him a fierce shake, then released him. "You've earned it."

"Well, so long as I have your blessing, my life is my own."

Laughing, she kicked his haunch. "You more than have my blessing. You can save that augment." She whistled, and Bresnyar slunk around the terrace edge, stretching and flexing his wings. "Take Bres...consider it another way of saying thank you." She grinned at him, the gleam back in her eyes. "And of letting go."

Hand to Bresnyar's steaming muzzle, Aden understood at last.

"You and Maleck," he murmured. "You aren't returning to Valgard when the time comes."

Smile fixed, she shook her head.

Aden didn't know when his idea of the future had begun to include all of them together, when family dinners had shifted in his mind from him and his father to them and Maleck and Ashe...and Mira and Nadeem. He only realized that impression was branded in his mind when he watched its embers flicker and fade, carried off in the desert wind.

"I wanted to tell you first, in case you decide to go back to Valgard while we're still here," Ashe added. "I know it—"

He embraced her, choking off the words, because if she spoke them he knew a piece of them both would come undone. "All I want is for you and Maleck to be happy. And if that's not with us in Stornhaz, it's all right. The beast-slayer and rain-dancer is not a creature to be tamed."

Ashe laughed hoarsely, hugging him back; when they drew apart, her grin was wider, but she no longer stopped the two damp tracks carving down her dusty cheeks. "Neither is the Lord of the Hive." She shoved him toward Bresnyar. "Get moving, will you? It's time for *you* to be happy."

"Certain you can manage Rion Bartos without me?"

"I'd be asking if he can handle *me*."

"Of course, my mistake." Aden backed away from her, sketching a showman's bow with arms flung wide. "The Lady of the Hive fights on."

Ashe shot him a vulgar salute, and Aden, chuckling, whipped around with a snap of his armored cape, striding toward Bresnyar. All at once, it cut free—a tether he hadn't even known was keeping him in place. He lunged onto Bresnyar's back, and with a mighty roar the dragon leaped from the scaffolding, casting off over the city in a sharp track to the north.

Toward home.

The sound of hammers and chisels greeted Aden long before he caught sight of the Citadel.

The wind grew sharply colder the further north they flew, and the imminence of dawn dragged a blanket of fog from the sea. He and Bresnyar had fallen silent miles ago, the dragon from the exhaustion of the long journey and Aden from anticipation. When the beat of Bresnyar's wings swirled the fog into torrents around them, revealing the Citadel's pale spire and Astoria spread out below, Aden's heart clenched with equal parts regret and relief—and something more powerful than either when they circled the Citadel's heights, searching for one balcony among many, and he caught sight of her beige dress, her dark hair and deep brown skin, her eyes turned south. Watching. Waiting.

The moment she caught sight of Bresnyar through the fog, she broke for the door to the inner Citadel.

Those last seconds of descent were the longest of Aden's life. The instant Bresnyar settled on the side of the southern bridge, he was down and running, harder and faster than he ever had in his life, toward the Citadel doors flung open by Wardens within. And there she was, skirts bunched in her fists, flying toward him with a smile so wide it seemed to hold the rising sun.

Those first golden rays flung over Aden's shoulder as he slowed, raising his hand. There was much to say, but all that emerged was, "I'm back."

She halted before him. "You are."

A silent question in her tipped head and curious, hopeful eyes. And Aden decided right then he was done with safety and sacrifice. His life redeemed, his family saved, the war ended…he was finished with penance.

Nothing had ever felt so right. So he closed the distance, took her face in both hands, and pressed his mouth to hers.

She melded into him like she'd always belonged there, arms strung around his neck, stretching into his height. His eyes rolled shut, his arm wound around her waist, and he pivoted them, seeking the bridge railing with his hand so he could lean them both against it. His world was consumed with vanilla and spice, the smell of her soap and the taste of her mouth. He sank deeper into her until there was nothing but their mingled breaths and the thread of her fingers in his hair.

All too soon, they had to breathe, drawing apart to drink one another in. The look on her face was nearly his undoing—fear, pain, and above all else, trust.

"I take it you missed me?" he teased.

She punched his arm. "*Nadeem* did." Then her fingers found his collar, winding into it. "Fine. *I* did."

He brushed his lips against hers, once, twice, three times. Each one reciprocated, full of the same hope that had carried him higher than any dragon's wings, all the way back to her.

"There's plenty to do," she said after the third kiss. "The repairs are underway, but Viktor's found more ensorcelled council members, and one man who confessed to giving Lady Eboni some of the drug for the Queen."

Aden sighed, pressing his brow to hers. "Is it always going to be like this—moments of passion interrupted by duty?"

Mira laughed, pushing him back again so he could see her raised brow and beaming grin. "Tell me you would have it any other way."

"I'd have *you* any way you let me."

Her laughter joyous, she kissed him again in the sunrise—a kiss that changed everything, flinging the doors of their future wide open.

CHAPTER FIFTY-NINE

I T WAS LONG after dark when Cistine escaped her daily duties for a moment of peace and solitude in the Palace halls. It had been like this ever since Thorne woke, her attention always pulled one way or another— meetings with the Wardens, councils with Kashar, sending notes back and forth from the border forts by carrier pigeon. These tasks were hers to fulfill because the King had not yet woken and the Queen never left his side.

Tonight, after head-splitting hours with Kashar discussing what reparations might be owed from both kingdoms, it was too much. Instead of going to the infirmary or her parents' private chamber, Cistine wandered.

She really did love this Palace with the threat of Jad no longer present. It was open and airy everywhere the Citadel was closed off in white stone, most halls looking all the way down to open sides where cloth veils could be lowered during sandstorms or summer rains. She enjoyed the freedom of it, the sense that she could never be trapped or caged here.

Except by duties that should've been her father's. The weight of those shackles grew heavier every day.

Her meandering feet brought her at last to a dance hall on the Palace's upper level, its inner wall made of mirrors, the one across from it nothing but vaulted windows, the ceiling dripping chandeliers and the floor a glimmering shell of blown glass in variegated shades. It reminded her of her coming-of-age birthday, of tea and dancing and scheming and everything she'd taken for granted back then.

She settled on the floor, spreading out the skirt she'd worn today—a fine silk piece Tatiana had given her, complementing her midriff top and long cardigan. She yearned for the protection her armor offered, but she'd chosen this instead, keeping her promise to Thorne: one terrifying thing every day. This was today's choice. Tomorrow...gods only knew. She was too exhausted to contemplate what tomorrow might bring.

She watched the moon rise, its pale dapples bouncing from the mirrors and setting the floor ablaze with silver-tinted color, like auroras and wistful summer daydreams. The ache in her temples faded while the silence thickened and her thoughts wandered. Worry for her father chased out every trace of exhaustion over time, leaving her wide-eyed and anxious while the light in the room changed from silver to core dark and back to rose-pink.

What if there was a change while she was away? Or what if there wasn't? How long before he opened his eyes and said their names again—if he ever did? And what would she do if he *didn't*?

The door whispered open behind her. "Feeling overwhelmed again?"

That husky voice jolted her halfway to her feet. "*Thorne!* What are you doing up?"

"Don't bother." He motioned her back down. "I need to sit." He lowered himself slowly beside her with a strained cough. "Here I thought I'd have plenty to do when I finally made it out of the infirmary. I should've known you and Aden had everything in hand."

Had. Cistine eyed him tentatively. "He's gone?"

"Back to Astoria last night."

Relief loosened a knot Cistine hadn't even noticed was wrapped around the base of her spine. "Good. I'll feel better with him there. How are *you*?"

"Tired from being on my feet most of the night." Thorne stretched. "But we both know I didn't need to be in that bed anymore."

She supposed that was true; but it had kept the harder conversations at bay, the ones she'd avoided with the excuse that he wasn't ready yet. In truth, *she* wasn't. But silence held them off now while they watched the sun creep over the horizon through those magnificent floor-to-ceiling windows.

"I went to see your father," Thorne said at length. "He seems..."

"Awful. I know," Cistine whispered. "I keep hoping there will be a change, but there never is."

"It will come." His hand slid nearer to hers on the blown-glass tiles, and Cistine let it. Two brave things today. "And when it does, I'll be here, *Logandir*."

It wasn't the name she wanted him to say, but he hadn't called her *Wildheart* since the night she'd told him he was beginning to sound like Julian, and it didn't feel right now. She hardly deserved to hear that precious word from his lips when she'd cast it back in his face so cruelly last time. Heart aching, she watched him fold his arms loosely on his knees and study the depths of the ceiling. "I'm sorry I didn't come see you tonight," she said. "Or him. I just..."

"You're carrying the weight of Talheim on your shoulders," Thorne said when she trailed off. "There's nothing to apologize for. You don't owe me or your father some added measure of suffering to prove your love. He won't know if you're there or not, and I know precisely why you couldn't be."

Gods, this man was determined to make her cry. "How was Mama?"

"As well as can be expected. She told me about Aden...and Eboni." Pain flashed in his eyes. "It's no wonder Rion's been a specter. I heard he's only come to see your father once, and Solene ordered him out."

Cistine winced. She understood why, but she wondered what repercussions would come from distancing Rion from the only two people he seemed to fear losing anymore. "Do you remember what you said to him when you were ensorcelled?"

Grimacing, Thorne shrugged. "Fragments. Jad made me confirm what your mother told him about how Julian died, and I know I told Rion. Beyond that, it's all shadows and pain until I woke up with Aden forcing the antidote down my throat."

Cistine rubbed a chill from her arms. "Do you think he'll try to finish what he started in the Parlor?"

Thorne was quiet for so long, Cistine knew it was one of those difficult questions—the kind where he didn't want to lie, but he didn't want the truth to add to her pain. "Most likely," he said at last. "Before we came to Masiya's defense, he told me no one who harms his family goes unpunished. I don't know what that will mean for your mother, killing Eboni...but I know what it means for a Valgardan."

"If he comes close to laying a hand to you, if he even *tries*, I'll have his head."

"Julian would never forgive you for killing his father."

"I don't care. Julian isn't here. If his father tries to hurt my husband, there will be Nimmus to pay."

A quiet chuckle slid from Thorne, followed by a short, hacking cough. Concern floated hot and heavy into her throat, but he was still smiling when he pounded his chest clear and shook his head. "I appreciate your ferocity, particularly on my behalf."

Cistine bared her teeth and growled, and his chuckle became a full laugh. Then she was laughing, too, and it felt good, the bounce and echo of their humor rising to greet the coming day. How had she let herself forget how precious moments like these could be? How had she given up the wonder of laughing with him, of simply *being* with him, until it was almost too late?

"You were right," she said when she caught her breath, and Thorne's head tipped slightly. "The moment you were gone, all I could think about was the things I did have with you that might be gone. Waking up in the same room. Eating together. Sitting on balconies and watching over Astoria. I took so much for granted, and you were right...I didn't look for happiness, I ran from it." She hugged her knees to her chest. "Every day, I realize how right Papa was, too. I'm not ready to be Queen. I just want to be Cistine Novacek. I want to travel to Valgard whenever the urge strikes, and I want to help my people without being the one making laws and decisions for the whole kingdom. And I'm terrified he's going to die and I'll *have* to be that person, even though I'm not ready and I might never be if he's gone."

"If it comes to that, I'll stay as long as I possibly can, until Bravis or one of the others comes down and drags me back to Valgard by force."

Shaky laughter burst from her lips. "Most likely it will be Bravis."

"Most likely."

Sniffling, she turned her cheek against her arm. "Will you do something else for me?"

"Name it."

"Will you forgive me?"

His eyes softened. "I already have."

Silent tears spilled over her lashes. "Then will you dance with me?"

If the question surprised him, it didn't show. "I'd be honored."

He stood, extending his hand; and though fear pounded in her temples, Cistine let her bare fingertips hover just above his when she rose before him.

Three brave things.

Silent and careful, Thorne backed away, and she moved with him, letting him lead her out onto the dancing floor. Every shred of sense screamed at the danger, but his expression never changed from that quiet faith she'd taken for granted. His hands settled near her waist and above her shoulder, and she made hers meet him—a breath of space between their upraised palms, her shaking fingers and his powerful arm.

"I won't let us fall," he said.

Cistine poured every scrap of faith she still possessed into her answer. "Neither will I."

And they began to dance.

She'd known Thorne was a good dancer ever since that long-ago tavern in Stornhaz where he'd taken her away from the pressures of responsibility for the night. But this was so different, so much sweeter; every step placed with care, every movement conscious and careful, gliding through the familiar motions of a Talheimic waltz she'd learned stepping up on her father's feet at festivals and balls. She knew it so well, she barely had to think of where her limbs went.

"Where did you learn this dance?" she asked.

"Your mother." His confession came with a sheepish slide of teeth. "She insisted I learn, in case..."

In case the curse ever lifted. In case they had that chance...or this one.

Shaking her head, she twirled out from him, then back in, keeping her fingertips just shy of his. They spun across the floor to the imagined melody of a piano, the floor alight in brilliant streaks under his bare feet and her flats, the sunrise shattering around the glass and through her skirt.

"I'll have to thank her," Cistine said breathlessly when they stepped together, her back nearly to his chest, close enough to raise the hair on her neck but still never touching.

Thorne's hand snaked around her body. "So will I."

She pivoted on the balls of her feet, then leaned back in the classic dip, well-trained muscles stretching into the motion. Thorne leaned with her, his palm an inch from the small of her back, his nose nearly brushing the column of her neck, lowering to the divot between her collarbones where he breathed in the smell of her citrus-and-jasmine soap.

Her core smoldered at the brush of breath on her clavicles. She straightened slowly, and he moved with her, carefully sensuous, his hand still hovering at her back even when she was upright again.

"You said your touch didn't kill Jad," he murmured. "Maybe it's changed, Cistine...not entirely, but enough."

"I still killed a plant afterward," she whispered.

"But I know what that augment feels like, when to withdraw from it. If you'll let me, I want to try."

Instinct told her to jerk away, but desperate longing kept her feet rooted, her gaze fixed on his. "What if I hurt you again?"

"I'm not one to tempt the gods." Thorne raised his hand, letting his fingers hover above her cheek. "But I'm willing to take a chance for us."

She let her eyes flutter shut, weak at those words, her head tilting almost of its own volition toward his hand.

The ballroom doors banged open so loudly both Cistine and Thorne recoiled, leaping apart and turning to face the commotion. Rozalie all but hung from the doorway, face so white her freckles popped like sand across her cheekbones. "You both need to come with me," she said, and Cistine's stomach began a freefall plunge. "It's the King. He's worse...the physicians say he won't last the day."

CHAPTER SIXTY

THE RUN FROM the dancing hall to her parents' chamber was a blur. She only knew she'd fallen and risen again when her knees ached and bruises thumped dully in her palms—and it didn't matter. Nothing mattered but reaching that room and hearing for herself that the physician was wrong, that he'd made some sort of mistake. As long as her father breathed, there had to be hope, just as there'd been for Thorne. There *had* to be.

She burst into the chamber to find it in chaos—physicians dashing to and from the bed with terse shouts, a guard restraining Solene who twisted and fought with all her might, sobs racking her body so violently she couldn't catch her breath.

Cistine froze in midstep, heart crashing, lungs shrinking to pinpricks. Thorne slipped around her with a snarl at the guard holding Solene. "*Take your hands off her.*"

Perhaps in terror at that voice, or weariness from restraining her to begin with, the man obeyed. Thorne caught the Queen by her shoulders when her knees buckled, driving her toward the floor.

Cistine's mind refused to make sense of what was happening—these physicians, their steaming pots and herbs, the way that bed swallowed her father's mighty figure like a grave.

"Healing augments?" she whispered when Rozalie's footsteps tapped up on her heels. "Why haven't we...why aren't the healing augments—?"

"The damage is already done," one physician said curtly.

She knew that. Thorne had taught her long ago on her balcony outside the Den how a healing augment administered too late might not be enough...but he had risked everything leaping into that chasm, they'd only been gone minutes, though it had felt like *hours* inside that augmented cage...was this the fumes? His lungs? The way his body broke on that ledge where Thorne found him?

It didn't matter. Something was taking her father away faster than she could think of a way to hold onto him. But she couldn't give up without trying one last time. "Get me a healing augment!"

At the command in her voice, someone obeyed, and in a rush of passing minutes a flagon rolled across the floor to her. Her legs gave way when she bent to reach it, and she crawled between the physicians to the bedside, fisting the duvet in one hand and pulling herself onto her knees to stare at the King's ashen face.

Open your eyes, she wanted to scream. *See me!* But those already-slow breaths grew fainter with every rise and fall of his chest.

Desperate, Cistine shattered the healing augment in her hand, not caring when it charred the first few inches of her sleeves off; she thrust the power out with all her might, pouring it into her father while the physicians worked their mortal methods on him.

It struck again within seconds, that rip tearing her wide open just like at the trench, and if she hadn't already been on her knees she would've fallen anyway. Bile surged up her throat, squeezing between teeth clenched around a scream. It felt like something was searing loose from inside her.

"Cistine!" Thorne roared. "*Stop!*"

She was bleeding; she'd bitten clean into her tongue, blood streaming hot and oily from the corner of her mouth. But she couldn't let go, couldn't stop trying, not until she *knew*—

The edges of the pain softened. A strange warmth spilled through her like a thousand hands hot with power, holding her palms above her father's ravaged chest. Wilder than any lightning augment, fiercer than any flame, yet the power soothed as it journeyed in and through her. It reminded her of orange-cinnamon scones and midnight eyes and desert spices.

Hal ulda viy. The words whispered through her racing mind, the voice neither male nor female, loud nor soft, a shout and a whisper all at once. Every syllable bloomed with infinite might and endless love. *We are here,* Logandir. *For him. For you.*

The Key's power rose to a wailing crescendo in response, something luminous and heartbreaking, a lonely note recognizing its symphony—a piece crying out to the whole from which it had been taken almost a year ago. Divine singing to divine.

The door crashed open. Cistine didn't have to look to know who'd entered; Rion Bartos still emanated a palpable presence, a fume of rage that pierced even the wondrous shell around her when he saw the power binding her to the King. She didn't know who'd summoned him, and she didn't care. She wouldn't have spared him even a glance if Solene hadn't exploded in fiery rage.

"*Get out!*" she screamed. "Haven't you done enough? Hasn't your vengeance cost us *enough*? If you'd been fighting beside him like you're meant to instead of feeding your own gods-damned grudge, you could've ended Jad *together* before he ever went to that trench!"

The augment guttered out of Cistine's grasp with a last yank of pain. The voices faded, that warming presence gone. She whipped toward them, heart racing in shock, terror climbing her throat; she'd never heard her mother's voice so enraged, had never heard so much hate spill from those lips. For a moment, she saw the huntress who'd won the Prince's heart, who'd defied Jad and his people during weeks of imprisonment.

"Solene," Rion rasped, eyes wet, voice shaking as he stepped again toward Cyril. "Leney, I—"

"*Get out!*" the Queen roared. "You have no place here!"

Rozalie laid a hand on Rion's shoulder, and he shrugged her off. Loathing battled the grief in his eyes when they found first Cistine, then Thorne, as if either of them might advocate for him. And once, she might have. But now...

She turned back to the bed, slumping to her knees again before Rion's footsteps retreated. Pain throbbed deep and low in her core, like she'd taken a blow to the stomach, but she didn't care. All that mattered was her father, his body still glistening with silver light.

Time slowed, and the world with it, the physicians moving at half their speed...half the pace of her racing heart. She didn't fully comprehend why until Rozalie whispered to the Head Physician, Ibrim, as if afraid a breath louder would break the tension holding this room together: "Why are your people stopping?"

"There is nothing more we can do," was the soft reply. "He is in Dyalmun's hands."

No, no, no...

"Papa, *please.*" Cistine's fists dug into the blanket so hard, the seams tore. "Don't leave us."

"*Cyril,*" Solene choked, and Thorne loosed the quietest grunt of pain. Looking back, Cistine found him crumpled on the floor, his arms laced tightly around her mother. She hung from his grip, gaze fixed on the bed, cheeks red and tearstained.

They'd given up. She was the only one holding onto this hopeless dream—a wish too great for her useless, death-cursed hands to manage alone.

So Cistine Novacek did the most unqueenly thing she'd ever done; she spun to her feet and *fled.*

She didn't know if they shouted for her, nor did she care. She ran without any sense of direction, her knees throbbing, her hands aching, her middle still torn from that augment. Hurtling up and down staircases, lost in corridors she'd never seen before, she escaped from that room and its pall and the knowledge that her father was seconds away from dying, and she couldn't watch him go.

Even if it was selfish, even if it made her cruel and cowardly and unfit to lead, she didn't care. She couldn't watch him take his final breath, couldn't brace enough for that blow or the memories that would unleash with it, the pain that would come after. She'd endured it with Baba Kallah, with Julian, even with Maltadova, and on the Deathmarch. But she would not survive it with him.

She crashed out through a pair of bright brass doors, stumbling when her feet encountered grass. She'd entered the *garriqah*, Arak Shehr's lustrous inner garden; and though her touch would spread more death, she darted out among the palm fronds and willows and olive trees, kicking off her flats just to feel the tickling against the soles of her feet. She sprinted on, losing herself in the dense foliage, the tunnels of ivy and moss, until she couldn't see the doors behind her or the *garriqah* walls.

And then, finally, her strength failed her.

She slammed to her knees, gripping the soil while the world pivoted wildly around her. Fear and grief surged up her throat in a spew of vomit; she let it come. What did it matter if someone found her sick and shaking among the plants? What did any of it matter if her Papa, her hero and guide, her first and greatest love, was dead?

Dead. The finality of that word was as final as the curse in her body.

Dead because of her. Dead because he'd borne Jad down into the pit to keep him away from her. Dead, gone, leaving Solene a widow, leaving Cistine a half-orphan, leaving Thorne without a father he could lean into and be proud of. Leaving Talheim without the leader it truly needed.

Tears heaved from Cistine, wild and retching, and somehow they formed words. A chant of *no*, at first, and *Papa*, and *please, please, please.* Then something snapped in her chest, and more words came—a familiar torrent, a breached dam, like speaking to an old friend after months of silence; like a tavern in Veran with Tatiana, like her bedside in the Den with Quill on her wedding day, like talking with Thorne in the infirmary.

For the first time since the Deathmarch, prayers poured out of her.

"*Please,*" she gasped, "please, oh, gods, I'll do anything, I'll give *anything* you ask, just not this...*don't let him die!*"

Her shaking arms gave way and she fell on her side, cradled by the soil, her eyes squeezed shut but powerless to keep the tears at bay. They ran into her ear on one side, painted her lips on the other, and the sobs that broke free with them were so painful her chest felt like it was splitting in two again.

"I don't want to do this anymore!" she sobbed. "I don't want to lose him, I don't want to be Queen yet! I want to be the Princess, I want to keep learning and growing, and I want—I *need* him to teach me! I'm not ready to say goodbye, please, *please*...stop this, fix it, make it right somehow, I'm *begging* you...*save him...*"

That was all it became, just a steady stream of *save him, save him, save him* while she lay in the dirt, tucked in the *garriqah's* deep shadows where no one could find her. She sobbed the words until she had no strength left, no voice; until all that remained was the sound of wind whispering through the fronds, and with her eyes shut tight, she listened, fighting to gasp in a full breath.

We are with you, Wildheart. The words were a breath within the breeze, an echo in the aching chambers of her heart. *Hal ulda viy.*

The pain in her middle eased at last, a comfortable, gentle numbness stealing over her like sweet relief. Her lashes peeled apart, her body shuddering with a dull, deep shiver; her aching eyes found a fat caterpillar crawling across the back of her hand like she was just another growing thing in its way, planted deep and waiting for her time to flourish.

She had been a small girl the first time her father took her out among the flowering plants in the Citadel garden; they'd eaten crisp, soft melon wedges while they walked, the juice staining her cheeks and dress even though she'd tried to eat with the dignity her Papa always possessed. They had sat in the shade while he gestured to the seedling plants and sapling trees.

"A kingdom is like a garden, little one," he'd told her—a name she'd shrugged off when she'd turned thirteen and stopped wanting to be thought of as *little*. "We step carefully through it and help everything and everyone in it grow to the best of our power. There will always be weeds to root out and dead growth to prune, but with enough love, care, and rain from the gods, anything can flourish."

Maybe that was what the gods demanded of her; maybe it *was* time to flourish. Their answer to her prayers might be nothing more than that she somehow found the strength to fall a princess here, and rise a queen who did not break—one who walked through the garden of her kingdom with head held high, even if her touch could kill every living thing in her path—

She blinked.

The caterpillar inched across her knuckles, then paused, choosing a finger to carry it down to the soil.

Slowly, Cistine pushed herself upright, bringing her hand to eye level. Confronted with the swift change in height, the caterpillar hurried up the back of her hand, climbing her wrist, then her sleeve. Cistine plucked him off and set him in the verdant grass, watching him scurry away, her heart scrabbling at her ribs.

It couldn't be. It wasn't possible.

And yet...

She snapped to her feet, stumbled deeper into the *garriqah*, and fell to her knees again beside a flowering rosebush. Plunging her hands into the soil at its base, she pushed with all her might, all her will, not daring yet to consider. To hope. To *believe*.

Nothing. Nothing.

Nothing.

Red rosebuds grinned at her like painted lips all whispering the same secret: *Yes. It's true.*

They were not dying. Like the caterpillar had not died.

The tearing. The separating she'd felt every time she'd used augments these past few weeks, like something was leaving her body—something she couldn't identify, something that had seemed so much a part of her she'd forgotten what she was without it.

Haval taking so long to kill the fish at the oasis and the Enforcer attacking Shathen—then failing to kill *Jad*.

Like it was fading. Tearing away.

"Cistine!" Thorne's voice shattered her stupor, pulling her head away from the flourishing rosebush.

His voice—he sounded *hopeful*.

"Cistine, I know you're out here, the guards saw you come this way!"

Undergrowth crunched below his heels. "You don't have to hide from me...something happened, the physicians can't explain it, but your father's breathing changed again! They think the healing augment..."

She didn't hear the rest of what he said. She knew it wasn't the augment itself...but the ones who'd gifted it.

Hal ulda viy.

"Cistine, where are you?"

"I'm here!" she cried, fingers still buried in the soil. "Thorne, I'm *here!*"

Twigs snapped and vines slapped aside as he plunged through the *garriqah's* densest parts to reach her; he came to an abrupt halt, the desperate hope in his face fading to nothing but shock when he saw her kneeling in the bright emerald grass, fingers sunk deep into the soil, life *living* all around her. Life singing from the smile on her face when her gaze locked with his.

His knees gave out, only his grip on the palm tree at his left keeping his feet beneath him. He stared at her with the widest, brightest eyes Cistine had ever seen, jaw gaping.

Stumbling upright, she gathered her skirts and ran to him, not caring about the dirt between her toes or the tears dried on her face or the soil clinging to her clothes. All that mattered were these steps, and this distance, and how it vanished when Thorne thrust himself up to meet her.

Cistine dropped her skirts and leaped, wrapping her arms around his neck and her legs around his waist, and they crashed back against the tree as her mouth collided with his—an abandoned meeting of breath, teeth sinking into each other's lips hard enough to bruise, one of his hands hitching her bare thigh under her skirts and the other buried in the hair at the nape of her neck. His gasps were a blend of her Name and the moans of a man coming back from the dead, and Cistine couldn't tell where his tears ended and hers began.

Then he spun her around, face buried in the side of her neck, kissing every patch of her skin his lips could find, pounding shivers through every last inch of her body. At last his legs gave way, and he fell, bringing her down with him, and he sobbed against her neck, his hands curling under her arms to grip her shoulders, straining the fabric with the tightness of a drowning man's grasp. She held him while he wept, the way she hadn't even dared dream of for months, resigning herself that she would never have this again.

Thank you. The silent prayer rose from her mind to the hands of the gods. *Thank you, thank you.*

"I love you." Thorne pressed a kiss against her forehead. "I loved you then, I love you now..."

"With my whole heart," Cistine laughed through her own tears.

"For my whole life," he finished against her mouth, her tongue swallowing that last word, drinking and tasting it from him. Tasting the truth of it.

They kissed themselves senseless, her back landing against the ground somewhere in the middle of it, Thorne bracing his weight above her, one hand beside her head and the other on her hip. His thumb traced the contour of the bone as he pulled back to gaze at her face, full of wonder and relief and a desperate, wild love that spun her head more sweetly than the aroma of crushed herbs and flowers around them.

"I prayed for this every day," he croaked.

She slid her hands into his hair. "I know. They heard."

His mouth dipped to capture hers again, but she tugged him back until their eyes met.

"Papa?" she asked, hardly daring to believe the gods might have given not one gift, but *two*.

Thorne laughed in joyous disbelief. "They don't know what changed. But when your mother touched his face, his breaths eased. He tried to open his eyes."

A huff of relief shook from Cistine's chest and she guided Thorne's brow down to rest against hers. "Ariadne was right. The gods are still here...still listening."

I can't thank you enough. She cast the prayer up from the depths of her heart to listening ears above. *I'm in your debt.*

We know. The whisper, gentle but solemn, filled her mind like the breeze answering—the same everything and nothing she'd heard at the bedside when the power joined her to them. *And someday, we will hold you to the oaths you've made today.*

A shiver tried to make its way through her body, but Thorne's living warmth blotted it out as he dipped to kiss her again. Someday, she would worry about all the *somedays*. But for now, she wanted to bask in miracles and mercy.

And she never wanted to let go of her *valenar* again.

CHAPTER SIXTY-ONE

Heads up, Mal!"

Quill's warning came far too late for the inevitable, and Maleck didn't even bother blocking this time; he turned and submitted to the crash of a scaled body colliding with his chest, flinging him to his back on the sand.

They'd been working for hours today, and for days before that, teaching Quill's dragon the different names and scents among the cabal. Maleck could think of no creature more different from Bresnyar, a slobbering pup to the golden dragon's dignified wolf; but it made sense that this would be the dragon meant for Quill, and Quill for him. Gazing up into those eager eyes, the *Tayir's* legs planted on his chest, Maleck truly couldn't see it happening any other way.

"Well," he deadpanned, "it would appear you've found me."

The answer was a needle-tipped tongue swiping his face.

Quill whistled. "*Shrike!* Go find Tati!"

Whooping that owl-like warble, the dragon spun and bounded away, and Maleck pushed himself up, massaging his shoulder. They would have to work on the eager jumps and voracious, if friendly, attacks. He had never more admired the Wingmaidens of Oadmark or better understood why they only rode the beasts bonded to them since hatching.

Jogging up with a grin, Quill offered his hand. "Any bleeding this time?"

"None that I can feel."

"Good! Thought Shei might cut off my head, the way you walked away from the last round."

"Think lower, *Allet*."

Quill pulled a face. "That woman is terrifying."

Maleck grinned. "I'm well aware."

"You know, you're a lot calmer than everyone else I've brought out for target practice." Quill raised a brow as they clasped forearms. "Why do I get the feeling you've done this before?"

Scoffing, Maleck yanked Quill down with him, twisted him into a headlock, and raked his knuckles over his friend's mismatched hair. Cursing and laughing, Quill broke the hold easily, plopping onto the sand at Maleck's side. They watched Shrike hunt along the well-watered plain outside Arak Shehr, studded with pale stone and hardy carob, olive, and almond trees. Bresnyar and Ashe watched his progress from a limestone crop, basking in the shade. It was some effort for Maleck to tear his eyes from his *valenar* and watch the dragon prance among the thick foliage in search of Tatiana.

"He's improving," he commented. "His tracking and his communication both."

"Seems that way, doesn't it? Bresnyar's not sure he'll ever learn the common tongue, but at least some of his noises are starting to make sense." Quill dug his heels into the sand, arms linked loosely around his knees. "Pip's really going to love him. She doesn't say it in her letters, but I know she misses Faer."

Maleck's heart twisted at the thought of Quill's sister.

"I was thinking," Quill added, "we could take her back to Starhollow sometime, visit Helga's grave. I haven't been there since everything—"

"Quill," Maleck interrupted quietly, "perhaps you and Tati should take her."

The silence dragged on. Quill wouldn't look at him.

Shrike let out a whooping huff, finding Tatiana behind an almond tree, and she slid out to throw an arm around his neck, then glanced at Quill and

Maleck. When neither of them moved, she sent the dragon to find Ariadne.

Maleck cleared his throat. "I'm—"

"Staying? Turning Talheimic?" Quill's tone was almost too light. "I've figured for a few months. The way you get along with the Wardens, how the Queen and Roz and Cistine treat you. Especially when the King gave you a command in the siege." He dragged a hand through his hair, turning it across his head. "But when were you going to tell *me, Storfir?*"

"It was never the right time. Asheila and I have discussed it now and then, but she knows how much Cistine needs her, and she knows I will never leave her side. I think it settled for her when we all reunited in Masiya."

Quill snorted. "I could've told you a long time before that. Shei thinks she's a nomad, but she's not. She's been Cistine's, maybe from the first time they ever laid eyes on each other. Whatever that looks like, their paths were always going to stay together."

Maleck didn't bother saying he'd once believed the same of himself and Thorne—before a fierce and fiery warrior, once a red-headed girl in the snow, had stumbled back into his path and changed everything.

He nudged shoulders with Quill. "You'll be all right. You still have Aden and Thorne, Tatiana and Pippet...and someday, I have no doubt, a family to keep you more than occupied."

"Ha." Quill fumbled out a cinnamon stick, sliding it between his teeth. "That's if we can stop fighting wars for two minutes." He waited exactly that long before adding, "We're really going to miss you."

"I'll only be a dragon's flight away." A vow—and an offering.

"Right. But you're leaving *me,* so *you* get to do the traveling for the first five or ten years."

"I can accept that."

"Then I guess I'll just have to accept the rest of it." Quill scrubbed a hand through his hair again, watching Shrike spin circles around a heap of stones before he finally barked Ariadne out of hiding. "I never figured, you know, back then...it was just supposed to be another ordinary caravan raid."

A chuckle rumbled deep in Maleck's chest. "Isn't it always *just* another..."

He trailed off, mouth slack. For there, approaching them through the olive grove, was something that should not be—something he had never thought he would see again.

Two heads of silver hair, Valgardan armor and silk skirts, bare feet and flats. A Chancellor and a princess coming toward them through the foliage, hands linked and shoulders pressed together, leaning into each other with every stride.

Maleck didn't even realize he'd risen until the shift in height under the setting sun set his head spinning. "Quill."

"I see it too." Breathing shallowly, Quill stood beside him. "Mirage?"

But the others had fallen silent, frozen as well. Only Ashe moved, sliding from the rock to land heavily in the stunted grass, and Bresnyar, raising his head to scent.

Cistine and Thorne halted, and her fingers flexed around his. He did not fall.

He did not fall.

"Before any of you ask," she said hastily, "it's real. The gods, I don't know why, really, or exactly *how*, but—"

That was all anyone needed. It was more than enough for Maleck.

They all reached her and Thorne at once, Quill's three-fingered hand twisting in Cistine's hair and his forehead digging into her temple, Tatiana peppering her cheek, her brow, her head with kisses from the other side. Ariadne's arm wrapped around her waist from the front, Ashe's circling her from behind, and Maleck pressed his lips to her crown as he fell with his arms around her and Thorne. If he was weeping, he was not the only one; he'd never heard so many tearful voices at once, a storm of questions that didn't matter but demanded to be raised. He thought Ariadne might be shouting prayers of praise; it was difficult to tell when Shrike crashed into them as well, utterly unaware of what was so wonderful but begging to be part of their joy.

"Quill, call off your lizard, he's crushing me!" Ashe finally gasped, and Quill slithered out of the heap, whistling. Shrike bounded backward, wings flaring, mouth agape in a draconian grin, and the others stumbled apart.

Tatiana gripped Cistine's hands and looked deep into her eyes. "Tell me this is real. I'm not dreaming?"

"It's really *real*, Tati." Cistine's grin was almost too wide for her cheeks. "I'm finally...I'm *back*."

Maleck offered his hand to her. "You were never gone, *Logandir*." When her fingers curled fearlessly over his, a fissure of pure happiness broke open in his heart. Her surprised laughter burst across the plain like the sweetest music when he swooped her off her feet and spun her three times across the rocky ground. "But," he added, setting her staggering on her feet, "I am glad we can do this again."

"And *this*." Ashe yanked Cistine from his grip to take her face and kiss the top of her head.

"And this." Ariadne butted shoulders with her, and Cistine shoved her right back.

"And this!" Quill jammed his fingers into her ribs, and she squealed, spinning and throwing a punch he caught by instinct on the palm of his hand.

Everyone froze again, even the dragons, nostrils flaring, heads raised at the shift in their tension.

A wicked smile curled across Cistine's face.

Then they were all sparring with her, the princess in a skirt and handkerchief top whirling through their midst, punching palms and throwing kicks, the cabal taking every blow and dealing them back. High above, the first watchful stars peeked out from the graying veil of coming night—guardians from a realm beyond, looking down on the work they had done.

A work that once again made the cabal one.

CHAPTER SIXTY-TWO

THE KING'S BORROWED CHAMBER was cozy, the crackling flame in its rounded hearth chasing out the cold of another desert night, and Cistine curled her stockinged feet under her body, snuggling deeper into the chair at her father's bedside. In one hand, she held his; in the other, a book of Mahasari romance. According to Mairin, these were the best in the kingdoms. Having sampled from all three, Cistine was inclined to agree.

It wasn't just the book she was enjoying, though; it was the quiet night, no battle councils demanding their time, no pall of death hanging above them. Her mother lay in the bed beside the unconscious King, head on his shoulder while she wrote a letter to Aden. Thorne, perched in front of the fire, scoured a text on dragons, looking up occasionally to catch her eye and smile.

The King slumbered on, as he had for weeks now, but his breathing was deep and even, his complexion healthy again. The physicians remained unsure if this was all a miracle or the work of that last healing augment; Cistine knew it was both—a girl and the gods working in tandem to restore what was nearly lost.

It was precisely what augmentation was meant to be, a meeting of giver, gift, and those they gifted it to, all weaving in perfect harmony. And of all the sensations she recalled from that day nearly a week ago when her life and her father's were both ransomed back from the Undertaker, that feeling stood out the most.

She wished she could scream it from the rooftops, could teach every Valgardan the true purpose of the power mined from their lands. But even now, nearly a week later, she was still sorting it out for herself. After hours of conversation with Ariadne, curled up in a Palace windowsill watching sunrises and sunsets over the city, they had made as much sense of it as possible.

The tearing she'd felt was the Death augment clinging onto her in the way only one of the *Stor Sedam* could. It had weakened as she'd used other augments over the past year, and particularly in these last few weeks, but it hadn't wanted to leave. When she had poured out her strength, her pain, her life for her father...death had held no more sway in her. The gods had peeled the rest away.

Cistine made sure to kneel in grateful prayer every night, even if it was just a mantra of *thank you* until she was too exhausted to keep her eyes open and crawled into bed with Thorne. She hadn't gone a single day without crying yet, but no one else had, either; least of all her mother, who was just today letting her sit out of reach of wandering feet or a hand stroking her hair.

A heavy gaze branded her across the room; she peeked at Thorne over her book again, then turned the page, slow and sensuous. She pretended to nod along to the words before her, raising her eyes and fanning herself at the scandalous content. He shifted in his chair, shooting her a filthy glare, and she choked on giggles.

A sudden, light brush at that sound. The subtlest squeeze around her fingers.

Breath catching, book forgotten, Cistine looked down to where her father's hand grasped hers—his thumb slowly, deliberately caressing her knuckles.

Her gaze flashed to his face, hardly daring to believe.

Dim slits of deep brown eyes watched her. Tears leaked from their corners, so silent not even Solene had noticed them.

For a long moment, Cistine didn't dare move or speak. She held her breath and drank in the sight of his eyes, the tears when he realized she was holding onto him.

Then Cistine threw down the book so loudly both Solene and Thorne jolted, and she scrambled onto the bed, flinging her arms around her father's shoulders, pulling him up to lean against her. His arm slowly dragged around her waist, and by the time he managed that, Solene was under his other arm, her face pressed into his neck, kissing his jaw and shouting his name. They jostled to find a way they could both hold him, and he them, tucked under his arms with their heads on his shoulders; then Cyril raised a slow brow at Thorne, lingering at the hearth and rubbing the back of his neck. A stern but soft look, full of knowing—a silent command.

With a sheepish snort, Thorne sat on the bed at Cyril's feet, only to be caught by the shoulder and dragged forward to bump foreheads with the King. They lingered like that, brow-to-brow, and from so close Cistine could see how tightly Thorne's eyes squeezed shut; she could feel how fiercely Cyril held onto him, his arm still wrapped around Cistine but that hand fastened onto the back of Thorne's neck like he might never let go.

The Novacek family, wounded and still healing in so many ways. But together once more.

Thank you, Cistine prayed. *Thank you, thank you. For this, for everything.*

The answer was a lick of remembered power along her limbs, a smell like orange-cinnamon scones, and three words she'd never believed more.

Hal ulda viy.

CHAPTER SIXTY-THREE

THE DAY AFTER Cyril woke, he insisted on a bedside meeting with Kashar. Though still weak and ill, the King sat up against a barricade of pillows Cistine had crafted behind him, the Queen straight-backed at his right hand, the Princess on his left. Thorne reclined at the door, keeping watch over Kashar, who shifted uneasily on his feet, occasionally glancing over his shoulder like he was waiting for someone else to arrive.

"I think it's time we discussed the future of our kingdoms." Sickly or not, Cyril commanded authority in a way that made Thorne acutely aware that more than twenty years of ruling experience separated them; Cyril had been King nearly as long as Thorne had been alive.

Kashar, too, shrank a bit in his shadow. "Your headstrong daughter has already been nipping our heels about that. We'll shoulder the cost to repair the border forts, naturally. And Middleton, whatever you think is fair once you have time to visit."

Cyril nodded. "And from that, *you* can extract whatever you consider fair pay for the hospitality you've shown us."

Kashar's head snapped to the side. "That's hardly necessary. You helped retake this kingdom."

Cyril's gaze softened slightly. "As far as anyone who was not in that Parlor or at the trench needs to know, Kashar az-Kyrian was the one who saw to Jad's end."

Cistine's gaze flicked to Thorne—a silent question. He dipped his head in reply. So long as she knew he'd fulfilled his vow to her all those months ago to end Jad's march of terror, he was content.

"You must present a strong image now," Cyril went on, "fair, but not too generous. Your people will be watching closely that you tend their needs better than your predecessor, and there are some who will take advantage of blatant generosity to another kingdom. This is a perfect opportunity to show them the sort of ruler you'll be."

Kashar's spine straightened, his hands folding at the small of his back. "In that case, perhaps you could eat a bit more cake to offset our tremendous debt to Talheim."

Solene burst into laughter, and Thorne bit back a smile. Cistine winked at Kashar. "I planned to do *exactly* that, how did you know?"

"Oh, my cooks are already warned to be on the lookout for Princess Novacek and her curly-haired friend who raid the kitchens at all hours."

She shrugged, utterly shameless. "If you don't want us to take advantage, you shouldn't make your cakes so tasty."

"Noted. For the next war, we'll ply them all with cake."

"Any war there may be," Cyril interjected, guiding the conversation back to somber ground, "as much as it's in this family's power, will not be with us."

"Nor with Valgard," Thorne added. "Our oath was to help bring Jad down, and we've done that. We want peace...a chance to catch our breath."

"That's all Talheim has ever wanted," Cistine agreed. "Peace."

"And you're willing to put that to paper?" Kashar asked. "An official treaty between all three kingdoms?"

A reverent pause took the room as the notion truly settled among those who had the power to bring that treaty to life.

"It's never been done," Solene murmured at last. "Not in all our recorded history."

"True," Cistine said with a grin, "but maybe the gods were just waiting for a time when the right rulers all sat in power at once."

"I can't do anything officially," Thorne reminded them. "Not without Bravis, Kyost, Valdemar, and Adeima. But whatever your scribes write, I'll return to Valgard for review and bring back with suggestions or signatures."

Kashar nodded. "And what reparations does Valgard demand?"

"Only one Mahasari ever made it past our borders, and I suspect she's been more than dealt with," Thorne said, and Cistine winced at the mention of Reema, the spy who'd tried to befriend her in Stornhaz. "Valgard asks for nothing more than the food and healing your people have already offered. And we look forward to a treaty of friendship."

Kashar's stern mask cracked, a faint smirk tilting through. "As does Mahasar."

"As does Talheim." Cyril nodded to the door, and Thorne sidestepped to swing it open. "Tomorrow, then. Bring your quickest scribes and finest pens, Your Eminence."

"The Treaty of Three Kingdoms, penned at a King's bedside." Kashar shook his head, laughing as he strutted out. "History being made every day in these halls!"

Silence descended in his wake, the Novaceks all looking around at one another; relief and happiness bloomed deep in Thorne's stomach when he met Cistine's shining eyes. It was truly happening; they would go home, not to war, but to the future they'd dreamed of having, with the peace and the treaties they'd all fought so hard and nearly given their lives for.

His heart was so full, it felt like it would burst.

They ordered supper up from the kitchens, where the rations were at last clean of Sorcel, and Cistine and Thorne dragged the room's lonely dining table close to the bed so Cyril could reach. Over roasted lamb skewers and flatcakes heaped with shaved onions and sour cream, the King demanded tales of Valgard—first the epics from which Sillakove Court derived its name and where the constellations were told, then of the cabal's exploits during their ten long years in the wilderness.

Throughout the telling, Thorne barely managed a single bite, but he didn't mind; not when his stories of Quill's first few hopeless attempts at wagon raids on the Vey and the disasters of early training in Hellidom had

Solene and Cistine in stitches and Cyril wiping tears from his eyes. And not when it brought everything so close—the past from which he'd finally escaped, and the future he was so privileged to be a part of, together in this room.

"You know, all of this might make me fear the man my daughter married," Cyril chuckled, gesturing at Thorne with a skewer, "if I hadn't been that exact sort of man at nineteen."

"Dashing off to Khorraris, you mean," Solene scoffed. "I've never known such recklessness."

"Well, I'd never known such love." Cyril caught her hand and kissed it.

The Queen's cheeks flushed. "Flatterer."

"I'm a King. It's required for the title. Where do you think the treaties come from?"

Thorne caught Cistine's eye down the small table and mimicked the words in exaggerated silence; she shot forward to swipe a streak of sour cream down the length of his nose. Laughing, he didn't hear the door open while he cleaned off his face; but he sensed the sudden, subtle shift in the air, as if a chill had wafted inside.

Cistine straightened, the humor falling from her features. Both the King and Queen stiffened. And Thorne pushed his chair back and turned to look at Rion Bartos, filling up the doorway.

His memory of what had happened in this Palace after Jad had ensorcelled him was blurrier every day, glimpses and flickers fading to nightmarish sparks. But when he looked at Rion, he remembered incensed eyes and spittle-flecked lips, a face set to murder.

No one harms my family and lives.

A flash like lightning, a flicker of Julian's face across Thorne's mind. His hand curled into a fist against his knee.

"Rion." Cyril's tone was something between pleasant and cautious. "Care to join us?"

Solene's lower lip quivered, but she didn't argue—perhaps recognizing, just as Thorne did, that this wasn't about them. It was just the King and his Commander, regarding one another carefully through the doorway.

Rion cleared his throat. "It's...good to see you awake. When I heard the news you were recovering, I could barely believe it."

"Well, I think I owe that to this one here." Cyril rested a hand on the back of Cistine's head, and she leaned into his touch.

"To a *healing* augment, you mean." A faint bite of scorn undergirded Rion's tone, and Thorne bristled.

"I wish you could've felt it, Rion." Despite the room's unbearable tension, Cistine's smile was like the stars, brilliant and ethereal. Something had shifted in her that day at the King's bedside, tangible and lasting, taking a part of her so high Thorne could barely reach it. But it awed him like the sight of every star that had ever mapped the course of his life. "Using augmentation the way it was meant to be used...we still have so much to learn, but it was *good*. If you had just seen—"

"But I wasn't permitted to see anything, was I?" His harsh interruption blotted out her enthusiasm. "I was told to get out."

"That may be. But you're invited now." Though Cyril's tone remained even, his eyes flashed.

"I don't make a habit of dining with *murderers.*"

And there was the accusation Thorne had been waiting for, bared like the first gleam of steel when a knife left its sheath.

"There are no murderers at this table," Cyril said calmly. "Men and women who've made mistakes, yes, that's all of us." Cistine squirmed a bit in her seat. "But not murderers."

"I beg to differ." Rion's gaze pierced into Thorne with all the killing might his sword had failed to impart in the Parlor of Winds. "I want justice for my son, for *my* family."

"If it's justice you seek, you shouldn't be looking at Thorne." Solene's voice trembled. "Look at *me*, Rion."

He wouldn't, though the tendons in his neck strained visibly. Perhaps he was afraid that if he laid eyes on the woman who'd delivered the fatal blow to Eboni, ensorcelled or not, his rage might shift to another target— one he couldn't strike without breaking Cyril's heart. "As far as I'm concerned, the only reason Eboni was unaware of what happened to you, the only reason you were taken and the only *reason* she is dead, is because she was bereaved of our only child." He gestured toward Thorne with a slice of his hand. "Because *he* led him to slaughter."

"Julian chose to go," Cistine snapped. "I was there. I told him...*Thorne* told him not to attack Salvotor. He chose to do it anyway."

"You'd *spit* on my son's grave to defend the man who brought about his death?" Rion roared so loudly Cistine flinched. "You never deserved him, you rat-romping—"

"That is *enough*," Cyril growled.

"No, it's not enough! None of this is *enough*...I want justice!" Now that he'd cut loose the tether of his rage, Rion was unstoppable; the maddened fury from the Parlor gleamed once more in his eyes, and Thorne laid a hand to the dagger belted at his waist, pulse kicking. "His life for Julian's, that is all I will accept. It's what's fair!"

"There is nothing fair about this. Not when a man is deprived of his only son," Cyril said. "But I will not put mine to the sword for the decision yours made. You need to grieve, Rion, not to seek vengeance."

"I have no use for grief! It's empty and endless, it solves nothing. Vengeance is the only thing that will bring me peace, and you owe me that, Cyril! After *everything*!"

"It won't end in anything but more heartbreak. I can't let you do it."

The words fell like the clatter of a gauntlet thrown down. Heat pricked Thorne's throat when he looked at this bedridden King whose trust he'd betrayed and confidence he'd taken for granted, standing between him and Rion in conduct if not in body.

The weight of that wasn't lost to Rion, either. Hand braced to his own sword, his chest heaved. "Then you're choosing them. Choosing the Valgardans over me."

Unbearable sadness gleamed in Cyril's eyes. "I am choosing peace. I choose my family, Rion. And you will always be part of that if *you* choose...but it's time to lay down the sword."

Rion's fingers flexed on his hilt. Once. Twice.

"No."

Frigid silence descended. Slowly, Cyril tugged back the blankets. His legs inched over until he sat on the edge of the bed. "*Excuse* me?"

With a swift glance, Thorne and Cistine came to their feet, braced with tension, his dagger and her Nail half-out of their sheaths.

"I will not stand by while Talheim becomes *infested* with Valgardan filth, while their murderous offspring roam free and their backwards ideals pollute the Cadre. I stood by as you made that treaty with them to discourage Mahasar, and look what good it did us, Cyril! Absolutely *none*! Solene was taken, you nearly died, *Eboni* was killed!" His voice cracked around her name. "What use is Valgard to us? Break the gods-damned treaty, give me my son's killer, and *then* we'll have peace!"

"If you kill a Chancellor, peace will *never* come," Cyril argued. "War or none, we still have much we can learn from Valgard, and them from us. I won't throw that away just to sate your hunger for revenge."

"*Much to learn*," Rion echoed scathingly. "Is this about augments? Do you really love those little jars of power more than you love me?"

"It's because I love you that I'm not giving you what you think you need."

"I would do it. If I was in your place, I would do it for *you*."

"That's why I'm King, and you will never be."

Rion's face paled, his expression crumbling like he'd been struck. Slowly, his head wagged, fingers peeling away from his sword. "You've gone down a path I can't follow, Cyril. Chosen fanatics and barbarians over your own people. Chosen my son's *killer* over me." Rion stripped off the Cadre emblem from his uniform and cast it onto the table. "The King I loved is dead. He died in that trench. My men and I will not serve an augur who defends murderers."

"But you will heed one." Cyril rose, slow and lethal, thunderous in quiet fury and not a flicker of weakness in his frame. "If you break this peace we have all fought so hard for, you will find the end of my mercy is a noose, Rion. You have been warned."

"So have you, *Brother*."

Rion stalked from the room, slamming the door at his back.

The moment it shut, Cyril buckled, and Thorne and Cistine lunged across the bed, catching him under his arms to keep him upright. Solene's arm wrapped his waist, and they lowered him gently onto the bed's edge together.

The King leaned back against his wife's chest—utterly spent, eyelids fluttering, chest heaving. Over his bowed head, Thorne met Cistine's eyes and found his fear reflected in her face. And in the echo of Rion's retreating footfalls down the outer hall, Thorne heard the whisper of Jad's parting threat.

What I began today will curse them for the rest of their lives. They will always have enemies carrying my shadow.

The game is not over…it's just beginning.

THE PRINCE

OF

BLOOD AND STARS

CHAPTER SIXTY-FOUR

Things were different after Rion Bartos left the city.

Much as Tatiana wished she'd had a chance to holler *good riddance* at his retreating back, she didn't even realize he was gone at first; the word came through Rozalie only an hour before Cistine and Thorne rallied the cabal to tell them about the argument at the King's bedside.

The morning after Rion's defection, he and nearly half the Wardens in Arak Shehr had disappeared into the desert wastes beyond the fertile plain; those who remained were confused and conflicted, desperate for answers about their once-loyal leader and his unprecedented feud with the royal family. Rozalie spent most of her time mustering them and explaining matters while Ashe and Bresnyar patrolled the skies, watching for Rion to rally and return.

But he never did.

Days dragged on, full of patrols, treaties, and so much stars-blessed *food*. Mahasar's spicy, savory dishes, now safe to eat with the *Alburi* cleansing the city, were nothing short of a revelation; Tatiana, Quill, and Cistine ate their way through all three districts, sampling so much Southern fare it likely broke laws. But sweetest of all was the joy on the vendors' faces seeing their fortune finally begin to turn under a new King with friends who could afford to eat their weight and then some.

"No wonder Jad ensorcelled his people through food and drink," Tatiana remarked one evening while she and Cistine slipped back into the Palace after dark, licking cinnamon and sugar crystals from their latest pastries off their fingertips. "I think I could be convinced to fight another war if it meant getting my hands on more of those...what did the vendor call them?"

"*Sukairgoth*," Cistine laughed, dodging a tide of servants' children sprinting down the hall. "You can't be spoiling for a fight already, Tati! It's barely been a month!"

Her feet almost stilled at that.

A whole month already since Jad had died. The time had passed strangely—a fortnight waiting for the King to live or die, then another two weeks since he'd opened his eyes and Rion had left. Like two separate lives with a cord cut between them. "Stars, it's really been a month. By this time after the Deathmarch, we were already knees-deep in the next war."

Cistine linked arms with her, tugging her down the ornate hall. "Maybe it's a good sign that next one hasn't started yet."

Maybe it never will.

They met the others in one of the sitting parlors, its deep amber walls glowing in the late-day sun. It had become a frequent haunt when duties with Wardens and augurs and meetings with nobles finally ended. They were nearly the last ones to arrive today; Maleck sat sketching on a sofa, Ashe and Rozalie discussing Cadre matters, Ariadne reading by the hearth and picking idly at a bowl of dates. Even missing Quill, Thorne, and Aden, Tatiana's heart swelled at the sight of them all together.

Cistine squeezed her arm and finally let go, moving to read over Ariadne's shoulder. Tatiana angled for the couch beside Maleck, but just then the parlor door swung open and a familiar metal-fingered grip latched onto her hip, twirling her straight into her *valenar's* lips.

There was something about how he kissed her she couldn't put a name to. How it felt, how it tasted, a blend of salt and ecstasy on his mouth...

She gripped his collar and pushed him back, meeting his feverish gaze. "What was *that* for?"

"Changing the stars." He winked, patted the breast pocket of his loose linen shirt like it contained all the answers to life, then swaggered toward the sofa. Tatiana raised her brows at Thorne, trailing in behind Quill with a crooked half-smile.

He spread his hands in a shrug. *Not my story to tell.*

Rozalie broke conversation with Ashe to ask, "Should we order up food from the kitchens?"

"*No!*" Cistine and Tatiana chorused, earning a round of skewed looks. Grinning, Tatiana patted her middle. "If I didn't know better, I'd think Mahasar was plumping us up for slaughter."

"Don't say that," Rozalie scolded. "Kashar's been awfully generous, all things considered. Putting up a clutch of foreign nobles for a month…"

"Well, his uncle did nearly kill us." Quill's tone was casual; the way he prowled up behind the sofa was anything but. "I'd say it all evens out in the end."

"At what point was *your* life ever in any real danger?" Ashe scoffed. "You got a dragon out of this!"

"Don't forget who *took* that dragon and flew him to the trench."

She tilted her head slowly. "Fair."

Grinning, Quill leaned over the back of the couch, grabbed Maleck in a headlock, and dragged him backward out of his seat. Seconds later, they were wrestling, pounding each other's ribs and flipping one another across the floor.

"Quill! Maleck!" Thorne kicked the door shut. "If you get blood on these rugs, you'll have to clean it out yourselves."

They both looked up—Quill with a bruise on his jaw, Maleck's nose bleeding slightly.

"Is there something you want to say, Quill?" Thorne added.

Tatiana arched a brow at her *valenar*. He grinned back, showing blood on his teeth, too. "Not yet. Just letting off some heat."

"Well, in that case."

Thorne dove over the sofa and piled on top of them, turning it to a three-way tussle. Ariadne and Cistine rolled their eyes, and Tatiana, laughing, snatched a crocheted blanket from a basket near the hearth and strolled to the wingbacked seat near the window, fully intending to nap off the evening meal and copious desserts afterward.

Her haunches had barely struck the plush seat when the door brushed open again; to her surprise, King Cyril entered this time, escorted by a Palace servant.

Rozalie whistled, and everyone snapped to attention, even the men, popping up from their wrestling match like someone had set the floor on fire. Tatiana bit back another laugh.

"Papa, what are you doing out of bed?" Cistine surged to her feet. "You should be *resting!*"

"It's been two weeks, Cistine. I'm doing my body no favors lying down all the time." Though he still leaned heavily on the servant's shoulder, the King *did* seem stronger, his tone even and his color healthy again. "I'm here to steal Ashe."

"Consider me a willing victim." She rose and stretched. "Better than sitting around discussing Rion. Or watching these bastards beat each other's faces in."

With a shadowy glance and a gentle pat to the servant's back, the King slung an arm around Ashe's shoulders instead, then cleared his throat and looked at the men: his son by marriage wiping his bloody nose on his wrist, Maleck cradling his ribs, Quill knocking his hair over to hide his scar. "The next time your bloodlust consumes you, I recommend taking it outside where no one can hear you, or Kashar might assume he's under attack again." Eyes dancing with mischief, he guided Ashe from the room, calling over his shoulder, "And then I would have to join in and teach you boys a thing or two about how to *really* brawl."

The door swung shut on that half-threat, half-challenge.

Quill checked Thorne's shoulder with his. Thorne punched Quill over against Maleck. Maleck shoved him bluntly back upright.

Cistine burst into uncontrollable giggles.

"All right, all right, I'm done. Don't feel up for tangling with kings today." Quill sniffed back blood and strolled to Tatiana's chair, offering his hand. "Take a walk with me, Saddlebags?" Now that he was calmer, there was a secret shining in his eyes, a gleam of nervous joy that stroked her own excitement like a lover's flirtatious hand.

Tatiana let him draw her up and lead her from the parlor. Her last glimpse within was of Maleck snatching up his sketchbook and going to sit by Rozalie, and Thorne sliding onto the sofa behind Cistine, wrapping his arms around her waist.

Contentment filled her chest when she and Quill walked hand-in-hand through the Palace halls. He didn't seem to be going anywhere in particular, just wandering, but the way his fingers flexed around hers made her heart bound and sink again and again. First that kiss when he and Thorne had entered the room, later than everyone else; then the wrestling; and now that look in his eye. "Quill—"

"Shh. Not yet. I want it to be perfect." He glanced over both shoulders, then tugged her through a doorway and out onto one of the west-facing balconies. The dark ridge of the mountains was still visible in the distance, a toothy grin reminiscent of their time in Ralathi Trench and the oasis at Shinar.

Finally, Quill released her hand, and she couldn't bear it anymore, spinning on heel to face him. "What *is* it, Featherbrain?"

The words tapered off on her tongue. Quill held something out to her, pulled from his shirt pocket; a small scroll, sealed and tied.

The last time he'd given her a gift that looked anything like this...

Her shaking fingers took it gently. "What is this?"

"It's where we're going when we return to Valgard. If you want."

Tatiana's heart pounded. "But our home in Blaykrone was destroyed. Thorne told me. *Heimli Nyfadengar* lost almost everything, too."

"I know." Quill's contrary eyes glinted. "Just read it, Saddlebags."

She slid the deep purple twine off the scroll and turned to the balcony railing, unrolling it against the stone to read. She read it five times, and it *still* didn't make sense.

"Quill," she breathed. "This is a deed to the *Den*."

"Strictly speaking, it never really had a deed. I think Thorne made this one just to keep things official." Quill laughed shakily. "It's ours, Tati. He wants us and the guild in Hellidom. We keep the Den."

Tatiana pressed a hand to her stomach, all that delicious, sugary goodness threatening to rise back up her throat. Her head spun at the thought of *their* Den, warm and comfortable and familiar, the smell of cinnamon and orange scones filling the air; of falling asleep to the sound of the watermills churning every single night like she had for ten years, only this time with Quill in the bed with her and Pippet sleeping down the hall.

The cabal coming to visit, all piled into their old rooms, except Thorne would be in Cistine's and Ashe in Maleck's, and Aden could take the loft. They would train and tend that garden and be with their friends—and never have to hide again.

The deed fluttered to the balcony as she whirled and lunged into Quill's arms, meeting his mouth with hers. He stumbled back against the Palace wall and let her kiss him breathless with all her gratitude and joy, his hands gripping her waist and digging in almost to bruising.

She couldn't stop smiling even when she pulled away to breathe, leaning back in his grip to meet his gaze. "Tell me you thanked him a thousand times at *least?*"

"I doubt anyone but Cistine's ever hugged him tighter in his life."

Laughing, Tatiana gripped the sides of his neck and shook him. "Quill. We get to go back."

He brushed the curls from her face, then tilted her head up with his thumbs at the hinges of her jaw and met her gaze with wild joy, the happiness in his heart a mirror for hers. "We get to go *home.*"

Home.

Memory cracked through Tatiana so suddenly she sucked in a breath, tugging away from his grip. "Oh, stars damn it, I almost forgot! There's something I need to do. Thank you for the reminder, Featherbrain!"

Quill sighed. "Care for some company?"

"Not for this. But if you want to meet me in our room..."

His eyes brightened. "One step ahead of you."

They parted just inside the doorway, Tatiana blowing him a kiss and

Quill waggling his brows in a way that made her yearn to return to him that much faster. She all but ran through the halls.

She knew precisely where to find Mahasar's new King; she'd learned his patterns fairly early on in their stay in the Palace, just in case anything went wrong...or in case she needed to demand a favor.

Tonight, it was purely the latter.

Thankfully, he was alone for once, leaving his usual meeting room while the clamor of upraised voices continued inside. Tatiana shadowed him through two halls, waiting for the weary tension in his shoulders to ease. Once she was sure he was in a more agreeable mindset, she lengthened her stride in real pursuit.

"Your Eminence!" she called, but he didn't turn. "*Kashar!*"

Slowing, he turned with a hopeful smile that fell into a pensive, disappointed frown when he laid eyes on her. "Ah...Tatiana, isn't it?"

She almost asked who he'd been hoping to see, but really, she already knew. And that was another story that wasn't hers to tell.

"That's me." She swaggered to a halt beside him. "Still getting used to the title?"

"To all of this." He waved a hand and sighed. "The Magnates are rightfully up in arms over the mess of these last few years. If I explain Sorcel to them one more time, I think I might run screaming from that chamber." Sadness shadowed his gaze. "I wish Tirz...Sacha were here, this was far more her strength than mine."

Sympathy touched Tatiana's heart. "Give it time. Anyone who deals with intoxication, those lost days can feel like they were stolen from you. I imagine it's a lot worse when you're drunk on something against your will." She clapped him on the shoulder. "You've been through what they're going through now, but you've had the chance to come out on the other side of it. Patience is the kindest thing you can offer them."

Kashar studied her for a long moment. "I suppose that's true. And what can I do for you?"

"I have a request—don't worry," she laughed when he pulled a face. "It's nothing you're not already doing, just...I hoped you might expedite something for me."

"Well, if you're going to hunt me down with sage advice, I suppose I can spare you my ear in return."

Tatiana grinned. "There's a family in an oasis near Ralathi waiting on reparations for the land Jad swindled from them. I think they could use some of the payment right away. And maybe a house set aside for them in Masiya..."

CHAPTER SIXTY-FIVE

CYRIL ONLY LEANED on Ashe until they were out of sight of the cabal's favorite parlor; then he straightened, pulling his arm from around her shoulders with a roguish wink. "Cistine and her mother would have a fit if they saw me walking without a crutch, but I think I can manage this on my own feet."

It really wasn't far to the room he and the Queen shared, so Ashe let him go, though she did keep a close eye on him all the way.

She hadn't visited him as much as she should have before his recovery, and she'd been occupied on patrol with Bresnyar after; maybe he wanted to know why. Maybe he thought her a coward, not wanting to see him wasting away in that bed. But she hadn't been ready to watch the King she loved, more like a father to her than anyone in her life, die before her eyes.

Steeling her spine, she ducked after him into his and Solene's room, where he went straight to the desk someone had dragged in for him to work from. Scattered with scrolls and papers, it looked just like every other desk in every other room he'd ever occupied. Nothing kept the King from his duties for long.

"How are you?" Cyril asked, sinking into his chair.

The question caught her off-guard. "*Me?* I'm not the one who dove head-first into a poisonous trench!"

"Fair. Though I didn't dive so much as somersault." Cyril picked up a peacock-plume quill—apparently the preferred writing utensil in Mahasar—and eyed it for a moment. Then he tapped the nib on the desk. "But I meant about Rion."

The name wrenched at something deep in Ashe's spirit. "I scoured the city for him and his deserters...the desert, too. Bres tried to track him, but after that dust storm..."

The short, violent squall the day after Rion's departure had erased every trace, as if the King's Cadre Commander had only ever been a mirage. In some ways, she supposed that was true. The man in whose shadow she'd walked, looking up to him all her life, was no more real than the enemies he'd always assumed he was fighting.

Perhaps the truth of Rion Bartos was always the Butcher, *Meszaros* of Cerne Mosiar; maybe he'd just finally shed his skin to become the creature he was born to be.

"I appreciate the effort you've put into the hunt." Cyril's eyes softened. "But I'm asking how *you* are, not how that's going."

"I'm..." She nearly blurted *all right*, but at Cyril's raised brow, chose honesty over image. "Furious. And concerned."

"That makes two of us." He groomed his brows with his thumb and forefinger. "It's possible I pushed him too far...demanded too much of him, fighting another war, and alongside Valgard no less. I knew he was still grieving Julian's loss, that Eboni wasn't well, but I didn't want to face this without him."

"It wasn't your fault. Look at the Valgardans...they went from one war straight to the next, but it didn't make them vengeful bastards." Ashe settled into the seat across from him, pressing her thumb into the Wingmaiden's rune on her palm. "What was broken in Rion has been that way for a long time. Too long for us to fix."

"He didn't *want* to fix it." Cyril angled his body to stare out the window. "I see that now."

For several minutes, silence embraced them. Grief slanted the King's mouth and tilted his brow; Ashe wondered for a panicked instant if he was about to cry.

"I'm sorry I never truly took into account your feelings about him," he said at last. "I knew there was contention between you two, and I put Rion first. I thought if I kept him close, gave him the title and place at my side he never really wanted to leave, it might...I don't know. Mend things." He dug his knuckles into his brow. "God's bones, it sounds *ridiculous* when I say it. What a fool I am."

"It's not ridiculous to fight for the people you love," Ashe protested. "But I don't think we can deny it anymore: Rion doesn't want to be saved, he wants a reckoning. He'll be back for it someday."

"I know." Cyril heaved a deep sigh. "I've been thinking about that, too. About the vulnerability he's left in our ranks. In light of all that's ensued..." His fingertips grazed the frayed Cadre emblem on his desk. "I find myself in need of a new Commander. And it appears that with all these defections, the likely candidates have deserted me. Except Viktor, possibly, but that can never happen with his past loyalties to Rion. Which leaves just one."

Ashe sucked in a sharp breath. "Are you asking *me* to take his place?"

Cyril flashed her a tired smile. "Would you accept if I did?"

She let the wave of shock, the old longing, and gratitude rise through her one last time; Cyril held out the patch, threadbare and stained with blood from countless battles, some of it possibly Thorne's. Possibly Maleck's. Marks of shame, but also of power, and the love once held between the Bartos family and the Novaceks. A legacy he was asking her to carry on.

Ashe hesitated a moment longer, asking herself if this was truly what she wanted, the future she desired.

Then she gently closed the King's fingers over the patch.

"I appreciate the offer, but it's been a long time since I cared to be Cadre. And I think I can serve better as a friend to the Novaceks than a Commander."

Cyril's arm fell, his face with it. "I won't say I'm not disappointed. But I'm also proud."

"You are?"

"You finally know what you want. And I'd much rather have a

Commander who serves out of desire for the duty rather than obligation to the crown."

Ashe grinned. "Well, if you're still accepting recommendations..."

"Please, God, *yes.*"

"It should be Rozalie Dohnal. She fought harder than most to save this kingdom, and she's proven her loyalty to the royal family a hundred times over. She'll serve you *and* Cistine well when the time comes." Pursing her lips against an even broader smirk, she added, "And I think she's gaining a good grasp of Mahasari decorum."

Cyril scratched his bearded jaw. "I'll speak with her as soon as I can do it without hunching like a man twice my age."

"Hunched or not, the rest of us still see a King."

His smile lighter, Cyril sank back in his seat. "What will you do, then? Return to Valgard? Head north to the land of dragons?"

"Honestly, I thought I might come back to Talheim," she admitted. "Open up a sword school for girls, maybe. Teach children to ride dragons. Or just live a quiet life."

They looked at one another for a long moment, then burst into laughter that sent the King hacking into his fist.

"You could take that open jester's position, telling jokes like that," he wheezed. "But it will be good to have you back home, however you choose...however long it lasts."

Strange that the thought of being in Talheim *did* feel like home again, for the first time in months. Perhaps because Rion was gone; or perhaps because wherever she went, Maleck would be with her. And that would be enough.

"We'll see what happens." She pushed back from the desk. "I should let you rest."

"Ashe," Cyril said when she turned to go. "It warms my heart to see you happy."

Happy.

With the war over, her cabal safe, her husband and dragon at her side, and her princess finally set free...she truly was. And that, too—over titles, over lands, over a place to call home—was more than enough.

As evening approached, Ashe found Maleck in the music hall.

They'd discovered it together, a place the Palace reserved for revelry—so it hadn't seen use in some time. The converted dancing hall stretched out to a broad mezzanine overlooking one of the Palace's inner courtyards; with the balcony doors swung wide, many of the apartments were visible, where augurs, Wardens, and *Alhuri* lived now, people of three kingdoms learning how to be one in purpose if not one in creed or race...and that purpose was peace. A better future, like Aden always said.

From inside the hall came the unmistakable sound of Maleck's playing. Ashe halted just around the corner, back to the wall, listening to the gentle strains of a Talheimic lullaby wafting through the halls—a song she'd sung to Cistine and Pippet, a song Maleck had learned from listening to her hum it over him during the war against his brothers. A song of moonlit dreams and the home she was going back to, but nothing like the home she'd left so long ago.

Everything was changing. For the better, she hoped.

A whisper of unease reminded her that Rion was still out there, but she shut it away; he'd stolen enough years of her life with his false love, withheld praise, and outpouring of prejudice. She wouldn't let his shadow hang over this happiness now that he'd finally removed himself from her path.

ASHEILA. IS ALL WELL?

She hardly realized she'd cleaved, but when Bresnyar's voice stroked through her like a soothing balm, she opened her eyes to endless golden dunes and blue skies paling to lavender in the twilight. The spectral feeling of wind brushed her cheeks.

Everything's perfect, Scales. Flying with Shrike?

TEACHING HIM TO BANK. HE'S PITIFULLY UNDERSCHOOLED.

No better teacher. She wiped her face against her armored sleeve. *Admit it. He's beginning to grow on you.*

LIKE A FUNGUS.

Laughing under her breath, Ashe watched the world pass through her dragon's eyes. Her chest ached for those open skies, for the breadth of the world and the freedom it promised. *Let's go for a flight tomorrow…no patrols, just for fun. We'll race Quill and Shrike, and when we beat them…*

WHEN? His thoughts echoed in amusement, a flattered prompt.

I don't know. We'll see where the horizon guides us.

TO THE HORIZON, THEN, ILYANAK. AND WHATEVER LIES BEYOND.

She had no fear of flying into the unknown; with him, she could always find her way back when it was time.

She sent that feeling to him, coursing down the cleaving bond between them, and what returned was the pure, fierce, and fiery love only a dragon could possibly possess.

Shrugging up from the wall, Ashe broke the connection and strode into the music hall, joining Maleck at the piano. His passionate refrain surged out into the courtyard, where balcony doors hung open, coaxing the sounds in with the cooling mid-evening air. Ashe grinned to think of him providing entertainment for the Three Kingdoms.

"Better than any symphony hall," she remarked, trailing her hand along the piano's top and halting at a box placed on its edge. "What's this?"

Maleck raised his eyes but didn't break his playing. "I thought you might want to join me after you spoke with the King."

She opened the violin case, fingers quivering with joy at the instrument within; beautifully lacquered in stripes of deep scarlet and ebony, its surface like pure cream to the touch, the bow perfectly weighed. When she tucked it under her chin and laid hair to strings, the first note alone nearly made her weep.

"What did he ask you?" Maleck inquired with false innocence.

"He wanted me to lead the Cadre."

Maleck's fingers skipped, missing the next note, his eyes flashing back to her face. "And what did you tell him?"

"That I'm not the woman for the job." Ashe winked at him. "I'm not looking for a title anymore. I already have everything I need."

She found her place in the melody and sank into it with him, violin blending beautifully into piano, both one and distinct. Excited shivers danced down her spine at the sounds they made together, a pocket within the world's harmony that belonged just to them. Her feet moved almost of their own accord, spinning and sidling around the piano, and Maleck laughed while he watched her—not the keys. He knew this song as well as she did by now, as clear as his own Name.

Outside the haven their music made, more doors opened. On one balcony, Thorne spun Cistine out into the open, dipping her low and kissing her jaw, and the princess's laughter rang like a bell on the cool air. All around them, warriors and Mahasari nobles emerged to lean on stone railings and listen, calling out to one another in half-mocking invitations to dance; and some obliged, Wardens leaping across balconies to sweep augurs off their feet, *Alhuri* forming up in lines for traditional jigs, joined by students from the northern and middle kingdoms, eager to learn what their new allies could teach.

Somewhere, the Kings and the Queen were listening; somewhere much farther away, lands were healing. A new day was dawning, moment by moment across the world. No matter what it held, Asheila Kovar was glad to be part of it—her music just one fragment of the joyous symphony filling the kingdoms, a song for the ages ringing across time and into the future.

To the next horizon. And whatever lay beyond.

CHAPTER SIXTY-SIX

Rozalie DID NOT sleep after the King sought her out privately for the evening meal; once dismissed, bathed and dressed in fine silk pajamas, she sat awake on the floor before her vaulted windows, staring up at the moon's shutting eye. Her pulse quickened with thoughts of titles and responsibilities waiting to be claimed, and she relived their discussion over supper so many times she could've had it back with herself, word for word.

She'd never expected any of this, as a brothel girl or as a low-ranking Warden or even when Cistine had asked her to take Ashe's place at her side.

Gods. Rozalie Dohnal. *Cadre Commander.*

Before sunrise broke, she donned her armor and hurried to seek out the one person who might understand the weight of unprecedented titles heaped on unprepared shoulders.

She found him in the *garriqah* he adored, lost between tendrils of creeping moss and stocky frond trees near a rabbit hutch. He cradled one of the animals in the crook of his arm, so small and tufted it looked like a stormcloud. He rubbed between its ears and snorted when it snuffled its whiskers against his wrist.

Shadow-Slayer, indeed.

He looked up at her approach, flashing one of those trained, royal smiles that melted into something more casually cocky and deprecating when her recognized her; he knew he didn't have to try with her, because she would neither like him nor be fooled into thinking he was royal no matter what he did. It made everything so much easier.

With a jolt, she realized it was the first time she'd seen him in a month.

"This hutch was a gift," he said after a moment, seeming just as bereft as her of ways to start this conversation. "Jad brought me to it and told me to pick my favorite of all the rabbits. When I did, he took it from me and snapped its neck."

Rozalie's jaw hung slack. Maybe the brutality shouldn't have surprised her after a year fighting Jad's forces, but it still managed to sting.

"*Caring is weakness*," Kashar said after a beat, his tone so like his uncle's it made her heart skip. "*Favoritism is weakness.* Those were the sorts of things he whispered in my ear when I was ensorcelled. *All that matters is the game.* That was what I told my sister when I tried to take her life." He slid the rabbit gently back into its hutch, then turned to her. Regret stormed his dark eyes. "I didn't get to beg her forgiveness for that."

"You didn't have to. She'd already given it," Rozalie said. "She loved you enough to face her own *ivrrans* for you."

"And that haunts me the most. As much as our kingdom has to heal, we each have wounds of our own we must mend." Tucking his hands into his sleeves, he reclined against the hutch. "How are you healing?"

She shrugged. "Fine. How's your head?"

His eyes narrowed. "You know, most would consider it bad form to taunt a king, *Raqian*."

"Still sore, then."

He laughed outright at that, amusement chasing away the shadows still lingering in his countenance. "You certainly *seem* fine."

It took effort not to crack a smile of her own. "More or less. Before last night, I felt like everything finally made sense again."

"What happened last night?"

"You might not believe me if I told you."

He cocked a brow. "Well, did you come here for the garden, or for me?"

"I don't even know why I came." Rozalie lowered herself onto a stone bench, cradling her head in her hands. "No, that's a lie. It's just...the King asked me to assume command of the Cadre."

Kashar's feet, sandaled and stockinged, shifted just within her line of vision. "Quite an honor. Will you take the position?"

A wry smile yanked her lips. "Are you asking me as the suspicious ruler of a newly-befriended kingdom who wants to know Talheim's inner workings?"

"I'm asking as someone who knows full well what it is to have responsibility suddenly thrust into your hands."

Breathing out her relief that he knew exactly why she'd sought him, of all people, Rozalie raised her eyes to his. "How are you managing it?"

He shrugged. "Who says I am? Last night I helped the *Alhuri* chart a journey to the aqueducts to spread the antidote in the water. This morning I threw a chamberpot at the wall and kicked my bedpost so hard I may have broken a toe."

"Ah. Hence the choice of footwear."

"You noticed?"

"My princess and one of her closest friends are very fashionable. I have learned *many* things in the past nine months."

A smile tugged at Kashar's lips as he joined her, settling onto the bench. "Imagine what you can learn in nine more. Particularly if you're a Commander at the time."

She glanced at him. "I'm not sure either of us deserves these positions, really."

"Perhaps not. But...try to think of it like an adventure. An unexpected second chance. Don't we owe it to ourselves and everyone we care for, especially those we lost, to seize it and make the most of it? After all, if we don't, who will?"

"Maybe you're right." She rasped her palms together. "Do you push through the difficult days for Sacha?"

He bobbed his shoulders. "Knowing what she sacrificed all these years to free me, what sort of man would I be if I didn't?"

"I can understand that," Rozalie admitted. "I had—*have* two sisters. I spent so much of my training trying to make them proud, even knowing I might never see them again."

Damn this man and the way his presence opened up her inner parts like a swig of Sorcel. Not even half the Wardens knew of the life she'd had before the brothel.

"*Two* sisters," Kashar whistled. "No wonder you're such a wildcat."

She cocked a brow at him. "Do you miss her?"

"I didn't have her back long enough to miss more than the idea of what we could've been when we were both free." When Rozalie went on staring at him, he sighed. "I miss the children we were and the glimpse of who she became. All the moments and memories we'll never have."

With an old, long-buried pang, Rozalie thought of her family's farm. "I can understand that."

They were quiet for a time, him staring at the rabbit hutch, giving her space to think.

She could do it, couldn't she? After all, the Wardens had turned to her when Rion vanished. She had Ashe's tutelage and the things war had taught her, and she had vowed long ago to give her life for the royal family if needed. Taking this title would just be another way of keeping that vow.

"I think I can do it," she mused. "I think I have to."

"Well, good! I'm glad that's settled, because I've used up all the inspiring things I have to say." Kashar stood and offered his hand. "May I show you something?"

She squinted one eye shut, pretending to ponder. "I don't know. As future Cadre Commander, it may be harmful to my reputation if I'm seen consorting with the Mahasari King."

"Well, fortunate we won't be seen, then." He wiggled his fingers with a sly grin, and when she clasped his forearm, he pulled her up and led her into the halls.

The Palace hadn't quite woken yet; even the servants were sparse along the way. Their stride was leisurely, going nowhere quickly, and after the past year Rozalie found she could appreciate taking things slowly.

Many things, she decided, glancing at Kashar.

"For what it's worth," he said after a time, "I think the title suits you. You'll make a powerful leader, *Raqian*—and a fair one."

"I hope you will, too, or it's going to be my job to start a war with you." He halted first, but Rozalie was a step behind him, hands perched on her hips. "Are you *ever* going to tell me what that ridiculous word means?"

His brows rose, and he chuckled. "Sunshine."

And just like that, it poured into the halls—dawn's first rays slicing through the keyhole corridors, bouncing wildly on the walls, turning the world to a prism and setting it on fire, just like he'd promised.

Right there with him, caught in ribbons of color and light painted by the gods themselves, her heart full to bursting with a beauty she'd never witnessed before, Rozalie Dohnal decided there was still much to learn and experience in the world. Much she'd never done—and had always wanted to do.

And she was ready to step into the next adventure.

CHAPTER SIXTY-SEVEN

Slowly but surely, the Citadel began to recover. With armor traded for rolled sleeves and dust-stained pants, and battle wounds for skinned palms and bloodied knuckles, the warriors of Talheim and Valgard worked side-by-side to mend the broken parts of the Talheimic capital. And while Aden labored with them, and attended council meetings, and paced the halls with Mira and a fussing Nadeem, he found the calm and balance that had deserted him in Mahasar.

Perhaps that was something he owed to Mira as well, but for this wild, wonderous *something* they'd found that day on the bridge, he wasn't quick to evoke names or meanings. He was content to simply let it be, and to enjoy her presence—the occasional hand slipping into his while they tended the boy together, a fleeting kiss when they passed one another in the halls, him on his way to the next meeting and her on her way to speak to the struggling warriors recovering from Sorcel.

It was less a fleeting kiss one day, and something much more demanding, leaving his shirt askew and lips sore when they finally parted ways again from behind another tapestry-hidden hall, that he smirked about on his way toward the barracks for a report from his augurs.

Winding down a staircase to the lower levels of the Citadel, he paused at the mouth of the Wardens' bedchamber corridor, across the round foyer from the Valgardan hall.

He knew that low, familiar curse echoing on the arched walls.

Cautious and curious, he changed tack, strolling into Viktor Pollack's private chamber—a mark of his rank when most Wardens shared cots in the lower rooms. He was muttering to himself still, hurling things into a rucksack, and didn't seem to notice Aden's arrival.

Clearing his throat, he slouched against the wall. "What is this?"

"Packing for a new mission."

Aden frowned. "I don't recall any dispatches in council today. Least of all ones that would take the Commander's second away from his duties."

"As if we owe Valgard an explanation for Cadre dispatches."

His hackles rippled at that familiar tone of contempt, absent ever since they'd subdued the lords outside the tavern. "What's the mission?"

"None of your gods-damned business, is what it is."

Jaw clenched, Aden watched him fling the last of his supplies into the rucksack and strap on his sword, then grip the upper sleeve of his uniform and separate a patch from it with a rip like sutures from a fresh wound. He tossed it onto the bed, shouldered his pack, and turned.

Aden stepped into his path. "I'm as responsible for the security of this Citadel as you. Tell me what this is, Pollack."

Viktor's gaze scoured over him in a way that reminded Aden of Ashe's belligerence and revulsion when she'd first fought him in the Hive. "All right, augur. You really want to know my business? The mission is from Rion himself. We're leaving the Cadre, all of us who are loyal. No one with an ounce of self-respect or love for the true heart of Talheim will be wearing that mark after today." He jerked his chin at the frayed emblem ripped from his uniform. "Not now that we know."

"Know *what*?"

"What our new *Prince* is guilty of." Viktor's smile curled with hate. "You were clever, keeping that from me when you asked for my help. I would've told you exactly what you could do with your *alliance* if I'd known you shared blood with the bastard who got Julian Bartos killed."

Bleak realization broke through Aden. "This is about what Jad revealed in his game."

"No, it's about what you Valgardans are capable of. What you'll always be at your core." He shook his head. "Gods, I should've remembered. You, him, you're nothing more than animals on leashes. Well, this time he snapped at the wrong hand...this one strikes back."

Viktor jammed past him, wrenching Aden's shoulder so viciously he had no choice but to turn from his path. The Hive Lord's fury rubbed against Aden's skin, begging for release—begging to make this man bleed for so many insults leveled against Valgard, against *Thorne*, just like the Tumult had done so long ago.

But this wasn't them, this wasn't Siralek. And even if it was, these people deserved to be saved, just like Nimea and her followers had before their hate ran its course too far.

"You asked me to warn you if I saw you were about to betray your kingdom," he called to Viktor's retreating back. "You're doing it now."

Viktor's heels snagged to stone. Then he turned, gaze full of loathing. "This is not betrayal. This is saving Talheim." He jabbed a finger at Aden. "Your bastard of a cousin murdered Julian Bartos. That boy was like a younger brother to all of us...he was *one* of us. Do you really think I'd serve a king who protects the guilty ones? That I would *ever* defend a princess rolling with the rat-eater who killed one of our own?"

"Julian Bartos made his choice. It was *his* to make."

Viktor flashed a humorless smile. "Well, now I'm making mine." He hitched his satchel over his shoulder. "Watch your back, augur. The next time I see it, I'll put my blade there."

He slipped from the room, and Aden dragged a hand through his hair, debating for one moment...but he couldn't let this go. Another traitor, another enemy in the Citadel halls.

Smashing the door open, he stepped into the parlor—and froze.

Viktor was gone like he'd never been there, slipping away swift as smoke through some side hall or another false corridor beyond sight. And with unease churning deep in his gut, Aden wondered how many hidden ways within this Citadel Rion Bartos and his followers knew about...bleeding wounds even the royal family didn't know how to seal.

He was in the barracks still when Mira found him deep in the night, pounding his frustrations into the fabric satchel Tatiana had crafted for Cistine. Good that it was in Quill's height and bulk; it made him feel like one of his cabal was with him, like this disaster wasn't his alone to bear.

"I spoke to Moravec," Mira said, slipping into the windowless chamber. "He told me what happened. That explains why you weren't at dinner."

He kept hitting; he couldn't think of a reply.

"Over one hundred Wardens defected in a single day." She lowered herself onto the dressing bench, gripping the sides of her neck. "You had no luck tracking them?"

He stopped the hail of blows with a last, vicious swing, sending the bag reeling away and back to him. "Ashe was right about the Warden tunnels. Wherever they disappeared, it was nowhere we knew. And most who went were high-ranking, those in Rion's confidence...the ones with intimate knowledge of the Citadel's deepest secrets."

"One hundred of the King's best. Not to mention the ones who aren't yet fit to return to duty after the siege. That's a great flank exposed."

Winding one arm around the bag, Aden leaned his weight against it, panting open-mouthed and watching her. "Do you think Bartos will strike now?"

"No, he's not the sort," Mira said with a calm certainty that eased some of the stampeding nerves that had first sent him down here, working to hone his blows just in case. "He'll lie in wait, nursing his grievances and drumming up support. And that may be worse. A man who strikes from emotion is easier to unbalance."

Aden joined her on the bench. "A man who plots builds a firm foundation."

"The old Vassoran saying." She shifted to make room for him, running a gentle hand down the back of his neck. "This wasn't your fault."

"I know." He unwound the wrappings around his fists. "I don't feel guilty. I do feel responsible."

"And that is the mark of a great leader. But these Wardens were far beyond rescuing, Aden. Everything you observed in Viktor and Ashe and the others, I believe it to be true. Rion Bartos chose his closest followers very, very well."

"And Cyril never thought he'd turn, so he never severed that bond between them all."

Mira tapped her heels thoughtfully on the stone. "Do you suppose Ashe would've followed him, had this happened a year ago?"

"I can't be certain. All I know is it's good she didn't. They'll need the former Lady of the Hive and her dragon guarding the capital until Bartos is found."

Mira was quiet for a beat. "Ashe and Maleck are staying here?"

He nodded, bringing her hand down from his neck and twining his fingers with hers, that dull ache thumping in his chest yet again at the thought of losing them both to another kingdom.

"Would you like to talk about it?" Mira asked. "About all of this?"

Looking into her eyes, gentle and full of compassion, Aden nodded. "You save me in more ways than you know."

Laughing, she pressed a kiss to their entwined hands. "I'm returning the favor." Then she took his hand and drew him up, leading him from this place of darkness and back into hallways full of moonlight and skies full of stars.

CHAPTER
SIXTY-EIGHT

THEIR DAYS IN Mahasar were drawing to a close. Every day, Cyril grew stronger; and every week, new batches of Enforcers returned from Talheim, dragged in by Aden's augurs and the *Alhuri* whose pride at serving their new King shone in their grinning faces. From the augurs' reports, Cistine and her parents learned the Citadel grew restless. Despite their best efforts, Aden and Mira were not Talheimic; the people craved the reassurance of their own royal family on the thrones, particularly after another hundred Wardens defected.

"We should've warned Aden," Ashe muttered after reading that note. She and Cistine sat in the training courtyard, hurling knives at a target hung between two pillars. "The minute Rion left, Viktor was going to follow. He's his closest supporter."

"After what Aden said about bringing down the lords together..." Cistine groomed the stunted training grass with restless fingers. "I don't know. I hoped maybe he'd change his mind and stay with us. That he saw Valgard differently, like you and Roz."

"Rion's always had two powerful arrows in his quiver: charisma and intimidation. He either charms you to see things his way or teaches you not to argue." Ashe hurled another knife into the target's center. "Viktor is both, intimidated and charmed. A few weeks working with Aden isn't enough to change years of conditioning like that...believe me. I walked that road in Siralek."

"I never knew how many Wardens he cowed. I never saw how much all of you suffered."

Ashe paused, weighing the next blade in her hand, mulling her next words. "Sometimes I wonder how much he intimidated Julian."

The knife embedded in the target with a dull *thud*.

The notion made Cistine anxious to return home, but a part of her was still unhappy to leave these hospitable halls, these warm climes—from weeks of healing back to the cold Middle Kingdom with her duties awaiting.

And once they went back, who knew how long the cabal would stay?

The thought woke her before dawn one day, desperate for the distraction of training. Thorne was already gone, leaving a cinnamon-sugar pastry on the bedside table for her. She stuffed it into her mouth while she pulled on her armor, mind already halfway to the training grounds.

"I'm utterly convinced your sense of grace and decorum comes from your father." Solene's familiar laughter drew her head up from fumbling with her boot; the Queen stood in the doorway, her usual dresses traded for light Mahasari pants, a long linen shirt, and a sturdy leather vest.

Cistine rose, covering her mouth with one hand and forcing a swallow. "Are you going shooting?"

"I was just on my way. I wondered if you might join me, but it looks as if you're spoken for."

She smiled sheepishly. "Quill and Tatiana want to meet in the *garriqah* this morning. What's the occasion?"

Solene stepped inside the room, skimming her hand over the armoire, the dressing table, then the gilded windowsill. "King Kashar's asked me to train a few of the *Alhuri* in our particular methods of archery before they leave to spread the antidote across Mahasar. I agreed, fool that I am...I forget how much a bow in my hand reminds me of Ebby."

Cistine hesitated, then reached out to touch her arm. "How are you?"

"Some days are better than others." Solene's gaze floated to the window. "Training helps. Archery helps, sometimes. Spending time with your father reminds me I haven't lost everything." Her knuckles grazed the round of Cistine's cheek. "And of course, being able to touch you like this is a gift. But I feel as if I'll never stop atoning for everything I did."

"Neither will I." Cistine leaned into her touch. "It sometimes feels like Sacha died and Papa and Thorne almost did because of my mistakes."

"Your father and Thorne are *alive*." Solene gripped her face in both hands now. "And Sacha died for what she believed in. That is not your fault."

"I know." Cistine wrapped her arms around her mother's warm softness. "But it would've been nice, having another princess to talk to after all this was over. Someone like me."

"From what you tell me, she never would've gone back to that life." With a gentle squeeze, Solene released her. "And besides, there are no princesses quite like you."

Laughing, Cistine stuck out her tongue. "There are no queens like *you*, either."

"Thank the gods for that." Solene pulled Cistine with her, guiding them both to the door. "Do you know what's given me hope these past few weeks, while your father was ill, and whenever I think of Eboni or Rion?" Cistine shook her head, and Solene halted, taking her firmly by the shoulders this time. "*You* do, Cistine. Hope that the generation that comes after us won't make the same mistakes we did. Hope that there will be peace in your reign when it comes, not war after war. I think of all the horrible things I've done, all the mistakes I've made, but then I see you and know I must've done *something* right...because you helped forge peace with the people your father and I have feared and hated most in the world."

Tears freckled Cistine's vision. "Well, that's what a princess does. She spreads hope."

Solene pressed a kiss to her brow. "Which is why I feel confident to say, alone or not, you are precisely the princess these kingdoms need."

She strode away down the hall, her words lingering like a sweet fragrance on the coming dawn, and Cistine hung in the doorway, pondering them.

It was true, Talheim *did* need a princess now. Not a second Queen who made laws from the porcelain throne, but a daughter of one with time to spare for them. A woman with duties, but also with freedom to sit in glass courtyards and take leisurely horseback rides, read and drink tea with her subjects, listen to their voices and hear their hearts, train and teach and learn and *be* with them. And one who could then go into her study, shut the door, and suggest laws and amendments that bettered their whole kingdom.

It wasn't one or the other, a cage of a throne or every hour of the day spent at her own whim. It was both. The people *needed* both—and when had they had it last? After all, Cyril had been younger than she was now when he'd returned from Valgard, a prince who became a king in fields of blood.

But thanks to Thorne's courage and the gift of the gods, Cistine Novacek had many, many years to be a princess...a girl of books and beauty *and* a student of bone and battle.

She was determined never to take that time for granted again.

A whistle down the hall startled her, and she ducked her head from the doorway to find Quill and Tatiana waiting at the end.

Hands slipped in his pockets, Quill jerked his head when their eyes met. "Training?"

Cistine grinned. "On my way!"

CHAPTER SIXTY-NINE

WHEN HE WAS eight years old, Thorne Starchaser had a dream.

The finer details had paled over time, but the impressions remained like sunlight's brand against his eyes; he'd dreamed of himself as a man, tall and strong, sitting on the Judgement Seat. The people who came to kneel before him genuflected in reverence, not with the fear they always paid his father on that same chair. Their eyes reflected love, not resentment and terror.

He'd had that dream the very first time because of a prince-turned-king marching through their streets, a victor of war, his loyal and loving warriors at his heels; a man who'd loosed the bonds on Kristoff Lionsbane's wrists and sent him back to his family injured but alive. A man Thorne had only glimpsed from afar, tucked behind Baba Kallah's back while the truce was struck between the Middle Kingdom and Valgard.

The first time Thorne had ever laid eyes on Cyril Novacek, he'd dreamed of the kind of leader he wanted to be. And he hadn't even remembered that conquering King, not really—his face, his name stolen by the blur of youth and the passing years. But that dream had remained of Chancellor Thorne, making just decrees in a world where Natalya, Aden, and Maleck didn't have to search Kristoff for crippling wounds that would strip his title before they could even celebrate he was alive; a world where his father didn't return in a rage from that surrender and take his fists to Rakel, to Baba Kallah, to his own son, turning that apartment into Nimmus itself—one of the longest nights of Thorne's life.

He'd woken in a fit of excitement from that dream despite his black eye and bruised ribs, gushing to Baba Kallah of the world he'd build them where people followed out of love, not fear; where men won wars with strength of arms and the loyalty of their followers, not just with gods-given power.

A world he'd spent twenty years fighting for. And now he was looking down at it, not just as Chancellor, but as husband and leader and friend.

In the *garriqah* below, his cabal slowly gathered over time; Ashe dragging Maleck out to spar with blades first, then Ariadne joining them, turning it into a three-way dagger match. Tatiana arrived next, Cistine clinging to her back, arguing something about fist-wrappings with Quill swaggering after them. Then Rozalie appeared, and to Thorne's surprise, Kashar, looking frazzled and unhappy but a willing participant for a duel. That had been nearly an hour ago; now all he heard from below was laughter, ringing steel, playful jeers, and whoops of victory.

And finally, from down the wall, Cyril came to join him, carrying two mugs in his hands. He settled himself, offering one to Thorne. "Would I be misguided to think you've been avoiding me lately?"

Thorne took the mug—steamed milk with honey and cinnamon—and sipped with a shrug. "Would I be misguided to assume you cornered me here so I couldn't anymore?"

"So, we've established we're both cowardly when it comes to discussing our feelings. Excellent."

"It's worth noting that our last two conversations didn't go particularly well."

"Are you referring to the one where I reamed you, or the one where you disobeyed my direct orders to leave me in that trench and save yourself?" Cyril asked mildly. Thorne held that shrewd gaze, so like Cistine's, and didn't answer. "It was brave, what you did. But also tremendously dangerous, not only for Cistine's heart, but for your kingdom. Do you truly want to deprive Kanslar of its first level-headed Chancellor in decades?"

"Aden would've made a worthy successor," Thorne said. "But I wasn't thinking of Kanslar. All that mattered was reaching you."

Cyril shook his head and laughed, swigging from his cup. "I wish I had ten men like you on my council. We need more nobility in this world...more love like that. The kind that would fling itself at the mercy of the gods to save what matters most."

"Maybe. But I did it for selfish reasons, too. I didn't want you to die hating me."

Cyril's eyed widened. "Is that what you...?" He trailed off, clasping Thorne's shoulder sharply. "Listen to me. I may have been angry, I may have been disappointed, but I never once *hated* you, not even for an instant. If our places had been reversed, I would've gone down into the trench for you, too."

Heat clouded Thorne's eyes. He coughed. "That will take some getting used to."

"I gather. Cistine's told me tales of the bastard who raised you." The cup lifted to Cyril's lips, then lowered again. "I remember him. We fought on the plains outside your capital. He battled with the strength of a man twice his age and training. I thought at the time it was because I had captured one of his people, but I take it that wasn't true."

Thorne shook his head. "My father couldn't stand to lose. He couldn't stand anything that made him feel weak."

Cyril turned his cup in his hand, sighing. "I'm sorry for any harm his defeat caused you."

It was such an unexpected, unbelievable apology, Thorne laughed aloud. "My cabal decided long ago not to hold others responsible for my father's actions. It just leads to misery."

"Fair. But on behalf of the battle-born King who didn't know any better about the complexities of the kingdom he defeated...I truly am sorry."

Thorne grimaced. "Apology accepted."

They were quiet again, drinking and watching the sparring matches below.

"What you said about your father being responsible for his own actions," Cyril murmured at last. "I wish Rion could've learned that lesson."

Sympathy simmered deep in Thorne's gut. "I'm sorry that happened."

"So am I...but I'm also not. These last weeks have given me plenty of time to think. It's become clearer than ever how wrong I was to invite Rion back for the war council, but I was selfish, too. And it *will* be better for Talheim, not having him in that position of authority."

He studied the King's bereaved face. "Are you all right?"

"Not yet. But I will be, in time. It was the same when I first convinced him to retire to Practica...I was sure I'd done the wrong thing for myself, but the right one for my kingdom." He raised his brows. "It's like we discussed about your mother. Some things that are necessary for the people are the most painful for us."

Thorne hadn't pressed on the bruise of hurt from her execution in weeks, too consumed with everything else, but fresh pain bloomed behind it now.

Sighing, he bent his elbows to his knees, gazing down into the *garriqah*. His dreams had never warned him of this; what a sad, savage thing it was to hold other lives in your hands, to cast judgement on the future. What a terrible, merciless duty it was to be a leader.

Cyril followed his gaze and gave him a nudge. "Shouldn't you be down there, too?"

Thorne smiled crookedly. "You know how it is when the ruler arrives. The backs straighten. The feeling shifts."

"Doesn't it?" Cyril chuckled. "Though I've met few rulers as much a part of their people as you."

Some of the ache eased from his heart. "That means more than I can say."

"You know," Cyril said, watching him watch the cabal, "I've spent so much time since we first met telling you how a family should be, I never stopped to ask you what *you* think it is. What you've learned from the one you built for yourself." His eyes brightened with an unspoken invitation: *I'm asking now.*

Thorne pondered, staring into the *garriqah* where Quill swept Cistine up, dumping her over his shoulder, and Tatiana pounced on her and wrapped her in a headlock, tickling her sides until she begged for mercy. Ashe, Ariadne, and Maleck paused their three-way duel long enough to laugh; Rozalie and Kashar, grappling under the palm fronds, didn't even look up.

"Love," Thorne said when Quill tackled Tatiana off Cistine. "Loyalty." Ariadne swooped to his *valenar's* aid, helping her up by the hand, and together they turned on Quill and Tatiana and brought them down in wrestling heaps. "And sacrifice."

"Giving one's life?"

"That. And being willing to live on, no matter how painful it is." Thorne watched Maleck disarm Ashe, spin her, and dip her into a kiss, ending their sparring game. "Making the choice to live through the hard days for one another...for the hope of a future." Chuckling, he enjoyed the sight of Rozalie knocking Kashar on his back and pinning him with a blade through the loose fabric of his sleeve.

"Hmm." Cyril laughed as well. "Perhaps you know a bit more than I gave you credit for."

Thorne tore his eyes away from them. "What do *you* think family should be?"

"Honest," Cyril said. "Fearlessly vulnerable. And above all else, we honor one another. That's what makes us good men, good women, good leaders. Honor, honesty, and love."

At those words, the boy's dream and the man's present melded in Thorne's mind. The first sparks of a rebellious sort of leadership, fanned to flame in him at eight years old by the sight of this conquering king, this true vision of Kanslar itself, embodied in a man he now called father and truly meant it; and the truth of the Chancellor that Thorne Starchaser had already become—and where he still had room to grow.

"I'd like you to teach me, if you're willing," he said. "To be a better leader than my own father. And to be part of a family that honors and loves one another. I know I've changed and learned...I owe much of that to

Cistine. But I still have far to go."

"Don't we all? But it would be my honor to walk that path with you." Cyril drew him suddenly into an embrace, clapping him on the back. "I owe you my life, and I will be grateful for that every day I'm privileged to breathe. *Thank you.*"

After a hesitant moment, Thorne returned the embrace. "You're welcome, Father."

At dusk, Thorne sought Cistine out, finding her playing cards with the *Alhuri* in one of the parlors. From the doorway, he met her gaze at the table; a small girl sat in her lap, men and women crowded at her sides.

When she looked up, he tapped his fist three times over his left shoulder.

She came to him, fingers wrapping through his, and they walked together down tier after tier through a city darkening but not quite sleeping yet. It was fully night when they passed the Enforcers at the outer gates and entered the fertile plain between Arak Shehr and the desert's distant gold dunes; but the moonlight paved them a path the opposite way, through the undergrowth to a waterfall and river at the foothills of the Ralathi Mountains, which fed the plain. Rich minerals from the black soil turned the water and rocks slippery with iridescent ultramarine light, and Cistine's face glowed at the sight, gaze leaping to him.

Thorne grinned. He'd chosen this place just for her.

They settled on the shore, feet dipped in the cool water, listening to the falls gush and the nightbirds trill in the olive trees and hardy shrubs.

"Why here?" Cistine asked. "Why tonight?"

"Because it's beautiful, and so are you." He brushed her hair behind her ear and kissed the side of her neck. "And you deserve beauty."

Fingers still wound through his, Cistine laid her head on his shoulder. "So do you."

He was finally learning to accept that; he had to, or else he'd never feel worthy of her.

"Papa wants to leave at week's end." A hint of melancholy slipped into Cistine's voice. "I'll miss this place. The friends we've made here."

It was just like her, making friends of a kingdom she'd once risked her life to foil. "We'll see them again. And it will be on peaceful terms." He tugged her hand, and they settled on their backs on the dense, spiny grass, staring up at the stars.

"Is something bothering you?" Cistine asked after a moment. "You've been quiet all day. It seems like you've been avoiding me."

Trust her to notice, though he'd just been gathering his thoughts and pondering his words.

It was finally time; with the King's admonishment about honesty, honor, and love, he could no longer keep it to himself.

"I need to tell you something," he said, and she squeezed his hand—a silent sign that he held her full attention. "I sentenced my mother to death during my season. It was...it *is* one of the most painful things I've ever done. I didn't eat for a week. I could barely get out of bed. I spent every moment questioning if I deserved to be Chancellor anymore. Kristoff finally had to drag me out of my room. That was the letter I couldn't send you."

Wide-eyed, Cistine rolled onto her elbow to face him. "Oh, Thorne. I'm...I can't even imagine what that was like. I wish I'd been there." Her fingers followed the curve of his cheek, the line of his jaw. "Would it help you to talk about it now?"

He captured her hand and kissed her fingertips. "How about this: I'll trade you a truth for a truth from this past year. All the things we haven't said yet...nothing secret between us. I want to be honest and true to you in everything, Wildheart. Even the parts that hurt the most."

Her eyes were impossibly soft in the moonlight. "You have a deal, Starchaser."

Her lips touched his beneath the black sky, a shower of stars cast across it like a banner of celebration—a thousand die cast, the lots all tossed in hope of what their future could be: three kingdoms in friendship, two joined by marriage, by blended blood and blended hearts.

This time, it felt like the gods were betting on them.

CHAPTER SEVENTY

THE DAY WAS finally here.

Cistine barely felt ready, still exhausted from their whirlwind return from Mahasar, from visiting Eboni's grave and touring the ruined Citadel and going with her mother to see Mira every day. But after a week, it was finally time; the people needed this.

And it was not just Cistine's duty this time, but the whole royal family's, to give it.

She caught her mother's reflection beside hers in the full-length mirror, full cheeks plump with a smile, eyes serene for the first time since their return to Astoria. Her fingers flew, forging a complex crown of braids in Cistine's hair, tugging the roots so hard they itched. "Are you excited, Mama?"

"I'm not sure that's the right word for it," Solene admitted. "But I'm glad this day is finally here. As glad as I was after the last war."

"Are you two almost finished?"

Cistine grinned, catching Thorne's gaze in the mirror. He stood in their bedroom doorway, one hand pocketed, the other scrubbing at his own trimmed hair, smiling as he watched them work.

"Why are you so eager to be done with today?" Cistine mock-pouted.

"I'm not. Just eager to borrow you."

"For what? The ceremony is in less than an hour!"

"The cabal has a surprise for us, but they won't say what it is unless we're both there."

Cistine blinked wide-eyed at her mother, who was suddenly deeply invested in wrangling the last few pins into her braid. Curiosity nipped her fingers; the moment Solene slid the last pearl-tipped pin into place, Cistine pecked her on the cheek, gathered the skirts of her jeweled gown, and hurried to the doorway. "There, done! Now, can I have my surprise?"

Laughing, Thorne slipped his hand into hers; it still felt strange when he touched her so casually, without death hanging between them, but always so wonderful. Ever since the night outside Arak Shehr when they'd knit shut the wounds of the tumultuous past year, she never wanted to stop holding his hand.

So that was how they walked the Citadel halls. The hearths were lit, ancient gossips gathering before them to whisper about wartime stories and who was sneaking into closets with whom. They'd been some of the royal family's greatest assets lately, gathering rumors about those still ensorcelled while also spreading the word of Cistine's broken curse to the people; as if anyone couldn't see it, with her and Thorne walking together, fingers enlaced everywhere they went.

The cabal gathered in one of the outer parlors, dressed in pants and fine shirts and gilded jackets. They looked more like royalty than they ever had, and Cistine's heart swelled at the sight of them—then clenched with suspicion. Their faces were all shifty, eyes darting nervously toward the doors to the northern bridge.

Slowing to a halt, she tugged from Thorne's grip, crossed her arms, and raised a brow. "What is going on here?"

They all startled at her arrival; Maleck actually *jumped.*

"Nothing is going on!" Tatiana chirped, tugging out her lilac skirts. "Why do you always start with accusations, *Yani?*"

"Why are all *your* nails bitten to the quick?"

She folded her hands behind her back. "Not the point. We're discussing *you,* remember?"

Cistine sighed. "Did Quill steal another entire case of powdered-sugar rolls from the kitchens?"

"*One time*," he muttered under his breath.

"Did Maleck and Aden destroy all our grainsack targets again?"

"A man makes a single mistake," Aden intoned to Mira, who bounced Nadeem against her side with eye-rolling sympathy.

"Did Ari get banned from *all* the temple grounds for lecturing the priests and priestesses?"

Ariadne's eyes narrowed, a quiet message conveyed: *It was worth it.*

Cistine flagged her arms. "*What is going on with all of you?*"

Quill cocked his head with an infuriatingly smug smile. "You'll see."

A lecture leaped to the tip of her tongue—then died. Slowly, she looked around at them all. "Where's Ashe?"

A whistle echoed through the seam of the doors, a quick two-note command Cistine recognized just as the Wardens drew open the doors, and a girlish shout of her name had her spinning to catch an assault of long limbs and black-brown hair within a ceaseless storm of chattering. "Holy stars, Cistine! It's true, isn't it? Ashe *said* the augment was gone and I didn't think it was real, but it *is* real, it is! Look, I'm not dead!"

"Pippet, *what* are you doing here?" Cistine laughed, pushing Quill's sister out at arm's length. "And who said you could grow this tall? You're like a bean sprout!"

"And you're so *muscley*!" Pippet squeezed Cistine's biceps, grinning. "I'd bet five mynts you could fight *Aden* now—where is he? *Aden!*" She launched herself past Cistine to hug him, then bounced to Maleck's arms, then Quill's, then Tatiana's, then Ariadne's.

When she got to Thorne, he spun her around, wrapped his arms around her elbows, and trapped her against his chest. "Calm," he coaxed. "*Breathe.*"

"*I. Can't!*" she shrilled, rattling in his grip. "Look at where we are! A real castle with *real princesses*! I want to go exploring! Quill, take me exploring!"

"You're not going anywhere until someone tells me *why you're here!*"

Cistine cried.

"It's a gift." The warm voice came from the doorway, accompanied by the creak of turning wheels. "To see the end of your war."

Cistine spun with a yelp, hands clapped to her mouth, as Kristoff rolled into the parlor in his wheeled chair. Ashe strode in behind him, windswept and grinning, shedding her cloak for her own fine shirt and pants.

"Kristoff!" Cistine ran to him, kissing his cheeks and wrapping her arms around his strong neck. He squeezed her tightly, his grip stronger than she remembered from a year of rolling himself all around Stornhaz. "I can't believe you're here!"

"Of course we are, there's going to be *cake!*" Pippet squealed, lunging forward in Thorne's grip so hard he swung her feet off the ground to draw her back.

"Ah, the guests have arrived!" Cyril's voice boomed from the winged staircase, and he descended, still slower than Cistine was used to, but with a smile bigger than she'd ever seen.

He halted at the foot of the steps, his eyes meeting Kristoff's. Neither man spoke; they simply gazed at one another, so intently Cistine's heart pounded with unease.

"*Athar?*" Aden said slowly. "What's wrong?"

"Nothing," Kristoff said. "Just admiring the King."

"Papa?" Cistine prompted.

Cyril started, shaking his head. "Yes. Right. Ceremony. Why don't you all go take your places?"

Cistine glanced helplessly at Maleck, who shrugged, and Aden, whose frown suggested he'd be interrogating his father later about that look and the crackle of history it contained. But he merely pushed Kristoff's wheeled chair ahead of him down the hall, the others falling into stride behind him.

Ashe sidled up alongside Cistine, wrapping an arm around her shoulders. "I'm sorry to be so secretive, but I thought you'd want them both here. They were such a part of everything, it felt wrong not to."

"It's perfect," Cistine said. "Thank you."

Ashe kissed her temple. "We'll see you in there, Princess."

Then she was gone, striding away with the others, leaving Cistine, Thorne, and Cyril alone in the entry parlor—the King grinning with wicked mischief. "Did you like your surprise?"

Thorne arched a brow. "You knew?"

"For days now. They asked me to keep it secret. Quite the friends you have, so unafraid to threaten royalty."

"I'm not angry," Cistine laughed. "Sometimes I don't think I'll be angry at you ever again."

"Oh, we'll find a way to knock heads. We're too much alike, after all."

That they were. The two Keys, first and second made; those bound to throne and crown. Father and daughter, woven into one another like two rivers, their destinies and hearts much the same.

"Are you all right, Cistine?" Cyril asked, and this time it felt like a deeper question—a more genuine one.

"I am, Papa. I think..." She chewed over the words, weighing their truth before she spoke them. "For the first time in my whole life, I think I'm perfectly content with who I am."

Thorne cleared his throat, smiling so broadly his cheeks plumped. Cyril squeezed her shoulder. "I love you. No father has ever been prouder of his child."

"Well, I don't know...you should hear Kristoff talk about his sons."

"And wait until you meet Tatiana's father," Thorne added.

Laughing, Cyril draped an arm around each of them and led them from the foyer.

They were quiet on the walk to the throne room, Cistine's pulse quickening with every stride. Passing servants bowed to them, their bright-eyed grins following the Princess, the Prince, and the King on the long journey to that familiar chamber; before they even reached it, the echo of chatter drifted from within, laughter and conversations raised in a blend of tongues. Not just Valgardan and Talheimic, but the Mahasaris, led by Esmail, who'd come to help them route the Enforcers; they would leave tomorrow, but for today, she was glad to have them here.

Solene greeted them at the door, her own dress of deep pine green bringing out the returning brightness of her gaze. She took Cistine's face in her hands and kissed her brow. "Having you here today, in this way, means more than you know."

"*You* mean more than you know," Cistine said, and Solene let out a wet half-laugh, kiss fiercening until it nearly hurt. Then she drew back and took Cyril's hand and Cistine's; Thorne took Cistine's other.

The King grinned at them all. "Are you ready?"

Cistine gathered her breath. "More than I've ever been."

At a gesture from her, the ballroom doors opened to the rising storm of cheers within, the people dropping to their knees in honor of the royal family striding down the aisle. At the very end, the temple priest stood before the four thrones: ebony, ivory, porcelain, and dark onyx, awaiting the royal family. And on each one, a thin circlet—one of them just forged the previous week.

Heart drumming, Cistine could hardly contain herself to a steady walk up the center of the room where the war table had once lived. When they reached the base of the dais, Cyril kissed her cheek and clapped a hand on the back of Thorne's neck, marching him up the broad steps. Solene and Cistine paused, mother's brow to daughter's for a moment. Then they joined their men.

The moment Cistine reached Thorne's side, the first traitorous tears slid free. Frowning, he brushed them away. "Are those for me?"

"They're for all of us," Cistine said. "Because I'm happy."

His hand fell to her chin, then dropped back to his side. But his smile stayed strong.

"The time has come at last, a day we have prayed for since the first tidings of war brought us all together," the priest announced. "King Cyril, by your decree, are the borders of Talheim secure once more?"

"They are." Cyril smiled toward the front row—at the cabal, and Esmail and Mairin. The captain was grinning; Esmail, far more reserved, dipped his head to Cistine, and somehow that meant more than any of the cheers.

"Then so, too, does the kingdom recognize its peace." The priest sidestepped, gesturing an arm to the thrones. "It's time."

Thorne blew out an audible breath as he turned beside Cistine, facing the onyx throne. She squeezed his hand, then tugged away to lift the iron crown from his seat, its single red gem forged precisely to honor him. His very own *Blaykrone*—a blood crown fit for a king.

The gleam of emotion in his eyes when she fitted the circlet to his hair told her he knew...and that it meant more than words could ever say.

Beside them, Solene did the same for Cyril; then the men for their women, crowns settled over their braids. A warm rush of relief surged through Cistine when the jeweled circlet touched her head again, marking the tradition consummated—the peace solidified.

It was finally over. Talheim was free.

They turned all together to a storm of cheers, above which the priest's closing words could barely be heard.

"I give back to you, in this peace, King Cyril and Queen Solene," he cried, "and Princess Cistine and Prince Thorne! Your leaders. Your rulers. Your royal family."

༄༅

A chilly wind swarmed up through the chinks in Astoria that evening when the cabal made their way down to the sea.

The Citadel glimmered jewel-bright at their backs, the day behind them full of nothing but celebration, good food and drink, laughter and love as they made the journey together: Pippet on Maleck's back, Quill beside them, Aden pushing his father's wheeled chair alongside Cyril and Solene, hand-in-hand while Mira carried Nadeem, all of them chattering like old friends. Tatiana, Ariadne, and Ashe took the lead, their laughter floating on the cool breeze from the Agerios; at the rear, Cistine stayed with Thorne, her dress's edges crimped and tied off around her hips, feet eager for dancing.

All around them, the city awakened with the first glimpses of the coming spring: vendors peeking out among the markets despite the late hour, ghostlamps flickering to life on the bridges. And ahead, the coast danced like a prism, bonfires of a dozen colors raising shimmering arms to the sky. Fiddles and violins and drums braided a wild melody into the smoke when the cabal reached the sand where their people swarmed.

Rozalie was at the nearest fire, dancing with Shathen and Lydie. Esmail and Mairin arm-wrestled while a knot of Valgardans threw down bets on them. A storm of cheers and hooting shouts followed a sparring match at the nearest fire where a Valgardan and a Talheimic leaped up, mouths bloody, arms around each other's shoulders, and swapped a mead bottle.

Joy bounded in Cistine, so breathtaking she almost sobbed. Everywhere she looked, warriors and Wardens danced in pairs and chains, teaching one another the songs of their own kingdoms. They mingled around the fires, trading drink and stories, sprawling on the sand in delirious laughter. It was impossible to see where any kingdom ended and the others began. Battle had broken down all the lines between them, and now the cabal joined in. Tatiana, Quill, and Aden raced each other to the betting circles. Maleck, Ashe, and Ariadne hurried off to the wrestling matches. Cyril and Kristoff gallantly escorted Solene and Mira to a flock of augurs and Lords circled around one fire.

Cistine drew in a deep breath of the briny air and shut her eyes. "This is where I used to come on my birthdays and dream of the north," she told Thorne. "I'd think about going there...about what it would be like, how it would feel to cross those borders. To be part of that world I knew absolutely nothing about."

Thorne wrapped his arms around her waist from behind and rested his chin against her temple. "This is what it looks like, *Logandir*. This is what we built. Everything we fought for."

He was right. This music, this light, this entire night and the people in it, and the ones who couldn't be: Julian. Baba Kallah. Helga. Eboni and Sander and Sacha and even Rion, and all the other friends who'd given their lives for this chance at peace.

Through all that pain, all that grief, Thorne had kept his promise, and she'd kept her vows to her kingdom—and to herself. Now here they were, Valgard and Talheim and even Mahasar, no lines between them. No death between them. No space between them at all.

"Thorne!" Pippet cried. "Will you dance with me?"

He glanced down at Cistine; laughing, she shoved the small of his back. "*Go.* I'll join you soon."

"Not if I join you first." He nipped her earlobe, and she pinched his side, heat swarming down her neck.

"You're such a barbarian! You never could stay away from me."

"That's true." He pressed a kiss to her forehead that curled her toes in her boots and sent her eyes tumbling shut. "And if that's *my* curse, I'm content to live with it for the rest of my days."

A whistle sounded down the shore, and Quill swaggered to join them, hands stuffed in his pockets. A knowing look passed between him and Thorne, and with a last squeeze around Cistine's waist, Thorne swept Pippet off to the nearest fire. Quill offered his three-fingered hand with a mischievous smirk. "How about a dance, Stranger?"

"If you think you can keep up," she winked. "I'll always be a better dancer than you."

"Debatable. You really think Tati could live a year in Talheim and not pick up a few dances?"

He snatched her out of the shadows and into a Talheimic waltz at the next fire over, and for a time there was just laughing and dancing with her head over his heart—and the silent admission that he *was* good at this, better than she'd imagined. Maybe her mother, not just Tatiana, had given him lessons, too.

"Say it," he growled playfully. "Say I could still teach you a thing or two."

"Never," Cistine laughed as he twirled her around the flames. Quill's damp hair flicked water on her cheek, and Cistine squinted at his face in the flames. So many new scars since they'd first met. So much new sadness—some that hadn't been there when they reunited in Masiya. "Tell me what you're thinking?"

Quill led her through a few more patterns before he said, "We're really going to miss you too, you know? Home's not going to feel like home without our Wildheart."

Tears fluttered across Cistine's vision. "I'll miss you, too, Quill."

"I figured as much. You're already pining after Thorne, and he hasn't even left yet."

"I don't mean that. I mean I'll miss *you*."

Quill pulled her closer as the music slowed, the violin's notes turning mournful as they eddied into the next song. "I know."

Cistine leaned her head into his shoulder. "Did you have any idea...when you saw me in that tavern in Veran? Did you ever think it would go like this?"

Quill snorted. "Not a chance in Nimmus. All I saw was a pampered, terrified girl—" Cistine planted her feet, twisted free, and swung at him, and he flashed up both hands, taking her punches, laughing. "A girl who was going to change all the kingdoms," he amended.

"I couldn't have done it without my *alletkai*."

Light danced in Quill's eyes again as he trapped her wrists and pulled her into a hug so tight, it made up for every wasted month since the death augment had stolen through her limbs. "You'll be all right. That crown may be heavy, but you're strong enough for it. You always have been. You just needed us to help you see it."

Cistine squeezed him with all her might, wishing she could hold onto him—all of them—forever. But when Quill drew back and slid a cinnamon stick into his mouth, Cistine's chest didn't ache quite as much anymore.

"I do see it," she said. "And I see you, Quill. I just want you to be happy."

He saluted with two fingers. "Always am, Stranger."

Then he vanished back into the crowd, leaving the faint trace of his scent on the air: cinnamon and steel, and just a hint of danger.

A moment later, Tatiana cursed at the top of her lungs, and Cistine burst into laughter, backing away while the next dance began.

This one wasn't for her.

She went down to the starkissed shores instead, watching the Agerios deposit glowing phosphorescent sea plants on the sand. Behind her, the world pulsed with music and laughter and voices, all so distinct and precious;

and as she stood embraced by light and darkness, still and quiet for the first time in months, she felt it again—that soft call, that tug in her chest.

On the fringes of firelight and shadows, Cistine swiveled to look north.

It was just a gentle whisper that grazed her mind tonight. Just a memory of silver light and power and a moment of oneness with the gods.

Someday, the call whispered over her bones. *Someday*.

And then it faded.

A different call took its place instead, turning her away from the north and back toward her cabal dancing around the fires, drinking and laughing with their friends. Three kingdoms, three tribes, a hundred blended hearts all woven together in the glow of the fires and the light of the stars.

And there was Thorne, coming back for her. Her husband, standing at the edge of darkness and light, hand open, beckoning. Smiling as he invited her into his joy, into the next dance, into all of it; into their future—the small slice of Cenowyn they'd built together.

Come. The call in her chest sang as she met Thorne's eyes and his grin took her breath away. *Come home, Wildheart*.

And with a smile on her face and her heart aching with joy, Talheim's princess heeded that call.

The End

A GUIDE
TO OLD VALGARDAN

Words:

Allatok – Heathen

Bandayo – Bastard (roughly)

Stor Sedam – the Great Seven

Yani – Sweet

Sillakove - Starchaser

Selvenar – Blended hearts

Valenar – Blended blood

A GUIDE TO MAHASARI

Words:

Iteilach – Flying

Ivrran – Demon

Raqian – Sunshine

Sahlah – Killer

Tayir – Snake

Alhuru – People

Asgaid – Free

Hasac – Whore

Brashiq – Brother

Aba – Father

Umma – Mother

Phrases:

Tawal marsinn Alhuru en-Asgaid – Long live the Free People

Ay, duin du fahi – Shut your mouth.

Items:

Sorcel – Mind-altering drug

Ivrran Salah – Strong alcohol

ACKNOWLEDGEMENTS

WELL, HERE WE are, readers. The end of the journey.

It's difficult to put into words what this book and the adventure of this series has meant to me—just know that I'm weeping even as I try.

WILDHEART was just a pipe dream when I first wrote it, a sendoff *I* needed but when I never thought would be published. Now I know it was the conclusion the story was always building toward—one of hope, and joy, and home, and family.

So it's only right I end off with thanking mine.

First, to my Father God, the One from whom every family in heaven and on earth is named. Thank You for not giving up on me when I gave up on myself, on my stories, and on the path You chose for me. I now know what it means to guide a little one who wanders and walks off in a hundred directions, and I have never been more grateful for Your endless patience and love. I now know belief runs both ways. Thank You for the gift of telling this saga, these stories, to these people.

To my earthly family: Thank you all for loving this series, and me. For reading, advising, supporting, tough-loving, gentle-loving, celebrating, and helping create this world alongside me.

And of course, a special nod and hug and a thousand kisses to JD, the "why" to my "what", my little buddy, my partner in crime, my little helper and the living heart outside my chest. Mama loves you more than all the words she's ever written can ever say, Little Man.

To Cassidy and Miranda: My sisters in heart and soul. Thank you for helping me see this series through to the end. For encouraging, inspiring, critiquing, reading, editing, songwriting, mug-making, listening, talking it out...all the uncountable ways you ladies made this series possible. If all I have ever gotten from STARCHASER was that it brought us together, that would be enough. Forever and always. <3

To Maja and Jessica: For the covers and maps that helped give this series a face and a scope that people have absolutely loved. I am so thankful for your talents and what they have brought to these books. I will always grin every time I see the covers and maps of this series!

To Atty: My first CP to ever tell me I could do this. It seems so long ago you read the first chapter of DARKWIND and said, "This reads like a finished draft", but you will never fully know what those words meant to me...how I learned to believe in myself in new ways, thanks to you. To close out this series, I hold you and your words forever in my heart. <3

To Holly, Jen, Joy, and Chief: You made this possible. I love you all, always and always.

To Katie and Meaghan: For helping me cross the finish line strong, if screaming, if in anguish. WE MADE IT, LADIES! Thank you for the videos and the aesthetics, the music and the love.

To Pam: Honestly, this series would not have begun without you and that silly song game. For that, I can never thank you enough. And for a million other things since I was a preteen sprout sharing your Walkman on the car ride up to Michigan...the words fail. Just know you're stuck with me until our dying day.

To Savannah: For being my weekend writing buddy, my coffee companion, my fellow dragon lover, my mentor, critique partner, coworker, and one of the best friends I've ever had. I prayed my whole life to know someone like you. I pray now that we spend the rest of our lives just growing closer as we tell stories together.

To so many friends who helped hold me up along the way: To Lina, Savannah, Holly, Heather, Kristin, Lucy, Zee, Tiffany, Blake, Heidi, Laura, the Katies and Brittan(e)ys and Stephanies and Sams and Meag(h)ans, Piper,

Mevia, Alli, Stephanie, Brina, Eve, Raine, Sydney, Renny, Lana, Bisa, Cristen, Clare, Allisa, Leeva, Teresa, Maddie, and so, so, so many more. Your love and lives have touched me in unforgettable ways, and I will never forget as long as I live just what a blessing each of you are to me.

To every reader who made it this far: God love you all. Thank you for the messages, the reviews, the screaming DMs, the posts you've shared, the giveaways you've participated in. Every word of encouragement you sent lives on in my heart, as I hope this series—this great big story—lives on in yours. You have changed me for the better, in ways beyond fathoming. I hope to spend the rest of my life creating adventures and stories you'll find joy, hope, and happiness in...even if a bit of raging and crying and despair happens along the way.

The end of a saga is always painful even when it's beautiful. But the grace of a closing cover means it's time to open another book.

I'll see you all in the next adventure. <3

ABOUT THE AUTHOR

Renee Dugan is an Indiana-based author who grew up reading fantasy books, chasing stray cats, and writing stories full of dashing heroes and evil masterminds. Now with over a decade of professional editing, administrative work, and writing every spare second under her belt, she has authored *THE CHAOS CIRCUS,* a portal fantasy novel, and *THE STARCHASER SAGA,* an epic high fantasy series. Living with her husband, son, and not-so-stray cats in the magical Midwest, she continues to explore new worlds and spends her time in this one encouraging and helping other writers on their journey to fulfilling their dreams.

Find Renee Dugan online at:
Reneeduganwriting.com
And on social media: **@reneeduganwriting**

www.ingramcontent.com/pod-product-compliance
Lightning Source LLC
Chambersburg PA
CBHW061340190726
48288CB00005B/1539